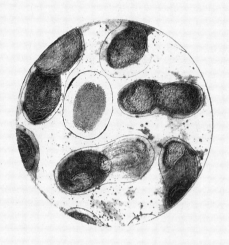

INTAGLIO - MICROGRAPH... *Albert*

Magnified........2.....diameters
Prepared...*C. A. Opius*. (*August 2007*)

Identity in context altered partly induced in uniform accent

2/8

C. A. Opius

I BURN PARIS

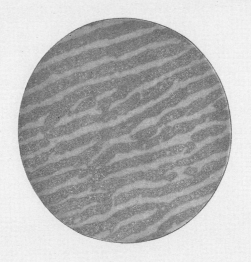

INTAGLIO · MICROGRAPH. *Ohngrade*

Magnified ......7...... *changes*

Prepared *C. A. Herrison 2.03.8)*

1/15

Ol. Opus

Bruno Jasieński

I BURN PARIS

translated from the Polish by
Soren A. Gauger & Marcin Piekoszewski

artwork by Cristian Opriş

TWISTED SPOON PRESS

PRAGUE • 2017

ISBN 978-80-86264-34-9

This publication has been funded by the
Book Institute – the ©POLAND Translation Program

To Comrade Tomasz Dąbal, a tireless soldier for the peasant-worker cause, I give this book, as a hand to clasp over the heads of Europe.

1

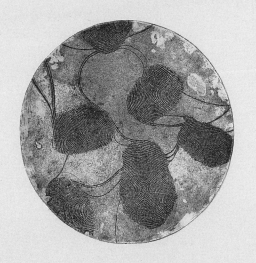

INTAGLIO - MICROGRAPH *Atrof. leg. fam.*
Magnified *322* diameters
Prepared *C. A. O. Novembre 2007*

stöt. deg. 2
reg. L. fem. i n. i
atrof. fem. 3.

2/15   *Ch. Opuez*

I

IT STARTED WITH A MINOR, SEEMINGLY INSIGNIFICANT incident that was decidedly private in nature.

One beautiful November evening, on the corner of Rue Vivienne and Boulevard Montmartre, Jeanette informed Pierre that she would most definitely be requiring a pair of evening slippers.

They walked slowly, arm in arm, intermingling with that random and unsynchronized throng of extras cast every evening by Europe's rickety film projector onto the screen of Paris's boulevards.

Pierre was gloomy and withdrawn.

He had good reason.

That very morning the foreman, measuring the hall of the factory with guttapercha steps, had stopped suddenly before his machine and, his eyes fixed somewhere just above Pierre's shoulder, told him to pack his tools.

This quiet angling had been going on for two weeks. Pierre had heard from his friends that France's lousy economic situation had made people stop buying cars. Factories were being threatened with closure. The workforce was being cut by half everywhere you looked. To avoid any commotion, people were being dismissed a handful at a time and from different divisions, staggered throughout the day.

When you came to work in the morning and stood at your workstation, you couldn't know for certain if you wouldn't be the next to go.

Four hundred agitated pairs of eyes, like dogs snuffling the ground, surreptitiously followed every step of the foreman's heavy feet as they moved slowly, deliberately, as it were, pacing between the workstations, and tried to avoid meeting his gaze as it slithered across all their faces. Hunched over their machines, as if wanting to become even smaller, grayer, more imperceptible, four hundred workers raveled out the seconds on their smoking machines in a feverish race of fingers, tangled and hoarse from silently screaming, that seemed to mutter: "I'm the fastest! Don't pick me! Not me!"

Day in, day out, in some corner of the hall, the cruel, sloped handwriting of steps would come to a full stop, and a flat, expressionless voice would break the tense silence: "Pack up your tools!"

Then a few hundred chests would heave a sigh of relief like a blast from a ventilator: "So it's not me! Not me!" Hastily, even more quickly, the trained fingers grabbed and grafted and wound second upon second, link upon link of the iron, eight-hour chain.

Pierre had gotten word: the politically suspect were the first to go. He had nothing to worry about. He kept his distance from agitators. He didn't attend rallies. During the last strike he had broken the picket line. The tub-thumpers had scowled at him. When he saw the foreman he always tensed his lips into a friendly smile.

In spite of all that, whenever the foreman began his silent, malevolent stroll through the hall, Pierre's fingers tangled in anxiety; the tools flew from his hands, and he would leave them where they fell, for fear of calling attention to himself. Beads of sweat moistened his feverish body like a cold compress.

But when the ominous steps stopped abruptly before his workstation that morning, when his gaze read the sentence from the sketch on the foreman's lips, Pierre unexpectedly felt something like relief: So this was the end!

Taking his time, he leisurely packed his segregated tools into his bundle. He looked at no one else as he started to remove his overalls and carefully wrap them in paper.

When his food tokens were being counted out in the secretary's office, it turned out that someone had stolen his micrometer.

The faultless mechanism of the factory administration transferred him to the office of the inspectorate. In the office, a bald, cross-eyed clerk laconically informed Pierre that the factory would be docking him forty francs for the lost micrometer. He had collected the remainder the day before yesterday as an advance. He would be getting nothing more.

Pierre gathered the symmetrically arranged, grease-splattered documents in silence. He knew all too well: The factory and the government were collaborating to deny laid-off workers their right to unemployment benefits by omitting the phrase "dismissed for redundancy" on the document. For a moment he still wanted to try, just to be sure. He glanced at the nasty, gleaming bald pate of the upright scribe, at the pair of thugs working for factory security, whose backs were turned as if they were occupied in conversation . . . He understood there was nothing to be done.

He trudged out the office.

At the gate, he was relieved of his pass, and the contents of his bundle were searched.

Finding himself on the street, Pierre stood for some time in helplessness, wondering where to go. A fat navy-blue policeman with the face of a bulldog, a polished ID on his collar, barked into his ear that loitering was not permitted.

He decided to go around to a few factories. But inevitably, wherever he applied, he was turned away empty-handed. The crisis was everywhere. The factories were only operating a few days a week. Jobs were being slashed. Hiring new workers was out of the question.

After running around all day, tired and hungry, he went to the warehouse at 7:00 to pick up Jeanette.

Jeannette thought she needed evening slippers. Jeannette was absolutely right. The following day was St. Catherine's Day. The warehouse was organizing a staff ball. Being thrifty, she had turned last year's dress into a new one. Now all she needed were the evening slippers. She couldn't very well go to a ball in her patent-leather shoes! Anyway, they weren't so expensive — she had seen some gorgeous brocade ones in a storefront for only fifty francs.

Pierre had exactly three *sous* in his pocket, and in gloomy silence he listened to the melodious chirping of his girlfriend, at whose sound something fluttered in his chest as if he were taking a hairpin turn on Devil's Mountain.

•

The next day's search proved just as fruitless. Nobody was hiring. At 7:00 p.m. a tired and dejected Pierre found himself somewhere on the outskirts, at the far end of Paris. He was supposed to be waiting for Jeannette to get off work. He was in no state to make it there in time. And what would he tell her? Jeannette needed evening slippers. She would cry. Pierre couldn't stand the sight of her tears. He made his way to town with a sinking heart.

On the way he thought about Jeannette. He decided he had behaved badly by not going to wait for her to get off work. The thing to do was explain it to her, make her see the whole situation. But instead, he'd abandoned her like a louse. She must have waited for him. Then she had given up and gone home. She'd be right to hold a grudge. Despite the lateness of the hour, he felt he had to go see her, to explain everything and ask for her forgiveness.

At her apartment he found out that Jeannette still hadn't returned from town. This information caught him off guard, a blow scattering the beads of sentences so painstakingly strung together in his mind.

Where could Jeannette have gone so late at night? She almost never went out alone in the evening. He decided to wait by her front gate. Soon his legs were sore. He sat on a rail, leaning against the wall. He waited.

Somewhere far off, in some invisible tower, a clock struck two. Slowly, like schoolboys who had learned their lessons by heart, the other towers repeated it from above the pulpits of the rooftops. Then silence again. His heavy eyelids fluttered clumsily like insects on flypaper, flapping upward for a moment, only to drop once more. Somewhere on the faraway bumpy pavement a first tentative cart began to rumble. Soon the garbage wagons would appear. The naked, coarse cobblestones — the bald, scalped skulls of the masses buried alive — would greet them with a long, clattering scream, passed from mouth to mouth as far as imaginable down the endless length of the street. Black men with long spears would run across the sidewalks, sinking their blades into the quivering hearts of lanterns.

The dry rattle of aching iron. The groggy, waking city struggling to lift the heavy eyelids of its shutters.

Daybreak.

Jeannette hadn't come home.

II

THE FOLLOWING DAY WAS ST. CATHERINE'S DAY. Pierre didn't go out to look for work. He made it to Place Vendôme in the early morning and, leaning on the gate next to the warehouse, waited for Jeannette to appear. A hollow anxiety filled his body. In his heavy, sleep-deprived head, vague images of the most improbable accidents rose like drifting islands of tobacco smoke in an airless room. He stayed that way all day, glued to the iron grille. He'd had nothing in his mouth for two days, but the sickly aftertaste of saliva remained a gustatory sensation that had yet to pierce his consciousness and become hunger.

Rain started to pour in the evening, and under the sluicing streams of water the hard contours of objects rippled gently, sinking into the depths, as if immersed in a swift, transparent current.

Dusk fell. The lanterns were lit and splattered colorless stains on the inky surface of the night, neither soaking into it nor illuminating it, an algae of shadows, the fantastical fauna of the bottomless depths populating the riverbed of the street.

The precipitous banks — full of the phosphorescent, magical grottoes of jeweler's windows, where virgin pearls the size of peas, shucked from their shells, slumbered on suede rocks — stretched upward, their perpendicular walls vainly groping for the surface.

Down in the wide valley of the riverbed, a tightly-packed school of bizarre iron fish with fiery, bulging eyes flowed past, swishing their rubber-tire scales, lustily rubbing against one another in clouds of bluish gasoline spawn.

Along the steep banks, straining to move, divers in the limpid gelatin of water waded under heavy wetsuit umbrellas with feet of lead. It seemed as though at any moment someone would pull at a dangling handle and gently glide upward, their legs tracing zigzags in the air over the heads of the frozen crowd.

From afar, with the flow of the river, an odd, flat wetsuit with three pairs of female legs slowly drew near. The legs stumbled their way along the slick ground, reeled with laughter, giving a gurgle of physical joy in overcoming adversity.

As the legs approached the gateway, Pierre saw that they were carrying three laughing heads under the wetsuit, and that one of the heads belonged to Jeannette.

Seeing Pierre, Jeannette ran to him in little hops, sprinkling him with the multicolored confetti of her chirping (Devil's Mountain). She was wearing her evening dress, an overcoat, and brand-new, sopping wet brocade slippers.

Why had she stayed out all night? She'd spent the night at a girl-friend's, of course. She had been up late sewing her costume for tonight's ball. Where had she gotten the new slippers? She'd been given an advance on her next paycheck from the warehouse. She still had a bit of time, so if Pierre wanted, they could go for dinner together.

A disgruntled Pierre snorted that he couldn't afford dinner. She tossed him a glance that was surprised and baffled.

No? In that case she'd rather eat with her friends. She had to hurry, because she still needed to pick up a few odds and ends.

She stood on her toes, gave him a quick peck on the mouth, and disappeared through the gates.

Pierre trailed off home. His legs were weighing him down, and now the acrid aftertaste in his mouth crept past the door of his consciousness, where it had long been rapping with stubborn and patient hiccups. He understood, and smiled at his own obtuseness. It was hunger.

The boulevards were already swarming with flocks of frolicking midinettes, entrepreneurial youths, colorful caps and sashes. In the shadows of impassive lamps, festively attired Pierres kissed the mouths of their little Jeannettes, who stood nimbly on their toes.

Gray Ménilmontant was as dim and gloomy as ever.

It was hard for Pierre to drag his body home. He was tired, and a single thought preyed on his mind: to stretch himself out in bed.

For some time he'd been carefully avoiding coming face-to-face with his grumbling, pockmarked concierge. His recent expenditures (Jeannette's fall wardrobe) meant that for the last three months he had fallen behind with the rent. Every evening he tried to slip unnoticed through the dark entrance hall and straight onto the stairs.

Yet this time his maneuver backfired. The shapeless profile of the concierge suddenly emerged from an alcove in the entrance hall, a phantom popping up to greet Pierre. He tried to slip past with a tip of his hat but was caught by the arm. He understood only one thing from the snide, phlegmy words: They weren't letting him into his room. He hadn't paid for three months, so his room had been rented out. He could collect his things when he paid what he owed.

Mechanically, without a word of protest, to the visible surprise of the concierge — who had stopped in mid-sentence — Pierre turned and went into the street.

It was drizzling. Pierre absently retraced his steps, not really knowing where to, along damp walls of houses swollen from the warmth of the people slumbering within. In cramped alcoves, in the embrasures of the houses, black, huddled men and women fashioned themselves accommodations, wrapping their extremities in scraps of newspaper to ward off the cold.

Collapsing from exhaustion, a castaway heading for the nearest beckoning light, Pierre turned toward the red glimmer of the metro station and made it to the corner of the boulevard.

A clock struck one. Drowsy workers drove the last, straggling passengers to the surface, along with the tramps lured by the warmth of the underground's tiled abyss. The gates clattered shut.

The stairs leading up to the sidewalk were packed, buzzing, stuffy. Unshaven, tattered people grabbed their place in a miserly rush, trying to huddle near the heated gate, carefully, solemnly, choosing their burrows. Nearer to the gate, dear God! The stifling, decayed warmth of Paris's wheezing breath blew through the gate. Wrapped in rags, they slowly arranged themselves along the stairs, heads resting on the comfortless pillow of the stone steps, clumsily covering their convulsing bodies with the frayed fringes of their hands.

Shortly the whole stairway resembled a forest leveled by winds. Only the places on the highest steps remained for foolhardy latecomers, who were left to the mercies of the rain and cold.

Pierre was too exhausted to wander further on. Shyly, meekly, trying not to trod on anyone, he stretched out in a free spot at the top, between two gray crones wrapped in rags, who greeted every new arrival with a menacing grunt.

He couldn't sleep. The damp paw of a fine, misty rain stroked his face, soaking his clothes with a sharp, slick wetness. The rain and sweat in his rags gave off a musty, acidic smell. The stone pillow of the spittle-covered stair jabbed his head. The sharp edges of the steps cut into his ribs, splitting his body into separate pieces that writhed in feverish insomnia like the segments of a severed worm. The lucky wretches at the bottom, fortunate to have reserved their places by the gate in advance, snored in a wide register of stifled breaths. Pierre, too, was gradually overcome by a heavy, delirious half-sleep.

He dreamed he was lying on no ordinary stairway, but on an escalator, which was ascending with a rattle (he had seen one like it at the Au Printemps store, or at the Place Pigalle metro station). From the yawning chasm of the Earth, the open maw of the metro, a never-ending iron accordion of moving stairs climbed upward in a hollow and rhythmic rumble. One after another, more and more steps clattered into sight, blocked by the row of ragged, helpless bodies. The summit of the stairs, where Pierre lay, was somewhere far in the clouds. Down below, many-eyed Paris shouted out into the soulless silence of the night with its billion lights. The stairs clanged in time as they rose higher. Pierre was overwhelmed by the cosmic vacuum of interplanetary infinity, the blinking of the stars, the limitless hush of space.

The escalator flowed from the bleak abyss of the open street into the gaping abyss of the heavens, carrying along a black mass of wretched, slumbering bodies.

III

HE WAS AWOKEN BY AN IMPATIENT SCRAPING SOUND. The metro was open.

The gray, drowsy flock, cursing and stretching, reluctantly cleared off the stairs. The depths radiated the thick, narcotizing warmth of the heated entrails of the city, digesting its first helping of light morning trains on an empty stomach. The people wheezed and yawned as they scrambled one after another onto the sidewalk, disappearing one by one into the prickly morning fog.

The first bistros opened their doors. The lucky owners of thirty centimes got to drink a cup of hot black dishwater while standing at a counter.

Pierre did not have thirty centimes, so he began wandering aimlessly up Boulevard de Belleville.

Paris slowly shook off its sleep. In the ruddy, moldering window embrasures of the stooping hotels, the profiles of old, disheveled, half-naked women showed themselves, majestic in their rotting frames, the phantom portraits of the great-grandmothers of this derelict neighborhood where prostitution is an ancestral dignity, like an inherited title or the profession of notary elsewhere.

A window is a picture nailed to the dead, stone rectangle of the gray wall of the day. There are still-life windows, strange, meticulous compositions by unsung accidental artists, freely composed of a chance curtain, a forgotten vase, or the bright vermilion of tomatoes ripening on a ledge. There are window-portraits, window-interiors, and window-naïfs — suburban idylls à la Le Douanier Rousseau — neither discovered nor appraised, ownerless.

When a train approaching the city at night passes the houses on either side of the tracks with their irregular, illuminated square windows set here and there and at various heights, then the window is a showcase for a strange, incomprehensible, even foreign life, and my eye — that of a lonely traveler — flaps as helplessly as a moth before the impenetrable panes of glass, incapable of entering.

When after a long and fruitless day in search of work Pierre returned down an empty and unfamiliar street, it was already evening, and the concave squares of the windows had started to grow phosphorescent with their internal, latent light. The street smelled of frying oil, the heat of unaired apartments, the holy, sacramental dinner hour. His greedy, tamed hunger lay at the threshold of his consciousness like a trained dog, without crossing over uninvited, content that every thought that hoped to enter his mind had to tread on *it* first.

Through the cloud of fatigue, Jeannette's name battered about inside Pierre like a scream trapped in an airtight container and unable to free itself.

He understood that he had to go to her and talk things over. But what he would actually say to her he did not know.

Before he had disentangled himself from the muddle of streets, night had fallen. He blundered in the dusk for quite some time, with no point of orientation, only barely making out the street signs. Suddenly he had the impression he had come off an unfamiliar field path and onto a safe, well-traveled road.

How often it happens that wandering unfamiliar side streets we suddenly hit upon a familiar road the mind cannot recall, and we pay no heed to our legs as they instinctively guide us forward, a sleepy team of horses pulling their slumbering driver down a path once traveled. Who's to say we haven't accidentally hit upon tracks we ourselves once laid, into which the feet step comfortably and firmly, like a dog tracking its own scent. The town we walk every day, the individual beads of images our gaze gels into the negatives of our memory, compose a uniform concept of the city only when strung together on that invisible thread of our scattered steps, that intangible map of our own Paris, so unlike the Parises of others — though their streets may be the same as ours.

When Pierre's meandering steps had finally brought him to Jeannette's home, it was already past midnight. Nonetheless, Pierre went upstairs and knocked. Her sleepy-eyed mother opened the door. Jeannette wasn't in. She hadn't been home since the day before.

Pierre spent a long time walking down the stairs before going back onto the street. Finding himself on the sidewalk, he didn't wait by the gate as before, but wandered heavily into the gloom.

On the corner of a bustling avenue, an open taxi drove past, splattering him with mud. A fat playboy was sprawled on the seat kissing the lithe girl clinging to him, his free hand brushing back her skirt to explore her slender thighs.

Pierre was unable to make out the girl's face, he saw only her dark blue cap and slender, almost girlish thighs, and with a sudden inner convulsion he recognized them as Jeannette's. He started to run, shoving disgruntled passersby left and right.

A moment later the car vanished around a corner right before his eyes.

He ran a few dozen more steps before stopping, winded. His murky, feverish thoughts suddenly flew off like spooked pigeons, leaving a gaping void and the flapping of wings in his temples.

He was on a narrow street that smelled of sauerkraut and carrots. He struggled to make it to the next corner.

On the abandoned fields of the spacious avenues towered gigantic green cylinders, red cones, white cubes, rough-hewn pyramids, a real kingdom of geometrical forms that had sprouted from the earth overnight. He was at the market stalls.

Gray, exhausted people in rags erected multistory buildings and towers from perfectly round heads of cabbage and bouquets of cauliflower. A sentimental cube of cut flowers shot up skyward. Everything that Paris would need for love and sustenance at daybreak had been gathered here during the night.

The pungent smell of freshly uprooted vegetables stopped Pierre in his tracks. The acrid, patient hunger that had been waiting in vain at the door to his consciousness started doggishly scratching with a paw.

Pierre moved closer. A man stooping under the weight of a gigantic armful of cauliflowers elbowed him and cursed. Pierre shifted meekly onto the sidewalk. Somebody grabbed him by the arm. He looked. A broad-shouldered, mustached, muscular man was pointing to a wheel-barrow filled with carrots . . .

Pierre took the hint and began to pile a formless tower on the street. A few other haggard people helped him out. He seemed to recognize one of them as his neighbor from the previous night on the metro steps.

The irregular red pyramid grew, drew even with the first floor, and rose higher.

When the empty wagons departed, all the vagrants were led into the depths of the hall. Taking a look around, Pierre noticed a mob, threadbare like himself, trailing behind. They all had filthy woolen rags wrapped around their necks, and their faces were bloodless, unshaven and sallow.

They were placed in a long line, and each was treated to a bowl of hot onion soup. Pierre also got a bowl and three francs cash. When he had slurped back the hot liquid, searing his mouth in the process, the bowl was snatched from his hands, and he was pushed aside to let others have their turn. Returning down the streets of this strange new city condemned to annihilation in only a few hours time, Pierre nicked a few big carrots still smelling of soil and greedily devoured them in an alleyway.

Dawn. Pierre was overcome with fatigue and drowsiness, lulled by the warmth of the aromatic soup he had consumed. He started scouting for a place to sleep.

Here, in the concave spaces of alcoves, in the recesses of the clotted homes, people slept balled up, coiled like orange peels. Pierre found himself a free crevice sheltered from the wind and planted himself in it, wrapping strips of newspaper from a garbage can around his freezing extremities, as he had seen others do. He was already asleep before he had managed to cozy up to the damp, mangy wall.

He was awoken by a short navy-blue man in a cape who had been patiently explaining to him for some minutes that lying down was forbidden and that he would have to move on at once. Pierre was not precisely sure where "on" might be, but nonetheless he obediently began drifting again.

The fantastical, laboriously built city of the night gave way like a Fata Morgana. Where a moment ago rose magical cubes and bulging cones of turnip heads, now the motorhome trams glided down their slick rails, their bow collectors impersonating smoke. It was now daytime . . .

Work was nowhere to be found. Roaming down side streets, Pierre entered garage after garage, offering to wash cars. He was greeted everywhere with the hostile faces and bloodshot eyes of workmen scrubbing autos, their eyes fierce, like dogs smelling a rival for a bone that will feed one at most. Nobody was in need of help.

When night fell, Jeannette's name trembled inside him — a new burning cramp more painful than the hunger. He instinctively started wandering in the direction of her apartment.

Jeannette still wasn't home.

The long streets multiplied before him, stretching into infinity like a rubber strap tied to his leg, they scampered from under his feet like lizards in the reflections of the dashing lights, they knowingly winked in the dusk with the eyes of a thousand hourly hotels.

Approaching one hotel, Pierre suddenly spotted a couple emerging. A broad-shouldered man and a petite, slender woman. He couldn't make out the woman's face in the darkness, but he recognized her silhouette as Jeannette's. He lurched toward them, shoving aside the passersby who got in his way. Before he managed to catch up with them, they had stepped into a taxi and driven off.

Before the doors of the empty hotel, he stood for a moment, helpless, in a powerless frenzy. The onrushing wave of pedestrians swept him further along.

He had not moved a hundred steps when he saw a couple leaving another hotel. The girl's silhouette was deceptively like Jeannette's. To get his hands on them, he had to cross the street. His path was blocked by a surging flood of cars. When he at last reached the opposite sidewalk, the couple was no longer there, they had dissolved into the crowd. In his helpless rage he choked on bitter tears.

All around hotel signs flickered on and off, suggestively flashing their alternating red and white lights, beckoning pedestrians inside. Jeannette could have been in any one of those hotels at that moment. Exhausted by the lusts of an insatiable muscleman, she was sleeping curled up like a child, her hands folded between her knees as though in prayer. The brute was stroking her white, frail, defenseless body. Pierre felt an inexpressible caring for her, almost tenderness.

His thoughts swirled, as tangled and twisted as the alleyways down which he drifted. On the thresholds of cheap hotels stood skinny women in shabby clothing, sheltering themselves from the rain under the rapidly blossoming palms of umbrellas. They stopped passersby with alluring staccato clicks of the tongue, just as dogs are called all over the world. In Paris, this is how people are called.

A slender, consumptive girl in soaked evening slippers promised him the most carefully concealed delights of her scrofulous body for only five francs. To emphasize an indecent gesture she meant to be seductive, she stuck out a white, furry tongue, as though she had indigestion.

Pierre shook from the cold and inner turmoil. From somewhere close by drifted the bouncy melody of a player piano. A small red lantern indicated it was a lively establishment.

Pierre recalled that he still had the three francs he'd earned during the night, and he decided to go in. He could order a *boca* with his three francs and sit in the warmth until morning.

He was enveloped by a wave of nauseating, staggering warmth, the powerful smell of powder, cheap perfumes, and cheap women. He groped his way to the first table by the wall and, utterly exhausted, slumped heavily onto the upholstered couch, whose springs produced a harsh lament.

When he opened his eyes into the dazzling light, it seemed to him that the couch spring beneath him was also the central spring of the whole mechanism he had unintentionally damaged.

The room in no way differed from the bar of an average public house, with tables and the piano now playing at such a slow tempo that Pierre could distinguish the vacuum between the individual tones of the gamboling keyboard, the pulse of a falling drop, a molecule of time.

By the wall, in the shade of the rachitic palms in green buckets, sprouted rows of speckled toadstool-tables, between which a dozen naked, voluptuous women circulated in languid, atomized movements, as though filmed in slow motion. Their plump, swollen bodies were visibly straining to break the air's resistance, rocking on the rubber pillows amid the flat, thickened clouds of tobacco smoke, the bodies of Renaissance angels, their faded sashes fluttering rhythmically and fanned out like the tattered wings of moths.

Pierre understood everything in a flash. The spring quivered, and a final bounce tossed him into a different reality.

Yes, this was paradise. Pierre saw this at once, though not being religious, he had never precisely imagined this institution before. He recognized it by the blissful torpor flowing through his veins, by the somehow familiar sounds, the paradisiacal music he seemed to know from a previous life, and by the rustling wings of the angels languidly circling him. But why did the clouds so remind him of tobacco smoke, why did the ambrosia distiller so resemble the bar of an ordinary bistro.

Suddenly his gaze fell on the corner, and Pierre died of humble ecstasy.

The Lord of Sabaoth, silent and still as a statue, towered over the wooden altar of the countertop. This was no Christian God with long white beard, it more resembled a bronze, serene Buddha, whose gigantic statue Pierre had once seen at a colonial exhibition. This was the same god precisely, matronly in shape, a puffy, wrinkled, feminine visage, yet from these ears hung the expensive votive offerings of massive earrings counterbalanced like the scales of an exact, mystical weight.

Men trickled one by one into the room with the chilly draft, fumbling and embarrassed, looking long and helplessly for the free table awaiting them.

At a few tables Pierre noticed other women, wrapped in the tight embrace of costly furs, like the sinners in the pictures of the old masters, who vainly struggled to cover their burning nakedness with the transparent fringe of their flowing hair.

From time to time a man would raise himself slowly, staring at one of the angels surrounding him, his eyes wide with astonishment — as though in her face he had suddenly seen that of another, someone familiar and long lost. Then the couple, taking each other by the hand and tracing slow semicircles with their feet, approached the altar of the counter, where in exchange for the mystical writ of a banknote the motionless Buddha of the puffy feminine visage made a ceremonial, liturgical gesture and handed the woman the symbolic ring of the number and the narrow stole of a towel. The betrothed then ascended in the majestic spirals of a twisting, celestial staircase, guided only by fluttering butterfly glances from the odd women wrapped in furs.

Pierre had all but fainted in the heavenly sensation of the penetrating warmth. He was overwhelmed by a sweet half-sleep; he soaked in it like a hot bath after a long journey.

He was brought to his senses by a voice battering itself long and persistently on the wickets of his consciousness. Reluctantly, he opened his eyes. Once more, the same view. He pricked up his ears:

"Don't you recognize me, Pierre?"

Someone was insistently, violently trying to wrench his head out from under the soft eiderdown of slumber. Pierre struggled to wriggle away from the voice, to let it blow past, like a man driven by a bullish alarm clock from the virginal undergrowth of sleep, but trying in vain to dig back into his warm, vespertine, tropical foliage. The voice glided somewhere above him, like a great bird at first oblivious to its prey, then turning a wide arc and swooping back as sudden as a knockout punch:

"Aren't you seeing Jeannette anymore?"

Pierre opened his eyes wide. The monotonous whimper of the player piano. Heavy, big-breasted angels paraded around the room like a hypnotic slow-motion film. One of them, entirely naked, her hair in a bun, was crouched on the edge of the couch, obstinately staring at Pierre.

"Don't you recognize me? I used to be a good friend of Jeannette's. We used to go to the pictures together. Remember, you'd always buy us candy? . . ."

Leaning over memory's booth like a stubborn fairground spectator, Pierre rummaged in the sawdust inside him, sometimes finding the sparkling pinpoints of scattered recollections.

Who was this nagging fly, struggling to bring him back to a reality he'd forever abandoned? Could it be just a trick of his imagination, still addled by earthly reminiscences? Then it would surely be enough to burrow deeper into the magical pillow of the all-cleansing slumber, washing over him like the tide.

But the meddlesome fly kept buzzing:

"I'm sure you're wondering how I got here. My God, it's so simple. I've never had any luck. I couldn't find a sugar daddy. It's not so easy to dress yourself and survive off two hundred francs a month. It's not the same if your boyfriend's as good as Jeannette's. I never had any luck. I got my health card. The warehouse threw me out on the second day, of course. I had to try working the street, but it's not as easy as it seems. The summer was okay, but when it started to rain . . . I get sick too easily. I caught a cold . . . I spent time in the hospital. When I got better, I came here. The work's not so tough. It's always warm. I earn less, but the pay is steady. Ten francs per guy, the house takes seven. They give us meals. It's a living. One day you earn more, the next day less, it depends on your luck. The day before yesterday, for example, I had fifteen guys — that's forty-five francs. Of course, you don't get that much every day. The work's a bit exhausting, but we get every third day off. Are you going already? Won't you stay just a while longer? I wanted to ask what Jeannette's up to. Isn't she your girlfriend anymore?"

Pierre suddenly stood up from the couch and sluggishly put on his cap. The spring leapt with a twang, setting the whole mechanism back in motion. It felt as though Pierre had poked the soap bubble surrounding him, and it suddenly burst.

The bouncing, breakneck lament of the Pianola. A dozen naked, perspiring girls turned around the room in quick orbits, adorned with cheap and tawdry bows. A few others were noisily cajoling some red sergeants into buying them beer. Smoke, tumult, stifling air.

At a few tables: lavishly dressed ladies in the company of gentlemen with shiny shirtfronts. Rather than drink their beer, the men were happy to generously give it to the girls swarming their tables and to admire their acrobatic skills. One of the guests would place a franc on the table and a girl would try to pick it up with only her genitals, without using her hands. The women in furs smiled approvingly.

Digging his three francs out of his pocket and leaving them on a saucer, Pierre shoved his way through to the door and, without responding to the affable farewell from the majestic Buddha-matron at the cash register, scuttled out to the street.

A fine drizzle was falling, punctuated by the distant blinking of stars. Over the frozen pool of the sky the Great Bear was shaking its shiny fur coat after its evening bath, and the chilly spray flew down to Earth.

IV

JEANNETTE STILL WASN'T HOME. Her old shrew of a mother, who had always cast a disparaging eye on her daughter's relationship with poor Pierre, one evening slammed the door in his face, claiming that Jeannette had moved out.

The city rumbled as always, an eternal ebb and flow. Inexhaustible crowds of people flooded into the street — paunchy, bloated men with salami necks. Any one them might have slept with Jeannette, maybe the night before, maybe only a few minutes ago. Any one them could have been the man he was aimlessly pursuing. With manic determination, Pierre stared into the faces of passersby, struggling to find some trace in them, the most minute convulsion remaining from an evening of delight spent with Jeannette. His keen nostrils took in the smells of clothing, trying to catch the scent of Jeannette's perfume, the subtle fragrance of her tiny body.

Jeannette wasn't there, she wasn't anywhere.

And yet she was everywhere. Pierre clearly saw and recognized her in the silhouette of every girl accompanied by her lover from the front door of every hotel, riding alongside in a taxi, disappearing suddenly into the nooks of the first gateway she happened to notice. A thousand times he ran, furiously shoving aside the pedestrians forever standing in an impenetrable wave between her and him. He always arrived too late.

Days turned into days in a monotonous play of shadow and light.

After barren weeks of wandering, he had given up looking for work.

For many days he had been carrying a greedy, sucking hunger in his belly as a mother does a fetus, lifting nausea into his throat and dissolving a leaden fatigue throughout his body.

The contours of objects sharpened as though outlined with pencil, the air became rarified and transparent under the bell jar of the urban sky. The houses swelled and became pliable, squishing unexpectedly into one another, only to stretch once more into an improbable and absurd perspective. People wore scrubbed and indistinguishable faces. Some had two noses, others two pairs of eyes. Most had two heads at the ends of their necks, one strangely crammed onto the other.

One evening the tide chucked him from the Montmartre boulevards and thrust him against the glass frontage of a grand music hall. A gigantic fiery windmill slowly turned its blades on their axis, summoning the ludicrous Don Quixotes of pleasure from the endless avenues of the world. The windows of the surrounding houses glowed with the bright-red embers of the unquenchable fever burning within.

It was time for the show to begin. The lobby was glassed in like a lighthouse, and around it a furious wave of cars crashed onto the side-walk, only to recede moments later, leaving the white foam of ermine capes and tuxedo mantles, shirtfronts and sleeves on the rocky shore of the pavement.

A vast black crowd, a roaring deluge, pressed into the side doors, jostling and crushing toes. Pierre had the impression he'd seen such a mob somewhere before, that he was a missing piece of it. It reminded him of the same idiotic stream of people that had squeezed into the market for a bowl of onion soup.

A new, towering tidal wave tossed him aside, smashing his face into a wall — which upon closer inspection turned out to be a soft human face, one suddenly familiar. The face, using hands to free itself from the unexpected pressure, was also inspecting him.

"Pierre?"

Pierre strained his mind to recall something. Now he seemed to remember: Etienne, from the ground-floor packing room.

They cut through the crowd to a side street. Etienne said something sharp and incomprehensible. Yes, he'd been sacked as well. There was no work to be found. Crisis. You had to find some way to eke out a living. He'd tried everything. He'd dealt coke. No good. Too much competition. He'd tried pimping his own Germaine. She always brought in a dozen francs a night. But times were very tough. Not many foreigners. Supply was outstripping all possible demand. You had to make a little extra on the side.

Now he was a "scout." A lot of legwork, but still, relatively lucrative. You had to know a few addresses and above all, not take any lip, that was key. You also had to know a bit of psychology. What attracts whom. Lots of competition as well, but if you were a good talker, you'd make out all right.

He specialized in older men. He knew a few houses where they kept fresh-faced little girls. That was a sure thing. Not far away, on Rue de Rochechouart. Thirteen-year-olds. Surefire goods. You just had to know how to serve them up. The presentation: short dress, a little apron, pigtails. A schoolroom upstairs: a picture of a saint, a child's bed, a lectern, and a blackboard, where they'd written in chalk: 2 x 2 = 5. The full illusion. No older man could resist. You got ten francs from the guy for telling him the address and five from the house. It was a living.

This was his turf. If Pierre wanted, he could work him in, whisper a few addresses in his ear. The key? Eloquence. And a keen eye. Knowing whom to approach. Best to wait in front of a restaurant. Maybe check out his old turf, in front of Hôtel de l'Abbaye. Surefire. As long as you didn't mess up the addresses . . .

A new whirlpool of pedestrians violently swept Pierre and carried him blindly. Etienne got lost somewhere. Pierre tried not to fight it and let himself be swept along. After a few hours' ebb and flow he was spit out at Place Pigalle.

A bright turnstile of advertisements. The flaming syllables of words written in the air by an unseen hand. Instead of "Mene, Tekel, Peres" — "Pigalle," "Royal," and "Abbaye."

"Abbaye . . ."

Etienne had mentioned that.

A slender, fancy-dressed porter stood there in his short jacket, frozen in front of the glowing entrance, until an obsequious bow doubled him over.

Two older gentlemen. Alone. Loitering on the corner. Smoking.

Pierre mechanically moved closer in. The gentlemen, absorbed in their talk, paid him no mind. Pierre tugged on the older, potbellied gentleman's sleeve and mumbled into his ear:

"A good time . . . thirteen-year-olds . . . little aprons . . . a child's bed . . . a blackboard . . . 2 x 2 = 5 . . . the full illusion . . ."

The older gentleman violently yanked away his sleeve. Both men involuntarily checked for their wallets. Hastily, almost at a run, they jumped into a passing taxi, fearfully slamming the doors.

Pierre was left alone on the corner. He was baffled. Leaning on a wall, he blundered through the night down a dark, deserted boulevard. A pane of glass. A mirror. A gray, sallow face covered with a tangle of beard emerged from the mirror to greet him — the red, searing lanterns of his eyes.

Pierre stopped in his tracks. He seemed to understand. They'd simply gotten scared off. No earning a living with a face like that.

In the middle of the boulevard strolled a couple locked in an embrace, kissing with every other step. A small, slanting cap. Long, slender legs. Jeannette!! The couple went into a corner hotel, kissing all the while. Again a car — a damned car! — cut in front of him.

With a single hop, Pierre landed on the other side. The hotel door gave off a matte gleam. Six tall floors. Where to look? In which room? No chance! Better to wait until they came out.

Exhausted, Pierre leaned against a wall. Minutes passed, hours perhaps. Surely they were undressing by now.

In a frenzy of self-torment, Pierre's mind went through all the successive stages of those caresses he so lucidly recalled, replacing himself with that other, faceless man with upturned collar.

He could now be quite certain they were lying in bed. The scoundrel's hands were roaming over her firm, white body. Now they were inter-twined . . .

Suddenly everything burst. A couple was leaving the hotel across the way. A paunchy, bloated fellow and a slender girl. Jeannette!! The girl, climbing on her toes (oh, how well he knew that pose!) kissed the bloated fellow on the mouth. She hailed a taxi.

Screaming and leaping headlong, Pierre landed on the other side of the road. The taxi had made off with Jeannette. The bloated fellow remained in front of the hotel, examining the contents of his bulging wallet by the lamplight. The flush of delight from a few minutes before had yet to fade from his jowls. Jeannette's parting kiss lingered on his revolting lips. The crumpled folds of his clothing still held the warmth of her touch, the singular, unforgettable smell of her body. At last!

The fist tore free from Pierre's frame of its own accord and landed square between bulging, encysted eyes. The hollow crash of a toppled body. The bull-like, flabby neck squished like dough between his taut fingers. The wallet fell from his hands and flapped to the gutter, helpless as a shot bird.

The night responded to the powerless, hoarse calls of the fat man with a sustained, plaintive whistle. In a flutter of cheviot wings, navy-blue bats descended from the night's recesses on all sides onto Pierre's scattered red mane, like to the flame of a candle.

The rhythmic swing of a vehicle carried him somewhere into the infinity of the horizon. The narcotizing flap of capes. On his face — like a cold soldier's shroud — the American flag of the sky, with stars upon stars.

V

EVERYTHING THAT HAPPENED NEXT JUTTED across the boundary of three-dimensional reality, like Chaplin's shack over the precipice.

The black walls streaming with twilight. A perfect cube of musty air you could cut with a knife, like a gigantic, magical Maggi bouillon cube. In the deep, barred well of the window — a gallon of condensed sky.

Pierre encountered a new, miniature underworld governed by its own peculiar laws on the margins of the giant, complicated mechanism of the world. An alien world of things undeserved: the narrow, comfortable cot under the drooping canopy of the ceiling, morning and evening — the mess tin of warm soup, flavored with a hunk of bread, free of labor. On the other side of the wall, in the neighboring cramped cells — a strange society of castaways, discarded like waste by the scrupulous, unforgiving machine of the world to this place behind the high wall on Boulevard Arago and, by someone's inconceivable will, tied and hitched to a new and bizarre mechanism governed by the new and bizarre laws of the World of Readymade Things.

The pointless walks around the symmetrical circles of the courtyard, regular as a carousel, under the low, sooty bell jar of the prison skies. The long string of the rosary manipulated by an unseen hand, of which each bead is the live, pulsating guts of human existence. The machinery built of cogs that had no place beyond the wall, but which unexpectedly meshed when thrown together in this monstrous lumberyard, clinging to one another and creating a new collective organism, functioning according to a new guiding principle, one scarcely conceived on the other side.

The days ever changed into other days, somehow different, longer, outlined by the inscrutable measurements of some strange manual.

Somewhere, in the stuffy vases of apartments, in the flowerpots of offices, slowly, leaf by leaf, the metaphysical flower of the calendar was blossoming. The long thousands of miles measured in the cell extended in one mental straight line, losing itself somewhere in the muddy, reed-covered banks of the Orinoco River.

Only at night, when the word "sleep" was illuminated on the blank face of the mystical regulator, whose electric light gave orders by suggestion, did dreams come.

The black coursing waves of reality from the other side, tethered in place by the indomitable wall of the day and the regulations, surrounded the island on Boulevard Arago from each and every side. The wall cracked and swayed. The towering river of bodies, paper money, actions, bottles, exertions, lamps, kiosks, and legs crashed above the rooftops in a throbbing wave, a rumbling din. Aged, unaired mattresses, slept on to the point of disrepair, poured out of the gaping maws of hotels like drawers from an open wardrobe, multiplying and rising up into a gigantic hundred-floor Tower of Babel with creaking, springy stairs. At the top, on the enormous, king-sized mattress of *Le Lit National* lay the tiny, defenseless Jeannette. A vast throng of men crept up the trembling stairs like ants: blond, brunet, redheaded, they all wished to ravish for a moment her weary body with their heavy, lust-soaked carnality, one after another, everyone, the city, Europe, the world! The tower creaked with convulsing springs as it swayed, bent, and fell, inundated by the waves of the furious sea, beating its shattering tide on the rocky wall around the shaven-headed Robinsons asleep on their island looking out onto Boulevard Arago.

•

One day, unexpectedly, as if one of the gears of the well-oiled machine had suddenly ground down, Pierre's lonely cell was crammed with a ruckus of people, their heads gashed and dried blood on their bandages and the collars of their blue shirts. There was the powerful odor of male sweat, gunpowder, and the acrid, indelible soot of factories. Heavy words fell everywhere, chipped like paving stones: revolution, proletariat, capitalism.

From the fragments of sentences, stories, and cries unraveled a solid four-day epic, written in blood on the asphalt, by the glare of electric lamps.

The table of contents was always, irrevocably, the same:

Unemployment. Pay cuts. Gloomy rallies. From the rally: a march through the city, with *The Internationale.*

They were harassed by the police. Cornered in side alleys. Beaten with rubber truncheons until they bled. The trampled pavement spat a hail of stones in reply.

The enraged soldiers charged. A single salvo paved the street anew. In response: the stony jaws of the street bared the teeth of its barricades.

A massacre. Sticky, dun blood on the sidewalks. Trucks loaded with people. The crowd, some tens of thousands, like a number crossed off a balance sheet, was hauled off to the margins behind gray and impenetrable prison walls.

Incredible numbers were cited. The prisons couldn't hold this oversized haul. Fifteen thousand were apparently packed into La Santé Prison. Fresnes Prison was said to have even more. The army surrounded the prison buildings. Rows of fifteen slept side by side on the floors of cells intended for a single man. Walks were held at various times of the day, in shifts, to avoid havoc.

The flawless mechanism of this underground world began helplessly spinning its gears like an overwound watch. The hands still traveled their familiar paths, but the loose cogs spun, dragging a muddled chaos of screws and springs behind them.

The prison telegraph tapped from cell to cell, day and night, with its one thousand tireless woodpeckers.

Those placed in the cells for general offenders demanded they be moved to the ward for political prisoners. The prison council denied the request. The prisoners replied with a hunger strike.

Huddled in his corner, wary as a dog, lapping up his portion of soup and greedily swallowing his bread, Pierre felt fifteen pairs of sober, steely eyes — enlarged by the atropine of hunger — on him, and under their gaze the tasty morsel of prison bread stuck in his throat, rising on the yeast of his saliva and turning into a hunk too large to swallow. The thick soup grew cold in its mess tin, coating over with a map-like skin.

At night, long discussions reached him from afar, as if through a glass wall. The words, chiseled like blocks, piled one on top of another, and soon a spired building shot up into the sky. If they could have gone outside and rolled up their sleeves, they would have built it from real stone, and just as spacious and proud.

Like a shoddy machine, the world destroys more than it produces. This cannot go on. You have to strip everything down to the screws, throw away whatever's useless, and after taking it apart, build it all over again, once and for all! The plans are ready, the builders' fingers are itching, but the old, corroded scrap iron won't give way. It has taken root, a coat of rust has formed in its seams, they'd have to yank out every screw with their teeth.

And in the black, smoky box of the cell, the myth of a new, reconstructed world unspooled like the reel of a hallucinogenic film.

Back in the factory, Pierre had heard long and monotonous stories about this new world, a world with neither rich nor oppressed, where the factories would be owned by the workers, and labor would change from a form of slavery to a hymn, to hygiene for the liberated body. He didn't believe them. No one would budge the diabolical machine, not even an inch! It had grown deep into the earth. It had been running since time immemorial, ever since it had been set in motion. Seize the cogs with your bare hands? It wouldn't stop, it would just rip off your hands. He saw blood on soiled bandages, hands bound in bloody rags, and he thought: another exercise in futility. The battered bodies were flung off the transmission belt and onto the sidelines, behind the wall, with a flick of the wrist.

Sometimes at night, a white-hot word of hatred would fly out from the huddled group, fall like a spark upon the soft sawdust of his dreams and then blaze up with a red flame: Go! Stand arm in arm with them! Storm! Smash! Take revenge!

Then Pierre awoke with a sudden jolt and sat up on his cot.

But the cool, glassy words of the blue-shirted folks piled symmetrically like bricks, and there was no anger in their words, there was no thick, destructive hatred, only the strong will to build — the pickax and the trowel.

No, these people don't know how to hate! They have heaps of plans for replacing one machine with another. Replace this one with that, and again they spin circles, cogs mesh with cogs, they pull, drag, carry the defenseless human splinters, and again they'll bloody their hands on the black spokes of the wheels, these terror-crazed Pierres, incapable of stopping the wheels, or stalling them for even a second.

Pierre's outstretched hand convulsed, retracted into the depths, his head rose from its pillow, slowly settled back onto his shoulder, then moments later fell onto the mattress, and there he lay pressed into the flattened straw — a man no more, just a tortoise in an impenetrable shell of solitude.

VI

ONE MORNING, WHEN THE VERDANT RAGS of foliage hanging from the heated wires of the branches released an acrid, burning fragrance, the enchanted gate suddenly opened before Pierre's astonished eyes, and he was violently shoved outside.

He stood there for a long moment, staggered by this improbable event, hardly knowing how to start, where to go, lost once more in this strange and incomprehensible world, where there were no comfortable cots, and to get a mess tin of soup you had to drag heavy loads of damp carrots through a long, sleepless night.

His first, instinctive reflex was to go back through the gigantic closed gate, but it refused to suck him back in. In this world of hostile and inaccessible things, entrance to the World of Readymade Things was possible only by extraordinary effort.

But then his disoriented thoughts, running down the twisting and comfortless alleys of this world, suddenly snagged on an old wound, and Pierre decided to seek out Jeannette.

It was the first time in months (years?) that he had set off walking in a straight line. He walked for a long time down paths of alleys intersecting at every possible angle, which some mysterious giants had strewn with the enormous gravel of cobblestones. Everything here was different. People jostled each other as they ran, unchoreographed and haphazard, free, it seemed, of any mutual regulations, as if circulating in a chimerical world of absolute liberty. Navy-blue police officers rose here and there at boulevard intersections like majestic statues, a single flick of their miracle-working fingers and the flood of vehicles were stopped and then set in motion, indicating that another mechanism was at work, one too complex and intangible to fathom.

When Pierre found himself at Place Vendôme, the clock was striking twelve, and through the half-open sluice gates of the warehouses a clamorous wave of midinettes came bubbling onto the street. Pierre desperately strained his eyes to find Jeannette amidst the crowd. The stragglers slowly began dispersing.

The warehouse was as stark as an orangery. He was told that Jeannette hadn't been to work for some time.

He went back out to the street feeling disconcerted, as though his last lead had failed him. He felt Jeannette had vanished into the black forest of the city, vanished forever, and he would never manage to find her again.

A crowd surge pushed him onto the road, then a wave of cars threw him onto a slender stone island where a haughty little man peered down onto the spray lashing below from the summit of a giant bronze column, helpless as a sparrow on a telegraph pole.

Across the way, along a wide stretch of road, a dense herd of huffing, breathless cars battered against the low embankments of the sidewalks, ready to boil over at any moment.

Behind the front-running, purebred, greyhound-sleek Hispano-Suiza, with its shifty headlight eyes and feminine gasoline juices, sped a motley, rabid pack of dogs, barking and squealing, snapping at one another, vainly struggling to stick their nostrils under its feminine tail: the majestic Rolls-Royces, stout as Great Danes, the Amilkars, squat as dachshunds, the Fords like dirty, stray mutts, and little Citroëns like short, docked fox terriers. The tumult rose above the street, a choking estrous odor, the scream of a maddened chase, the stupefying vapors of a scorching summer afternoon.

Pierre watched this frenzy of bodies with eyes wide in horror, searching in vain for some missing thread, a trail leading out of this deluge of rampant carnality that had him caught, irrevocably, with no hope of salvation, unable to resist.

Warm waves swept him away like a splinter of wood and carried him off blind, with no compass.

Thus began again the pointless days, the aimless drifting over the swaying oceans of the streets, the nights underneath the mystic umbrella of the stars, a loneliness unknown to even Alain Gerbault, that laughable Sancho Panza rocked on the shoreless sheets of the Atlantic for months on end.

The old, familiar hunger was building itself a nest in the sinews of his bowels. Like a gull in the tangled rigging of an abandoned ship, it gave him not a single moment's rest. Pierre made no attempt to shoo it away. The useless pneumatic vacuum of entrails he carried around inside him was like a city whose entire population was quarreling, and there would be no hand to toss in a crinkling packet of food.

One night, wandering down the knotted labyrinths in search of a warmer recess to sleep, and drawing close to something he at first took to be a comfortable crate, Pierre spotted a dark, hunched figure in the gloom. The figure leapt to one side, flashing the ominous whites of his eyes and baring a predatory swath of teeth. From the recess wafted the heavy, nauseating odor of decomposing waste. Then Pierre realized that what he had taken for a crate was in fact a row of enormous garbage cans, emptied in the morning by the sanitation vehicles that circulated through the city.

The figure rooting through the containers came menacingly toward Pierre, his body shielding the foul contents. From his bared teeth came a hoarse rattle:

"Scram! It's mine! Go look somewhere else!"

Then, like a bolt from the heavens, a simple revelation struck Pierre: The garbage cans in building gateways surely contain scraps of food!

He obligingly went back in search of other gateways. Yet he soon discovered that in a democratic society a revelation was not the sole privilege of the individual, it was common property. In each and every gateway he was confronted by the same ominous whites of the eyes and bared teeth of first finders, rearing up from redolent containers filled with mysterious treasures.

Passing by a long line of alcoves, Pierre finally hit upon one that was . . . empty! The bins that lay inside had been ransacked top to bottom, a clear sign that some lucky fellow had beat him to it.

Pierre was undaunted — he greedily threw himself upon them, carefully digging through everything once again.

His trophy for this long search was a box of preserved meat with some scraps left, and a veal rib that could still be gnawed. Placing this paltry meal on a low wall, he licked it eagerly, in no way taming his hunger, only jostling it out of its numb stupor.

Exhausted and resigned from further searching, he drifted down a boulevard and plopped down on the first bench he came to. Sleep tucked him in under a tattered, hole-filled rag.

Through the holes in the rag he saw the stars twinkling high above, blinking on and off with the flick of an invisible switch, advertisements for remote heavenly hotels, summoning lovelorn souls through their gates, couples gone astray in outer space.

VII

A POWERFUL TUG FORCED HIS EYES OPEN. Instead of a navy-blue policeman, Pierre saw a healthy, ruddy face with a high forehead staring down at him from under the visor of a cap.

It was already day. The man bending over him had clearly been shaking him for some time. The young, happy voice revived him like a stream of cool, crystalline water.

"Pierre! Why, of course it's Pierre! I recognized you at once!"

The voice was familiar, round and polished like a billiard ball that, having ricocheted around the table of his consciousness, suddenly arrived at the right pocket, as if it had been specially carved out for the ball to land in. But when had it been carved out there?

Pierre squeezed his eyes shut, vainly trying to peek through the pocket into the depths. At first he saw only blackness. Then when his inner eyes adjusted he started to make out a slender, tentative shaft of light. It seemed as though he were starting to distinguish the vague contours of objects, like staring through a keyhole:

The narrow, extended silhouette of a bell tower in a red top hat of burnt roof tiles. A thin straw man in a black perforated cap, tipped rakishly onto the spot where the left ear is normally located. A scarecrow with ragged clumps of straw peeking out of his shirtsleeves, standing erect before the green background of a creaking, freshly painted window shutter. A crooked well green with age, its crank hunched astraddle, all wrapped in the links of a ruddy, rusted chain, a wooden pail at one end, reeking of damp. How comfortable it would be to ride it down into the depths of the black well, with its smell of decay and moldy earth, the creak of the ascending chain, eyes trained on the small, round window of sky up above, the heart pounding fiercely, a chill of fear running down the spine, and in the breast — such joy that the throat contracts, so long as the burble of water down below doesn't let you know with a sudden, terrifying shudder that it's time to yank on the chain for all you're worth. Then the centuries-old, geriatric chain, groaning and lamenting, pulls you slowly, laboriously upward, along the black, moldy, fungus-coated walls, toward the sky, toward the flat space, rolled out like dough as far as the eye can see, toward the jolly, chuckling voice, ringing so wide across the panel of the horizon, round and smooth like a gramophone record.

Now the sound of the unexpected voice, situated in space and groping to situate itself in time on the line of their intersection, started slowly reworking itself into the contours of a defined human being, until, translated back into the abstract language of sound, it crystallized into the few syllables of a hastily uttered name.

Pierre experienced a remarkable sense of relief. He felt as though he had been pulling a bucket full of precious liquid from his depths for endless hours, like from a dark, deep well bearded with fungus — he was afraid it would slosh, and he pulled with all his might, feeling that at any moment it would slip irretrievably into the black abyss — and now he was holding it in his hands, raised onto the surface, unspilled, intact.

The person thus raised so laboriously from the depths was clearly unaware of the difficult process that had just been accomplished, and he smiled broadly, and in-between his broad smiles he showered Pierre with shards of disjointed sentences that pricked like broken glass.

Now this was a surprise! He'd recognized Pierre at once, though it *had* been some time. How could he not recognize a childhood friend? True, he'd changed a good deal. In fact, he had heard long ago that Pierre was in Paris, but there had been no way of tracking him down. He'd heard some rumors . . . Truth to tell, he wasn't looking so hot. Out of work, huh? He'd heard. He was going to have to get by somehow. Above all, he couldn't go plopping himself down here, on this bench. If he didn't have an apartment, he could stay with him for the time being.

For his part, he couldn't complain. He was getting by all right. He worked as an attendant in a bacteriological institute. Easy work, an apartment, days off. Pierre could have a look for himself. He lived nearby. They'd be there in a moment.

Pierre mutely and obediently wandered down the unfamiliar streets, dragging his feet, following the yarn of the unexpected voice, the ball of which he had lost (so long ago!) at the bottom of a green village well he knew from his childhood.

VIII

THE UNPREDICTABLE ROULETTE OF FORTUNE had spent hours stubbornly skipping past the baleful number on which the gambler-fatalist had staked it all, stripping him in turn of his possessions, his convictions, and his woman, things that could not be won back, until finally, his shirt already lost, when he was just getting up to leave the table, the ball stopped on the long-awaited number — but as usual, it was too late.

Pierre found work. A water tower at a city filter station in Saint-Maur. From eight to six. Every morning the stuffy, packed suburban trolley car. A narrow, eight-cornered room with bird-patterned wallpaper on Boulevard Diderot. Breakfasts and lunches. The long, slender sticks of bread rolls, vanishing into the insatiable orifice of the mouth, like fire-brands down the gullets of fairground jugglers. Warmth and sleep.

In the evening, having returned from work, Pierre lay for hours stretched out on his soiled mattress, relishing the passive pleasures of digestion, his gaze fixed absently on the uncomplicated arabesques of the wallpaper. Freed from the tyranny of the mind, his gaze devoted itself to pure, useless creativity, industriously combining random fragments of patterns — the beak of a bird torn from its head, leaves from a branch, and the immaterial smear of a shadow — into the contours of human figures, fantastical, predatory profiles, a new realm of objects, unsettling and surreal.

In the depths of his idle consciousness, congealed motionless like a cornfield on a windless, scorching Indian summer afternoon, lurked the vague, hollow presentiment of an open wound, deep and black as a mine shaft. His languid thoughts, drifting on the surface like lazy gusts of wind, instinctively tiptoed past this spot, as if afraid that one misstep would send them hurtling into the void. Left to its own devices, his vision assembled shifting outlines from cutout fragments, and some blind internal instinct kept it from merging the treacherous contours into a certain faded feminine profile.

On the first Sunday, Pierre was visited by a ruddy René, the accidental perpetrator of his recent prosperity, who invited him out for a stroll around the city.

The inactive, dusty tedium of the day off made the streets teeming, stifling, and dull. It was the stretch of the Parisian summer following the Grand Prix, when the last corpuscles of blue, or even dyed-blue, blood evaporate from the heated body of Paris along with the sweat and water, condensing in receptacles seemingly built for that very purpose — Dauville, Trouville, and Biarritz — and Paris's blood takes on a color that is decidedly red, the red of the urban working-class parvenu.

It was the eve of July 14, Bastille Day, and tricolor flags and paper lanterns were hastily strung about the city. The streets were flooded with crowds in festive attire, giving off that special odor of a French holiday: cheap wine, tobacco, and democracy.

After meandering a few hours, Pierre and René found themselves before the gates of the institute, where René was to work a night shift. The institute was empty. A damp chill blew from inside, and with it a complex smell of chemicals, such as one finds in country pharmacies.

René offered to show Pierre the laboratory.

Up a wide, stone staircase, dark as a tunnel, they went.

The laboratory was filled with the same rejuvenating chill. Along the walls, from the depths of cabinets, strange, unknown creatures made of glass and steel stared out at Pierre with one thousand glassy eyes. Their mysterious shapes filled him with apprehension.

René returned a moment later in a white laboratory smock.

He was one of those creatures, at once simple and complex, encountered most frequently on the lowest rung of the social ladder, in whom a sixth sense had developed, unbeknown to those around him, through constant, direct contact with a hermetic world of objects — a sense of forever foreign, silent matter — often found in those spending long periods of time among deaf-mutes.

Living in this practically irreal world — a transparent world of glass, of fantastic, inconceivable apparatuses — as though it were a normal environment, René could glean the unique individuality of objects, sense the unique in even identical objects, mass produced to appear the same to us, much like the faces of Europeans appear identical to a black man from Senegal.

Holding them gingerly every day, dusting and polishing them, René shuddered in fear as he registered their fragile lives, which dangled on one careless move of his coarse fingers. Taking root in him was a horrible instinct of responsibility for the preservation of this illusory world of helpless and mysterious creatures left to the mercies of his unschooled hands.

Whenever he happened to smash one of the instruments entrusted to his care, he suffered it more than he would have the death of a living creature.

When one of the institute's laboratory assistants — a person he got along with splendidly and who even showed him empathy — poisoned himself one day on a microbe and died in terrible agonies, René appeared to show not the slightest grief; on the contrary, it seemed to give him malicious satisfaction. The assistant had had the ill fortune to break one of the retorts the previous day, something that René had been unable to forgive. He believed in his heart of hearts that the assistant's demise was his just deserts.

This in no way altered the fact that René had an exceptionally good heart and would not have harmed a fly.

Collecting the fragments of the broken instruments and trying in vain to piece them back together, René bitterly thought:

"Let men harm one another — a man is no loss! A man can defend himself. A *thing* is a different matter. Only a scoundrel would harm a thing. A thing is defenseless."

This feeling of innate responsibility for the lives of hundreds of these fragile creatures outweighed his human sentiments.

In moments of great cataclysms and revolutions people of René's ilk are capable of the greatest acts of heroism and devotion to the safety of an endangered machine, while watching with indifference as human blood is spilled before their eyes.

That awareness of constant responsibility for the life of a miniature world, over which he felt himself lord and caretaker, nevertheless filled René with a deep sense of pride and a feeling of personal significance, which his colleagues clearly derided. In the fictitious hierarchy of this world's administrators, René was a person of the lowest grade.

The whole afternoon's visit and stroll around town was all in all a carefully planned maneuver to get Pierre, offhandedly as it were, to the door of the institute, to dazzle Pierre with his miniature kingdom.

Guiding a dumbstruck Pierre past the glass cabinets as though before the ranks of a sparkling army under his command, René reveled in his delusional might.

In front of one large cabinet where large and small test tubes filled with liquid were visible in rows of stands, he found himself compelled to deliver a brief lecture on bacteriology, illustrated by the colonies of silent microbes imprisoned in the hermetically-sealed glass.

"Here, behind this seemingly inconspicuous pane of glass, we keep a unique menagerie. All the possible plagues of the world. In that test tube on the left, you've got scarlet fever; a little further on — tetanus; in this one — spotted fever; in that one, way in back — typhoid fever; there, sixth from the end — cholera. Quite a collection, eh? You see those two test tubes on the right with the white, opaque liquid? That's the apple of our assistant's eye — the bubonic plague. He's been working on it for a year, sustaining it on nutrients of his own devising, and he says that some incredible strains have been developed. Bacteria like stallions. This autumn he will be presenting his brood at a bacteriological conference. He's boasted that he'll start a revolution in bacteriology. So, what do you think of the place? Not bad, eh? Just imagine if you were to set all these bugs loose while walking through town — what do you think, would there be much left of our Paris?"

Pierre nodded absentmindedly.

The visit lingered into evening. It was already late when Pierre finally bid his hospitable friend farewell and, shown out through the gate, was back on the street.

He was supposed to have the night shift, at midnight, at the water tower, and he needed to make it to Saint-Maur by then.

It was now dusk, and the streets were illuminated by the matte moons of electric lamps.

After the memorable encounter with René on the boulevard bench, Pierre had conscientiously avoided being in the city at night. At nightfall, the familiar daytime cube of the city, so devoid of mysteries, shed its familiar contours, burst with a thousand alleyway cracks invisible by daylight, and became populated by armies of blazing lamps rushing about in a panic, ominous phantoms of glowing inscriptions, and the screeching of monsters with fiery, bulging eyes.

Venturing into this labyrinth, Pierre felt his head spin, and he immediately lost his bearings. The old, familiar waves snatched him up like a ball.

He got to a small island with the remains of his strength and leaned against the stone portal of the Saint-Denis gate. The streets were already ablaze with colorful bubbles of paper lanterns for the next day's celebration. Here and there people started dancing. The sidewalks and streets swarmed with throngs of couples in a clinch.

Pierre suddenly felt as though an underground current, dammed somewhere deep down by bricks jammed tight over the previous few days, was welling up inside him, undermining the masonry. He felt the jostled bricks popping out one after the other, the scrape of the mortar breaking apart — the floors of his daily affairs, erected as painstakingly as swallows building a nest, sinking into the tide one by one — and a warm red stream slowly flooded his eyes. He shut them, wracked with pain.

When they opened, he saw only the blinking of the countless hotels, the swarm of blood-red, bloated necks and the thousands of feminine profiles, as identical as photo-reproductions of a face he remembered so well.

Through every doorway, pressed tight to their apoplectic suitors, dozens and hundreds of Jeannettes came and went in a feverish haste, one identical to the next, Jeannette in an enchanted hall of mirrors, in a living forest with tree trunks of flabby, bulging necks.

Pierre's seething hatred made him start to swoon and choke. There hovered for a moment, like a distant reflection, the vision of his taut hands clenched around the neck of the fat man from the Montmartre hotel, the lardy folds seeping between his fingers, and then it disappeared, without leaving the satisfaction he craved.

No! Not enough! What good would *one* do! One thousand! One million! All of them! The city! Where to find those gigantic hands, those mile-long fingers, to throttle those phlegmy, jiggling throats with one squeeze? All of them! Crumple! Topple! Imbibe their powerless gurgle! Hands! Where to find such hands?

Suddenly an unexpected clarity, a blinding magnesium flame, illuminated his brain, and he stood there baffled, stunned, and silent. For a moment he was thunderstruck, then he turned on the spot and started back the way he came, straight through the crowd, like Christ walking on water, giant and majestic, as though bearing aloft the beaming monstrance of his hatred. He felt people stepping aside for him, opening before him a long stretch of road unto a vanishing point.

Finding himself once more before the door of the institute he had left just moments before, Pierre calmly rang the bell.

René opened the door, surprised at the unexpected repeat visit. Pierre calmly explained that he had forgotten his cane, which — as far as he could recall — he had left in the laboratory.

They went up the wide, stone staircase, cold as a tunnel.

The cane wasn't in the laboratory. Pierre asked René if he would check the other rooms, while Pierre had one last look in all the corners.

When René returned empty-handed after a few minutes of fruitless searching, he found Pierre still poking behind one of the laboratory cabinets. The cane wasn't there.

Pierre admitted he might not even have left home with it — he would have to check the following day — and for the second time he said goodbye to his hospitable friend, who was earnestly surprised by this remarkable display of absentmindedness.

The third-class carriage on the train traveling to Saint-Maur that evening was full of smoke, noise, and suburbanites excited by the approaching holiday. A slim, red-headed man sitting on a corner bench stood out in the hum of the general conversation as he took no part in the chitchat and seemed to be eavesdropping, silent and distracted.

The man got out at the Saint-Maur station. The conversation continued.

Arriving at the water tower, Pierre noticed he was a full five minutes late, and he ran upstairs to relieve the day shift.

The engineer on duty appeared, finishing his nightly rounds. In a moment the last footsteps below faded to silence.

Then Pierre dipped his hand into his pocket and took out two small test tubes. He carefully held them up to his eyes. The test tubes contained a thick, whitish liquid. Pierre shook them gently under the light.

Then with the test tubes in one hand he approached the big centrifugal pump, powered by a diesel engine.

A door slammed somewhere below. Pierre stopped and listened carefully for a moment. Complete silence. Then Pierre took a big wrench and started opening the faucet of the enormous funnel pump that served the reservoir, setting the water in motion. While opening the faucet, he tried to uncork the first test tube with his fingers. The cork was tight, it wouldn't budge. Exasperated, Pierre clenched it between his teeth.

Uncorking both test tubes, he carefully poured their contents into the wildly splashing larynx of the funnel.

Down below, the water burbled in rhythmic time to the beat of the diesel pistons, a measured rising and falling like the valve of a gigantic heart, forever pumping new supplies of clear, transparent blood into the starving arteries of faraway, slumbering Paris.

2

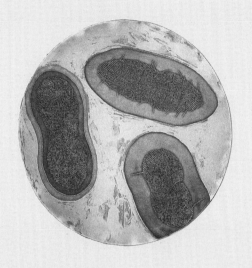

INTAGLIO - MICROGRAPH *Nucl. Fen.*

Magnified...........²..........diameters

Prepared. C. A. S. September 2006

1/15

I

THE FOLLOWING DAY WAS THE 14TH OF JULY.

Paris's intrepid shopkeepers, those who had stormed the Bastille to erect in its place an ugly hollow column "with a view of the city," twelve bistros, and three brothels for average citizens and one for homosexuals, were throwing a party in their own honor, as they did every year, with a traditional, republican dance.

Decorated from head to toe in sashes of tricolor ribbons, Paris looked like an aging actress dressed up like a rube to star in some folksy piece of trash at the church fair.

The squares, illuminated with tens of thousands of paper lanterns and light bulbs, slowly filled with the strolling crowd.

With the coming of dusk an unseen switch was flicked, and the gaudy footlights of the streets exploded in a gala show.

On platforms cobbled together from planks, drowsy, grotesque musicians — rightly assuming that a holiday meant a day of communal rest — blew a few bars of a fashionable dance tune out of their strangely warped trumpets every half-hour or so and then rested long and extravagantly.

The gathering crowd, stuffed into the cramped gullies of the streets, thrashed impatiently like fish about to spawn.

Dancing broke out in places. With no space to dance in, the entwined bodies were reduced to a sequence of ritual gestures, soon thereafter performed in the solitude of the only truly democratic institutions, the nearby hotels, which were not observing this holiday of universal equality.

Over it all rose the odor of sweat, wine, and face powder, the ineffable, translucent summertime fog exuded by the surging rivers of crowds.

The smoldering houses endlessly perspired more residents by the dozens. The temperature rose with each passing minute. In the scorching frying pans of the squares the crowd started to bubble like boiling water around the improvised lemonade and *menthe glacée* booths. Chilled glasses of the greenish and white liquids were snatched from one hand to another.

Clearing away the crowd with the oar of a hoarse siren, the packed arks of the tourist companies floated down the streets in regular intervals, bearing aloft on the waves of this flood of democracy chosen couples of the pure and the impure — generally of the same Anglo-Saxon stock — curiously observing the well-fed, tame, and amiable conquerors of the Bastille through their opera glasses and binoculars, in silent, though profound conviction that the whole French Revolution was in actual fact little more than another ingenious concoction of the immortal Cook, a pretext for sumptuous annual celebrations, reckoning on tourists and calculating a margin into the cost of the bus ticket.

Dancers were generally far fewer than spectators, and one disappointed gentleman aptly informed his embarrassed guide that the Parisians didn't put much enthusiasm into their holidays.

The foreigners' districts — Montparnasse and the Latin Quarter — were, however, pulling out all the stops for the 14th of July.

Eight jazz bands were scattered across the tight square between La Rotonde and Le Dôme, their sharp cleavers of syncopation quartering the live meat of the night into chopped bars of entrails. The multilingual crowd of Americans, Englishwomen, Russians, Swedes, Japanese, and Jews showed their boundless joy with spasmodic dances, all for the storming of the grand old Bastille.

A few streets down, on dark Boulevard Arago, La Santé Prison was celebrating the holiday in silence, surrounded by a military cordon, with larger-than-usual portions of food. La Santé, to be sure, was not the Bastille, and holiday celebrants could dance without fear, knowing full well that the walls on Boulevard Arago were high and secure, the military detachment well-armed and obedient, and that in a democratic and civilized society certain excesses — though permissible during the era of the *ancien régime* — could in no way be repeated.

A garland of faded letters hung on the prison frontage, courting passersby with their blackened inscription: "Liberty–Equality–Fraternity," like a discolored mourning ribbon for the abandoned tomb of the Great French Revolution.

The paper lanterns rocked gently like water lilies on the shiny surface of the night.

Sweaty, ruddy-faced waiters only just managed to keep the cool, clear lemonade flowing to the tables that had miraculously proliferated for the festivities, spilling off the sidewalks and taking possession of the streets.

Above the jazz band, a breathless Negro shattered invisible plates of noise on the heads of the listeners with the motions of a hapless juggler, shaking in cataleptic convulsions over the empty dishes of the cymbals. Sixteen other Negroes hollered their throats raw shouting the magic incantations of faraway continents into the brass speakers of trumpets loud as Jericho's, confirming with horror that not only were the walls not tumbling down, they seemed to be rising higher in jagged lines of flickering windows.

Cool, crystalline water flowed with a gurgle from thousands of taps like cut arteries, and an exhausted Paris went pale, wilting in the sweltering heat.

The first ambulance was observed at ten o'clock that evening at Place de l'Hôtel de Ville. The crowd, shunted and smothered by the endlessly drifting tour buses, at first mistook it for another bus and greeted it with a scowl. The error was soon recognized, and people swiftly moved aside. The band was just starting up a third Charleston. The dancing continued unabated.

Not twenty minutes later a second ambulance showed up, only to disappear into the black crevice of a neighboring alley. Nobody paid it any mind.

The third, fourth, and fifth arrived just after the second, filling the festive square with the echoes of their ominous sirens.

The first minor disturbance was seen around eleven o'clock. In the middle of the fourth Charleston, one of the dancing couples fell on the slippery asphalt and showed no signs of getting up. They were surrounded by laughter. The pair shook in convulsions. They were brought to the nearest pharmacy. Five minutes later, an ambulance arrived and collected the unfortunate dancers. For the first time someone dropped the word "epidemic," which clattered like a coin and rolled through the crowd. Nobody believed it, and the dancing resumed.

The next dancing couple to collapse showed strange symptoms of poisoning, and they were picked up from Place de la Bastille. The third from Montparnasse, in front of the veranda at La Rotonde.

A few dozen cases were reported before midnight, and though there was more muttering about a strange epidemic, the dancing did not stop.

A Negro playing in the jazz band on the terrace of Le Dôme Café crashed spastically onto his drums halfway through a bar, kicking his legs up in the air to comic effect. The amused audience rewarded this new trick with a spontaneous round of applause. But the man did not get up. His face turned skyward, he was dead.

The ominous horns of ambulances wailed in the black tunnels of the streets like a lonesome scream for help. The dancing stopped here and there, and the unsettled crowd quickly dispersed to their homes. In Montparnasse, the Latin Quarter, and in a few other districts inhabited by foreigners, the dancing continued.

The horns howled relentlessly, mournful and terror-stricken.

•

The next day, Paris awoke in fright at the wet ink of the morning gazette. On the front page, in big black letters, ran the spine-chilling announcement: PLAGUE IN PARIS!

The news was alarming. Over the night of July 14, eight thousand cases of plague were reported, almost all fatal.

The day rose pale from emaciation, dry and sweltering. Feverish crowds had been roaming the streets since morning, snatching shreds of special newspaper editions from one another's hands. The hollow, piercing horns of the hospital vehicles wailed incessantly and simultaneously on all sides of town. People began dropping in the streets by the dozens.

When evening fell, attempts were made to dance in Upper Montmartre and Montparnasse, in spite of it all. Dancers were few.

In denial over the loss of their traditional holiday profits, the café owners managed to slap together new bands, and hearing the bouncy beats of the Charleston, excited crowds of pedestrians swooped from the dusky streets to flood the abandoned terraces. The musicians going wild in front of La Rotonde blew the last shreds of their lungs out through their saxophones, vainly trying to drown out the cheerless jazz of the ambulances.

In the blink of an eye, the tight rectangle formed by La Rotonde, Le Dôme, and La Coupole was populated with swarms of dancing couples.

The frenzy erupted unexpectedly, and relatively late. It began as it had everywhere else. In the middle of a dance, a girl suddenly toppled to the ground, dragging her partner with her. Nobody noticed them at first. Trapped by the crowd, the other dancers were still undulating to the music. Another couple stumbled over the fallen pair. In the space of a minute, a mound of bodies was thrashing about in the center of the square. Pandemonium erupted. The music broke. The crowd gushed onto the sidewalks. The dancers struggled to their feet, running after the rest of the crowd. The square emptied.

Only a slender girl was left on the asphalt, writhing in zigzags of inconceivable pain. Her short pleated skirt was hiked up, revealing a small, almost childlike pair of knees wreathed in luxurious garters, and the shy white of boyish thighs, peeking out like supple, frenzied snakes from a thicket of cream-colored lace. The pointed heads of her slippers quivered unabated.

The dancers pressed themselves against the wall in panic.

Cutting through the crowd and clearing a path with his fists, a lanky, redheaded man in workman's clothing emerged from the mass, making for the other side of the street, probing the eyes of the throng as he went. He walked up to the girl stretched out on the pavement, stopped, bent over, and looked carefully. Another painful convulsion jerked the girl's face upward. The redheaded man let out a strange shriek, a rooster's crow, and sat abruptly on the ground. Grasping the girl by her slender arm, he made a futile attempt to lift her. The girl flailed in violent paroxysms. The redheaded man took her in his arms and got up, but with another thrust of her body he staggered and fell with her to the ground. Leaning over her on all fours, muttering inarticulate sounds, he covered the twitching body of the girl with hot kisses.

This extraordinary spectacle lured some onlookers down from the terraces of the cafés to the edges of the sidewalks, forming a tight circle around the odd pair. The despair of the redheaded man was so palpable, so unbridled, he immediately won the sympathy of the ladies observing the scene in their décolleté dresses.

The man, vainly trying to still the girl's twitching body in his arms, was hoarsely repeating the same word between his kisses. The audience edged closer. The first to hear hurried to share the news with those nearby:

"He's calling out her name. I think it's Jeannette."

"His girlfriend, no doubt."

"So young!"

"And so elegant! While he's . . . a simple worker . . ."

"Her brother, maybe?"

"Hardly! Have you ever seen a man kiss his sister like that?"

All these speculations were to remain unresolved. The girl suddenly shot up in the air with her whole body, struck her head on the asphalt with superhuman force, and fell silent. The crowd shuddered. A hush reigned. Even the excited ladies went silent, without having finished their stimulating exchange. The filigreed legs, wrapped in an imperceptible cobweb of stockings, froze stiff, the aghast heads of her slippers protruding upward.

Bent over the girl in silent despair, the redheaded man had also fallen silent. When he lifted his head a few minutes later, his face was disfigured from fighting back the tears. The crowd was expecting him to sob and groan, to hammer his head against the asphalt. A policeman had been drawn by the crowd, and was discreetly squeezing his way in from the back.

The redheaded man took in the crowd with a glassy stare. A jealous motion of his hand pulled down the girl's skirt, covering the exposed legs and lace *dessous*. His angry, canine gaze scanned the faces of the men surrounding him, and rested on the policeman's and the polished number pinned to his collar.

"I'm the one who killed her!" he said in an indifferent, raspy voice, his eyes fixed on the policeman.

The crowd rippled with excitement. The policeman bristled.

The redheaded man pressed his face once more to the face of the motionless girl and remained in this position for a long while. Vaguely sensing the solemnity of the moment, the policeman decided to show restraint. Finally, finding the mute scene to be dragging on a bit too long, his hand delicately touched the man's arm.

When the redheaded man turned to face him, everyone felt a wave of unease. His tangled, disheveled hair hung in his eyes in clumps. Two black veins pulsed on his forehead, like cords binding his bursting skull. The blood rushing to his face turned it crimson.

The crowd retreated in panic. Even the fearless policeman preferred to take a few cautionary steps back.

The redheaded man raised his fist and shook it at the retreating crowd.

"You'll all croak, you bastards!" he screamed in a hoarse, shrill voice, waving his fist in the air. "There was no way to punish you! I am your punishment! I'm the one who's poisoned you like rats! I stole the test tubes of plague from Pasteur! I poisoned the water supply! Run! Save yourselves! There's nowhere to hide!"

The crowd inched backward in panic and terror.

"You'll never escape! This is the end!" roared the redheaded man, shaking his fist at Boulevard Arago. "If you don't croak from the plague . . . THEY will come out from behind the walls! Thousands of them! Tens of thousands! For me! For my wrongs! For everything! Not even a pile of stones will remain! Bastards! Swine! Scum!"

His face flushed scarlet, the redheaded man made straight for the well-lit veranda.

The guests knocked over chairs in panic, rushing to the back. Glass shattered. Women squealed and took cover under tables. Someone gave a long holler:

"Help! Marauders!" and suddenly fell silent.

"The police! Where are the police? Are there really no police?" echoed the voice of a hysterical woman.

Then, amid the general confusion, a well-built gentleman rose up from behind a corner table, an athlete to judge by his broad shoulders, and aiming a heavy champagne bottle as if it were a tennis racket, flung it at the redheaded man. Glass flew. Blood mingled with wine and gushed onto the terrace in a sparkling, foamy stream.

"In one throw!"

"Do it again!"

"*We* are supposed to croak? What about him?"

"Maybe he really did poison the water? The papers reported that test tubes of plague were stolen from Pasteur!"

"He definitely poisoned it! The bandit! You can see it in his face!"

"Pound the maniac!"

"Hit the scum!" roared dozens of savage voices.

"Gentlemen — this is clearly a madman!" someone yelled, but the shout sank like a stone in the sea of tumult.

"Where did the plague come from?"

"What about the test tubes?"

"He obviously poisoned it!"

"Kill the dog!"

Struck by a third well-aimed bottle, the redheaded man staggered and collapsed onto the sidewalk, spurting blood. He was smothered by a wave of rabid people, a forest of raised sticks, the crash of breaking bottles and the piercing shrieks of women.

When the tide ebbed, there was no more than a motionless, red splotch left on the sidewalk.

The majestic policeman — he had gotten lost somewhere and was suddenly located — looked the other way with a grimace of disgust. Five minutes later the café was evacuated.

At one o'clock a.m., bulletins from the prefecture were hung up all over the city calling an end to the festivities and banning gatherings. They appeared, as usual, after the fact, at a time when the streets were more or less already empty. Ambulances had already taken the last stubborn dancers, still spinning in convulsive contortions, to local hospitals.

The nightly newspaper editions, which by now only the newsboys read, noted sixty thousand new cases on the day of July 15.

A hollow vacuum reigned in the streets, practically the only cars driving through them were those flying Red Cross flags.

On July 16, a second proclamation from the Parisian prefecture appeared on the walls. The prefecture announced that in the interest of containing this exceptionally pernicious epidemic and preventing its spread throughout France, Paris had been surrounded by a military cordon over the previous night. Any attempt to leave the city was futile and would carry the death penalty. The prefecture urged the residents to stay calm and rational, and not to leave their apartments.

The day arrived pale, shaky and scorching. Stores remained closed. Café chairs sat motionless in the streets, as if frozen where they had been strewn.

Cheap paper lanterns swayed over the abandoned streets like bubbles over a petrified whirlpool. Half of the newspapers went unpublished.

The radio reported that by noon one hundred and sixty thousand fatal cases had been recorded. Even when every city and municipal vehicle had been converted to ambulances, it was still too few for all the victims. All public buildings were hastily converted into hospitals, and a mandatory confiscation of private autos by the Red Cross was anticipated.

At six p.m., the Eiffel radio station broadcast political news.

Having spent his vacation at the seaside, the President of the Republic arrived in Lyon, where he immediately summoned the majority of vacationing deputies and senators, as well as the members of parliament enjoying some recreation in the provinces. An emergency assembly of the Chamber of Deputies was to be convened at midnight in Lyon, presided over by the president himself, to discuss the lamentable events of the past few days.

Paris was perishing softly, with dignity, to the clamorous funeral march of car horns and the jazzy clattering of bells. Eiffel Radio reported half a million fatalities.

On the fifth day, in defiance of the prefecture's ban, Parisians who had been impatiently crammed in their apartments — from which many corpses still awaited removal — wandered irresolute into the streets. Somebody decided that alcohol was the best antidote to the plague. The bistros pulsed. Corks flew. Jazz bands rattled. Hotel signboards once more began flashing. A possessed Paris numbed itself with wine.

Down the riverbeds of the streets, down the slick ribbons of asphalt streams, flowed a flock of cars like dead, powerless birds carried along the surface of a glossy, black current.

•

Bells rang from Sacré-Coeur.

Notre Dame, Madeleine, and all the small, scattered churches responded with the rueful echo of Paris's bells.

A religious psychosis was slowly but systematically taking hold of a growing segment of the population.

Overhead the hollow, moaning bells beat their cupped bronze chests with lead fists, and the church interiors replied with the rumble of convulsively clenched fists and a spiteful, pious murmur. The Host was continuously raised by waxen priests, swooning from exhaustion.

In the Orthodox church on Rue Daru, a metropolitan in gold trim read the Gospels in a dignified, throaty bass, and all the bells rang as though it were Easter.

In the synagogue on Rue de la Victoire, candles burned over the striped crowd in tallithim. The congregants, like the tongues of invisible bells, swung in a pendular rhythm, and the air, like a bell, replied with a lament.

In the face of the leveling strickle of death, the people dissolving in the giant vat of the city clung spasmodically, in a blind centrifugal urge, to every shred of their individuality, crowding together around the temples of their own rites, like iron filings around the poles of a magnet. Like so many lightning rods, the spires of the cathedrals, Orthodox churches, and minarets sent heavenward a magnetic current of separatism that grew with each passing moment, amassing the scattered human herd into self-contained racial and religious complexes.

The first eruption took place in the milieu that was the most distinct — due to the very pigment of its skin — and had no lightning-rod temple of its own.

A WINDOW IS A PICTURE NAILED TO THE DEAD, stone rectangle of the gray wall of the day.

The buildings on Place du Panthéon have thirty-six windows apiece: six rows of six. In building number 17, the sixth window in the third row is always lit during the day with the white glow of an unpainted canvas, with the matte smear of a latched shutter, disquieting as the milky-white eye of a blind man stubbornly fixed on the solemn profile of the Panthéon.

The evening patrols of the morgue vehicles had already passed through the streets, collecting the dead from the homes and streets and alerting the living to this fact with their unnerving bells, when P'an Tsiang-kuei, in pajamas and house slippers, pushed open the paralyzed wing of the shutter and appeared in the square of the frame, his face half lathered.

Finishing his shave in front of the mirror, P'an Tsiang-kuei carefully wiped his face, hands, and the whole of his body with a transparent solution, gargled long and scrupulously, and spritzed his laid-out underwear and clothing with an atomizer. Having performed these preparatory activities, P'an Tsiang-kuei quickly got dressed, slipped on a pair of gray gloves, wrapped his neck tightly with a scarf (the least possible surface area of skin was to come in direct contact with the pestilential air), and quickly ran downstairs.

It was crowded and bustling in the small Chinese restaurant at that time of day. Finding a free table was out of the question. After a moment of indecision, P'an Tsiang-kuei sat himself at a corner table occupied by a lone and elderly gentleman — not Chinese — wearing gold-rimmed glasses and a disheveled goatee that resembled a grayish feather duster.

In silence, without bothering to look at his chance neighbor, P'an Tsiang-kuei bent over his favorite dish: a steaming bowl of bird's nest soup.

He was just lifting the last spoonful to his lips when he felt someone's sharp fingers clutching his elbow. The gray man with the goatee was hunched over the table and staring at him over the tops of his glasses and, reddening in the face, said in a decided, though somewhat quavering voice:

"Forgive me if I've startled you. May I have a word . . ."

•

If the miles of film of the average human life could for once be played in reverse, the eye, like an all-seeing probe plunged into the fathomless stream of human consciousness, would hit upon a point somewhere deep down, a hard bedrock, a fact, an event, an image, an undefined and flickering sensation. It would be tattered and faded, yet inflected with such a strange hue that the current of time flowing through one's life would absorb its indefinable color for good.

In P'an Tsiang-kuei's life, at the core of all his impressions, experiences, and mental scaffolding, lay one such image.

It was from long ago, so long ago that sometimes, when his memory ventured into those fields, groping around in them, it would get lost in wisps of all-leveling fog, from which emerged the disjointed fragments of some other world of objects, like the contours of precious, fragile toys from layers of cotton padding.

Little P'an was dressed in motley, shredded rags, busy making dams in the gutter of one of Nanjing's narrow, dirty alleyways, when he spotted his father running down the street. The skinny, barefoot rickshaw driver, hitched up to two narrow rods, ran at a trot, struggling to pull his cart holding a man dressed in white — and with a face just as white — along the chipped cobblestones. The rickshaw driver's bare heels passed each other in midair as narrow streams of sweat ran down his strained face.

P'an Tsiang-kuei was then struck for the first time by the wide, incredibly white, seemingly swollen face of the gentleman, his strange bulging eyes with their cleft eyelids, and the expression of calm dignity and self-satisfaction set on his round features.

Long, exhausting days and brief, gentle nights. The image became worn and faded, vanishing somewhere in the back of his mind in the wisps of fluffy, cottony fog. He was left with a sour, fleeting aftertaste, enveloping the world and its objects forevermore in its immaterial covering.

That broad face with its bloated cheeks, its flared eyelids upon unnaturally bulging eyes, lost its hard corporeality; it became a symbol, a reservoir for the burning, acidic hatred that seeped from all his pores.

When three years later, on an enervating hot June day, the motionless and glassy-eyed rickshaw driver, having been felled on the road by a sudden hemorrhage, was brought from town and laid heavily on the floor by his merciful neighbors, little P'an neither cried nor clung to the feet of his neighbors, who were hurrying back to their jobs. As if out of curiosity, he carefully studied his father's gaping black mouth, an inconceivable, mysterious grotto with red dangling stalactites, his thin, bony legs topped off with a pair of enormous feet like worn-out slippers, and with earnest deliberation he waved his child's fist at someone by the window as a coolie named Pao-Chang had the day before at the shopkeeper Ling-Ho, who had wronged him.

Then he squatted on the floor and, with a broken fan found somewhere on the street, he began shooing the flies drawn by the scent of blood, swarming around the dead man's gaping mouth. The corpse's glassy eyes were dully fixed on the ceiling and they gave a murky shine. No terror, no pain shown in those eyes — only boundless, silent astonishment.

Perhaps the body had started to dry out from the unbearable heat, or perhaps a gland had simply burst from inside, but a great tear rolled from the dead man's right eye and slowly crawled down the yellow, wrinkled face.

Little P'an had never seen a weeping corpse, but it didn't occur to him to investigate this unusual phenomenon. In a panicked terror he got to his feet and dashed out of the room. He ran down narrow, twisting alleys amid the chattering rickshaws, with no destination in mind.

That evening some sailors found him by the docks between sacks of rice. They spent some time kicking him back to life, then gave him some scalding sorghum wine to drink and left him in a storehouse to sleep it off.

P'an Tsiang-kuei was seven years old at the time.

He had long been used to living with hunger — he had never known his mother — but now he would have to get by on his own mettle. In summer, he slept by the docks, under the stars. During the rainy months, he took to strange nooks, garrets, or storehouses. When caught, he was beaten long and hard. He would not scream, but he did sometimes bite. He sunk his teeth so hard into the hand of one Mandarin who had tugged his ponytail that the man screamed to the heavens, at which his neighbors came running, and had a funeral procession not appeared at just that moment they would surely have beaten P'an to death. He ate what he chanced to find, which wasn't much. He robbed dogs of their bones. The dogs tore his rags to shreds and sometimes slashed his body. When they saw him coming from a distance, they bared their teeth. His diet was mainly vegetarian. He gathered grains of rice left scattered on the docks after a loading. He had nowhere to cook them. He ate them raw, slowly chewing and savoring each grain.

Nonetheless, he carefully avoided the temptations of the crowded markets, where pudgy stall-keepers treated pedestrians to tasty soup with tea or pungent rice wine for a few coppers, where the stalls were piled high with fruits, cakes made with sesame butter, pieces of sugarcane, and other such delicacies. Even just walking past, the spicy, sugary-sweet smell tickled his nostrils and he couldn't resist nicking the plumpest sugarcane, and then — run for it! — but there was no getting anywhere between the tightly packed stalls, like a condemned soldier — through the rows, vainly shielding his back from the blows of the furious traders. After such escapades his back hurt for a week and his stiff loess bedding seemed even more uncomfortable.

In the daytime, when he wasn't playing with the other homeless urchins, he liked strolling through the merchant districts, gazing at the complicated drawings of the characters, the intricate calligraphy on the dangling signboard sashes. Fanciful and marvelous, the characters swung like fragile matchstick houses that might tumble down at any moment, yet held tight, immovable, built by some unknown architect magician. He spent hours on end searching out familiar contours in the incomprehensible hieroglyphics. Oh, that character was frivolously raising its little leg like a fairground ballerina, and that other one, as if irritated, was cocking its "nose" in the air. Those capricious compositions of lines and hooks, clear and familiar to some, wild and absurd to him, fired his young brain with their riddles.

Sometimes he wandered to the outskirts, where in an openwork, pillared house forty boys rocked back and forth with their eyes trained on mysterious designs, vying with each other, screaming out the incoherent, monosyllabic, nasal sounds, prompted from a pulpit by a wrinkled lemon in glasses and a long robe. Lurking behind the veranda, P'an greedily fished through the rumble of the scattered voices. The bespectacled lemon was indoctrinating the children of wealthy merchants into the hidden meanings of the enigmatic symbols.

In time, he stopped by another place more regularly. Not far from the market, on the street, under a tattered, faded parasol, an old, gray calligrapher painted slender, serpentine characters with a thin brush on long silk scrolls. Little P'an plastered himself to the wall and followed the complex movements of the nimble brush, his eyes wide with delight. The sticks grew, branched out, combined into elaborate figures, characters crawled under other characters and hefted them onto their shoulders like acrobats, a second later an even, tottering pyramid shot upward and the calligrapher smiled with pride, weighing the magical brush between two fingers.

He was the only person who didn't chase little P'an off, and seeing the boy's cleverness, his enamored and curious eyes, he gave a friendly smile.

On days few with customers, when the wise maxims flapped aimlessly in the wind, vainly struggling to tarry those rushing past, he'd give the boy a brush and a scrap of scroll off the ground and teach him to draw his first characters. The scribbles that came from the strokes of the reverently trembling, unschooled child's hand struggled to keep their balance, and soon crumbled into a heap of line fragments.

The child's wisdom soon grew. His sticks, joined by invisible hinges, held fast: Just try to blow them down! He made a real pagoda with six pillars and a roof, all first rate, held up by one slender leg, keeping perfect balance. Instead of a mysterious, complicated tangle of lines — words. Here — a tree, here — the earth, and here — a man, running, unstoppable, so vigorously the momentum was swinging his legs.

With time it became clear that both words and objects were but appearances. The essence of things was not to be found there but in the lines. Not in the ones snaking out from under his brush, but in other mysterious and inscrutable ones.

In his many free hours the old calligrapher enlightened his soul by reading the *I Ching*. Sixty-four lines — the *kua* — were carved on the shell of a tortoise, and these contained the entire riddle of existence. Nobody had been able to fully decipher them, not the all-knowing Fu Xi, not the enlightened Confucius, not the one thousand four hundred and fifty commentators who had been puzzling over them for centuries. How could our poor calligrapher dream of penetrating the secrets, even if he knew all the combinations of lines by heart, including those that appeared in the sacred patterns of the *kua!*

Little P'an understood none of this, or rather he understood it in his own fashion. He ran outside of town to catch tortoises, and searched their shells long and hard for the sacred pattern. Not finding it, he would smash the shell with a stone, to see if it wasn't hidden inside. He found nothing. The all-knowing Fu Xi turned out to be a common swindler.

Returning to town, P'an didn't share his discovery with his teacher, not wanting to worry him. He struggled with his thoughts in silence. He couldn't allow his teacher to go on being tricked! He weighed his options for some time and finally decided. When his teacher nodded off in the heat and began snoring soundly in his chair, P'an carefully snatched up the source of all the errors, the holy *I Ching*, and spirited it off to the riverbank. Waiting for the right moment, he surreptitiously flung it into the water.

The calligrapher couldn't find his book when he awoke, and he gave a loud lament. Onlookers surrounded him. Neighbors were found who had seen young P'an hurrying to town with the book under his arm.

P'an was caught. He was flogged long and hard. They wanted him to admit that he had sold the book. Not getting anything out of him, they threw him onto the street, half dead.

Rubbing his bruises, he thought carefully. Fine, they had beaten him — he was used to that. But how could it be that his good calligrapher uncle had stood by and watched everything without lifting a finger? So he was no better than the rest? There was no point in worrying about his mistakes, no point in stealing books. No point in making friends. If you tried to take the smallest bone from people, they bit you like dogs.

But how could you get by without people in the big, crowded city? In the city everything was a riddle. Who would explain things? He would need to make compromises.

He wandered to the east side of town. The streets were wider here. Stone houses piled on either side, symmetrical as boxes. Glass boxcars raced along the tracks, the rumble constantly in the air. But stranger than the houses and the boxcars were the incredible carriages that sped along the streets with no rails, horses, or rickshaw drivers, powered by an incredible wheel hovering in the air, never touching the ground.

One day, passing a warehouse, P'an noticed something: a wagon, loaded with colorful boxes, and at the front, instead of a shaft, there was a large crank. How could he resist turning it? He scanned the street — not a soul in sight. He couldn't restrain himself. He ran up and turned the crank with all his might. The wagon snarled resonantly, as though a whole pack of dogs were responding from inside.

A man in a greasy leather apron came out of the warehouse. P'an cautiously leapt across the road.

"Was that you, grub-face? You want a ride? Get in, we'll take a drive."

The slanted eyes of the man in the apron gave a friendly smile.

P'an tensed his body: "I know that trick! First they get you to come close, then they give you a smack you'll remember for years!" Nonetheless, he didn't run away. He studied the owner of the snarling vehicle from a safe distance.

"What are you afraid of, kid? Get in, I won't eat you. Let's go for a ride."

Little P'an obviously did very much want to take a ride. He decided to risk it. If he got a whack on the head, who cares. A bruise or two, big deal. What if he really did get a ride? He inched up to the car.

"Climb in here. Don't be afraid. Get on board."

He sat down. The nice guy touched the wheel. The vehicle moved.

On the road, the man in the apron opened up. His name was Chow-Lin. He was from Kouei-Tcheou. He'd had a son there just like P'an, but the boy died in a lean year, during his trip to Europe. His wife died as well. Now he had settled in Nanjing, and he worked as a deliveryman for a big department store.

He was chatty and straightforward. He gave P'an a banana and drove him around till evening, dropping off the colorful boxes at stores around town. He asked about the boy's parents. He felt sorry for him. When he said goodbye, he slipped him an orange and added:

"Drop by the warehouse tomorrow. We'll go for a spin."

That was how they became friends. Every morning, on the very same corner, P'an would wait for the heavy vehicle with the colorful crates, nimbly jump into his seat, take the bunch of bananas waiting for him, sometimes even a piece of sugarcane, and, chewing it slowly, stare at the passersby from above.

The talkative man's stories about the faraway countries he'd visited in his youth were even tastier than the bananas or the sugarcane. Apparently (at least according to his globetrotting uncle) the Earth wasn't flat at all, and it didn't end at the sea — it was round like a ball. A man leaves Nanjing, travels the whole world round, and comes back again to the place he started from. All this struck P'an as strange and improbable. But the man swore it was the truth, and there was no doubting him — he had seen everything with his own two eyes. He said white people had proven all this long, long ago.

Once he even reached into his pocket and pulled out a nicely bound notebook, with a picture glued at the back — not a picture per se, but a map of the whole world. Two round hemispheres, like the shell of a tortoise, and on the hemispheres, like on a shell — an infinite tangle of lines: earth, sea, Nanjing, China, the world.

Yes, this was no doubt the same mysterious *kua* — the sixty-four holy lines that he, stupid little P'an, had vainly sought on the shell of that treacherous tortoise. The white people had solved the riddle of the wise Fu Xi!

If the old calligrapher hadn't done him wrong, P'an would have immediately run to share this dazzling discovery. But recalling his bruises and bloody nose, he shuddered. The beatings were still fresh in his mind.

The enigmatic white people, on the other hand, whom everyone hated, including the gentle old calligrapher, grew in his eyes to the proportions of magical, all-wise creatures. Chow-Lin said many incredible things about them.

Somewhere, many, many *li* away, there are gigantic, monstrous cities, where white people live in multilevel crates, and in those crates, instead of stairs, boxes shuttle up and down, able to lift the residents to the very top in a single instant. Boxcars flash through long underground pipes like lightning, taking travelers dozens of *li* in the space of a minute. Giant machines work day and night in factories, spitting out ready-made things for the white man, so that he needn't wear himself out. You want clothing — you take it and put it on. You want a rickshaw — get in and go. No buggies, no horses. It's all machines. A strange, heavy word, almost bursting with hot iron. The white people had even apparently come up with special machines for killing their enemies — not one at a time, but by the dozens.

Once a startled P'an asked:

"But then why do the white men come ride in our uncomfortable rickshaws if everything is so good where they live?"

Chow-Lin laughed:

"White people like money. You have to work for money. White people don't like to work. They like other people to work for them. Where they live, machines and their own kind, whites, do the work for them. But there's never enough money for the white people. That's why they came to China and yoked up all the Chinese to work for them. The Emperor and the Mandarins helped them. That's why Chinese people live in such poverty, because they have to work for both the Mandarins and the Emperor — and above all, for the white people, who need lots and lots of money, and so there's nothing left for us."

So the white people had to be fought? They were invaders, like the old calligrapher had said. But how could you fight them when they had discovered the essence of things, they even had solved the mysterious *kua*, over which the wise Fu Xi and the enlightened Confucius and one thousand four hundred and fifty commentators, and even the old calligrapher himself, had all wracked their brains? When they had machines for doing everything and machines for killing? How could you fight such people?

Chow-Lin said: For the time being you can't. You have to learn from them. The Chinese nation is the most populous of all. If it knew how to do everything the white people can, it would be the mightiest nation in the world, and it wouldn't have to work for the white people. Little P'an's head spun from such conversations, his pulse hammered in his temples. At night he dreamt of enormous iron cities, gigantic, monstrous machines with gaping steel maws, pouring out torrents of ready-made clothing, hats, umbrellas, rickshaws, houses, streets, cities ... and waking up in the middle of the night, P'an had reveries: he'd grow up, get over there — on foot was impossible, let's say by ship — he'd spy, track down and smuggle out the white people's secret, bring it back to China, build enormous machines everywhere, and he'd set white people at the machines (Chow-Lin said workers were needed even at the machines), the ones who didn't like to work, and he'd force them to work day and night, so that the cowed, tired, and starved Chinese could finally rest.

Sometimes he and Chow-Lin would drive to settlements outside of town to drop off crates, and Chow-Lin would laugh and let P'an take the wheel, teaching him how to steer a vehicle. It turned out to be not so hard. One touch of the child's trembling hands and feet and the truck moved obediently, turned, slowed down or sped up, as if it didn't notice that it was being driven by little P'an and not Chow-Lin. Its name was incomprehensible: *Au To Mo-bil.*

Later P'an figured out that this was its last name, not its first. It had many first names. Riding about town, Chow-Lin taught P'an to know the first names of all the vehicles by their markings. These names were peculiar, and he had trouble learning them: *Bra-Zye, Pa-Nar, Dai-Mler, Na-Pyer, Re-No.*

Once out on the road they passed a polished black car shapely and sleek like a magical palanquin, with curtains in the windows and soft, gray, velvet pillows. It had an even stranger name: *Mer Ce-des*. Chow-Lin followed it with eyes aglow:

"A machine like that could take you around the world!"

This got P'an's attention.

"Could you even go to Europe?"

"You could even go to Europe."

P'an stared with delight. But the car was no longer there. It had disappeared.

In those days, P'an lived mainly on Uncle Chow-Lin's bananas, though sometimes he managed to earn a few coppers. While wandering about, sometimes a fellow would stop him, and a bargain would be struck: Run a letter to the other side of town and return in a flash with the reply. He was known for his unusually strong and nimble legs (he had obviously inherited them from his father, who had been known as a first-class racer). He would run at a trot through two or three neighborhoods, and then right back! The coins went into his pocket.

That day looked as if it would be much the same. Some fat confectioner had sent him off with a letter to his partner. The reply was worth two coppers and some cake to boot. Off he galloped.

It was far away. Outside of town on a pretty, squeaky-clean road: greenery, blocks of villas in the middle of the foliage like dainty white cubes. He had never seen anything like it. He went bit by bit, forgetting he was in a rush. Then — he stood as if thunderstruck. In front of the closed gate, it stood there black and shining like a marvelous palanquin, softly snoring, the enchanted *Mer Ce-des*. There could be no doubt, he recognized it straight away. It was standing there alone, softly snorting in the sand. Even the chauffeur had wandered off. It would just be a matter of jumping in the front seat, stepping on the right pedal and . . . he'd vanish into thin air! Right, left — the lines of the road branching off like the mysterious *kua* on the holy tortoise shell. In the distance, over the hills and down the valleys — the gigantic iron city of *Eu Ro-pa*.

He almost dropped his letter from excitement. He looked around — nobody there. Chow-Lin's voice rang in his ears.

"A machine like that could take you around the world!"

He hesitated, a swarm of bees in his head.

No, there was no holding back. He crouched like a cat and then sprang into the front seat with one bound. He feverishly switched on the engine. He jerked the wheel. The car began gently rolling. He picked up speed. On either side villas and trees flashed by in a frenzied dance, a fan of pickets unraveled in a whiz. Through the countryside and into infinity ran the long strip of road. People had covered the globe with roads, like a cracked pot wrapped in wire. Farewell Nanjing, prodding elbows, goose eggs, half-chewed bones, evil calligrapher, Yangtze, carrying the holy *I Ching* on its waves, and Uncle Chow-Lin — Farewell!

Suddenly he went numb. He distinctly felt the weight of a heavy hand on his shoulder. He looked around and was paralyzed. A white, pungent-smelling man with a furious face was crawling through the open partition window from the back seat, trying to get up front. A steel hand grabbed P'an by the collar like a pair of forceps. The car dashed like an arrow, hopping lightly on the bumps. Finally climbing into the passenger seat, the white man grabbed the steering wheel from P'an's hands and began to brake the car.

P'an's first reaction was to be frightened, and in his sudden terror he let go of the steering wheel. Bit by bit, however, he came to his senses. The white man had clearly been sitting behind those curtains the whole time, perhaps waiting for the chauffeur. It hadn't even entered P'an's head to look through the little window! And now all was lost. He would kill him, surely. His one hope was to slip through the man's fingers and bolt into the bushes.

The car stopped. P'an struggled with all his might and tried to bolt, but the white man held him firmly by the collar, shouting something in an incomprehensible language, probably cursing. P'an understood only the word "thief," which the white man repeated in Chinese. Holding P'an by the neck with his left hand, the white man swung the auto around with his right. They were driving back. P'an tried to bite the hand that held him and received a solid fist in the jaw. His ears rang.

They drove on in silence. The white man stopped the car in front of the fateful gate and began shouting. People ran out from the villa and surrounded the machine. The white man kept shouting his incomprehensible words. P'an struggled hopelessly, was seized and carried inside, and soundly pummeled on the way. A moment later, a dazed P'an found himself in a dark cell underneath the stairs. The door was bolted shut behind him.

He bitterly stroked his painful jaw. He battered at the door — it was solid, no way. No sense in even trying. All was lost!

After an hour they came, dragged him out of the cell, and carried him upstairs. In a huge, grand hall, where the floor shined like the lid of a lacquer tin, sat the white man from the car, a few more white men, and a potbellied Chinese man, a Mandarin or a merchant, in a richly embroidered silk gabardine.

The Chinese man immediately proceeded to interrogate him in Chinese:

Why did he steal the car? Who had put him up to it? Name the conspirators, and we won't do you any harm. If you don't name them, we'll thrash you so badly you'll spew everything out onto the table.

He was silent. How was he to tell this potbellied man about the tortoise shell, about the iron city, about the white man's most carefully guarded secrets?

Servants were called. Two Chinese men with thick bamboo rods entered, spread P'an out on the table, and beat his bare heels with the rods. He howled.

"Hand over the conspirators!"

The potbellied man hopped about like a frog, croaking:

"If you won't tell us, they'll tan your hide all the more!"

They beat him long and hard, pausing to rest. He didn't scream, clenching his teeth until he bled. Even the Chinese men got worn out. They got nothing out of him. The potbellied man, spreading his hands in defeat, jabbered something to the white man in a foreign tongue. The Chinese men gathered P'an up in their arms and carried him back to his cell. Along the way, they tenderly stroked his face. They asked: Did it hurt very much? Then added, as though in self-justification:

"When the white man tells us to hit, there's nothing we can do."

In the evening they surreptitiously slid a bowl of rice and a big piece of dumpling into his cell:

"There you go, don't cry. Gather your strength."

He ate, greedily licking his fingers. He squatted in the corner, deep in thought. They'd beat him again. Tomorrow for sure. It figured — the white men were his enemies. And the potbellied one? You could see from his clothes that he was rich. And he was on their side. He barked at their command. So he was an enemy, too. Chow-Lin was right. It wasn't only the white men. The Chinese ones, too. The Emperor, Mandarins, the wealthy . . . they were all in it together. It was oppression. They didn't let you live. Everyone complained about them . . . The white men had apparently invented machines for killing. When he grew up, he would strike back with that kind of machine — and the ones in the embroidered gabardines would be the first to go.

He fell asleep with clenched fists.

The next morning he was dragged out of his cell and again carried upstairs. He tried to put up some resistance. It didn't help. The potbellied man was already there, standing straight as a ramrod. This time there were no threats. Grinning perfidiously, he started asking questions:

"Where's your father?"

"I don't have a father, he's dead."

"And your mother?"

"She's dead, too."

"Do you have any relatives?"

"No."

"Who do you live with?"

"Nobody."

He repeated it all to the white man in the foreign language. They consulted for a long time, shaking their heads. P'an looked suspiciously at the servants, to see if they were holding the rods. They weren't.

Having chattered his fill with the white man, the potbellied one spoke to P'an in Chinese:

"As you're a thief, we ought to hand you over to the police, so that they put a cangue around your neck like they do to thieves. But the white man is merciful. The white man takes pity on orphans. He has put many homeless Chinese orphans in charity reformatories. That's why he's decided to pardon you, and not only will you go unpunished, but in his benevolence, he'll also place you in the Christian missionaries' orphanage, so that under their guidance you may find the true faith and learn to praise the great Christian God, who will teach you that stealing is a capital sin. Now go kiss the hand of your benefactor."

Having finished this solemn tirade, the potbellied man dragged P'an by the collar to the hand of his benefactor, but the boy was so clearly baring his teeth that the white man, recalling the previous day's bite, swiftly retracted his hand.

Then P'an was led once more through the hall and shoved into that cursed auto. The potbellied Chinese man and a stranger climbed in with him, and the car began moving in an unfamiliar direction.

P'an was carried struggling from the car into a white stone house filled with many white people in long, bizarre dresses. In a spacious hall, on a wall, P'an noticed a strange, flat tree of large dimensions, with three widely splayed ends, and on the tree, impaled through the hands, head lolling to one side, was a naked man with his body curled up. So this was how the white people punished thieves! Soon they'd be doing the same to him: Why had he stolen that car? The potbellied man spoke clearly: The white god forbids stealing!

The huge windows of the hall looked out onto the garden, and there P'an saw the same white people in long trailing dresses.

The potbellied Chinese man and the stranger were conversing near the window with a tall man in a dress. P'an felt a slick, icy fear radiate from the white walls, from the strange man nailed to the tree. The men were caught up in their conversation and had their backs turned to him. The door to salvation loomed blackly, only six steps away. Counting to three, P'an shot over to it in one hop. At that same moment the door was thrown open wide, and P'an fell into the arms of the long-skirted hulk coming in. The hulk lifted him up and carried him, despite his desperate resistance, into the depths of the chilly white corridors.

P'an had a sudden and lucid flash that all was lost, that they would lock him in the white, shadowy cellars and he would never again see the clattering buggies, the long glass boxcars, Uncle Chow-Lin's gaudy, colorful crates, the magical palanquins on their chubby hoops that moved without a sound, and in helpless despair he finally let loose with the loud sob of a child, a sound mocked by the narrow, bleach-white corridors.

P'an Tsiang-kuei was ten years old.

In the evening, his situation became a bit less murky — this hell wasn't going to be as dreadful as what had come before . . . At least he wasn't alone. In a long hall, with beds lined up in two rows, there were a few dozen other boys. There just might be someone to talk to.

They bathed. They washed. They draped him in a long shirt that stretched down to his heels. In the evenings, before he went to sleep, the long-robed man got everyone down on their knees at their bedsides, and everyone chattered some suspicious vows in chorus. On the wall, that same curled-up little naked fellow nailed to a forked tree twisted his mouth into an anguished grimace.

P'an questioned the occupant of the neighboring bed. Do they beat you a lot? He replied: Not much. What do they do? They teach you a foreign language and lots of other things. He complained about the food: they only got dessert once a week, on Sundays. In general, it was boring.

In came "Father" in a long cassock. In a flash his neighbor buried himself into his pillow, pretending to be asleep. He faked it so cleverly that before the rounds were finished he was snoring in earnest. The other questions would have to wait till morning.

For the first time in his life P'an stretched out in a real, clean bed. It seemed to him rather uncomfortable. The pillow somehow didn't fit his head. He pushed it aside. The blanket, on the other hand, was very much to his liking — it was warm. The silence in the room, cushioned with the boys' soft exhalations, helped him think things through.

Ah, it's not so terrible after all. If the runt is telling the truth, then it looks like this is just a school. They teach you a foreign language, and other things, too. It never hurts to learn. Except where did these white folks get the idea of teaching Chinese kids? It must be some kind of con. Nothing to worry about, they're sure to guard their secrets pretty closely. Anyway, I'll have to poke around. The most important part will be to learn the foreign language. Then I'll be able to listen in on the white people's conversations. They might divulge something. Got to stay alert. Not let anything get past me. Root out what I can.

He slept curled up like a hedgehog — a captive behind enemy lines.

Then days and weeks. Strangeness and bizarre tales. It turned out, for example, that the man nailed to the tree wasn't a thief at all, nor even a man, but rather the true — the truest — God. Pudgy Father Francis liked to say that this god had turned into a man on purpose, to suffer for everyone, even for him, for little P'an. Apparently they gave *him* a fairly good beating as well. It was all so hard to swallow. Why would a white man — even if God himself — have suffered for all the Chinese?

Father Francis told lots of funny stories about him. For example, when he was beaten and slapped on the cheek, he didn't return the abuse, but presented his other cheek instead. Here you go, hit it, give it all you've got! Just like a clown at the fair. Father Francis said humility was a great virtue. But what good was humility when they were beating you? If you don't defend yourself — they beat you to death. Apparently they killed that guy as well. A nut, basically.

But then again, he wasn't just any old nut, as it might have seemed, he was clever. He kept up the humility. Don't fight evil. Give unto Caesar what is Caesar's, and unto God what is God's. And unto God . . . well, God doesn't need much. Not so with Caesar. Caesar is your enemy, as everyone knows. He helps the Mandarins and the white men rob the people, so that Uncle Chow-Lin's children died of hunger. What kind of honest and just God could order the Chinese not to fight Caesar? A white one, obviously.

Oh, as Father Francis said not more than a week ago: "Easier for a camel to pass through the eye of a needle than for a rich man to enter the Kingdom of Heaven." And every Sunday he accepted all sorts of presents from rich white people, wine and fruit, and spoke with them cordially for hours at a time, and when they finally left he would see them to their cars, not troubled in the slightest that they wouldn't be entering the Kingdom of Heaven. Clearly it wasn't so terribly important if someone was entering the Kingdom of Heaven or not, if the rich folk weren't so eager to get there, and Father Francis didn't see much of a problem with it. Obviously this Kingdom of Heaven wasn't anything special if only the poor folk were being sent there. No, P'an didn't much care for this docile god. The rich folk and the Caesars had clearly bought him out, so that he would convince people to be subservient. He could set an example by letting himself be beaten to his heart's content. If he was in fact God, it would hardly hurt. And he could die as much as he liked. No, you couldn't believe in a god like that. That kind of god was a scam.

But he pretended to believe. He ardently crossed himself and recited long-winded prayers by heart. Everyone praised him. Even gloomy Father

Seraphim, withered like the bark on an old log, would sometimes slip an orange or a pretzel into his hand. This P'an was an unusually devoted lad!

He studied diligently. He spent hours with his eyes shut, cramming the strange foreign words into his head. He had his multiplication tables down within two weeks. The further he went, the more outstanding his work.

At year's end, Father Gabriel himself arrived, the eldest of the Lazarists. The whole shelter was cleaned and swept for two days before his visit. He arrived fat, obese even, scarcely capable of making his way up the stairs. Two brothers led him by the hand, showing him around. He spoke with P'an. He inquired about this and that. His interest was piqued. He started to ask more precise questions. He checked how well he knew the catechism. He praised the boy. Upon leaving, he extended his hand to kiss and gave him a kindly pat on the head.

Skulking behind the door, P'an heard the fatso talking to Father Francis:

"A very, very bright lad. Mature beyond his years. It would be a shame to send him to a trade school. He should attend a gymnasium. I'll bring it up with Father Dominic myself."

And that was how he came to attend the gymnasium in Shanghai.

The gymnasium students were both Chinese and white. It turned out they were all learning the same things. He studied harder than before. The white students kept to themselves. They stared at the Chinese with contempt. They would scoff: "Hey, Chink! Where'd you leave your ponytail?" But they weren't so revolted by them that they didn't copy their homework. They would share a bit of croissant under the desk. But when recess came — get lost! The same boy who had copied the homework and shared the croissant would smirk: "Beat it, chump!"

Once P'an overheard that they were going to change the marks in the grade book during recess. A freckled kid with a mole on his cheek had stolen the keys to the office. He changed all the marks. They caught on. There were interrogations: Who was to blame?

Freckle-face stood up:

"It wasn't us, it was the Chinese. They changed our marks on purpose so we'd get a hiding. I saw that Chink myself steal the key to the office."

He pointed at little, innocent Hu.

Father Paphnutius grabbed little Hu by the collar and rapped his knuckles with a ruler:

"Scram!"

P'an couldn't bear it. He leapt on the freckled kid and gave him one right in the mouth! It took some effort to pull them apart. Freckle-face's nose was bleeding and a welt like a great plum appeared under his eye. He shuffled home with a bashed face.

P'an was grabbed by the ear and locked in an empty classroom.

Freckle-face's father pulled up in his car after lunch. Handsome, fragrant, a little red jewel in his buttonhole. In Father Dominic's office he screamed and stomped his feet:

"Expel him at once!"

P'an heard everything through the wall. Father Dominic begged forgiveness. It came out that it was in fact the freckle-faced boy who had tampered with the marks. The boy's father simmered down a bit:

"Punish him in my presence! Fifty strokes, and not one less!"

Guards were called in. P'an was hauled into the office. He was stretched out on the bench. They started counting the lashes. The white man with the little jewel in his buttonhole tapped out the time with a slender foot clad in an elegant shoe, snorting with irritation. After the fortieth stroke the cane snapped in two. The man with the little jewel didn't press it further. He went home, slamming the door behind him. Father Paphnutius lifted the flogged P'an onto his knees and had him turn to face the wall. He remained there until evening.

The following day he was told he'd been spared only because of his dedication to his studies. If this ever happened again — out he'd go!

It never happened again. He bit his lip. He didn't respond to the white boys' jeers and taunts. He walked past the freckled boy without looking him in the face. But he didn't let anyone copy his homework again. He didn't take any croissant. And they didn't offer him any. They kept their distance.

A year passed.

One day, right out of the blue, Father Paphnutius announced from the teacher's desk: "The people of China have overthrown the emperor. From now on, the Chinese state will be a republic."

On the streets it was as though nothing had changed. The trams rushed by as they always had, cars howled, sweaty rickshaw drivers sped past in a flash of heels, pulling after them carts with corpulent white gentlemen. In the gymnasium, the lessons dragged on, the Lazarist monks recorded marks in the grade books, and during the recesses drank strong, aromatic tea and nibbled bread and butter. How could this be? The Chinese people had overthrown the emperor and everything was business as usual. The white people weren't fleeing the country, quite the opposite: with every passing month there seemed to be more of them, and they spoke calmly of the coup, with approval, as if it were a shrewd business transaction. Clearly the emperor had nothing to do with the situation. So who was it, then? Chow-Lin had also mentioned the Mandarins. P'an wasn't sure if the Mandarins had kept their old positions, and he had no one to ask, but it seemed as if they'd stayed put. In any case, the rich people and the merchants in their opulently embroidered gabardines were still around. There must have been some mistake. Dethroning the emperor clearly was not enough, the people in embroidered dresses also needed to be overthrown, and those people had been overlooked. How could this have happened?

P'an didn't understand it, he couldn't understand it, there was no one to explain it to him, and without this explanation life became incomprehensible and senseless.

But little P'an's doubts were not reflected in his studies. He conscientiously devoted himself to his studies just as before, as if in the difficult mathematical problems he might find the solution to the riddle that plagued him. He had to learn everything the white people knew, and then everything would become simple, comprehensible, clear.

Months went by.

Years went by. Long, laborious, exhausting years that passed leaving no trace in the memory, a void, not because they somehow lacked the singular, remarkable events that fill every day of boyhood — it was as if a hole had formed in the crammed sack of memory and all the contents had trickled out. A man looks over his shoulder, starts to reminisce, he can recall some years, practically day by day, in the most precise detail, and suddenly a blank crops up. A year, two, three — he digs, searches, but nothing remains. Generalities: I was going to school, I was working in a factory. Doing this and that. Then a stop. From the soupy fog of non-existence emerges a small and insignificant episode: a lost wallet, a word overheard somewhere, an image — a tree, a bench, a house — and then it all fades like so much steam. How many of these blanks were there, where did they come from, who could say? And isn't it a hundred times stranger to think that all those tiny trinkets of odd, half-aged feelings come from memory's neglected, ransacked drawer, forever confirming that the small freckled urchin, feverishly playing bottle caps and up to all sorts of pranks, and you — a mature, staid, reasonable fellow — are two links of one and the same chain, bound with the dubious glue of a surname on a certificate?

A sizable library was housed in three long hallways on the third floor of the Lazarist fathers' gymnasium. Strong oak shelves stacked with the spines of solid, leather-bound volumes stretched from floor to ceiling. It was like wandering through a forest with not a single clearing to be found. The pathways and hidden roads were known to one man only, the librarian, Father Ignatz. Students were only admitted to this seclusion from sixth form on, and visitors could easily be counted on the fingers of one hand. Most were intimidated by the impenetrable thicket of books.

When P'an arrived here for the first time, at sixteen years of age, his heart sank. So many books — and he had to read them all? Would there be enough time? He soon took heart. At first there seemed no way to get a handle on them all, but the numbers gradually began to diminish. Others had come to grips with them, why couldn't he? Above all, there was no time to waste. He could get by with less sleep. Six hours a day was enough. That was already two extra hours. He decided to begin at one end and systematically work his way through all the shelves. He soon started to be more selective. He could pretty much skip all the Jesus folklore. The shelves slowly began to thin out.

Amid the treatises, the dissertations of saintly fathers, he stumbled across a book that interested him more than the others. A pious "father" was exposing a contemporary heresy that went by the name of "Socialism."

He read the book carefully, and when he finished, he began all over.

There are people, a cult, who want to measure everything by work. The principle was straight out of St. Paul: "If any would not work, neither should he eat." Take the riches away from the rich and turn it into public property. Do away with private property and divvy it up among everybody according to their work.

He considered this for a long time. Then he began diligently searching for more detailed information. He combed the whole library. He found nothing. By chance, in the notes inside a bulky volume, he came across another mention of the mysterious cult. The author quoted bits from a work that was clearly written by the ringleader and founder of this dangerous heresy. His name was Marx.

He decided to find the book at any cost. He flipped through the entire card catalogue himself. The quoted author was missing. For a long time he debated whether to ask the librarian. Finally, he plucked up the courage. He asked. Father Ignatz flapped his arms:

"It's a sin to ask for such books! All that is the devil's work. Say more prayers and don't forget to fast!"

That was all he found out.

He decided to ask around in bookstores. Easier said than done. He had no money. Nor anywhere to get some. He had nothing to sell — he didn't own anything. What to do? He thought for a long time, but couldn't come up with a solution. Then he got up and went into a corner, toward some dusty shelves that even Father Ignatz never browsed through. The shelves were piled high with messes of thick folios in old, musty bindings. He took down the first book in Old Chinese and weighed it in his hand. He smiled to himself. Theft? Some witty Romans in a hostile land had once called it "acquiring fodder." It would be interesting to know the history of the book, how it got there. One might assume the methods were not entirely Christian. A smile on his face, he tucked the book under his shirt and slipped downstairs.

The half-dark room of the secondhand bookseller's in the remote Chinese district reeked of mildew and centuries of decay, and the dust on the potbellied porcelain vases lay piled in layers, as befits dust, until you could read the genealogy of the centuries in the number of layers, like the rings of a felled tree. The bespectacled, myopic bookseller scrutinized the book for a long time, running his nose across it, as if judging its antiquity by its smell. He paid three *taels* and carried the book off to his lair.

P'an ran with the money to the European bookstores. But the book was nowhere to be found. Feeling discouraged, he wandered deep into the Chinese district to search for it. In one of the Chinese bookstores that sold European titles, the bookseller said:

"We don't have any in stock. We can order one from Europe. But I can't tell you when it'll arrive, because a war's going on there."

Put down his name and wait for months to see if it would arrive? No, he wasn't interested.

The obliging bookseller gave him a tip:

"If you don't want to wait, there's a student group around here. They ordered a few copies through me. Try going to them and asking — maybe one of them will loan you theirs."

He wrote down the address on a scrap of paper.

P'an hurried there with a new spring in his step. It was nearby. He ran up to the third floor, taking the steps two at a time. It was opened by a scraggy young man in glasses. P'an told him why he'd come, mentioning the bookseller. He was ushered in.

A lamp gave off a dull glow in a small, modestly furnished room. His host was affable and polite, and asked about this and that: where he studied, what year he was in, what the conditions were like in the school, if the Chinese students were oppressed, were there many white students? They chatted awhile.

He went to a shelf and pulled down a book.

"Marx should not come right away. It's not easy. You won't keep up. Read this book first. It's easier. Get to know the subject. The time will come to tackle Marx."

He didn't want any money.

"We don't sell things here. Give it a read. When you've read it, come back and I'll give you another."

"The Fathers won't be mentioning this in their lectures," he smiled.

P'an thanked him and gave him a firm handshake, feeling abashed. He really liked the scraggy guy. He'd never been able to talk so frankly to anyone before. He raced home fast as a bullet — if only no one had noticed his absence!

He devoured the book in one gulp. The unfamiliar economics terms stuck in his throat like fish bones. He read it a second time. It seemed easier and clearer.

If the book could be believed, it wasn't just in China that oppression and poverty were rampant. In Europe, the same tens of thousands of white people were oppressing and robbing tens and hundreds of millions of their own white workers and peasants. The root was not the color of the skin or the crisscrossed state borderlines, but the strata of class, joined by their common interests and goals, in spite of their differences in language and custom. The workers and exploited around the world were one big family. Both the white and the yellow-skinned were fighting and suffering for the same thing. Likewise for the bourgeoisie. It wasn't by accident that the rich Chinese were always walking arm-in-arm with the white invaders.

All of this was unexpected and astonishing, the newness of it made his head spin. His cheeks burned from the thoughts bursting his skull. His eyes now wide open, he saw the world differently, as if armed with new glasses, boring right through the clutter like drills.

Having read the book from cover to cover, he ran back to the scraggy guy to ask for the next one. They talked about what he'd read. The scraggy guy explained the words he hadn't understood. He gave examples to illustrate the more difficult passages. All of a sudden they were talking about current events. About the war, imperialism, and so on. Why would it be better for China if Germany won? One way or another, the imperialists' colonial appetite would surely taper off after a while. Yet another danger lay in wait: a Japanese invasion. They were ousting the white people on all fronts. They couldn't wait to get their paws on China. In no way were they better than the others, maybe even worse. They were shamelessly exploiting the workers in the factories and paying them pennies, much less than the British.

He gave P'an another book and invited him to drop by more often.

He exchanged one book for another, and the more he read, the more he understood. He read in secret, during the night — the nights were clear and bright. In the morning, the dawn woke him lying on an open book. His eyelids drooped in his daytime classes. He even started neglecting his studies. The Lazarist fathers asked about his health. They shook their heads knowingly.

When he finished a book, he was itching to bolt off to the scraggy guy. He met other people at the scraggy guy's apartment. Students. Educating themselves. Long, heated, nighttime discussions. Courses, lectures, gatherings. He envied them. He wanted to dive into this new and alluring world as soon as he could.

After a few months they got used to him, they'd taken his measure and had visibly started to trust him. One day, the scraggy guy made a suggestion:

"Would you like to prepare a lecture on the role of the Christian missionaries as tools of American-European capitalism in the process of yoking colonial peoples? The topic should be familiar to you and in line with your interests. You can speak at the next gathering."

P'an leapt for joy. He wrote a lecture that was lengthy and exhaustive. Unfortunately, he had no opportunity to deliver it. Father Paphnutius had noticed his mysterious excursions. He worked out what he was up to. One day he groped around under P'an's straw mattress and found a dog-eared copy of *The Communist Manifesto* with notes scribbled in the margins and the lecture on the missionaries. Crimson juices flushed his face. Panting heavily, he trotted off to see Father Dominic.

P'an was summoned from his lessons. Father Dominic, by now a purplish-blue, was sitting in his office with the unfortunate lecture in his hands. In his rage he forgot what he was going to say, and could only give an inarticulate hiss:

"Begone, you wayward lamb!"

P'an said calmly, "Please return my book! Don't you dare rip it!"

"I'll show you, you delinquent! Down with his pants!"

Two guards grabbed P'an by the arms. A third promptly yanked down his pants. They threw him onto a bench. He scratched one of them in the face. They called in a janitor to help. They beat him alternately with two canes. Father Dominic screeched:

"I'll teach you some gratitude, you yellow devil!"

The flogged boy was thrown to the floor.

"Take off his shirt! And all the rest of it! The shoes! It's all ours! Our benevolence! The long underwear! Take it all off!"

So they did. They left him lying naked on the floor. A guard named Vincent rummaged out — who knows from where — a torn, ragged Chinese gabardine.

"Put 'em on!"

So he did. Everything inside him seethed. They grabbed him by the arms.

"Get out!"

P'an struggled. He wanted to lash out. His hands were twisted until the joints cracked. In his powerless frenzy he spit so vigorously into Father Dominic's face that the holy father squealed and stamped his feet, wiping his face and soiling his entire cassock.

They clambered down the stairs, through the garden, threw the gates wide open, and tossed him brusquely into the street. He landed in the middle of the road. The gate clattered shut.

A policeman appeared:

"And what might you be doing here?"

P'an picked himself up and, shamefully covering the holes in his rags, made his way down side streets to the scraggy guy's home.

The scraggy guy washed his bloody welts with the corner of a towel. He dug a few pairs of underwear out of a drawer and some old, worn clothing out of a corner. He helped P'an get dressed and let him stay the night.

A few days later P'an was set up at an English cotton mill. From eight till eight. Pay: two *maces* a day. You couldn't live off plain rice for that amount. They found him a room. After that, he was on his own.

He came to work spry, filled with enthusiasm. Now he'd finally come face to face with the real workforce, with ennobling physical labor. With the pickax of exertion he'd chip out underground tunnels of organization into that airtight, faceless human mass.

At eight o'clock he left the factory, deaf and dejected, an absurd and bulging scream shooting up his throat. This he could never have imagined. What were books, dull misery, starvation, and tables of abstract statistics next to this? Here for the first time, his eyes wide with terror, he spanned the whole abyss of human distress and disgrace, the entire enormity of the average man's suffering.

An unbearable heat swam in the factory, and the people worked half-naked, streaming with sweat. White foremen brandished whips as they paced the hall between the machines, and every other moment a serpentine whip cracked as it rose over the bent back of an unwary worker and fell with a mournful groan. Red streaks appeared on the arched backs, like hours being ticked off, staining the sweat crimson. Over half the workers were women and children, some not even ten years old, and beads of sweat as big as tears poured down their strained faces, like those inconceivable, terrible drops that fall from the helpless, astonished eyes of tortured animals.

The enormous machines were like monstrous two-headed dragons, swallowing gray skeins of oakum as filthy as smoke, then spitting them out in long, fibrous saliva, swiftly wound on the spinning tops of spools. Then the iron fingers grabbed and unwove the fibers for the hundredth time, pulled them apart in infinite slender threads, and these threads, strained till they groaned, broke in the air with a snap, where they were caught in mid-flight and tied in a split-second knot by the women's lively fingers. The spools dribbled from the slobbering maws of the machines into the spittoons of gigantic baskets, and the filled baskets were carried off somewhere into the fog by spindly-legged boys, straining under the terrible weight.

In the evening, when the people were numb from exhaustion and felt their movements begin to flag, to grow sluggish and more fitful, like the stubborn grinding of unlubricated gears, the lines of the apocalyptic red pencil ticked off each row of backs in turn, as though an enraged mystical censor were crossing all the helpless verses of human beings from the Book of Creation, one by one.

A cloud of down hovered in the air, and in the acrid smoke the naked human figures convulsed with barking coughs, like the thrashing death agonies of the condemned in catechism illustrations.

This was precisely how medieval painters had envisioned hell, except theirs, it seemed, had no children. Or perhaps the subtle Christian god, already bored of torturing adults, had created a special new hell for children, a dogma the priests were keeping from the faithful.

He returned to his hovel feeling as though he'd smoked opium, his head full of chaos and his feet full of lead.

That night he dreamt of the striped backs, the mouths wrought in anguish, the eyes wide with terror and inhuman yearning, amid suffocating billows of smoke. Then red tongues of flame began piercing the smoke, everything exploded in a blinding fire, and amid the flaming tongues the white pockmarked foreman from the drying house, a harp in each hand, performed a snake dance. Ultimately it all dissolved into streams of chaotic nonsense; sleep began the work of rhythmically flooding the red-hot poker of his brain.

In a month he'd toughened up, grown used to it. The blows, the coughing and howling, the acrid cloud of down, none of it made his head spin. His eyes were calm and stern from behind the bars of their lashes. He got down to work, organizing a group. This was extremely difficult. There could be no thought of talking to anyone during the day. Every step was marked and accounted for. In the evenings, the workers, reeling from exhaustion, listened without comprehending.

He tried to make contact on days off. The older workers glared fearfully at him and scowled. They were afraid of even sighing aloud in the factory. They were dismissed for the slightest word, let alone outright resistance. Who could even think of opposition in those circumstances? They avoided him and observed him cautiously: He was clearly up to no good. Even so, by the end of the second month he managed to gather a small group of young workers. The work loped onward. Most of the young people were illiterate. He set up basic evening classes. Few came. After twelve hours of exhausting work their eyelids drooped low. They were asphyxiated by the smoke of fatigue and couldn't get the difficult letters through their skulls. How to teach these people? His powerlessness made him lose heart.

One, a sixteen-year-old spool worker named Chen, turned out to be surprisingly clever. An extraordinarily bright girl, and she studied hard. Top of the class. Passionately campaigning among her friends, she brought over a dozen workers into the group.

P'an liked her a great deal. She asked about everything in detail. Memorized things avidly. Her questions became acute, adult, thoughtful, and precise. Her slanted, rational eyes were gentle and open.

Once, on the way home from the factory, she told P'an her short life's story. She'd come from the countryside. There were thirteen of them at home, and only two *mu* of land. Hard times. When she was only thirteen, her father sold her to an old man. She ran away. Made it to the city on foot. She had worked in a Japanese factory — the pay was low, survival impossible. Now she was employed as a spool worker. That was rough, too, but a bit better at least.

P'an hadn't met any girls before. Even though there had been no chance to at the Lazarists', he had unconsciously started to despise them. They were slaves, breeders, nothing more, reflecting ages of discrimination, the legacy of generations. The word "woman" was a slur.

But this one struck him with her childlike, unconquerable gentleness, her keen and ungirlish mind, her eagerness to discover, her conscious will to fight, which was so inconceivable in such a miniature frame.

They spoke long into the evenings, forgetting their meals and their fatigue. Returning to his little hovel after the group meetings, stretched out on his straw mattress, P'an recalled words both mild and honest, eyes wide from curiosity, and in his mind he repeated: My darling! And here he caught himself. And what was this now? Love? What a laugh! And what is love exactly? Copulation and children? No, that's not it. Something else. Just a nice, kind comrade — that's all. But he knew all too well this wasn't it either! And he fell asleep more quickly if he tried not to think.

One evening after work (he had the night off), P'an stood in front of the female workers' exit. The last ones dispersed.

Obviously he had missed her. Chen was probably busy. She was teaching a few workers by now. He wandered off home: he'd work on his own. He didn't waste his nighttime hours.

Meanwhile, as Chen was leaving down the narrow corridors of the factory, her path was barred by the stocky, pockmarked foreman. He had been molesting and harassing her for some time. This time she didn't even manage to scream. He covered her mouth with a big, hairy paw. He dragged the flailing girl into his cell. In her helpless misery she bit his nose. He knocked her out with a blow of his fist, as if pacifying a horse. Then he threw her on the floor and raped her while she lay there unconscious.

He walked away wiping his nose with a handkerchief.

A few days later P'an met Chen at a group meeting. He was astonished by the change that had come over her. She'd been tiny to begin with, but now she seemed even smaller, as if someone had knocked out her supports from within. Her eyes were wide and astonished, like those of a wounded child. Once they'd been open and brave, and now they fearfully avoided his gaze.

He went up to her when the meeting was finished and asked what was going on, if she was ill. She gave a rueful smile. Hard to say if she was smiling or about to cry. She mumbled something about a headache.

P'an felt agitated. She was worn out. It was natural. How was a child like that supposed to cope with such infernal labor?

From that day on, they met infrequently. Only at group meetings. She studied as diligently as ever. But you could see that something inside her had snapped. He tried talking to her. Her responses were evasive. She was tired. And in a hurry. She had a smaller female workers' group next. She couldn't be late — everyone was exhausted. He couldn't get any more out of her.

Until suddenly — a great and unexpected joy. Delivered by the newspapers. A workers' revolution in Russia. Power was in the hands of the soviets. The Communists were in the vanguard. If only they'd hold out! A socialist workers' state right next door — this was a powerful ally! With this thought in mind, it was easier to work, to bear the failures, discrimination, and the pulverizing, inhuman oppression.

Months passed.

Work in the factory progressed quickly. There were already three older workers' groups. He had no one to help him. Everything on his own. He could hardly keep up. He had to shelve his own studies for the time being.

In spite of it all, when alone at night he would secretly yearn for his old conversations with Chen, for her bright and trusting eyes, for the soft exaltation of her voice.

Then one evening — a few months had slipped by unnoticed — as he was leaving he saw some workers congregating in the courtyard. He went over and asked what had happened.

"A spool worker drowned . . . in the well . . ."

He shuddered. Pushing aside the gawkers, he squeezed in closer. His heart drummed an alarm. He recognized her from afar. There she lay, tiny, her face bruised and swollen. In her half-open eyes — the terror of a child.

He roamed the streets late into the night, shaken to the bone, vainly trying to unravel this grim puzzle. What could have happened? How could he not have noticed anything, not have taken care of her, not stopped her?

Late that night he returned to his room feeling a mess. On the table in his room — a letter. He opened it with trembling hands.

"My dearest! Don't condemn me for what I've done. The white pockmarked devil has disgraced me. He's infected me with a terrible disease. How can I go on living? If I had confessed it to you, you might have killed him. He'll get what he deserves, no matter what. I've written the authorities that he's to blame. I'm so afraid to die! My one and only, my dearest! I love you . . ."

Overcome with rage, P'an dashed to the door. At the threshold he paused. Where was he going? To kill the pockmarked man? One way or the other, he'd have to wait until morning. He crouched on a sack, not bothering to get undressed. His thoughts ran in circles. And inside him — a physical, gnawing pain.

Gradually his thoughts sifted themselves from the chaos and found some precision.

Who was this pockmarked guy? A pawn. A wheel in a huge mechanism. Kill the individual? Nonsense! If an oak is blotting out the sun, why tear off an acorn? You've got to hack down the whole tree. Dig it up by the roots. When it falls, all the acorns will tumble to the earth. Provided he had the strength to keep hacking! Don't give up. Become the ax himself. Whittle his hate until it was sharp as a blade and watch that it never grew blunt.

A red-hot needle of pain turned his thoughts back to Chen. Such a tiny thing! So wise! Wanted to know everything and wasn't aware of such simple things, like the fact that only the Chinese punish those who cause a suicide. White people were above Chinese law. They scoffed at it. Who would think to punish the murderer of a tiny Chinese girl?

He squatted there until morning.

In the morning he showed up for work stiff, calm, composed. In the evening, at the group meeting, he explained things forcibly, responded precisely to questions and, feeling ten pairs of slanted eyes trained on him, reached a hard full stop:

"Death to the oppressors!"

That fall he managed to organize the first opposition in the factory. The workers sent delegates to the factory administration. To raise salaries. To abolish corporal punishment. Equal payment for the children and women who did equal work.

The delegates were beaten and thrown out of the factory. The workers responded with a strike. Management lost its head. An army detachment was called in. Soldiers surrounded the factory. Police arrived to dispose of the instigators. P'an Tsiang-kuei and a few other workers were arrested and taken to the police station. Their shoes were removed and their heels lashed with bamboo sticks until they fell unconscious. P'an passed out and was thrown into an isolation cell.

He escaped. He'd known beatings since childhood. They didn't scare him. Like a cat thrown on the ground, he'd learned to land on all fours. Now it was the same. Scaling a high wall, he dusted off his clothing and, like nothing had happened, marched over to the district committee.

Then — faces, factories, cities . . . image after image, like a high-speed film. No way to retain it all. Groups, meetings, strikes, demonstrations, prisons. The flesh on his heels stripped to the bone. Two months in the slammer. Two death sentences. Two jailbreaks.

He joined Sun Yat-sen's party. Took a look around. The Kuomintang was swarming with nationalist-leaning bourgeoisie. Take away the foreigners' privileges, force them to rewrite bad treaties. Otherwise — same old story. What could P'an have in common with them? For the time being, one thing only — a common enemy, the imperialists. You've got to use whomever you can against them. For now they were allies. Later, it would be up in the air. After the foreigners were sent packing, then maybe it would be their turn. The important thing was to forge ties with the working masses. There was always work to be done.

He had to abandon his studies. His only luxury was the newspaper. It rarely brought much comfort. More often it disturbed him. Something had gotten tangled up in the West. The Entente Cordiale had conquered Germany. Their own "socialists" had swallowed up the workers' revolution. Something like a German Kuomintang, apparently. The winners bellowed their victory with a triumphant howl. Just watch, they'll start pouring in again, China will be taken overnight, it'll be flooded by swarms of new, insatiable carpetbaggers.

They descended. Even more brazen, even haughtier, even more bloodthirsty. A weary China greeted them with a strangled moan. But things were already seething down below. The first timid explosions — the hollow, faraway rumble of an impending storm.

In China the air was getting thinner. White-skinned and yellow-skinned spies nipped at the heels of the Chinese like greyhounds. He had to slip out by night, sniffing out the nooks, like back in his childhood, when he had to look for rundown hovels to sleep in. It was getting harder to work. Exhaustion and sleep deprivation made his eyes fall shut, made his lashed heels ache.

Help arrived unexpectedly. Arranged by his friends. The Kuomintang was sending him and a group of students to study in Europe.

On a stuffy, sweltering evening, when the overloaded ship swayed heavily on hunched, foam-fringed waves, a cumbersome wardrobe carried by porters on strained backs, P'an Tsiang-kuei stood on deck, and his gaze took in the contours of his receding homeland for the final time. A lump swelled in his throat. China drifted away in the dusk like a giant galley shunted into the distance by the measured strokes of invisible oars. It seemed that at any moment the choked and protracted howl of the slant-eyed rowers, the rattle of chains, and the crack of a white slave driver's whip would break the silence. The East was just a black smear of night. P'an leaned on the railing in a quandary. Where was that hapless country floating to? Did it have far to float in this dusk? And would it someday float off into freedom and sunshine, or was it never fated to see the long-awaited sun, whose misshapen orb the emaciated and anguished workers embroidered by night on the white flags of the Kuomintang?

He arrived in Europe tense and alert, like he'd been as a child when he'd gone crawling into treacherous doghouses in search of bones. Now he was crawling into the enemy's cave to carry off his most precious and jealously guarded bone — knowledge. This enemy was far worse and more vicious than those he'd known before. In comparison, his old bloated employer seemed like a clumsy leech stuck to his side, ready to be torn off and tossed aside. In China he'd already felt a sharp repugnance, as if his entire epidermis were stuck with thousands of aphids. It was simply impossible to tear them all off. They trailed endless threads of telegraph wires in long and supple tentacles, circling half the globe and going astray somewhere in the unexplored stone jungles of a foreign continent. After years of childhood dreams, an enchanted seafaring Mer Ce-Des had finally carried him to their secret lair.

Plunging the negative of his consciousness into the reagent of one capital city after another, P'an Tsiang-kuei came to feel like a man inoculating himself against a disease, feeling the bloated and frenzied bacteria coursing through his arteries, and whose terrified body, like a machine pushed into overdrive, began firing off ready and waiting antitoxins by the thousands.

The achievements of European culture, once so dazzling to his child's mind, no longer blinded his jaded and naturally squinting eyes, which studied everything carefully and ruthlessly, taking what was essential and material and dismissing everything superfluous with a bat of his eyelashes.

The little boy who had read all the books in the Lazarist Fathers' library had bequeathed an unquenchable desire to learn about absolutely everything, to know the whole complex apparatus of the foreign culture from the ground up.

He studied with passion, swallowing the books whole, discarding the finished ones like husks. Like a sleepwalker on the scaffolding of a six-story building, he crossed through the shadowy corridors of Europe's universities without once losing his balance.

In the evenings, he avoided the rumbling boulevards, preferring to roam the workers' districts on the outskirts, sparsely lit by the occasional fires of lampposts. He would blend into the muddy, threadbare crowd, staring into the emaciated, angular faces, jaundiced from poverty, their bones jutting out over the caverns of their cheeks.

In the ruined, gray face of a coachman he caught a flash of the spokes and the naked heels of a downtrodden rickshaw driver, dashing at the same moment somewhere down the sweltering alleys of Shanghai. Stooped under the crushing weight of a sack, a porter dripped the yellow sweat of a Chinese coolie. The swollen, drooping eyelids of women, staggering under the weight of their infants swathed in rags, narrowed their eyes to oblique slits.

For the first time P'an Tsiang-kuei saw what those books he'd read so thoroughly described: apart from the China of his homeland, with its Yellow Sea façade, there were other Chinas, internationally, everywhere, where backs are crooked, jaws are strained taut, cracks of eyes are narrowed with hatred, and where a fat, majestic employer presides.

In the cities he passed through he appeared as a delegate at meetings of local workers' organizations, flinging his lasso — the thrilling call of international solidarity — over the rippling sea of heads.

Showers of red sparks flew from the faraway flickering firebrand of Moscow, Lenin's incendiary words fell like glowing cinders on the oppressed masses and peoples, on layers of class consciousness that had been kicked and trampled under the feet of conquering armies. Explosions from the shifting plates deep down below shook the ground beneath their feet. News from China came choppy and muddled, like a flock of spooked birds from the East, fearful harbingers of a brewing tempest.

And finally it happened. The white-hot cauldron burst with the hysterical shriek of startled parliaments and the dismal lament of telegraph wires. Lava spewed from the cauldron, melting everything in its path, innumerable yellow columns spurted forth, a gathering, unbridled wave washing over the world. The red sun of the Kuomintang with the hammer and sickle and the five-pointed star. A triumphal march to the north. A winged word flew on the telegraph wires, arriving ahead of the bullets: Victory!

The shrapnel from the mighty explosion sprayed all over the world, eventually reaching as far as Europe. Puny white people with suitcases. Undigested fear and astonishment in their eyes. They blundered across the whole continent in terror. Along the boulevards the enormous stampeding and shimmering letters of illuminated gazettes, whipped up by a lashing gale of bulletins, formed themselves into one harsh, prickly word: "intervention."

Upon first hearing of the revolution, P'an Tsiang-kuei shuddered, snapped shut a half-finished book, and wanted to dash off to the train station. He was prohibited. He was ordered to stay at his post, give up his studies, forge closer ties with local workers' organizations, prepare the European proletariat's resistance to the armed intervention of the imperialists.

He acquiesced: he understood the center of gravity wasn't there, it was here. In London, in Paris. In the smoke-filled rooms of the Foreign Office, in the salons of the Quai d'Orsay. Thin lines stretched from here to the enemy's headquarters: francs, pounds, directives, steel buildings floating on the water — battleships. Snap the enemy's back with a single blow to the spine, a slender telegraph cable stretched between London and Paris, break it with the resistance of their own white working masses, under the flag of defending the Chinese Revolution, in the name of the luminous slogan of worldwide solidarity of the oppressed!

Instead of the crowded libraries and the chill of the laboratories, now it was stuffy and overcrowded halls, meetings, conferences, demonstrations, fiery articles on scraps of paper torn from notebooks, black, swinging railcars, apartments, overnighters, the watchful eye of police surveillance. He was deported from London. In Paris, on the stairs, on the tram, in cafés, searching eyes scrutinized him. He was sick to death of it. The usual hiding spots in the subway, between the exits, the entrances, and the corridors. He gave them the slip. Thus passed the weeks, the months, a year.

Finally vacation. He was allowed to travel to China. Again the ship swayed, hefted upon the muscular shoulders of the waves like an orator on the shoulders of a frenzied crowd. At the Chinese shore his path was blocked by the gloomy towers of battleships observing the banks through the long telescopes of their cannons. A dreary shadow fell upon the sunny March day. But the shores were bathed in sunshine, and on the bank, hoisted high above the pyramid of crowded buildings, flapped the radiant flag of the Kuomintang. P'an's spirits rose at the sight.

Shanghai greeted him with swelter, the mournful beat of drums, the alcohol of a frothing crowd, the lament of sirens, screams and jabbering. Chucked out of their apartments, fear-crazed, barefoot and in their underwear, people leapt past firebrands like phantoms, only to vanish moments later in the burbling yellow flow of the crowd without so much as a scream. Ceremonially dressed rickshaw drivers triumphantly paraded the heads of yesterday's passengers impaled on stakes.

He went to a meeting of delegates. Their speeches throbbed with a victory more heady than rice wine. The majority were leftist Kuomintangs and Communists. Arm the workers. Form a leftist provisional government. All power to the delegates! The nationalist delegates objected to arming the workforce. They left in a huff. Forget it! They'll dance to our tune yet!

After Shanghai came Nanjing. The Shandong armies were retreating in disarray. On the streets, the dense celebrating crowds overflowed, swirled, thrashed. The sun blazed and suddenly the ice cracked open. It seemed that at any minute, snatched up by the swift current of the crowd, the bulky frames of houses, palaces, and pagodas would tear free from the ground and float by, rushing forward, colliding and whirling to the open outlet — toward victory. The sun on the spread wings of flags, in pupils joyfully dilated, in the timid spring green of trees, in the warble of drunken birds, on the façades, on faces — a golden sunny soot.

And then . . .

A hollow rumble. What's that? The first peal of a spring storm on the horizon? A shell burst with a crack over the heads of the startled crowd. A frantic commotion, screams. A whorl of bodies, a sudden, mad outpouring. The river was dammed and the gathering waves flushed back to strike. In the air, shells flew like smoking rockets. They're firing at the city! Who? The Shandong soldiers? No, not them.

The first messengers came running in a panic.

"Gunboats! Landing troops! The American and French armies are coming ashore!"

Everything seethed. Shells sailed over the city like meteors. To the left, to the right — the crash of tumbling buildings and red fountains of flames. The defenseless crowd blundered between the collapsing walls like a blind herd of horses in a burning stable.

People came running, disheveled and wheezing:

"Everyone to the arsenals, to the weapons!"

P'an Tsiang-kuei kept his head. Snatching a machine gun from a baffled soldier, he led a few dozen people toward the port. Groups of armed workers and soldiers were already rushing from all sides, firing in the air as they ran. On the shore, a skirmish. Reinforcements came in time. A bramble bush of human bodies. Dough. P'an pressed into the malleable blue mass with all his momentum. A gunshot cracked. A British sailor leveled his bayonet at P'an. P'an wriggled away. A fist to the back of his shaved head. The sailor's blood-smeared face got hooked onto the catch of his rifle. P'an tore away the weapon. On the catch, red pulp. He grabbed it by the barrel. The butt came down full force onto the starched white caps. He cleared a spacious field around him, like a lumberjack. Reinforcements came. The sailors dispersed along the stone steps of the wharf. But more were coming from behind. On the boulevard, a new skirmish. P'an hurried toward it, leaping through the bodies. Suddenly he stumbled. In his eyes — shards, a red swirl.

He crumpled gently, without a scream, straight and supple, like an acrobat falling from a trapeze onto the stone net of the wharf stretched out below.

He came to three weeks later, in a filthy wartime hospital that stank of iodine and the cloying sweat of soldiers. In his chest was a burning needle.

The doctor consoled him:

"We thought you weren't going to make it. One inch below the heart."

P'an asked about the news. It came as a blow. In the Kuomintang: division and treachery. The right was chumming up to the imperialists. The traitor Chiang Kai-shek was starting a bloody liquidation of workers' organizations in Shanghai and Canton. The slogan: the fight against Communism. Mass shootings and slaughter everywhere. Nanjing was still holding strong for the time being, but the new Kuomintang was riven by squabbles. The left wing was in on the anti-communist conspiracy. Just wait, they'd cross over to the counterrevolutionary camp. And so on. A long litany of unhappy incidents, and names and dates of disgrace. His eyes drooped in fatigue. Well, hadn't he known in advance that their time would come, too? He just hadn't suspected it would be so soon. Maybe it was for the best. He liked it when all the cards were on the table.

He was soon released from the hospital. A bit unsteady on his feet, he dove into the whirlpool of work. Now for the countryside. New directives. Take charge of the peasant unions. Help the existing peasant organizations develop. Get young people involved. Break up the *Meituan* networks. Form an alliance with the Red Spades. Guiding principle — agrarian revolution. Hubei. Hunan. Mud huts. Levies. Endless waterlogged roads. By the roadside ditches, the dates of bitter and harrowing events cropped up like milestones. Wuhan. Nanjing. The workers' insurrection crushed in Canton. Shooting. Executions. Sticky, innocent blood.

The one bright spot: the revolutionary ferment of the peasant masses was swelling, gathering like a wave. May it continue! Burrowing under the dams like a patient mole. They would break and wash everything clean. Then it would be time for revenge.

Only one thought sustained him: the gigantic Soviet Union sprawled out to the north, occupying one sixth of the globe. It had survived interventions, blockades, years of starvation and demoralization. Bound by a ring of imperialists, alone, unaided, it had taken root and was growing, floor by floor, upward. It made accusations, reproached, and urged with the irrefutable digits of statistics. "Hold on! Don't back down! Build! Failure, hardship — it's all part of the transition! Before us lies victory, a wide expanse! Don't lose hope!"

All the difficulties, discomforts, and adversities clouded his mind. An old wound flared up. He was out of commission. Sent to the head office. Then back to the hospital. An old bullet they'd overlooked. He quickly recovered. The day before he left the hospital he received his orders. The Party was drafting him to Europe as a secret agent, as someone who knew the ropes, to expose the counterrevolution on site.

He was reluctant to leave, but he made no protest. He arrived in Paris incognito. He was soon sniffed out. More creeping around at night. Shut up in a tiny room in a hotel on Panthéon Square, P'an Tsiang-kuei pushed forward the clock hands of his daily routine. He slept during the day and went out into the city only late at night, when the telltale color of his skin was obscured by the yellowish glow of electric lamps, and the long slits of his eyes vanished under the wide brim of his hat.

In Paris, the Latin Quarter was swarming with nationalist students. He imperceptibly slipped in among them. He was taciturn and serious. He slowly earned himself acceptance. By spring he was the heart and soul of the whole movement. His facetious nickname: "the dictator."

He first heard about the outbreak of the plague from a short bellboy. His first impulse was to be pleased at the unexpected ally. It was more fun than any intervention, and would put the kibosh on Europe for a good few months — no battleships, no armies, no suitcases stuffed with money. If only it held out long enough, until his men had managed to settle the score with their own and the others!

The accidental herald of the sinister news raised his eyes and saw to his surprise that the stony face of the Chinese gentleman had for the first time cracked in a smile, like a ripening fruit. It suddenly seemed to P'an Tsiang-kuei, as he bent down over the frightened bellboy, that in the boy's wide eyes he could make out other eyes, narrow and slanted, and through the contours of his face, as if staring through a veil, another face, the Mongol grin of the plague.

And indeed, the hotel boy died that night. He was one of the plague's first victims.

•

In the tiny Chinese restaurant, the grayish man with the goatee was bent over the table and staring at P'an over the tops of his glasses, and reddening in the face, he said in a decisive, somewhat tremulous voice:

"I'm sorry if I've startled you. May I have a word . . ."

P'an Tsiang-kuei raised his eyes from his plate and stared at the stranger in surprise, trying to recall if he'd seen his face somewhere before.

"You don't remember me, of course," said the older man without lifting his gaze. "You're too Chinese to be able to tell European faces apart. All the more so given that, strictly speaking, we are bound by no formal acquaintance. You studied bacteriology and biochemistry with me at the Sorbonne some seven years ago. I was your professor. A relationship that hardly obliges you to remember me. In my case it's different. I have always observed your people with great interest.

"The morning you people arrive here, while you're still standing on the train steps, and before your foot has even touched our soil, you're already throwing yourselves, as if headfirst from a diving board, into the pool of our knowledge, yearning to swim its length at top speed, as if the other side held some magical prize known only to yourselves. You cram your alien and ill-matched mindset into the new forms of European thought with as much passion as your women squeeze their mangled feet into the tight holes of their shoes. My impression is that if you found out one day that people with longer legs were able to see more clearly, you would not hesitate to cut off your own legs and replace them with longer prostheses.

"You are our fastest-learning, our cleverest students, and at the same time our most ungrateful. Armed with the seven-league boots of our knowledge, you leave them on your doorsteps like a pair of slippers, only to walk barefoot on the stone floor of your traditions, carpeted with your superstitions.

"You were one of my best and most inspired students. But of course, this alone is hardly cause to renew our acquaintance after so many years, in such totally different circumstances.

"When you vanished from my sight like so many of your people before you, I thought our paths would never cross again. I forgot about you, as one forgets a pedestrian one collides with on the street, who vanishes with a polite tip of the hat. Unfortunately, things went differently. Our paths crossed once more, and now nothing could untangle them, unless . . . unless by a radical incision . . ."

P'an Tsiang-kuei stared at the old man with growing astonishment.

"Excuse me," he said mildly, "but it seems as though you've mistaken me for someone else. Even if I did once study bacteriology and biochemistry with you at the Sorbonne — as indeed, I once did, I believe — I can tell you with total confidence that I have never seen you since."

"You needn't tell me," replied the gray man, peering over the rims of his glasses. "I'm well aware of it. You have in fact never come across me since. It is I who came across you. I met you in Nanjing in 1927. If you recall, that year mass outbreaks of Asian cholera were reported in a few Chinese provinces. The Bacteriological Association delegated me to travel there to conduct scientific research. I was all the more willing to go as it meant seeing my only child, who had volunteered for a unit of assault troops. At the time his battleship was stationed off the coast of China.

"The civil war that consumed the provinces I was researching forced me to seek asylum in Nanjing. And I indeed had the opportunity to see my son, as his ship was moored at the port entrance. Riots broke out, however, a few days after my arrival. That was when I spotted you for the second time. I saw you at the head of a frenzied mob that attacked the landing troops defending the trading post. You hardly resembled the shy and industrious Sorbonne student I once knew, but still I recognized you at once.

"The English trading post where I found sanctuary was being looted by retreating Chinese soldiers, and so we were woken up, and hastily evacuated in our underwear to the English cruiser waiting in the harbor, under army escort. Among the officers in one of those units was my son. From on deck I observed the ensuing battle through a telescope with tense anticipation. I saw how the savage mob charged out of every crevice of the Chinese city, pouring over the entire shoreline. Spearheading the throng was you. Pressed by the barbarous rabble, our soldiers began to retreat. Then I spotted my boy. He was running with a revolver in his hand, stopping those who were escaping and forcing them to turn back. The rabid horde fell upon him. And then I saw, with my own two eyes, how you leapt upon him first and smashed in his skull with the butt of your rifle.

"I lost consciousness and was taken to a cabin.

"Since then I've been entirely alone. You took everything from me in one fell swoop. Science, which had always been the very air I breathed, became a loathsome business. Whenever I tried to sit down to work, the image of my boy always hovered before my eyes, and I was incapable of writing a single letter . . .

"Taking into consideration my service to the field of science, I was given retirement as an infirm old man, and reluctantly granted a professorial pension. Now I am vermin, of no use to anyone, gnawing at the carrion of my own many years of work.

"Through those years, sitting alone in a dark room like a mole, I often thought of you. I spent long nights searching for the footbridge that would lead from that industrious Sorbonne student, burning with holy admiration and an almost fiery love for our centuries-old culture and knowledge, placing the stiff flowers of his zeal upon that altar, to the savage Asiatic, massacring his recent teachers and welcoming hosts in the wild dementia of his hatred. Roaming the streets in the evenings and spying on the slit-eyed students leaving the Sorbonne with their schoolbooks under their arms, I tried to decipher the secret of their hatred from their faces. But their faces were smiling and as taut as masks.

"One evening I went to see a friend, the rector of the Sorbonne, and over the course of a long conversation I tried to convince him that European culture grafted onto Asian soil, like a bacteria transplanted into a new environment, would be murderous for Europe, that in recklessly enlightening Asia, Europe was setting the stage for its own annihilation. I showed him that not a day was to be wasted, that all the European universities should shut their doors to Asians. He took me for a madman, and steering the conversation down another path, he gently guided me home.

"Over time, all concrete images of you were eroded from my memory and, sitting for hours with my eyes squeezed shut, I tried in vain to summon them back. Your face had slipped out somewhere through my memory's filter, only your slanting, narrowed eyes and prominent cheekbones remained, like a stencil whose gaps I'd have to fill in myself.

"Until one evening, I came face to face with you in the street. I recognized you at once. You were walking quickly and didn't even notice that I stopped in your path, as though rooted to the spot.

"I spent the whole night mulling over various schemes for revenge, which came to me on their own. At dawn, unable to wait for the day, I headed straight for the police and demanded they arrest you. They hemmed and hawed. They pointed to the lack of evidence and promised to conduct an investigation. I realized that taking you to trial would be futile, because many people considered me a loon.

"At that point I understood that I had only one recourse: I had to kill you. On my way home I purchased a six-shooter and went in search of you.

"I started to frequent Chinese restaurants, estimating that the greatest chance of meeting you was there. My expectations did not fail me. Two weeks ago I did indeed finally come across you in this very restaurant. That evening I found out, however, that it is far less easy to kill a man than one might expect. Clearly a certain inborn predisposition is required, or at the very least some training. I have neither.

"For the past two weeks I have been tracing your footsteps, I have been waiting for you in the evening outside your hotel, I have been dining with you in this very eatery, I have been at your side like a shadow. And I do not know how to kill you.

"Others do it off the cuff, on a whim. Maybe you've got to avoid thinking about it and then it comes by itself, instinctively. But I can't stop thinking about it. As I walk you home, I swear to myself that tomorrow I'll do it for certain. But 'tomorrow' always ends just like 'today.'

"I've found myself in this position for the first time in my life. I've never tried to kill anyone. That's just how it's turned out. I've never even been to war. Reading the descriptions of dozens of murders in the newspapers, I didn't imagine that it could be so difficult. In the morning, having seen you to your hotel (I've adjusted to the hours you keep), I return home, pull some old newspapers out of the corner and carefully read descriptions of various sorts of killings. I reasoned that certain preparations are necessary for everything, even if on an elementary level. In this case, however, studies aren't much good. Much as a knowledge of the history of painting in no way teaches you how to paint, a knowledge of the history of every murder since the creation of the world cannot teach you how to kill a single man with your own two hands.

"After two weeks, I had practically lost all hope that I would ever manage to kill you.

"The outbreak of the plague cheered me at first — it was such a simple and unexpected way out of the situation. I counted on it coming to my rescue, that upon arriving at your hotel the following evening with my daily intention of killing you, this time for certain — I'd come across a stretcher bearing your corpse. I've come every evening, right on time for the arrival of the dead-carts.

"Yet the plague has spared you. At first I enjoyed shadowing you, I observed you wandering aimlessly through the empty nighttime streets like a rat caught in a trap. The certainty that sooner or later you would have to die from the plague was the only consolation when I returned home unsuccessful. But time is passing. I myself could die, if not today, then tomorrow. It could easily happen that I die before you. It could also happen that I die and you altogether survive. This I cannot allow to happen. Today I swore to myself that I would kill you, without fail. I came here early on purpose to occupy the table behind the one where you normally sit. I deduced that killing you from behind would be easiest. But today you came late and sat down right at my table for the first time. I feel that once again, I will not be able to kill you.

"I've decided to use the last means at my disposal. I feel that I shall never be able to kill you as long as I know that you are unsuspecting. When I'm convinced that you know the danger at hand and have your guard up, then I believe it will go more smoothly. This is why I have decided to get everything out into the open. Get ready! Defend yourself! Today I'm going to kill you as you leave this building!"

The professor fell silent, clearly agitated, his gray eyes staring over the rims of his glasses and not straying a moment from P'an Tsiang-kuei. P'an Tsiang-kuei observed him for a moment with curiosity.

"Shall we leave at once?" he asked calmly, wiping his mouth with a napkin.

"As you wish," the professor courteously replied.

P'an Tsiang-kuei silently settled the bill and got up from the table. He made way for the professor to go through the door. For a brief moment they stood on ceremony, both hesitating to be the first to go out. Eventually the professor went first.

Finding themselves on the street, they walked side by side in silence. After five minutes, the street they were walking down suddenly came to an end, hitting the stone balustrade of the shoreline like a head colliding with a wall. Down below, the Seine glittered with specks of light.

P'an Tsiang-kuei and the professor stood there, not knowing what to do.

"Tell me," the professor finally said, wiping the misted lenses of his glasses with a handkerchief, "tell me, if you'd be so kind . . . I simply don't understand. Why is it exactly that you despise us so implacably when you owe us so much, when you are endlessly taking from us. I think about this constantly, and I can't find an answer. If I killed you, I'd never know. Please explain why, if it makes no difference to you . . ."

Under the arcades of the bridge with their feminine curves, black, sparkling water babbled with a million mouths in prayer.

Leaning on the stone balustrade, P'an Tsiang-kuei spoke in a measured and passionless voice:

"Asian-European antagonism, a subject on which your scholars have scribbled whole volumes, searching for its origins in the depths of racial and religious differences, plays itself out entirely on the surface of everyday economics and class struggle. Your science, of which you are so proud and which we travel here to study, is not a system of tools to help man conquer nature, but rather to help Europe conquer non-Europe, to exploit weaker continents. This is why we despise your Europe and why we come here to study you so fervently. Only by mastering the achievements of your science will we be able to shed the yoke of your oppression. Your bourgeois Europe, expatiating far and wide on your cultural self-sufficiency, is no more than a small parasite latched onto the western flank of Asia's gigantic body, sucking its juices dry. It is we, planting our rice and growing cotton and tea, who are — along with your own proletariat — the real, though indirect, creators of your culture. Its complex aroma, spreading the sweat of your workers and peasants all around the world, mingles with the smell of the Chinese coolie's sweat.

"But today the tides are turning. Your gluttonous Europe is croaking like a mare who has broken its leg before the final hurdle. It's croaking without having swallowed everything down, its gullet clogged from the greedy mouthfuls it's taken. It's no accident that it's being killed off by the plague, an old friend of ours in Asia. The stomach of European capitalism has found Asia indigestible.

"How sweet it is to watch the death of your enemy, sneaking up behind him, to see miniature reflections of your face in his terror-dilated pupils. I saw one of your plague victims. He was practically blue when the health service carried him out of his house. When they wanted to put him into a vehicle with other people, he burst out screaming: 'You're not putting me in there! Those people are infested!' They had to use force. He thrashed, kicked and bit, and when he was finally pushed inside and the doors were bolted behind him, he suddenly turned blue and stiff. His fear of death advanced death's slow progress.

"I looked into those eyes wide with lethal horror, and then I understood that precisely this fear was the engine and the mainspring of your whole vast culture. That dread, that drive to endure at any cost, against the logical inevitability of death, has pushed you to superhuman effort, to carve your faces into such summits as could not be wiped clean by the all-consuming river of time. I also thought that perhaps only with an injection of the serum of European culture could our Asia be torn from its thousand-year coma under the Bodhi Tree of Buddhism. Thus far Europe has only sent us her merchants and her missionaries. Christianity was once a venom Asia inoculated into Europe, a venom that destroyed the rich Roman culture and plunged Europe for many centuries into a barbarian darkness. But Europe proved capable of assimilating even this poison of powerlessness, kineticizing it, sucking out the venom and turning it into a tool of oppression. Today Europe is getting its belated revenge by exporting it back to Asia. Unable to colonize us outright, they want to turn us into a colony of the Vatican. Christ is a salesman, a paid stooge of the profiteers.

"Today, however, it can no longer do us any harm. Europe is dying in its last convulsive spasms. No *cordon sanitaire* will save it. The plague will surge unstoppably across the whole of the continent when it's done with Paris. To tell the truth, its meddling in our age-old conflict is entirely superfluous. The absurdity of this intervention would almost convince me of the existence of your god, whose tricks — if we are to believe the authors of the Holy Book — were never exactly distinguished by an excess of intelligence. The years were already numbered for your imperialist Europe one way or another, and there was no need to hurry the conclusion with such extravagance.

"Two years from now, on the nameless, abandoned tomb of your rapacious Europe of exploiters, a new Europe would have arisen, a Europe of workers, who would have easily communicated with Asia through the international language of labor.

"The unwelcome intervention of this pointless natural disaster might bring about the death of both Europes in one go: the one that was dying and the one that was yet to be born.

"The old usurer hasn't even had time to put her last will in order. But the will — though unwritten — still exists. We are its inheritors, along with your own proletariat. Fate has cast us here, to the metropolises of Europe, to tear the keys from its ossifying hands."

P'an Tsiang-kuei fell silent. For a moment the only thing audible was the splash of water breaking against the base of the pillars supporting the bridge.

"You are mistaken," said the professor at last. "Your people are too weak to carry the weight of the inheritance upon your shoulders. If Europe dies, if her intelligentsia dies out, the fruits of her culture and technology will die with her. Then as soon as the one incentive to awake is gone you shall fall back into your age-old coma. Do you seriously believe our common rabble could really fill that role, that you'll manage to take over the treasuries of our culture with them as allies? What are those instinct-driven, unenlightened plebs good for, apart from mindless destruction? Without their master employers the 'working masses' will find themselves a flock without its shepherd. Pitiably helpless, they'll fall back into the gloom of barbarity. Incapable of any creative exertion, they won't be up to the inheritance of even one Paris, and will not be able to protect it from falling into ruin."

"And yet that's how things will be, I assure you, and very soon. You'll have the chance to see for yourself."

"Nonsense. I'd bet that I won't."

"You're on."

"The wager is too abstract for either one of us to stand much chance of winning."

"We can easily make it more concrete. If, with the current progress of the epidemic, we have not taken Paris within a month, I will consider myself beaten."

"I accept. One condition: the moment you lose, you will fire a bullet into your head without my assistance."

"Done."

"It may occur that I die before our bet concludes. This in no way alters things. The bet carries on just as before."

"Just as before."

"And if you win, well, then I promise to put a bullet in my head."

"Entirely unnecessary," P'an Tsiang-kuei responded with a smile. "If I win, you are obliged to return to your scientific work and become a loyal director of the laboratory to fight the plague in our proletarian Paris."

"Done. Deadline — one month. Just in case, in order to obviate any difficulties that might arise in keeping to the conditions of our bet, allow me to offer you my revolver straightaway. It might serve you as a fetish."

P'an Tsiang-kuei smiled as he tucked the revolver into his pocket.

"From this moment on, you should take scrupulous care of yourself and take every precaution not to fall ill or die. As an honest gambler, you don't want to prove insolvent. I will ask you for a calling card with your address, so I know whom to remind to pay his debt when the moment arrives."

The professor wrote his address in pencil on a piece of paper and tore it from his notebook.

Under the arcades of the bridge with their feminine curves, black, sparkling water babbled with a million mouths in prayer.

Bells rang from Sacré-Coeur, relentless, tearful, helpless.

In the face of the leveling strickle of death, the people dissolving in the giant vat of the city clung spasmodically, in a blind centrifugal urge, to every shred of their individuality, crowding together around the temples of their own rites, like iron filings around the poles of a magnet. Like so many lightning rods, the spires of the cathedrals, Orthodox churches, and minarets sent heavenward a magnetic current of separatism that grew with each passing moment, amassing the scattered human herd into self-contained racial and religious complexes.

The first eruption took place in the milieu that was the most distinct — due to the very pigment of its skin — and had no lightning-rod temple of its own.

On July 30 a radio station broadcast some incredible news. During the previous night the yellow-skinned inhabitants of the Latin Quarter had staged a coup. All the white inhabitants had been pushed to the right bank of the Seine, and the Latin Quarter had been declared an autonomous Chinese republic.

That evening, on the walls of the abandoned Latin Quarter, the first long strips of hieroglyphs appeared: proclamations in Chinese.

The provisional government informed the yellow-skinned residents of Paris that an independent Chinese republic had been established in the area of the former Latin Quarter to act in self-defense against the European plague. The provisional government declared that every white person caught in the territory of the republic would be expelled as a plague-sower. The government further forbade, under penalty of death, any yellow-skinned inhabitants from crossing the borders of their republic. With the aim of tightly fencing it off from the infected city, the republic was surrounded by a new Great Wall of China, this one built of barricades.

In a brief appeal to the people, the provisional government recommended that its citizens safeguard the valuable libraries located on the territory of the republic, which, as inviolable treasuries, were to safeguard the fruits of European culture for future generations.

The proclamation was made in the name of the provisional government and signed by P'an Tsiang-kuei.

III

IN THE SHADOWY DEPTHS OF THE OCEAN, beyond the reach of the currents, whirlpools, and the splash of waves, in the motionless greenish water, still as the water of an aquarium, amid the forests of gigantic algae, antediluvian sigillaria and liana, lives the flounder fish.

Somewhere, hundreds of feet high above, white-maned waves rush in an eternal, tireless chase, the hulls of massive steamships plow yards of black furrows into the aching surface of the sea, gelatinous medusas flutter in the murky jelly of the water, and the long, sleek bodies of fish slice through the depths with their scaly daggers like the cool shine of headlights in constant, relentless pursuit.

Down below is silence, cool, hard sand, and orchards of infertile trees, whitish like clouds seen from an airplane. The bottom is like the sky, like a reflection of the sky in a convex, measureless drop of ocean, with a cosmos of its own shifting starfish, of spine-tailed comets — a chilly postmortem refuge for exhausted wayward travelers.

On the bottom lives the flounder fish. Someone took a fish, sliced it in half along the spine, and placed one half on the sand. The flounder has only one side — the right side. Its left side is the earth, the bottom.

When an organ is unused, the organ disappears. All the flounder's organs have migrated from the left, non-existent side to the right. And on the right side, a pair of tiny, passionless eyes sit one beside the other, staring always upward.

The eyes always stare upward, both on the same side, monstrous, incredible, bizarre; and the left side — does not exist at all.

In the enormous city of Paris, in a red, speckled house on Rue Pavée, lives Rabbi Eliezar ben Zvi.

Rue Pavée lies in the heart of the Hôtel de Ville district, of little

Jewish Paris. It was brought to the center of this international city, to the middle of France, from someplace East, from the arable fields of the Ukraine, from the puddle-filled towns of Galicia, and ran aground here, silting up for a few decades to form a modern ghetto devoid of traditions, durable, insoluble, isolated.

In the great multilingual city, hundreds of languages and dozens of nations and races grind each other to dust, fertilizing the frozen French soil with a new, fecund manure. Poured into the solution of the city, the Polish and Russian Jews, with their particular talent for non-assimilation, always float to the surface, like a uniform oil slick.

In Paris, the masses seethe, governments rise and fall, events collide and vault over one another at a breakneck pace. Here we find silence, shiny black asphalt, shimmering like Berdychev mud, a yeshiva and a shul, a Friday-to-Friday week, and on every Friday dwarf trees are set on tables by the windows, blossoming with the orange flames of candles.

Here they have their own events. Hershel the baker is to welcome his son from America in a red auto, but it can't wriggle through the tight crack of Rue Prévost. A new party of Jews turns up from Iaşi, fleeing a pogrom. The daughter of Mendel the junk dealer runs off to the city with a black jazz musician from the Rivoli Street Café and returns to her father a month later, giving birth to a child, a little black boy. Utterly humiliated before the neighbors, old Mendel hangs himself in his entrance hall. In the narrow, husked alleyways a thick and gelatinous air descends, becomes motionless and transparent, and in the evening the shadows of lanterns swing somnolently like gigantic algae.

Rabbi Eliezer ben Zvi has two eyes set close together, and these eyes are always trained upward. Passionless, tiny, identical, they are turned toward the heavens, in which they seem to see things only they can perceive. When an organ is unused, the organ disappears. Rabbi Eliezer ben Zvi sees many things invisible to human eyes, but he does not see the simple things; he has only one side — the one turned toward heaven. And the one turned toward Earth is not there at all.

For many years, for as long as the residents of Hôtel de Ville can recall, Rabbi Eliezer ben Zvi has been a permanent resident of the house by the synagogue, never leaving it. There is a direct passage from his home to the shul, and Rabbi Eliezer ben Zvi doesn't need to go out into the street to recite *maariv*, the evening prayers. The street does not know Rabbi Eliezer. The only ones who see him are those who come to him for advice, which means all of Hôtel de Ville know him, because who wouldn't go to Rabbi Eliezer ben Zvi, to a man wiser than all the wonder rabbis, to whom even merchants from the distant shores of Paris drive to settle disputes.

Rabbi Eliezer ben Zvi has never seen Paris. He came here fifty years ago from his small town and at once took up residence in the house by the synagogue. And his wisdom in solving complicated quarrels could not be praised enough by the Parisian merchants.

Rabbi Eliezer ben Zvi has his own old shammes, the only one who could speak of the holy life of the rabbi. But the shammes is reluctant to speak, and spends days and nights on end at the rabbi's side. The shammes says the rabbi is very ill, and he won't let anyone in unless he is first convinced the matter is important and requires private consultation. One thing is for certain: those to whom Rabbi Eliezer gives his kerchief-wrapped *ksyba*, a handwritten benediction, though they may be afflicted with the deepest sorrows, return home carefree and happy as a lark. Thus the rabbi's door seldom stops swinging, and the old shammes's tattered velvet wallet is never short of money when he goes out shopping on Fridays.

Rabbi Eliezer ben Zvi has two tiny eyes planted close together, both on the side that looks toward heaven. Once in private, the shammes told old Hershel that the rabbi often speaks with God. God and the rabbi tell each other tales for hours at a time. And the Jews know: the rabbi can speak with the Lord whenever he pleases. It's as though he has a hotline. Ordinary Jews might try calling God their whole lives and never get through, so many want to talk to Him at the same time.

Sometimes a Jew manages to contact Him once in his life, for just a brief moment, and then he has to make his request very quickly before someone else cuts in.

You might say that Rabbi Eliezer has a private line at his disposal, and he could speak with God at any time of day, without being worried someone will interrupt him. Rabbi Eliezer knows the Lord doesn't like to be bothered when He's busy, just like any Jew, and he knows by now at what times of day he can speak with Him most freely. For this reason the Lord has a soft spot for Rebbe Eliezer, and He hasn't yet had cause to refuse him anything.

And so passed many, many years. How many? Even the old shammes had lost count.

By that year Rabbi Eliezer ben Zvi was already feeling quite weak. He often spoke of death with the shammes and received people only in very exceptional cases.

One evening the shammes returned from the city later than usual, almost delaying the rabbi's dinner. The shammes was quite terrified. There was word in the city of a terrible disease haunting Paris. The children of Levi the tailor had gone to a dance on the French holiday — as the young will do — and had died in horrible agonies a few hours after their return. That same night the wife of Symche the shoemaker also died in fits, as did three other Jewish women. Twelve Jews dead since morning. A great lament filled the town. The shammes, who recalled the cholera epidemic in Zhmerynka, recognized all the symptoms, though the papers were calling the new plague something different. The Jews were extremely alarmed and gathered to seek the rabbi's counsel.

Rabbi Eliezer ben Zvi listened to the shammes's report in silence, clearly disquieted by what he heard, judging by the fact that he did not even finish his dinner. Scrubbing his hands, he asked for his tallith and went down to the synagogue.

The synagogue was already filled with sobs and laments. Another thirty Jews had died over the course of the evening. Names were passed from lips to lips.

Rabbi Eliezer, bent over his pulpit, prayed long and hard. When he closed the *sefer* and turned toward the faithful, his face was mild and luminous. He ordered a wedding to be held at the cemetery the following day, as was the custom in times of plague. A young bride and groom were sought on the spot. Shiya the mercer and Sender the hatter agreed to provide the young couple.

The wedding took place the following day at Bagneux Cemetery in the presence of Jews from all over Hôtel de Ville. After the wedding, the young couple were taken home.

The young woman died with plague symptoms that very night. The shammes, to whom the terrified Jews came running with the news, was too frightened to tell the rabbi for a long time. Finally, fearing the rabbi would find out in shul, he confided what had happened with the greatest trepidation. Rabbi Eliezer said nothing, but his face, which was the color of his milk-white beard, grew even paler, and the shammes perceived that this bad omen had made a deep impression upon him.

The lament in the synagogue rang even louder than the day before. Another sixty Jews had died during the day, including all those who had washed the previous day's corpses. Moreover, twelve Jews had died from performing the burial rituals, going to visit the families sitting in mourning. Word had it that Parisians were falling in the street by the thousands.

Prayer services in the synagogue lasted all night, only interrupted by reports on the spread of the pestilence. Every other moment someone in prayer would hear of the plague in their own home and run out of the synagogue wailing.

Rabbi Eliezer prayed fervently till morning, hunched over his prayer book. By morning he was struggling to keep on his feet, and the gabbai and the shammes had to carry him upstairs by the arms.

All the next day Rabbi Eliezer ben Zvi shut himself up in his room and forbade the shammes from letting anyone in. A sobbing crowd squeezed into the stairwell. The pale shammes, his finger to his lips, stood on guard before the door. He knew all too well that the rabbi was speaking with the Lord and was not to be disturbed.

Late in the evening the rabbi called in the shammes and requested that he report the news. The news was terrible. One hundred and thirty more Jews had died over the course of the day. Corpses lay unwashed in apartments, because all the corpse washers had caught the plague and died. The families of the deceased were sitting shiva on an empty stomach, because all the members of the burial society had died. The families sitting in mourning were dying themselves. Of the ten people in the family of Symche the shoemaker, whose wife had died on the very first night, nine were now dead, and only the father was now sitting shiva.

The rabbi nodded his head in silence, listening to the shammes's horrible reports. Then he asked for his tallith and went down to the synagogue. The shammes ran after him out of obligation and curiosity.

When Rabbi Eliezer appeared in the synagogue, a great hush ensued. Everyone knew the rabbi had been speaking with God the whole day and that he had come to say something of import. All eyes were on him.

Standing on the steps of the altar, Rabbi Eliezer ben Zvi turned his face to those gathered and started to speak in the solemn voice of a legislator:

"God has opened my eyes, and in the book of His wrath He has allowed me to invoke the *pekuach nefesh*, the obligation to save human life. For as long as this plague continues, Jews shall be absolved from sitting shiva over their dead and from performing the rituals of burial. During this plague the bodies shall be stitched in canvas without prior ceremony and carted off to the cemetery. God is putting us to a grave test, and only through prayer shall He be appeased. The Angel of Death, *Malach HaMavet*, has entered Jewish homes, and our mezuzahs have not protected us. The houses he has touched shall be unclean for forty days and must be evacuated. Pray and beg for mercy."

Rabbi Eliezer, pale and swooning from weakness, descended the stairs and, supported by the shammes, left the synagogue, rumbling with a thousand feverish voices in his wake.

The events of the following days did not appear to show that God had been appeased. The *pekuach nefesh* somewhat reduced the number of corpses in the next few days, but the number never fell below a hundred daily. Plague-free apartments were swiftly becoming scarce. On the tenth day the housing crisis took on alarming proportions.

Rabbi Eliezer ben Zvi had shut himself up in his apartment all this time, neither showing his face in the shul nor receiving anyone, entrusting all his affairs to the shammes. The besieged shammes could only tell folks that the rabbi seldom spoke to him, choosing to spend hours at a time conversing with God in his room.

On the tenth day, when there was no longer a single apartment in Hôtel de Ville that had not been infested by plague, the ten most elderly Jews came to the rabbi as a delegation. The shammes was bought off, and he tiptoed in to inform the rabbi of the men's arrival.

After a long moment, the rabbi himself came out to see them. His face was more glassy than usual; it was terrible to think that his life was hanging by a thread.

When the shammes had brought chairs, it was old Mekhel, the biggest wholesaler in all of Hôtel de Ville, who spoke up.

"Rabbi," he said in a defeated voice, "Rabbi, we have done everything as you said. You read out the *pekuach nefesh* from the book of divine wrath, and since then we have not sat shiva over our dead, and the bodies have been stitched up in canvas and sent to the cemetery without ritual burials. You said that the homes visited by the plague were to be considered unclean for forty days and evacuated, and we have followed your words. Yet the plague continues, and not a day passes when several dozen Jewish families do not fall victim to it. Our apartments are spilling over. Soon every single home will have been afflicted by this pestilence. There are no more apartments in all of Hôtel de Ville. Families of the infected are sleeping on the streets. What can we do, Rabbi?"

Rabbi Eliezer ben Zvi smiled kindly, and his two eyes, trained somewhere beyond Mekhel, not seeing him, as though he were transparent, shone with the same smile as he replied in a faraway voice:

"There are still a great many apartments in the Jewish quarter, they are there for the taking."

The elderly Jews exchanged glances. When the rabbi spoke of the important things his eyes saw, it was impossible to perceive them with an ordinary mind all at once. A momentary silence fell. Finally old Mekhel gathered some courage and said:

"Rabbi, our minds are no match for yours. Your words are unclear to us. Which apartments do you have in mind that are there for the taking?"

Rabbi Eliezer was silent a moment and then responded as if to himself, in deep rumination:

"There are many apartments in the Jewish quarter whose doors are not protected by mezuzahs. It is through these doors that the Angel of Death has come to us."

A long silence fell. Then the rabbi spoke further, as if thinking more out loud:

"Rabbi Hillel, wisest of the wise men, once said: During the times of Rabbi Ezra, when the Jewish nation was split asunder, and the plague of Christianity raged all around, the Jews surrounded their communities with high walls to protect themselves and preserve their order. Our contemporaries have given such Jewish towns a name: 'ghetto.' But the time came when the Jews grew weary of their fathers' warnings and longed to spread their order amidst the foreigners, much to their own disgrace. Then they destroyed the walls surrounding their homes, and from then on the calamities of the Gentiles became their calamities as well, and God's wrath has turned upon them. Until the Jews surround themselves once more with a wall impenetrable to all who are not their own, then the pestilence shall devour them, and *Malach HaMavet*, the Angel of Death, shall linger at their threshold."

Whereupon Rabbi Eliezer ben Zvi made a sign with his hand to indicate that the audience was concluded, requesting the shammes to show his visitors to the door.

•

On July 30, at five in the afternoon, special editions of the newspaper appeared on the boulevards, announcing a new separatist movement. The Jewish population of the Hôtel de Ville district had seized the town hall and expelled all Gentiles from the whole of the area. The apathetic Christians generally offered no resistance. The only decisive opposition to the Jews came from the Saint-Paul neighborhood, inhabited by the poverty-stricken Polish population. Fired by their innate anti-Semitism, the Poles put up an armed defense. This led to some bloody skirmishes, with losses on both sides, until the Jews' superior numbers brought them victory.

The supplements made mention of a proclamation plastered on the walls of Hôtel de Ville, addressed to the Jews of Paris. It apparently announced the constitution of an independent Jewish territorial community to be walled off from the rest of the city, to hold back the Aryan plague. It called upon all the Jews of Paris to move to this territory, expressing the conviction that the plague had descended on Aryan Europe for their centuries of oppressing the Jewish nation and would now spare the Jews if they maintained the strictest isolation.

This news caused quite a stir in the city. In the evening, long lines of cars laden with suitcases were seen driving from the western and northern parts of the city toward Hôtel de Ville. Nobody tried to bar their way.

At the entrance to the Hôtel de Ville district, a people's militia, a Hashomer, frantically fortified the barricades in the event they should have to be defended.

Yet no attack was being planned.

·

In the ruddy, speckled house on Rue Pavée, the old, hunchbacked shammes walked up softly to the door, on tiptoe, and put his ear to it.

Rabbi Eliezer ben Zvi hadn't left his room for three days and hadn't been taking any food. He had only been praying and speaking to God. The shammes heard his monotonous, wavering voice. Rabbi Eliezer sat over his open, grease-splattered book, and his arched, transparent body swayed like sugarcane blown by the breath of God. For the first time, doubt entered Eliezer ben Zvi's mind.

And how could he not doubt? He had taken the whole burden upon his shoulders, and it exceeded a single man's strength. He had invoked the *pekuach nefesh* from the book of divine wrath, and since then the Jews had not sat shiva over their dead, and Jewish corpses had been going to death's womb without ritual being observed. All for nothing.

Black, grotesque letters shuffled before Rabbi Eliezer's searching gaze, like travelers waving handkerchiefs from the window of a leaving train.

"But the Lord will make a distinction between the livestock of Israel and the livestock of the Egyptians, so that nothing shall die of all that belongs to the Israelites . . ."

Rabbi Eliezer ben Zvi swayed lower, pendulating over the book. He had proceeded as the Lord had commanded, he had isolated the flocks of Israel with an impenetrable wall, and here the plague was spreading among them just as before, and there was no cure for it.

The black letters, like drops of a martyr's blood, trickled onto the book from the grimacing mouth of Rabbi Eliezer:

"Throughout all the land of Egypt the hail struck down all that were in the open, both man and beast; the hail also struck down all the grasses of the field and shattered all the trees of the field. Only in the land of Goshen, where the Israelites were, was there no hail."

Rabbi Eliezer doubted. He had taken the whole terrible responsibility

135

upon his shoulders. He had surrounded the Jewish town with a wall, depriving it of even its own cemetery, and the Jewish corpses had begun to rot in their chambers.

Rabbi Eliezer had revealed a *pekuach nefesh* unknown in the history of Jewry: as corpses could not be buried in the earth, they were to be consigned to the flames.

And the plague remained within the walls of the Jewish town.

Yet the Lord said:

"They shall take some of the blood and put it on the two doorposts and the lintel of the houses in which they are to eat the lamb.

"And the blood on the houses where you dwell shall be a sign for you: when I see the blood I will pass over you, so that no plague will destroy you when I strike the land of Egypt."

Rabbi Eliezer ben Zvi had doubts for the first time in his life. He bent under their weight like a branch that holds a bird. His parchment lips mumbled:

"Lord, why have you burdened me thus? I am old, and frail is my back."

The old, grease-stained book, like a sieve filled with valuable liquid, fell upon the parched sand of Rabbi Eliezer's soul in a rain of black letters:

"And the Lord continued, 'I have surely seen the plight of My people in Egypt and have heeded their outcry because of their taskmasters; yes, I am mindful of their sufferings. I have come down to deliver them from the Egyptians and to bring them out of that land to a good and spacious land, a land flowing with milk and honey . . . Come, therefore, I will send you to Pharaoh, and you shall free My people, the Israelites, from Egypt.'

"But Moses said to God, 'Who am I that I should go to Pharaoh and free the Israelites from Egypt?'

"But Moses said to the Lord, 'Please, O Lord, I have never been a man of words, either in times past or now that You have spoken to

Your servant; I am slow of speech and slow of tongue.' And the Lord said to him, 'Who gives man speech? . . . Now go, and I will be with you as you speak and will instruct you what to say.' But he said, 'Please, O Lord, make someone else Your agent.' The Lord became angry with Moses . . .

"This Moses and Aaron did; as the Lord commanded them, so they did. Moses was eighty years old and Aaron eighty-three, when they made their demands to Pharaoh."

Rabbi Eliezer ben Zvi made no protest. He knew God's verdicts were inscrutable. He at whom God points the finger seeks to avoid his fate in vain. No, Rabbi Eliezer would not whinge, like Moses: "Please, O Lord, make someone else Your agent." He was too used to being heard. He closed the book with a sure hand. He rose. He straightened his back. He called the shammes.

The frightened shammes understood: something important, something imperative had occurred. The rabbi's narrow, waxen face blossomed from the coils of his gray beard, like the white plumes of sacrificial smoke. His eyes shone with an inner glow. They stared without seeing.

Rabbi Eliezer ordered that the elders be sent for.

Down the narrow, darkening streets, where the shadows of streetlamps swayed in prayer like enormous algae, ran the old shammes in his flowing robes. He climbed winding stairs and passed his whispered bulletin through a door, opened just a crack: a message from Rabbi Eliezer.

•

"Hello! Grand Hotel? Please put me through to Mr. David Lingslay. Hello! Hello-o-o! Is that Mr. David Lingslay? This is the presiding secretary of the Council of Commissioners of the Anglo-American Territory. The presidium kindly requests your attendance at a closed council session at eleven a.m. That's right, in one hour. Can we count on you? . . ."

David Lingslay rolled over. The light slicing through the gap between the curtains hit him square in the eyes, making him squint, and he was forced to roll back over. He would have slept so sweetly had it not been for that diabolical telephone. In an hour he had to be at American Express. Time to think about getting up.

David Lingslay stretched out once more in his comfortable, king-sized bed. He suddenly jerked up and sat on the edge. Tossing off the blanket, he scrupulously fingered his stomach through his silk pajamas, and then, raising his arms one at a time — his armpit glands. After a thorough examination he stretched out again.

He rose every day with an instinctive terror of the moment his healthy muscular body would feel the animal fear of being woken with a gnawing pain in the pit of his stomach. By day, David Lingslay tried his best not to consider the sorry fact that an elementary calculation set his odds of survival at ninety-nine to one. He safeguarded that wretched formulation of hope, that one percent chance of salvation, somewhere deep inside him, like a nestling coddled in his bosom.

Each morning, however, when his sleepy body still hovered in that irreal void, in the sudden transition from sleep to waking, before the slackened gears of his will could mesh their teeth once more — the fear pressed in his throat like a coiled spring, and he could only punch it back into its cell, where it would lie in wait until morning.

In those brief moments, David Lingslay would remember that in the nightstand — only an arm's reach away — lay a small steel object anxiously awaiting that one particular morning. Curled up and invisible, it waited, counting the inaudible pulse of the cracked pocket watch lying on the tabletop, which somewhere, deep inside, in the trembling finger that marked the minutes, concealed the fatal hour, known to itself alone. It had counted out precisely such-and-such a number of revolutions and performed them daily, cloaking its headlong rush with a feigned indifference.

At such moments David Lingslay felt such a burning hatred toward the whole world of objects that only his inborn self-control and even temper kept the morning cleaning maid from coming in to find a demolished suite.

The lofty, cool panels of mirrors, taking every gesture he tossed at them like a slap, with servile humility, all the wardrobes and desks, indifferent and pulverizing in their irrefutable mathematical certainty that they would remain unchanged, that they would reflect other gestures, faces, and grimaces upon the polished surfaces of their wooden skins when no trace remained of David Lingslay — with their calm, arrogant superiority they might just have driven him insane. He had an overpowering urge to stomp on them, smash them to pieces, discredit their unshakable superiority, feast his eyes on their powerless shards.

At such moments David Lingslay just pressed harder on his soapy razor, under whose kiss his face emerged like Aphrodite from the sea foam, with the dazzling nakedness of well-pampered skin.

He shoved the watch into his vest with a dull loathing, put the small steel trinket into his back pocket, and went out into the city. He tried to remain in his room as briefly as possible.

David Lingslay, king of an American metal trust, owner of fourteen major newspapers in New York, Boston, and Philadelphia, had stopped in Paris on his way to spend his summer in Biarritz, as was his custom. During the few days of his stay in Paris, the plague had struck.

All his efforts to leave the plague-infested city had amounted to nothing. He was not helped by the gravity of his surname, his impressive connections, or by writing checks for astronomical sums. Fear of the plague had leveled social stratification, shaken the indissoluble spiderweb of fail-safe acquaintances, and surrounded Paris with an airtight and impenetrable wall overnight.

After two weeks of fruitless attempts, David Lingslay was forced to give up.

Like all who play the stock market, David Lingslay was a fatalist, and having realized the futility of all his efforts, he stared himself in the face in his luxurious hotel room and sincerely confessed that he had lost. He had succeeded extraordinarily well thus far in life, in all things. Once in a while, upon ascending to a higher rung of the financial ladder and casting an eye downward, he would experience a slight vertigo to think that his number, too, might one day be up.

When he was fully convinced that this time there was no way out, David Lingslay put his last will in order — as befitted a gentleman — telegraphed it to New York, locked the files with his recent affairs in a desk drawer, and waited.

The plague was evidently playing hide-and-seek with him. On the third day, his personal secretary died in terrible agonies. David Lingslay awaited his turn. Days passed. A week later, the black ambulance collected the typist from the neighboring room. The adjacent suites were being emptied, one by one. By the end of the second week, Lingslay was the sole occupant of the entire second floor. With lightning speed, like a stone tossed down an elevator shaft, they all silently vanished: elevator boys, service staff, *maîtres d'hôtels*. New ones cropped up in their stead. If, after giving the porter an evening request, David Lingslay came across a different porter the following day, he asked no questions. He merely repeated his request and tried not to bother his head with trifles of this sort. He drank his hot morning coffee in small sips and went to visit his mistress.

For many years David Lingslay had kept a Parisian lover, to whom he gave not only a collection of dazzling jewelry, but also a small palace on Champs-Élysées that was not entirely wanting in taste.

David Lingslay visited his lover twice a year, though he never once stayed with her, preferring to live as a bachelor in the Grand Hotel. His business compelled him to behave this way, and of course, as a gentleman and a husband, he was not keen to advertise his liaison.

On each of his sojourns in Paris, he had so much business to attend to that when he came to sit in his train compartment, taking from his attendant the customary packet of new novels his lover had sent to the station, he barely registered that during the whole of his stay he had spent less than six hours with her, and solemnly vowed to make it up to himself next time, in six months.

Having sent his last will to New York, David Lingslay realized for the first time the meaning of the shopworn expression "vacation," and he regretted it would pass so quickly. Come what may, he resolved for the first time in his life to devote it entirely to love. This was a part of life he had never had sufficient time for, a part he had had to squeeze in between telephone calls, always in haste, and always at the wrong time.

Years before, on the ritual honeymoon night, when he thought that just this once he would devote at least the twelve hours his wife legally deserved, he received an offer for an extremely profitable and complicated transaction at the very last minute, one he'd been pursuing for ages, and for the whole of his honeymoon night he fulfilled his conjugal obligations like a model gentlemen and responded absentmindedly to the peevish questions of his young spouse while he plowed gigantic abacuses of figures through his head, formulating the answer he would have to give by telephone bright and early the next morning (pray he didn't oversleep!). And so, whenever David Lingslay struggled to recall his honeymoon night as other people do, the film of his memory revealed only those long rows of figures — the rest had vanished like the background of an overexposed photograph.

For the first time in his life, perhaps only a week before his death, David Lingslay was able to give himself wholeheartedly to love, and every day was a true honeymoon.

Though he kept a lover in Paris for snobbish reasons — like his two Rolls-Royces, like his reserved cabin on the *Majestic*, to have a companion for the theater and then dinner at Ciro's, to draw jealous stares from other men with her uncommon beauty, or so he took it from others on good faith, not ever having had the occasion himself to realize it — this lover turned out to be a marvelous creature indeed, a sensitive and ravishing instrument that played inexhaustible scales of delight.

David Lingslay now spent entire days, evenings, and nights with her, discovering within himself — at forty years of age — an extremely affectionate *amour*. Like a sybarite yearning to whet his passion for tomorrow's meal by refraining from today's, David Lingslay did not move in with her. He kept his suite at the Grand Hotel so as to return from a few short hours' separation with his appetite stoked, in love for the first time — and madly so.

Love is a question of free time. Who would suppose that the bloated frames of the paunchy businessmen walking among us — those paradoxical slaves, their legs strapped by an invisible chain to the hands of their own pocket watches — in fact enclose the shells of fiery lovers.

Yet even on this occasion David Lingslay was not destined to fully fling open the storehouse of his pent-up eroticism. This time he was interrupted by a sudden seismic trembling, which was soon to send cracks through the psychological crust of plague-infested Paris.

On the day of July 30, almost simultaneously, two districts — the Latin Quarter and the Hôtel de Ville — split off from the uniform body of Paris in armed coups, in a spontaneous show of self-defense against the Aryan plague, creating two independent city-states on the old map of Paris: one Chinese, the other Jewish. The ethnic relocations were followed by social ones.

On the day of August 4, the workers' populations of the Belleville and Ménilmontant districts, invigorated by a sudden and irrepressible urge to seize some meager control of the lives they were watching trickle through their fingers, declared their territories an autonomous Soviet Republic. The army defected to the insurrectionists' side.

On the same evening, as a sign of protest, the royal Camelots, backed by the Catholic inhabitants of the Saint-Germain district, took control of the Left Bank of the Seine, from Place des Invalides to Champ de Mars, and thus proclaimed the restoration of the monarchy.

Taken off guard by the rapid series of events and sensing their properties at risk, the Anglo-American population of the central districts felt it prudent to take a firm stand against them and implement security measures. An unprecedented meeting of gentlemen was called in the Opera House to discuss the events of September 8. It was unanimously decided that, in self-defense against the Bolshevik districts of Paris, the districts inhabited by the English-speaking populations would be declared an autonomous Anglo-American Territory while the plague ran its course. An armed youth militia was to erect barricades around the new territory and defend it in the event of an invasion from one of the renegade districts.

The issue of the native French population inhabiting the newly declared territory was a source of lively discussion. A segment of the gentlemen firmly insisted on the displacement of non-English-speaking factions. The majority of votes, however, were received by the levelheaded proposition of Ramsey Marlington, who put forward the motion of using the French residents of the territory — after their wholesale disarmament — for service duties, recruiting indispensable hotel and private servants from their ranks. The only ones exempt from these duties, according to Mr. Marlington's scheme, were to be the shopkeepers and bistro owners, as their establishments served the public, as well as those Frenchmen whose yearly salaries exceeded one hundred thousand francs.

Ramsey Marlington's recommendation was implemented. The French populations of the central districts, long accustomed to living off tips from the British and American tourists, offered no resistance to Marlington's scheme and reconciled themselves to their new roles quite amicably, thus sparing the new territory's government any unforeseen complications.

This first gathering established a Council of Commissioners for the territory's board of directors, comprising twelve outstanding financiers: six Englishmen and six Americans. The American Express Company building was temporarily put at the disposal of the provisional government.

David Lingslay was among the six American potentates selected in the voting for the Council of Commissioners. The weight of his name and his social standing forbade him from declining this honor, though state and administrative matters clearly clashed with the overall canvas of his activities and affairs, and thus he resolved to devote as little time and attention to them as possible.

On the day in question, having returned to his hotel at five o'clock in the morning, filled with the most melodious strains of a passionate storm, whose lightning plowed him with deep and insatiable urges to sample life's delicacies, and prematurely awoken by the alarm of civic duty, David Lingslay felt the full burden of his social role more than ever before, and in a particularly sour mood he slowly went about dressing himself in his tailored suit.

He was just finishing shaving in front of the mirror when a knock announced the entrance of a slim, ever-beaming bellboy, the onetime head secretary of a great insurance concern, which had lost its raison d'être in the new order. He reported that two men wished to see David Lingslay about an important matter.

On any other day Lingslay would have suspected some tedious business and would no doubt have declared himself unavailable. Today, however, he decided to drain the cup of civic responsibility to the dregs, and with a resigned gesture he requested they be shown into the salon.

After spending a long minute knotting his tie, David Lingslay appeared in the doorway to the salon. Rising from their armchairs to meet him were Rabbi Eliezer ben Zvi and an older, corpulent gentleman in American eyeglasses.

BELLS RANG FROM SACRÉ-COEUR.

From Saint-Pierre, from Sainte-Clotilde, from Saint-Louis, from the small, scattered churches of the Saint-Germain district, Catholic Paris replied with a rueful clanging of bells.

The dull, weepy bells fought it out over the city with their fists of lead in their hollow bronze chests, and the church interiors responded with the din of hands convulsively wringing and a bitter, pious murmur. The adoration of the Sacrament continued without surcease, administered by waxen priests swaying from exhaustion.

In the Orthodox church of the Passy district, the metropolitan in gilded robes read from the Gospels in a rich, sonorous voice, and all the bells rang as if Easter Sunday.

Paris again burst open along the wide seam of the Seine, where it had once been hastily stitched with the white threads of bridges.

On either side of the Passy Bridge, flags fluttered from a lamppost: the tricolor flag of the Russian Empire and the flag of the Bourbons, white with gold lilies — the provisional border between two monarchies.

Four boys with rifles slung over their shoulders — two on each side of the river — marched to the middle of the empty bridge and back again, their strides resonant and measured. On the caps of the boys in long green shirts glistened tsarist eagles pulled out of mothballs and rubbed in chalk. They stared down on the meager, blackened lilies of the juvenile Royal Camelots.

Vasya Krestovnikov impatiently propped his rifle on his shoulder. The gun was heavy, it hurt his arm. Maybe let it drop? No, that won't do. Vasya paced the bridge, a spring in his step, a serious expression fixed to his chubby red face.

Nonetheless, he decided to let it drop. He only needed to make it to the middle span, and there he could set his rifle on the ground and rest on the barrel without losing any respect. It made him look serious, even striking. He'd seen pictures of soldiers on sentry duty in that very pose.

So Vasya, unflappable and indifferent, leaned picturesquely on the barrel of his rifle, casually sticking his right foot forward, its leather boot glistening like a samovar.

But whenever his eyes met those of the navy-blue sentinel across the way, Vasya was unable to resist, and an impish smile cracked through his mask of solemnity. How comical: just yesterday they were pals, playing blackjack under their desks and tennis after school, and today they were guards for two separate states on either side of the bridge — not hostile, even allied to some extent, but still separate.

Following Vasya's example, the trim navy-blue Camelot dropped his rifle, too, and leaned nonchalantly on the barrel. He'd have liked to smoke a cigarette, but duty first!

The two sixteen-year-old boys, leaning on their guns, their backs to the balustrades, let their eyes wander out into space: two tin soldiers on a cardboard bridge with a marvelous paper backdrop, so much like the Paris of adults.

"What was that racket and shooting I heard over there yesterday?" the navy-blue Camelot asked, trying to enjoy a little soldier talk.

"Ah, nothing, no big deal," Vasya replied in French, his tone emphasizing that it was hardly worth mentioning. "Just creaming a couple of Jews. They gobble our bread and spread the plague while they're at it."

Vasya checked around to see if anyone was looking, then dug his hand in his pocket and pulled out a huge, gold cigarette case. Who could resist a bit of bragging to a friend?

"See what I swiped off one of them? I bet he nabbed it in Russia, state security guy, a Chekist. Holds twenty cigarettes."

And noting a contemptuous sneer on the corner of his friend's lips, he hastily added:

"You have no idea what crooks they are. Yesterday my mom spotted her own necklace on a Jewess. They stole it from a safe in Moscow. Or they prefer to use the word 'confiscated.' They 'confiscated' all my mom's jewelry that way. All she's got left is her wedding ring."

The Camelot stared with mild contempt. He knew you weren't allowed to take valuables, not even from Jews — that was theft. He knew something else, too: these Russians were savages. And Camelot d'Escarville's lips twisted into a malicious, disdainful grin.

At that moment, a group of soldiers appeared at the foot of the bridge on the French side, escorting a man dressed in gray. Camelot d'Escarville slung his rifle over his shoulder and slowly walked toward them, with even steps. Vasya looked on with interest. D'Escarville and the group of Camelots approached the middle span.

Vasya could now clearly make out a thin young man in an ash-colored jacket and a conspicuously Semitic nose. Camelot d'Escarville explained: "He fled from your territory during the night and made it to our side. A patrol caught him in town and we're turning him over."

Vasya's eyes practically bulged with delight: A Jew! Escaped by ducking the guards!

"Hand him over, I'll take him to the captain."

The Camelots saluted and headed off. Vasya left his post to his fellow soldier. The fugitive was his.

The tall, thin Jew, maybe a year older than Vasya, said nothing. He just hunched down a bit and tucked his head under his arm like a frightened bird. His nervous gaze chased after Vasya like a dachshund.

Vasya took the rifle off his shoulder and released the catch:

"March! Don't try to escape, unless you want a bullet in your skull!"

The Jew didn't try to escape. He walked forward obediently. He only buried his head down deeper, and his two long arms dangled helplessly by his sides like clipped wings.

Meanwhile, Vasya dreamt: he himself, in person, would bring the prisoner to Captain Solomin. The captain would take one look, crack his riding whip on the tops of his boots and say: Go-o-o-od. Vasya puffed out his chest with pride and satisfaction. He would've walked through fire for Captain Solomin. All the young people idolized him. A brave officer. Fought the Bolsheviks back in Wrangel's army. Those who knew him say he was brave as the devil. And what a shot! He could kill a swallow in midair. Vasya saw it yesterday with his own two eyes. He was sitting on a table on the veranda of a café on Rue de la Pompe and he gave the Jews five hundred paces to get away, and then he popped them off like ducks with his seven-shooter. He didn't miss once! Good times were in store! Now to the right, just around the corner.

Vasya saw them from afar. Solomin was sitting in the company of four other officers on the veranda of the bistro across from headquarters. They'd been drinking since the previous night.

Vasya crossed the square with a bounce in his step and came to a halt in front of the veranda.

"*Vashe Blagorodye*, I'm here to report that I've brought a fugitive. Last night he ducked the guards and snuck off to the other side of the Seine. He was caught in town and handed over to our border post."

"Go-o-o-od!" said Captain Solomin, raising his eyes, and under his gaze Vasya went taut like the string of a violin.

"Bring him closer!"

The officers knew this would be good. The captain was a real card, he knew how to have fun. Curiosity pulled them closer.

The thin, freckled Jew trembled like a leaf.

"Closer," repeated Captain Solomin indifferently. "Respond briefly and to the point. What creed?"

The Jew was silent. Why speak? All was lost anyway.

"A disciple of Moses?"

The officers, sensing there was about to be some action, snorted with laughter.

"Have we a mute here? Maybe I should be more direct. I'm asking: Jew?"

"No . . . ," the boy stammered, his lips pale.

A volley of laughter from the amused officers.

"Hold on, gentlemen, do you see something funny here?" said Solomin in a drawl. "The nose is no solid evidence. Sometimes birth defects do occur. If he says he's not, then he's not."

The officers were splitting their sides, gazing at the captain with eyes full of adoration.

"Cross yourself," slurred the captain.

The boy tried to make the sign of the cross, his fingers convulsively twisted. His trembling hand missed his arm, went astray, and ended up making a kind of odd squiggle in the air.

A loud roar of laughter from the delighted officers.

"Not quite," said Captain Solomin with unruffled calmness. "But it happens. Out of practice . . . Once more, slowly and precisely."

The boy traced a more or less accurate zigzag with his hand.

"Yes, now see, that was much better. Didn't I tell you? The nose proves nothing. You can tell straightaway he's Russian Orthodox. But just to dispel any final doubts, down with his pants, men!"

With a bashful, almost delicate gesture the boy clasped his hands over his privates. Vasya and two other soldiers threw themselves on him and forcibly undid his pants. The boy struggled helplessly. The pants slid to the ground in two shapeless pretzels, raising another hoot of laughter.

"What's this?" Solomin shouted in mock indignation. "Here I am, shielding you with my very own chest, so to speak, taking your word for it, and you, brother, are lying to me? Befouling the holy cross with an unbaptized hand? Denying your own faith? This I did not expect."

The boy pulled up and fastened his useless, unruly pants. It took him some time to find the right button.

"Search his pockets, boys!" ordered Captain Solomin.

Three pairs of greedy hands groped his chest, turning his pockets inside-out, tearing out the seams of his elegant clothing, and triumphantly removing a booklet — a Soviet passport — handed it over to the captain.

"Soooooo . . ." drawled the captain. "You should have said so right away. Come and ask: a pass to Belleville, please. Why not? Who ever heard of slipping off like that during the night, and with a passport stitched into your jacket to boot. It's just foul! Oh, if only it were the last time!"

Captain Solomin returned the passport.

"Put it back in his pocket! And now — scram!"

The boy didn't understand, and his bulging eyes stared at the captain.

"Scram! I don't want to see you around here anymore!"

The Jew took a hesitant step forward, as if wanting to fall to Solomin's feet, stopped himself, stared at the officers' grinning faces, turned around, and started to run along a wall, slowly at first, but then faster and faster. He was almost to the corner.

"Wait!" Captain Solomin called after him.

The boy stopped and turned around, terrified and undecided.

"Wait, I forgot to stamp your passport," said Solomin, sending a bullet from his revolver after him.

The Jew fell flat, his arms awkwardly splayed.

Vasya figured out the game; he was a quick learner. Slinging his rifle over his shoulder, he ran to the corner where the boy lay and bent down to him. He pulled an object from the boy's bosom and, waving it in the air, ran back to the officers.

"Right through the middle!" he shouted from afar, shaking the small red booklet.

The shredded Soviet passport had a bullet hole exactly in the middle, and around the hole, blood had formed a red halo to make a stamp.

The officers passed the small red booklet from hand to hand, murmuring their appreciation.

"Well, time to get some sleep," said Captain Solomin, pushing back his chair and tapping his riding crop on the tops of his boots. "I advise you gentlemen to do likewise. In two hours we've got to be at the Bourbon Palace. A man needs his rest sometimes. So long — until evening."

•

A thick chill and the murk of lowered blinds hung in the luxurious, single-story palace. An orderly opened the front door, Solomin came in and stretched out on a soft chesterfield, ordering his boots to be removed. The servant tiptoeing around brought a cushion and vanished from the room, closing the door without so much as a click.

Solomin wallowed in the soft bliss, in the plush carpet of silence. It was not so long ago that he began taking advantage of this salubrious atmosphere of comfort, and each time he immersed himself, he dissolved like a saccharine tablet in a cup of strong, prewar Russian tea.

From this vantage, his chesterfield drowning in carpets under the milky moon of a crystal lampshade, his long years of roaming seemed to him like a bad German film seen in a third-rate, smoky cinema. The stories in those films were simple, full of clichés that stung like cheap tobacco, the kind of films that were screened by the dozen in suburban movie houses to jerk the tears from the eyes of softhearted seamstresses.

The son of a staff officer. Some property near Moscow inherited from his mother. Childhood (normally shown in the prologue): expensive toys, governors and governesses. Boyhood: gymnasium, books, stamps. Summers in the countryside — duck hunting. The first amorous thrills. Mainly farm girls managed by an experienced steward. And everything was just *so*.

University. "Moscow by night." Filling gaps in his erotic education. And then suddenly, at what we might call the sizzling climax — mobilization.

Military college. The front lines. Injuries. The hospital in the rear. Nurses. The oblivion of lusty frenzies under the modest habit of the good prioress. Back to the front. Second line. The tedium of plundered villages. Alcohol and card games. And in moments of starvation for ecstasy — Jewish girls. Hollow rumors from the rear. Revolution. Committees and "comrades." Leave of absence. Moscow. The allure of the uniform and the raptures it produced. Then more upheavals — October.

Roving from apartment to apartment. Hideouts. A soldier's gray overcoat, his hands covered in soot: no manicure, and blisters a *must*. Papa's shot. His estate turned into a soviet seat. Every inch of land parceled out. The manor of his carefree childhood now a school full of grubby village brats.

Flight. Falsified documents. The Crimea. General Wrangel. On the offensive. To avenge a "disgraced Russia." Towns recaptured. Counter-espionage. Settling scores with the Bolsheviks. Firing squads. Communists and Komsomol members. And in-between — Jews. Jewesses: a rifle to the temple and everyone gets a turn. Pasty, stinking blood.

Hurried evacuation, a humiliating retreat. Cities and people. Constantinople. Sofia. Prague. The abolition of relief payments. Hunger. In Paris, word was, they're recruiting white officers for Zhang Zuolin's army . . . Paris. Drivel, no chance! No way to make a living. Making the rounds of the émigré committees. Relief withheld. Hauling suitcases at Gare du Nord. Sweeping floors in Renault factories. Cutbacks. Pounding the pavement again. Nights under a bridge. One-time relief payment. A driver's exam. And to top off the many years of wandering — the immortal, canonical taxi.

Surviving off a driver's salary was feasible. The humiliation was much worse. Paris was swarming with acquaintances, both his father's and his own. Not everyone had come empty-handed. Some of them, of course, had known how to smuggle in a little something. Paris is never short on money. They set up companies, worked a business. Many already had their own cars. Others broke up their days and nights with cab rides. Shameful, humiliating predicaments. Having driven acquaintances, he would turn his face as he reached out his hand for a tip. He kept a notebook filled with addresses of all the pubs and brothels.

It wasn't just male acquaintances, often female ones, too. In the evening, drunk outside the Florida, accompanied by well-plucked Frenchmen — taxi to a hotel. Others didn't even manage to hold out till the hotel — they got right down to it in the cab. The seats were soft, there were all the amenities. The polished mirror over the steering wheel was a full-blown Le Chabanais every evening: all the positions. The cab reeked of semen from a mile off. In Moscow, the ladies were like school girls in pigtails who couldn't bear to hear foul language in good company, had their high-ranking papas in the state administration, fiancés to boot, everything just so. But here — they climbed into his cab and spread their legs on command: Parisian women! All of Étoile was one giant whorehouse. Show them a hundred francs and they'd suck you to death. He wasn't condemning anyone. Maybe they really couldn't make a living any other way? Everyone earned money as best they could . . . Until he had that single most humiliating encounter.

He'd had a fiancée in Moscow. Tanya, the daughter of one General Akhmatov. Eyes of azure. Otherworldly. She was all Balmont and Severyanin. Played the piano like an artist. They got engaged before the revolution. When he left for the front, she kissed him full on the mouth, and two warm teardrops rolled down his cheeks, forever to be stored in the small vial of his heart.

They were among the first to flee Russia. It was rumored they were in Paris. The prudent general had placed his money in a foreign bank account. Apparently he'd doubled his money playing the stock market in Paris.

Arriving in Paris that summer, Solomin tracked down their address. He was told: Gone off to Nice, no knowing when he'd return.

Then, upon dropping off a client at a brothel, he spotted something: it was her, coming out of the gate. He could scarcely believe his eyes. She got into the taxi and absentmindedly tossed out an address.

As he drove he drafted a plan in his head. He wouldn't say a thing, he'd merely remove his cap when she paid, so she'd recognize him. In front of her house, however, he caved in. Pulling over, he turned to the back seat and, taking off his cap, clearly enunciated:

"Earn a lot this way, do you, Tatyana Nikolayevna?"

She gave a start and then burst into tears. A fountain of words: Papa was stingy, he counted every penny. It wasn't easy going around in darned stockings. They'd been through so much . . .

"Where, if I may ask? In Nice?"

She furrowed her brow. Slammed the door. She didn't have to justify herself to some cab driver. (That's exactly how she put it: "Some cab driver" — Solomin remembered the exact words). She tossed him ten francs and vanished through a doorway.

He wanted to run in after her, throw the ten francs back in her face, give her a piece of his mind. He saw a butler in a starched white shirt standing at the door. He suddenly felt embarrassed by his driver's uniform, embarrassed by the whole laughable situation. He drove off. He vowed to return the money by mail.

That evening he drank heartily at a Russian cabbie's pub with a nasally "Volga" coming out of the gramophone, longing to sink to the depths of his bitter humiliation, his wretchedness ("stomped in the mud").

But he couldn't forget that slap in the face. Of the thousand and one insults he'd received, he always remembered that one. He hung it around his neck like a small, greasy scapular, and from time to time he'd pull it out to fuel his venom, to keep from forgetting. And in the long evenings, his mind constructed a complex, fantastical plan of revenge.

In the evenings he spent his whole day's earnings on a third-rate girl from Avenue de Wagram. It had to be a Russian girl, and after performing her duty he would press twenty francs into her hand and beat her face, hurling the most vile abuses. Soon no girl from Avenue de Wagram would go with him, not for any amount of money.

Months went by, then years. His return to Russia, gun in hand, at the head of an imaginary White Army, a return he dreamed of every evening, cultivating this dream inside himself like an antidote to his daily debasements, became more and more problematic. In fact, he had stopped believing in it. Only the émigré gazettes were still stubbornly making promises. He understood the editors had to make a living somehow, too. He stopped reading the papers.

Those Bolsheviks had made themselves at home, settled in for good. They'd raised a ruckus over their tenth anniversary and were gearing up for their hundredth. Nobody even imagined gunning them down. One could still entertain thoughts of going back after two, three, or four years, but ten years on? This seemed out of the question.

Some had returned anyway, begging a Soviet passport from the consulate. Even the officers returned. Every time he heard about a new renegade, Solomin gnashed his teeth and spat with contempt. He wouldn't dream of going back to Russia under such terms. He hated the Communists with every inch of his thick skin. They'd ruined his life. Murdered his papa. Confiscated his property. Ruined his youth, his love — everything. Turned his fiancée into a prostitute (he could also safely tack the humiliation in the taxi onto their account). They had forced him to endure months half-dying from starvation, to drive painted floozies about Bois de Boulogne, to scrounge for tips. To be a simple cabby, him, Captain Solomin, son of Colonel Solomin! And who had forced him? A rabble of mangy Jews and the swarthy populace. No, he wouldn't forget! Go back? Work as a farmhand for Leon? No, a hundred times better to spend his whole life carting around these rouged-up whores, dropping off those corpulent French johns at the bordellos, rather than disgrace himself. And his officer's pride swelled within him.

Life made less and less sense. Fine, he could drive a cab for the time being, a year or two, ten years. If he knew it was limited to a certain time. But to think: I've become a cabby for good, for my whole life, this is my life and nothing will change — Captain Solomin somehow could not get this through his head. He clearly felt that something had to come — an explosion, a cataclysm, a catastrophe — to shuffle the deck of cards. Things couldn't go on this way.

And every morning, woken by the bell of his alarm clock, pulling on his grease-stained driver's clothing, Captain Solomin bitterly resolved: not yet.

He greeted the outbreak of this plague like a long-awaited cataclysm that had promptly shuffled the cards. His cab was appropriated after the third day for transporting the ill. His life became more roomy. Like a solution into which a powerful reagent had been poured, Paris began disintegrating into its constituent parts before his very eyes.

Expelled from the various emerging mini-states, the rudderless Russian émigré community followed the lead of the other nationalities and dug their heels into Passy, declaring the district White Russian territory. The slapdash government of the new territory resurrected the White Guard to defend its borders.

Three days later, Captain Solomin was dressed in gleaming riding boots, epaulettes, and a cap with a ribbon. He moved into a confiscated palace, in the company of a newly assigned orderly, and gave a laconic telephone command to purge the Russian territory of its non-Russian elements.

But this bliss was too perfect to last. This was unambiguously fore-shadowed by the plague, which waved playfully in the guise of Red Cross flags on vehicles passing his window. Captain Solomin understood: One had to survive for as long as possible and settle old scores, putting nothing off for later.

Unfortunately, the biggest scores he had to settle were with people hundreds of miles beyond the cordon, inaccessible and elusive. He would have to content himself with substitutes. And Captain Solomin suddenly recalled there was a Soviet mission on Rue de Grenelle, and a whole office of "representatives." Not many, it was true, but at least they were authentic, totally authentic, those "responsible." Those bandits didn't send just anybody to Paris.

By an unfortunate turn of events, Rue de Grenelle and all its buildings had become part of the improvised Bourbon monarchy. When word got out, the personnel of the Soviet mission took up residence in peace and comfort in one of the buildings of Saint-Germain that had swiftly been turned into a jail, and under the protection of the French Guard they openly ignored the proximity of the rightful rulers installed in neighboring Passy.

It was Captain Solomin who first submitted a petition that unequivocally demanded that the French authorities hand over the Soviet prisoners to the White Guard, on grounds that they were subject to the Russian court, the only institution competent to determine their fates.

Captain Solomin's resolution met with a warm ovation from headquarters and the unanimous support of the army. A special commission was immediately selected, whose members included the creator of the scheme. This commission was assigned to start immediate negotiations with the representatives of the monarchy in Saint-Germain.

The French put up some obstacles. In principle, they had nothing against handing over the Bolsheviks, but they did require the Russian government to pay hefty damages to some Semitic-looking French citizens residing in Passy who had recently fallen victim to pogroms. The matter dragged on.

Yet in spite of everything, an end finally seemed to be in sight. At the previous day's session, the Russian government had eventually been made to concede to the conditions set by the adamant French. The definitive signing of the protocol was to take place at ten o'clock that morning, on French territory, in the onetime Chamber of Deputies building — now once more the Bourbon Palace.

•

At ten a.m. sharp a cushy six-seater Fiat showed the relevant transit papers and drove across Jena Bridge toward Bourbon Palace.

The official on duty led the Russian delegation through chilly, well-worn corridors to a small conference room where four gray-haired men in black were waiting at a table piled high with files. They immediately began to negotiate on the specifics. The French had invented some additional clauses; they didn't agree to being paid in installments, demanding an immediate cash settlement. The session stretched out interminably.

Captain Solomin took no active part in the discussion and maintained a dignified silence, yawning discreetly into his hand and letting his bored gaze roam about the ceiling.

At just the moment when the bargaining seemed to be winding down, a gray-haired, needle-nosed gentleman pulled a watch from his pocket and declared it was time for lunch.

The head of the Russian delegation, rattled by this new delay, tried to offer an objection, explaining that they only needed half an hour at most until the deal was finalized, that it should not be left to hang, and that after matters were concluded everyone could relax and enjoy their lunch all the better. The gentlemen with Bourbon noses did not see fit to acknowledge his remarks and rose from the table as if on command, after which the gray-haired gentleman announced in a steady voice that the meeting would resume at two o'clock. The Russian delegation could only bite their lips and go for a stroll while waiting for the meeting to resume.

Captain Solomin blundered through the endless corridors in search of a lavatory, and then spent a long time wandering in search of the way back. When he finally made it to the stairs and found himself on the street, his colleagues were no longer in front of the palace. They had tired of waiting and left for town without him.

Captain Solomin set off down the quiet streets with their glassy asphalt, walking at a leisurely pace. He knew this neighborhood well. This was where he had only recently driven elderly rich men with Legion of Honor ribbons in their buttonholes after a night at the theater. The worst passengers! Always pulling tricks — they'd pour you a handful of change you could count till day's end and still not reckon the full amount — and then all you got was a five *sous* tip.

Because of his involuntary occupation, Captain Solomin was nursing a powerful grudge against the French as the personification of all the attributes diametrically opposed to the "generous Russian spirit."

By force of longtime habit the captain — though having exchanged his driver's uniform for a cavalier's tights — had not ceased to rate people by how they tipped. This was in no way symptomatic of any kind of solidarity with the class of pariahs whose ranks he had only just left, but rather one of those grooves of accustomed behavior that had been carved in his mind, into which thoughts flowed automatically, like tears down the lines of a furrowed face.

For the first time he was walking the streets of this district a free, full-fledged pedestrian, looking down from the heights of his golden epaulettes onto the people passing by. One might say that along with his officer's uniform he had put on a new pair of glasses, and the city, so unbearable from behind the steering wheel, was now seen for the first time, and from the vantage of the sidewalks it suddenly seemed friendly, attractive, and not entirely lacking in a peculiar charm.

He paused in contemplation before the display window of a great restaurant, swimming into the depths of a tunnel of mirrors and a shady solarium, exotic and bizarre, where slender fans of palm trees swayed above the whiteness of tablecloths, scattered about like snowflakes.

He used to hurry past these places, and only occasionally, when he happened to be dropping tuxedoed guests off in front of the glassy tunnels, did he surreptitiously cast an angry, jealous glance inside. This was a foreign, closed, permanently inaccessible world, a city within a city, walled off from the rest by only a thick plate of glass: visible, yet off-limits. You only got in by slipping on a tuxedo, much as one did scuba gear for diving into the depths of the sea.

Frozen in front of the window, Captain Solomin was suddenly struck by a capital idea. Indeed, who was there to stop him from going inside if that was what he desired, who would stop him from sitting in the shade of the exotic palms, amid those black gentlemen in their fine suits, popping out from the ice floes of the tablecloths like trained seals, absentmindedly ordering something, and thus compelling the tuxedoed waiters to orbit around him, obsequious grins stitched to their faces?

This flash came so suddenly that Captain Solomin found it hard to act out a small comedy of nonchalance.

As if the whole city were watching him at that moment (the street was entirely empty), Captain Solomin casually pulled out a thick gold watch. As if noticing only now that it was already mealtime, he made an indefinable but clear gesture that would have led someone to understand that, as long as a restaurant was here at hand, then some lunch wouldn't hurt, and with the indifferent, bored expression of a man of the world, he pushed open the massive mirrored doors.

He was swathed in the pleasant chill of starched tablecloths, air splashed with the atomizer of a fountain, the sickly international smell of comfort. Over the small altars of the tables, people bent in pious concentration accepted the Host of veal and lamb cutlets, to the prayerful clatter of the plates held by the anointed choirboys — the waiters.

With the absent expression of an old regular who prefers an out-of-the-way table in his own discreet corner, Captain Solomin found a cramped place behind a pillar, which gave onto the entire room like the view from a theater box, and seating himself comfortably, he studied the menu.

The appearance of a guest in an exotic uniform did not go unnoticed, and feeling himself the focal point of many stares, Captain Solomin nodded to a waiter, showing the murderous nonchalance and coolness that distinguishes a real regular from the novice, and began to order a long and complex lunch, asking about the wine list with the air of a connoisseur. Having selected a range of dishes with the most sophisticated and solemn names, he struck a relaxed and photogenic posture on the armrest of the ottoman, his apathetic gaze wandering around the room.

The room was practically empty at this time of day. The gentlemen scattered here and there at only a few tables had long stopped paying any attention to the exotic guest and were now entirely absorbed in their food and conversations.

Three clean-shaven gentlemen sitting behind the pillar at the next table were sipping black coffee and having an animated discussion. With only the pillar between them, Captain Solomin was unintentionally privy to their conversation, observing them unnoticed.

The talk was dominated by a man with a pince-nez:

"But surely, gentlemen, you will admit," he said in a voice filled with grief and bitterness, "that the events we are witnessing must have a dispiriting effect on every sincere democrat. In the violent and unforeseen clash of powers taking place before our eyes, French democracy has shown itself to be a *quantité négligeable*. We are observing a phenomenon that would recently have been considered improbable and unseemly — the restoration of the monarchy — and even worse, we are forced to admit that it has taken place without a single shot being fired, without visible opposition from the wide ranks of our bourgeoisie. I trust you will agree this is a highly embarrassing turn of events."

"I don't share your pessimism," retorted a staid gentleman, whose perfect bald patch made it impossible to establish his age. "Times of general anxiety, like the present, lead us to exaggerate and generalize sporadic and exceptional events. We are forgetting that outside the sphere of Paris, which is undergoing a contagious fever full of hallucinations and oddities, there exists all of France proper, sincerely democratic and bourgeois. All it will take is for the epidemic in Paris to be eradicated, and feverish delusions like the Bourbon monarchy and Soviet republics will vanish in turn. The first division of the French Republic's army that crosses into Paris will set things back on track."

"I beg your pardon," the man with the pince-nez excitedly objected, "but following your conclusions would have us wander into the thickets of sheer metaphysics. Judging by the statistics to date, it would be irrational to suppose that any of the current residents of Paris will live to see the moment you describe. Everything seems to indicate that the reality in which we are living is and will remain the sole reality that will be given to us. For us Parisians, citizens of a plague-infested city, the borders of France have shrunk to the city limits. To speak of the existence of this France, this Europe, or a world beyond the limits of this city, which we might only leave in a coffin, is tantamount, at present, to speaking of the reality of life after death.

"You say that France and Europe really do exist, although we cannot confirm this for the time being with the faculties of our senses. You say that we saw them with our own eyes not long ago, that we receive radio broadcasts from them? But do the mystics not speak of the origins of an existence before time, which we encounter through pure recollection, and do the spiritualists not receive communications from the spirit world just as freely? And yet, perhaps you'll agree, the afterlife does not therefore cease to be a question of faith, and a sociologist who bases his sociological concepts on the fact that such an afterlife does indeed exist would at best be called a mystic, and a statesman who built the politics of his nation on the hopes of aid from the world beyond would simply be thrown into a madhouse. Is the belief that the Republic's armies will come and restore Paris to its old order really any different, then, from waiting for manna to drop from the heavens?

"I reiterate: for us the world, Europe, and France have, like a scrap of wet cloth, shrunken to the city limits, to the outskirts of Paris. The issues of our social and political life have remained the same, only their dimensions have changed. We have to solve them now on another, reduced scale. But as we do so, we mustn't deny that we are witnesses to the formal partition of France, and that in the face of this partition French democracy has proven itself worthless in the moral sense. Up till now, only inertia has kept French democracy on course, having long squandered its moral capital. The instant they began to reorganize the various estates, when communism and that shoddy monarchy made their bids — without a second's pause or any kind of struggle, French democracy relinquished the place it had occupied since the Great Revolution, and at a bargain price, to the darkest reactionaries for the crown, just to maintain its annuities in all their inviolability."

The bald gentleman glanced about anxiously to see if anyone happened to be listening, and lifted a finger of caution to his lips. It is unclear if he wanted to offer a rebuttal, because the third gentleman, a man whose shapely head was cleft like a walnut with the incision of an impeccable part, cut in and broke his silence.

"You are most certainly correct on many points," he said, weighing his words with the dignity and restraint of a born parliamentarian. "Yet I cannot share your pessimism. It is no doubt possible that the population of Paris, should it continue to shrink at the present rate, will die out entirely before the epidemic's course can be altered. But this is ultimately just a hypothesis that is no more or less likely than its antithesis. We ought to consider it, but we are not justified in raising it to the status of a certainty. Tens and hundreds of scholars and doctors behind the cordon are working around the clock in the struggle against this death-dealing microbe. None of us can guarantee they won't succeed — if not today, then tomorrow.

"Regardless, we can't deny that the events before us are in all respects symptomatic and instructive. We are forced to concede that, indeed, our democracy did not pass muster in its attempt to reorganize itself on this reduced scale — if you will permit me to use your expression. But the conclusions we draw from this mustn't be too far-flung. We all know the principle that a ruling class ages at the speed with which it consumes the revolutionary capital that brought it to power. The French bourgeoisie is not and *cannot* be an exception. But it would be premature to suppose that the French bourgeoisie has played out its role in history and must now quit the stage. In this day and age, when our science is so near to solving the mystery of the human aging process, why shouldn't we be tempted to stop the aging of an entire class? Take note, the anti-aging process will be a good deal easier. The ruling class needs only renounce its privileges and become a ruled class for some period of time. Nothing is quite so rejuvenating as a touch of resistance. This is a fact we all know from parliament.

"The French bourgeoisie, which has long squandered the moral capital it earned through the Great Revolution and lost every bit of trust the working classes had in it, needs this operation more than any other class of any other nation. A coup d'état or restoration of the monarchy should have been staged long ago in the interests of preserving its position of supremacy, to help the bourgeoisie again play out its role as liberators. We can only take satisfaction from the fact that this state of affairs has come about on its own.

"I am currently drafting a memo that I would like to present to the government in Lyon as soon as the epidemic is quashed. I contend that the immediate liquidation of the Paris monarchy would be an unforgivable error. On the contrary, I hold that for the sake of government and democracy we should make every effort to spread the monarchist system all across France, thus helping to stifle our shared implacable enemy — communism. Only a revolution that is pre-staged and skillfully conducted at the right moment, which the bourgeoisie will be capable of performing — without the aid of the other classes and without bloodshed, naturally — will restore its moral revolutionary trust among the masses, raise its authority and shield its breast with new armor against the danger of communism . . ."

Whether the bald gentleman and the gentleman in the pince-nez responded to this harangue, and in what way, Captain Solomin did not hear. He was suddenly overcome by a wave of infinite boredom. It all reminded him of the Moscow meetings in the Kerensky days, of speeches long as tapeworms, wherein the word "democracy" was repeated no less, only in a strong, sibilant Russian. The mention of communism had reminded him of those creampuffs comfortably snoozing in their French prison cells ("They'll sleep tight with us all right!").

He glanced at his watch: Two o'clock. He'd wasted time once again! And without finishing his carefully selected repast, he paid the extortionate bill and headed for Bourbon Palace through the desolate, suddenly charmless streets.

This time the bargaining moved along briskly, and less than an hour later, as he was laying down the curlicues of his signature upon the clause-blackened document, Captain Solomin allowed himself to smile inside — at last!

The final hitch was the timing. The French wanted to hand over the prisoners the following day. The leader of the Russian delegation wanted to make it at once. Impossible — formalities, and so forth. (What other kinds of godforsaken formalities could there be?) They had to agree to the following day. The Russians wanted to send two officers to fetch the prisoners. The French objected. They would bring them to the bridge themselves and hand them over when the border guard signed a receipt.

"All right, so be it. Well, till tomorrow morning, eleven o'clock."

The delegates shook hands in silence.

The black, six-seater Fiat softly rolled along the semicircle of the shady bank and onto Jena Bridge.

V

"COMRADES! NOT ALL AT ONCE! Please sign up to take the floor. We've got to maintain some sort of order!"

"So maintain it, comrade! That's your job. That's why you've been chosen chairman. Sign away. Only make sure everyone gets to speak their mind. You've got your opinion, I've got mine. But shaking a bell like they do in the capitalist parliament so that no one gets heard — what kind of order is that?"

"Comrades! Please calm down! Comrade Lerbier has the floor."

"Comrades, I will not take much of your time. As Food Supplies Commissioner I have no reason to beat around the bush. The state of the republic's food supplies is catastrophic. If we keep handing out quarter loaves of bread as we have, there'll only be enough for three more days at best. And this is assuming the population continues to drop at its present rate. Yesterday we handed out our last sack of potatoes. In three days, comrades, nobody will have anything to put in their mouths. The republic is doomed to die by starvation."

"And the way out? What is the solution?"

"In my view, there is only one way out, comrades. Breach the Anglo-American territory and seize their provisions. As I see it, comrades, the British and American imperialists haven't died of hunger since the world was made. They have surely hoarded up a decent store of supplies. We must be prepared, naturally, for their fierce resistance. The British militia is armed to the teeth, and in order to cross into their territory we'd have to force our way through two lines of barricades and wipe out a good few thousand gentlemen. But I don't see any alternative. The people will happily go along when they find out we're expelling the British from Paris. Obviously this is no solution to the problem, but it will at least postpone it for a while, for as long as the American provisions hold out.

If one of you, comrades, has a better idea, I'm all ears. I've said my bit, comrades. That's it."

"Remain calm! Please remain calm! Comrade Laval has the floor."

"I must disagree, comrades, with the speaker's opinion. Certainly, mopping up a few thousand British capitalists and cleaning out downtown Paris would be useful, no argument there. But now is not the time. The plague will do the job for us more cleanly and efficiently. No point in killing for the sake of a few days, but above all, comrades, because I do not believe in these food provisions Comrade Lerbier expects to find there. Where could the British have gotten them? Money is another matter. We would doubtless find piles of money. But why do we need money at this juncture, comrades? We can't buy bread with it. It's not worth the proletarian blood, comrades, we would have to spill. Even if there ever were provisions, they would have been eaten long ago. We won't feed ourselves there. And it is still too early, comrades, for cleansing Paris. Until the city rids itself of this plague, it will be of little use to us. No, comrades, searching for food in Paris won't do a bit of good. We'd only lose half our proletariat at the barricades, and they are dwindling in number as it is. With what forces, comrades, will we take control of Paris once the plague has been eradicated? We must guard, comrades, every drop of proletarian blood with our lives, and not help the plague do its work."

"But if we don't help it, then starvation will! Without bread we won't last long!"

"I know, comrades, we won't last long without bread, but one hunk won't get you far either. And we must find that hunk of bread elsewhere, where we know it to be for certain, and not where we already know it *is not*. We must seek it, comrades, beyond the cordon."

"But how, comrade, through the cordon? You can't just reach your hand through the cordon. There's no way of breaking through."

"Just a moment, comrades, allow me to finish. I have a plan. We don't need to break through the cordon to force the imperialist French government to give us provisions. It will suffice, in my opinion, for the Council of Delegates to send a telegram to the government: either they provide us with so many freight cars of flour, potatoes, and whatever else, delivered to our side of the cordon in two days, and continue to provide us with such supplies in the future, or we'll break through and tear their cordon apart. Even if we don't manage to break through, at the very least the army will be infected grappling with us, and from the army the plague will run riot all across France. We'll wait two days — the choice is theirs."

"They won't respond!"

"As I see it, comrades, they will respond, and mighty quick at that. There's no threat so effective as the fear of plague. They'll figure we have nothing to lose. They'll get frightened. They won't want to risk it. What if we do manage to break the cordon and come in contact with their soldiers? That's their worst nightmare. They wouldn't want to risk infecting all of France over a dozen freight cars of supplies. And it wouldn't hurt to send a second telegram to the French proletariat on the other side of the cordon: the Parisian proletariat are dying of starvation, they call out to the proletariat of France and the whole world to put pressure on the French government to force them to send aid. On one side the plague, and on the other a general strike. Before two days have passed we'll have a first-rate food shipment across the cordon. That, comrades, is the way I see it. I've said my piece."

Dozens of voices rang out at once.

Late in the evening the Workers' and Soldiers' Council of Delegates of the Belleville Soviet Republic, having voted in the majority for Comrade Laval's proposal, sent out two telegrams into the void.

Silence was the only reply.

•

Two days later, the Council of Delegates reconvened and accepted the conclusions of Comrade Lerbier, who recommended that the Council work out a detailed plan for taking the Anglo-American territory by force.

Leaving the session, Comrade Laval pulled his cap down low over his forehead, which always meant he was deeply upset, and set off into the dim and winding streets. A light rain fell.

The fiasco of his proposal had cut him to the quick, like a personal affront, filling him with a hollow rage.

"The bastards! Ignoring our threats! Leaving us to starve to death!" he muttered through gritted teeth.

He knew them all too well: the imperialists. How could there be any negotiating with them? They weren't the slightest bit moved by the fate of the dying proletariat. But he had been counting on their fear of the plague. That they wouldn't want to risk it. No, they weren't afraid. One could see they felt mighty sure of their cordon. They'd butcher the proletariat like dogs. Wouldn't let them get within one mile of the cordon.

A hollow, powerless rage swelled in Comrade Laval's heart.

He hated those bandits with every fiber, just thinking about them made his throat constrict in painful convulsions. Their heavy jackboots had already trampled the Paris Commune. And now they were calmly standing by while everyone died of hunger and the plague, to take over a disinfected Paris once more, smother it in police, drown it in democracy by opening the floodgates of futile parliamentary blather, set up snares for criminals, lock the city in iron manacles. And the swarthy, browbeaten people driven from their fields would again flow into the factories to forge for them their peace, their luxury and idleness by the sweat of workers' hands. Everything would continue just as it always had, and there wouldn't be the slightest indication that only months before Paris had had a commune, a workers' and soldiers' government, the Council of Delegates, a rugged workers' epic.

At the thought of all this Comrade Laval clenched his teeth tighter, until his jaws cracked a warning. The heavy boot of powerlessness pressed even harder than the yoke of plague.

Comrade Jacques Laval, captain of the Red Guard of the Soviet Republic of Belleville, had been a sailor on the *Victory* in the period prior to the revolution, that is, four weeks hence. He'd been in the Party for eight years, from the moment when, as a twenty-year-old ruddy-faced farmer's boy from the Combé sawmill, he was assigned to the navy by the draft board, and, thrust into that black floating dungeon, he began shoveling heavy lumps of coal into the huffing maw of the furnace, his coarse fingers probing the first burns on his naked, muscular torso. His twenty years of knowledge flipped a somersault, and the firmly grounded, orderly world swirled around in his head like a ship's deck in a raging gale.

From the vantage point of the Party everything suddenly took on a glassy transparency, and looking back Comrade Laval found he now understood a thing or two. Old Combé drove himself to the sawmill once a week to ask: Is everything OK? And old Frost, who had lost his sight measuring fractions of inches, was declared "unfit" by the foreman and given the boot by the factory police. The *Victory* had cannons, armored towers — it was a military vessel. The slick naval officer and old Combé were one man, two faces with the same torso — the white international. While setting the cannon at a 25° angle, Private Laval dreamed: corral the whole mob from all over the world, along with their cars, epaulettes, and cassocks, into one big space and — Kaboom! Comrade Laval's face lit up in a grin.

Comrade Laval had come to Paris on holiday and the plague had trapped him. When the plague sparked the first riots, the ground shook, splitting the various class strata at their seams, and Comrade Laval thought: there's no way we're dying like dogs, like we did before. As long as the imperialists were across the cordon, and the plague was blocking access to Paris, it was time to demolish this old ramshackle house and lay the foundations of a free people's republic.

And pushing back his beret, Comrade Laval was the first to head briskly back to the barracks, only to emerge an hour later at the head of a blue division, which had swiftly acquired — no one knew how — a red flag.

The following days were filled with organizational work. The plague interfered. It stole his best comrades from him. Otherwise, Comrade Laval would probably have scarcely noticed it; he was totally absorbed in organizing the workers' councils on the southern outskirts of Paris. Hygiene and precautions a must. The rest is up to the doctors. The plague was even useful to some degree. It purged the downtown and western quarters of their bourgeois elements. Now the outskirts had to get on their feet, so that the moment the epidemic was eradicated all of bourgeois Paris would awake to the clamping jaws of a proletarian blockade. Taking control of the plague-weakened city would be easy as pie.

But the plague showed no signs of abating, it decimated the proletarian ranks with sinister efficiency. It was extremely difficult to work in such conditions. Each day one had to start from scratch. And on top of everything — famine. The young, developing commune was sentenced to die by starvation. The remaining ranks of the Parisian proletariat, already thinned out, would die fighting for a morsel of bread at the barricades of the Anglo-American territory. Moreover, Comrade Laval didn't believe such substantial food supplies would be found over there in the first place.

Everything was turning to rubble before his very eyes, under a cruel, unswerving ax. The last threat they had sent those imperialists filling their bellies in peace and abundance across the cordon, patiently waiting until plague and famine finally killed off the last Parisian, had failed. What was left? Capitulate and wait for death with hands folded over one knee, or charge at it headfirst, at the barricades of the plague-infested Anglo-American territory?

Comrade Laval silently hefted tons of stubborn, gloomy thoughts, as he once had shoveled coal.

·

Long after midnight there was a knock at the door of Comrade Lecoq, commander of the Soviet Republic of Belleville army.

Comrade Lecoq groped for his pince-nez on the chair by his bedside, stuck it on his nose, and throwing his greatcoat over his underwear, went to the door, turning on the lights as he went.

"Is that you, Comrade Laval? What's happened? Is it urgent?"

"I've come to you on business, Comrade Commandant. And my business is urgent. It's not personal, it concerns the whole commune. I couldn't hold out till morning. Please don't be angry . . ." said Comrade Laval, crumpling his cap in his hands.

"Not at all, not at all!" said Comrade Lecoq, bustling about. "Come in. I'm at your service. If it's important, the time of day doesn't matter. Sleep can wait. Have a seat. Cigarette? I'm all ears. What's the matter?"

"I've come, Comrade Commandant, with regard to the commune's provisions. I can't allow the last proletariat to be sent to charge the Anglo-American barricades. We won't find any food there anyway. It's sheer suicide."

Comrade Lecoq nearly lost his pince-nez in surprise.

"How can this be, comrade? It is the resolution of the Council of Delegates. You already made this motion at the session. Your proposal was already tried. It brought no results. We had to pass another resolution. And now that this resolution has been passed, it's too late to turn back. The timing is not the best. If each of us began to criticize and overturn the Council's resolutions, where would we be? You know perfectly well why this particular resolution was passed, and at the time you didn't protest. You understood there was no alternative."

"There is an alternative," Comrade Laval said grimly. "I didn't see it then, but I do now. That's why I've come to see you so late, Comrade Commandant."

"What have you come up with so suddenly? You've seen they weren't intimidated by your telegram. They didn't bring a single railcar of food by the deadline. What should we wait for? Who's going to bring us food?"

"That's why I've come, Comrade Commandant. I'll bring it," blurted Laval.

"You?"

Comrade Lecoq leaned forward in astonishment.

"What do you mean, you? Where are you going to get it?"

"Where I get it is my business. Obviously it'll mean crossing the cordon."

Comrade Lecoq coughed with impatience.

"Comrade, have you come to make jokes? What does that mean, 'crossing the cordon'? We have no time here for jokes."

"It's not jokes I have in mind, Comrade Commandant. I've come to tell you that tomorrow I'm coming back with provisions for the commune, and I've come during the night because the matter is urgent, to my mind, and there's not a moment to lose."

Comrade Lecoq studied his guest carefully and responded only after a long pause:

"How, may I ask, are you going to get food for the commune across the cordon by yourself?"

"By breaking through the cordon, obviously. A whole army couldn't do it, but a few men might be able to slip through. Especially by water."

"So what if you slip through and return with a loaf of bread? Is the commune supposed to feed itself off that? Do you know how much it will take to feed the commune? Freight cars! How are you going to slip back through with them? Carry them on your back?"

"Not on my back, but it won't be hard to carry them by water."

"What water?"

"Just regular water. There's no cordon on the river. They haven't bricked up the river."

173

"And what about it. They guard it day and night. A fish couldn't get through."

"I haven't come to you for nothing, Comrade Commandant. I've checked everything. I know what I'm talking about. You can get out by river."

"How?"

"Not during the day, but at night."

"But you know they shine floodlights on the Seine to make sure no one sails down it at night."

"They do light it up, but not the whole of the Seine, only for one mile. Two floodlights. One on each side. There's no other floodlights in the area, and why should there be? It's as bright as daylight."

"So how do you think you'll be able to sail through?"

"Sailing through won't be too hard, even with more than one ship, as many as you like. You've only got to shut off the floodlights."

"How do you intend to do that?"

"Again, it's very simple when you know the exact positions of the floodlights. Two shots from a five-inch gun should do the job. We pulled more complicated stunts in the navy."

"Let's say you manage to knock out both floodlights. They'll have them repaired in half an hour."

"In half an hour I could get all of Belleville through, if you want. Especially now. The nights are dark as pitch."

"OK. And on the way back?"

"The way back will be harder, of course. We can always try. On the way back they won't catch on right away who's going where. And if they catch on at the first cordon, I don't suppose they'll do much shooting. The cordon is meant to keep people in Paris. Whoever chooses to enter the wolf's lair can go where he pleases. Why shoot? They'll fire twice to give us a scare and then leave us alone."

"All that sounds well and good. But where do you intend to get your hands on the food?"

Comrade Laval drew in closer:

"If you sail straight down the Seine, some thirty-five miles from Paris, there is a place called Tansorel. My hometown. I know every pebble by heart. A steam mill stands a verst from the shore, a huge one that grinds grain for the whole area. At this time it should contain a good dozen freight cars of flour. We should be able to collect three barges with two hundred sacks, give or take a few. A tugboat couldn't haul more. I thought about taking empty barges from here as well, but it will be easier to slip through with a single tugboat. And we'll pick up the barges there from the local sawmill. They used to transport lumber to Paris by barge. But now they no longer use them and the barges are just sitting idle. We'll load up three of them, be back before dawn. Six hundred sacks, two hundred pounds apiece. Not too much — but it'll feed the commune for a month. After that, we'll see. Maybe the plague will be over by then, maybe the proletariat will bring reinforcements? We'll have bought ourselves some time."

Comrade Lecoq did not respond right away.

"It's a romantic notion, this expedition of yours. Even if you do manage to make it to the other side, I don't see them letting you back in. They'll sink you and all your cargo."

"No harm in trying. If they get us, they'll be wiping out ten men. Ten men isn't the whole commune. The Anglo-American territory isn't going anywhere. If they sink us, then go search for your bread over there. We've got to try."

Comrade Lecoq pulled on his cigarette in silence.

"You see, comrade, we haven't even gotten to the catch yet. Let's say you managed to get through the cordon and returned with the provisions, which seems to me rather unlikely. One way or another, comrade, we have no right to carry the plague outside the cordon, even to save the whole commune from starving to death. Threats are one thing, execution another. If you succeed in your expedition you'll have to disembark on the other side of the cordon to search for provisions and come in contact with the locals, which means we have to consider the possibility of the plague spreading. We have no right, comrade, to put the whole proletariat and peasantry of France at risk of the plague to save the ten thousand citizens of the commune. I cannot give you my permission to go on such an expedition."

"What you say is just, Comrade Commandant. But I have taken all this into account from the very beginning. I've found a way to avoid docking. We arrive, stop in the middle of the river, collect the provisions, and then take off! You see, this is why I'm not taking any barges with us — we'll use theirs. We just need to hitch them up and go!"

"So you simply think they'll carry their flour out to you, load them onto their own barges, and then let you haul it away with their blessings?"

"How did you guess, Comrade Commandant? They'll load it up themselves. I have a plan, you'll see yourself, it's simple and straightforward, but you haven't let me finish."

Comrade Laval took a pencil from the table and traced it along a sheet of paper, explaining his plan in detail.

●

By the time Comrade Lecoq was alone in his room it was already dawning outside, and the street's tiny universe was incrusting itself into pale, frosted stained glass upon windowpanes streaked with the soot of the night.

Comrade Lecoq threw off his greatcoat and stretched out on his bed, trying to sleep. Sleep had spirited off, however, and would not return. Lecoq reached for the shelf and selected a book. He opened it. Lenin: "The Tasks of the Proletariat in the Present Revolution." He tried to read.

The thoughts, like tiny barnacle worms unable to burrow into his brain, sulked back between the black crops of the lines. Comrade Lecoq replaced the book and stared at the ceiling.

From somewhere, from his memory's mirror, like a delayed reflection, emerged a swarthy, wind-lashed face, and simple, smiling words rang out: "If they get us, they'll be wiping out ten men. Ten men isn't the whole commune. We've got to try."

Comrade Lecoq smiled. Ambition? Recklessness? Or perhaps a genuinely fervid love for the commune?

He'd met with these people every day for years, face to face, even back at university, when the bookish son of an impoverished gymnasium teacher ran from the student cookhouse to an assembly to see how the black digits of statistics looked in real life. He learned to look into those eyes, to decipher deep, unhealed, real injuries from wrinkles and the tone of abuse in the contours of nonchalant, sacramental words — "proletariat," "imperialism" — to estimate the digits of cut salaries, the weight of humiliations received. And suddenly here — bright blue eyes, a smile, and death. The effects of romantic literature? Heroism?

The telephone clattered on the desk.

Comrade Lecoq got up, listened to a report, then dictated a few directives into the black bowl of the speaker. And stretching out once more on his hard military bed, his face to the wall, he closed his eyes to sleep, and thought:

"They'll crush him, no doubt. It's a shame. When the plague blows over, we'll have to rebuild the commune, and we'll need as many like him as we can get."

His drowsy lips mouthed a trained phrase he recited every evening: "But by then I'll be long gone . . ."

Sleep would not come. Turning from side to side, Comrade Lecoq smoked a cigarette. He glanced at his watch. Four o'clock. Finishing the cigarette, he got up and turned on the light. He went to the desk. He reached under some reports buried deep inside the desk drawer, took out a thick notebook with an oilcloth cover, and opened it on the table.

No one knew Comrade Lecoq was writing a history of plague-infested

Paris. Few knew he had once been a man of letters. He'd written poems in his youth. Apparently they weren't bad. But he'd long stopped writing them. He was ashamed of his literary talents, as he was of his erudition and his roots in the intelligentsia. He'd bristle like a wildcat at crudeness, at the barbs of a soldier's vocabulary, at curt and gruff manners.

The relentless progress of the plague had made him certain that the Parisians were condemned to die in the ring of the cordon, that not a soul would be spared.

Nonetheless, from the first moments of the republic's existence there had been the liveliest attempts to fight the plague, as mandated by the Central Committee. Taking advantage of the confusion in the stunned bourgeois districts, the Belleville Republic had made a daring raid on the Pasteur Institute and trucked off all its inventories to their own territory. In well-equipped laboratories, dozens of scientists committed to the proletarian cause worked day and night in a superhuman effort to defeat the deadly virus. Every day new vaccinations were tested, though these refused to produce the desired results, like all those that came before.

After a month of fruitless struggle, Comrade Lecoq stopped believing in success. He watched the events taking place around him with the curiosity of a natural scientist observing the atrophy of cells. It troubled him that so much documentary material was being squandered in vain, that it would never be a part of the legacy of humankind. This thought tormented him at night.

Everyone will die off, no one will be left to tell future generations of the unforgettable and chimerical history of this city.

So at last he decided he would secretly write its chronicle, based on gathered information, oral reports, and first-hand observations. He would die, everyone would die, but his chronicle would remain. The plague would pass, new people would arrive, they'd find it, shake off the dust, and this piece of history, so full of valuable experiences, the unique vicissitudes of this macabre period, would not be forever lost.

In the nights, surreptitiously, during off-duty hours, he would record the news of the day in the thick notebook, adding to and rearranging the endless documents and clippings.

Opening the notebook to where he left off, Comrade Lecoq thought once more of Laval. What a superb specimen! Such people deserved an epos. He'd have to wait till the end of the expedition. What a melodramatic chapter! He absentmindedly flipped through a couple of pages. He paused on the last entry, about the uprising at Place Pigalle and the surrounding streets of the new autonomous African Republic, founded by the black people of Montmartre (jazz musicians and doormen) as a protest against the anti-African authorities ruling the central quarters. According to eyewitnesses, any white person caught in the area of the new state was beheaded by the Africans, with ceremonies borrowed from the Ku Klux Klan.

Comrade Lecoq turned the page, took out a fountain pen, and in his thoughts thumbed through the day's material. Then carefully, at the top of the page, he wrote out the title for a new chapter in an even, crimpy hand:

THE TALE OF THE NAVY-BLUE REPUBLIC

No one really noticed or bothered their heads much about the little blustering fellows in navy-blue capes who suddenly went missing from the street corners, where they had been planted for decades like natural, inevitable fixtures.

But we all know that nothing in nature ever truly perishes.

The disoriented and superfluous police, repelled in turn from each new state, by force of habit flocked to their barracks on Île de la Cité, which was bordered on three sides by independent republics: the Chinese, Jewish, and Anglo-American.

Île de la Cité lies embraced between the two arms of the Seine, and thus cut off by nature herself, it seems to constitute a sort of independent territorial unit.

On that day it swarmed with unemployed blue men.

Left to their own devices, the police found themselves for the first time in a troublesome quandary. Suddenly stripped of the compass of the law, unable to decide which of the emergent governments should be considered lawful, and realizing the fictitiousness of any government outside the ring of the cordon, the unemployed blue folk swiftly came to realize that they were less real creatures with every passing day, becoming metaphysical fiction, pure nonsense, insubstantial, like the very concept of "police for police's sake."

On the third day, Île de la Cité bore witness to the first demonstration of unemployed policemen in the history of the world.

The crowd of jobless blue folk spread all across the island, flowing into the square below the prefecture. At the head of the procession demonstrators carried placards with slogans: "The Republic is dead — Long live the Republic!" "We demand some form of government!" "The police without a government is like an electric tram without a power plant!" and so forth.

An impressive meeting was held in the square before the prefecture. After long discussions on how to save the police as such, it was decided to turn to the various governments of the new states one at a time, offering law enforcement services.

"This is not about the color, or even the national status of a government," claimed the man who devised the idea. "In order to win back their raison d'être, to return from the land of fiction and onto the lists of real institutions, the police have to immediately support a government of any sort, even the *idea* of government. Without the notion of law and order, we are but shadows."

The project was unanimously accepted and messengers were sent bearing letters to all the governments, except to the Soviet government of Belleville.

All the governments gave their refusal for fear of introducing foreign elements into their territories, explaining their positions by their inability to feed any new arrivals, on account of their low food supplies. ("We have enough of our own mouths to feed.")

In a final spasm of self-preservation, one policeman's motion was accepted: a random civilian was to be forced to proclaim himself dictator of Île de la Cité. A manhunt was hastily organized.

After a fruitless half-hour search, a patrol showed up at the end of a street carrying a strange, paralyzed old man. The old man displayed sure signs of terror. When he was carried into the prefecture, he began to cry and tried to tear himself free — ineffectively, of course.

In the prefecture's office, a delegate of the police informed him that he was now the dictator, and as such, he ought to give out a few decrees to restore the notion of lawful authority.

The old man sat apathetically in his armchair, not responding in the slightest to the honors and power bestowed upon him. They tried to elucidate the matter in the simplest terms possible. In vain. As it turned out, he was deaf.

They finally managed to get through to him in writing. The head office put together a proclamation, which the old man, after a great deal of hesitation and with a revolver put to his head, finally decided to sign.

An hour later, the first proclamation of the new dictator appeared on the walls of Île de la Cité. The new dictator proclaimed he was seizing power over Île de la Cité, establishing his jurisdiction over the territory. Anyone who dared oppose the power of the new dictator would be held in contempt of the law and would be subjected to the most severe persecution. The proclamation was signed: Mathurin Dupont.

On that day the island breathed a collective sigh of relief. The institution of the police, as such, had been saved. The elated policemen jauntily stamped their feet, ringing their heels against the asphalt, as if to confirm their own irrefutable realness.

Unemployment was not eradicated, however, with the release of the proclamation. No one had any intention of acting against the authority of the new dictator, and thus the notion of lawbreaking remained, for this new state, in the realm of pure theory.

After a few days had passed, the old man saw that no one was doing him any harm. He became more talkative and could even be persuaded to have a closer look into state affairs.

The first self-motivated proclamation of the new dictator was to hold a great parade on the square in front of the prefecture. Overjoyed by these vital signs from their dictator, the policemen got in file with verve and enthusiasm. From high up on his balcony, the dictator greeted the review, clapping his hands in delight.

After this first show of life, however, he fell back into his old apathy.

On the third day, the head office informed the dictator in his morning report, after the conventional assurances that peace was reigning in the state and that there had been no incidents of crime, that a new definition of "lawbreaking" was urgently required, along with the designation of a few lawbreakers, because without said lawbreakers the police were starting to entertain doubts as to their reality.

In response to the report, the old man unexpectedly became animated and, for the first time, requested pen and paper of his own accord.

Half an hour later a decree appeared on the walls of the Cité, generating extraordinary excitement on the sleepy little island. By force of this decree, all the island's blond inhabitants were declared enemies of the state, as opposed to the law-abiding citizens — those with dark hair. The lawful cadre of the police force was ordered to liquidate the new criminals as quickly as possible, and be none too scrupulous about the methods they employed.

By that evening Île de la Cité was back in fine form. Armed punitive patrols left one after another from the gates of the prefecture and vanished into the dark alleyways. The blond offenders were barricaded inside their dwellings. The roundup lasted three days, and in some places bloody skirmishes broke out. By the end of the third day the wrongdoers had been flushed out and put under arrest. Peace reigned once more on Île de la Cité.

Exhausted from this considerable burst of energy, the dictator fell once more into such a state of apathy he could not even be forced to read the daily reports.

In concluding the above summary of events, we feel compelled to express our doubts as to whether the resourceful little island would have succeeded in rescuing the indubitably useful institution of the police had the somnolent dictator not been relieved by the equally somnolent, but more reliable, plague.

VI

IN THE CHILLY CONFERENCE ROOM OF THE INSTITUTE, at a gigantic table covered with a green tablecloth and stacked with reams of paper, P'an Tsiang-kuei sat in a presidential armchair, dressed in gray gloves and a scarf around his neck (to ensure that only the smallest surface area of skin came in direct contact with the pestilential air).

On either side of the table two stenographers simultaneously tapped out the texts of the two circulars he was dictating. The telephone on the table punctuated his work every other minute with the sharp lament of its ring, the black barrel of its receiver spitting out reports from various parts of the state.

The reports were seldom comforting. In spite of the extreme precautions, the plague was spreading slowly but surely across the newly founded state. P'an Tsiang-kuei decided to deal with it Asian style.

On the fourth day of the new republic's existence a decree appeared on the walls of houses; the words were alarmingly frank. Contending that the plague in its currently rampant form had in practice proven incurable, and that those infected with it, being artificially sustained, were only spreading the epidemic, the decree declared that henceforth all those showing signs of infection would be subject to immediate execution. Healthy citizens were obliged to report every case of illness they came across, without fail. Those found guilty of concealing plague victims would likewise be shot.

The laconic voice over the telephone constantly reported new executions. The plague met the challenge. Bets were placed on the baize table, though it was orders, not cards, that were dropped. Sunk in his high-backed armchair, P'an Tsiang-kuei put the zigzag of his name on decree after decree, as if tossing down trump cards. From somewhere afar, through the tube of the telephone receiver, his opponent responded with new casualty figures.

Having dictated all the circulars, P'an Tsiang-kuei dismissed both stenographers with a wave of his hand and was left alone in the thickening gloom. Worn out from the lopsided and sleepless struggle, his mind demanded rest. The telephone coughed up another tally of executions. P'an Tsiang-kuei angrily flung down the receiver, slamming it onto the table. Its helpless mouth gave a vain, spiteful hiss.

P'an Tsiang-kuei suddenly needed air. He'd been nailed to his chair and hadn't left the room for three days. Pulling his cap down over his eyes, he locked the door behind him and ran quickly down the wide stone steps to the street, past the erect, Asian guards.

The streets were deserted. Solitary Chinese slipped here and there through the narrow, empty roads.

Walking down familiar streets, P'an arrived at the Luxembourg Gardens, which had been turned into the state crematorium. He was greeted by the dry crack of a salvo from somewhere deep below. P'an frowned and walked faster.

By a strange ricochet of associations the professor suddenly popped into his head, and a rare smile formed on his lips.

On the night of the coup the professor, as the only white man, was arrested by special decree, interned in one of the palaces of the Latin Quarter and kept in the strictest isolation.

The palace had been equipped with a model laboratory, where a dozen Chinese bacteriology assistants and students labored around the clock under the professor's personal direction to find the grail of the vaccine to immunize against the murderous disease.

He had to confess that the professor had been diligent, working day and night without rest. Caught up in dicing with the relentless plague, his academic pride had been piqued. Though reluctant at first, each new failure spurred him on, and he vowed that he would triumph over this insidious microbe that had thwarted his academic ambitions and scoffed at the power of modern science. The more his attempts failed, the more obstinate the professor became in his impervious resistance. In the end, he had almost stopped sleeping entirely. He spent every moment in the laboratory, and stubbornly refused to eat unless force-fed. Shut up among his microscopes, test tubes, and retorts, drawn and yellow from the sleepless nights and exhaustion, his beard disheveled and wild, he resembled a medieval alchemist obsessed with discovering the philosopher's stone, undeterred by any number of failures.

Ten days after the coup, P'an Tsiang-kuei visited the professor in his new apartment to ask if he needed anything. He found the professor feverishly shuffling test tubes and hovering over a microscope.

"I shall kill that cursed bacteria," he cried, shaking a test tube under the light. "Swear to me, though, that the vaccine I discover will not be used only for the yellow districts, that you will distribute it to the white ones as well. I have no intention of rescuing only the Asians from death and leaving my white brethren to their doom."

"If that's your only concern, you can rest easy," P'an Tsiang-kuei responded with a smile. "Though not every white district will benefit from the vaccine, it will certainly be shared with the most populous one: the workers' district of Belleville. *À propos*, in case you haven't heard, I might inform you that the workers' districts of Paris — Belleville and Ménilmontant with its outlying boroughs — have recently separated from the rest of the city to create an independent Soviet workers' republic. At present they have laboratories every bit as good as our own, where your colleagues are working to eradicate our common enemy. I suspect that information on their progress should interest you and that a mutual exchange of observations would not go unappreciated on either side. I have managed — at no small expense, I admit — to establish telephone contact with them. We had to run wires through all the districts in-between, which was no mean feat given Paris's present fragmentation into independent states. We struck upon the idea of using the metro tunnels. This evening we'll give you a telephone that will connect you to the Belleville Republic's laboratory."

The professor could not contain his delight:

"Incredible! That's a brilliant idea! It will take a huge load off our work. If they have a well-equipped laboratory, we'll be able to carry out simultaneous experiments. This will definitely speed up the results of my work. Yes, an excellent idea indeed."

"Any other requests?"

"Of course. Please order the radio to be removed. The assistants can listen to the news, if it interests them, in some other room. I haven't the presence of mind for it right now. It distracts me from my work."

"As you wish."

They shook hands like two old friends.

Going downstairs to the exit, P'an Tsiang-kuei bumped into an assistant, a small, chubby-cheeked Japanese man. They had once been friends at the Sorbonne. The small Japanese, spruce and fastidious in his grooming, not a speck of dust on his clothing, always reminded him of a carefully polished trinket.

The Japanese man was apparently waiting especially for him. P'an Tsiang-kuei was struck by his pale resolve, the determination with which he barred the way.

"What's wrong? Do you have something to tell me?"

"I must ask you for a great request, an enormous request . . . ," the Japanese man mouthed through his thin, strangely out-of-sync lips, and those lips suddenly quivered, dove, and fastened themselves to P'an Tsiang-kuei's bony, coarse hand.

P'an Tsiang-kuei tore his hand away in astonishment.

"Have you gone mad? What's going on?"

"I must ask you for a great request, an enormous request . . . ," the assistant repeated, quickly chewing his words and slicing each one with his white buck teeth. "I'm sequestered here in total isolation. I'm allowed no contact with anyone. I got a call today from the city . . . My wife is ill. Pains. It might not be the plague at all. In fact, it definitely isn't. She must have eaten something rotten. Her neighbors informed on her. She's been taken to the barracks. She'll be shot this evening at eight o'clock. You understand? This evening . . . If we could wait even just till tomorrow. We're testing a new vaccine. The results will be in tomorrow. Everything seems to point to her testing positive. Tomorrow the plague may be curable. You understand? You can't kill her today, not under these circumstances. Anyway, it might not be the plague at all. The first symptoms can be misleading. It might be a simple stomach flu. We have to wait it out, do some tests. Isolate her for a few days. Isolation won't put anyone else at risk. The execution just needs to be suspended. Your order by telephone . . . You understand, comrade . . . Her name is . . ."

P'an Tsiang-kuei stared at the assistant with surprise.

"I don't understand you, comrade. Or rather, I believe I'm starting to understand you," he said roughly. "Unless I'm mistaken, you want my support. You're asking that we break the rules of our struggle with the plague in order to prolong the life of an infected individual by a few days, owing to the fact that this individual is your wife. You've forgotten, it would appear, that every day dozens of our best workers are dying, and that only through implementing this law to execute the infected have we managed to decrease the mortality rate by over 50%."

The Japanese man quickly batted his eyelids.

". . . We're testing a new vaccine . . . The results will be in tomorrow . . . Tomorrow the plague may turn out to be curable . . . Stop the whole firing squad today . . . If the experiment fails, you can execute them tomorrow. But maybe we can save them? And I'm certain my wife doesn't have the plague . . . Just a simple stomach flu . . . If she were to be isolated . . ."

P'an Tsiang-kuei abruptly cut him off:

"Always the same old song and dance. If your wife wasn't infected before, she certainly is now. No one leaves the plague barracks. Anyway, we can't make exceptions and foster plague-sowers. None of the serums have had any effect so far. We have no reason to assume this one will fare any better. We would have to put off the executions from one day to the next and house the infected, and we wouldn't be able to keep them from coming in contact with the healthy, because we don't have the sanitation staff to deal with that. In other words, it would mean hiking the mortality rate back up to the level it was before. I'm surprised at you, comrade."

The lips of the small Japanese man silently quivered.

P'an Tsiang-kuei ran downstairs and through the gate. On the street the little squeaky-clean Japanese man appeared once more before his mind's eye, the corners of his ashen lips twitching.

"Infect everybody for the sake of one skirt!" he thought bitterly. "People like that ought to be shot . . ."

But a moment later, the whole incident was already forgotten.

Two weeks went by. Caught up in the affairs of the miniature republic, P'an Tsiang-kuei had not checked in on the professor until now. He had been receiving detailed daily telephone bulletins on the old scholar's work, which had stubbornly refused to produce the desired results, in spite of his tireless efforts. Seizing a free moment, P'an Tsiang-kuei decided to pay him a visit.

His trained legs led him down the crepuscular alleys to Panthéon Square. The window on the third floor of house No. 17 was illuminated, as usual, with the white of a closed shutter.

Rain suddenly started to fall, veiling the homes with curtains of glass beads. P'an Tsiang-kuei went to the open Panthéon to wait it out.

The Panthéon was empty; a chilly silence blew from its high cupola and from its shadowy naves. The empty ticket office was aglow, as always, with its uninviting inscription: "Entry 2 francs." His lonely footsteps on the stone floor mimicked themselves with long, reverberating echoes. From all sides, famous figures stared at the arrival with eyes of solid white . . .

•

The rain had long ceased when P'an Tsiang-kuei reappeared in the entrance to the Panthéon.

Meanwhile, a group of Chinese men had gathered about the railings, greeting the dictator with shouts of enthusiasm. Bowing awkwardly, P'an Tsiang-kuei flipped up the collar of his trench coat and quickly vanished in the twisting alleyways.

Dusk had already fallen; the decks of the sidewalks were shrouded in darkness, and Chinese lamplighters were hastily hanging the intricate balls of paper lanterns, multicolored ornaments from some phantasmagoric Venetian night.

A nauseating, bathhouse air had settled in the professor's laboratory, turning all the contours into wavy double lines. The drowsy, languid assistants staggered around like flies under a thick bell jar.

The wild-haired professor was pouring a cloudy whitish fluid from retort to retort, mixing it with substances in a row of test tubes, preparing a reaction. He mumbled incoherently in response to P'an Tsiang-kuei's questions, impatiently shooing him away. There was no getting a word out of him.

The assistants, insensible from exhaustion, appeared not to understand his questions. Their answers were delayed and incoherent.

Having made his rounds, P'an Tsiang-kuei cast a glance at his watch. It was seven o'clock, time for his evening report. P'an Tsiang-kuei hurried toward the exit. At the door he collided with a small assistant in a white smock. Glass shattered. Liquid sprayed across P'an Tsiang-kuei's face and clothing. The little assistant apologized. P'an Tsiang-kuei stared at the neck of the smashed beaker still in the fingers of the assistant, and lifted his gaze to the pale smear of the face before him. It seemed somehow familiar. He tried to jog his memory. The narrow quivering lips. The little squeaky-clean Japanese. He had pleaded for his wife's reprieve . . .

The Japanese man apologized profusely. P'an Tsiang-kuei looked him sharply in the eye and met a pair of cold, piercing pupils. For an instant he thought he saw taunting sparks inside them. Without another word, he turned on his heel and vanished into the depths of the laboratory. He took a large bottle of corrosive sublimate solution from the medicine cabinet, splashed it over his clothing, and washed his face and hands thoroughly. Then, without so much as noting the assistant still muttering apologies, he quickly ran downstairs.

Returning to the institute, P'an Tsiang-kuei busied himself with taking reports and issuing orders for the following day. The hands of the big clock were steadily approaching twelve when the dictator dismissed the last courier and turned off the harsh lamplight.

By the wall in the corner of the room there was a narrow cot that had been brought there three days earlier and for three days had remained untouched. P'an Tsiang-kuei made it himself and began to undress for the first time in a while. When he was completely naked, he carefully slathered his entire body in a transparent solution. Arriving at his armpits, he stopped a moment and, lifting an arm, examined them carefully. His underarm glands seemed somewhat swollen. He inspected them scrupulously with his fingers.

"Autosuggestion . . . ," he mumbled tonelessly, and throwing on a nightshirt, he dove quickly under the covers. He fell asleep in an instant.

That night he dreamt of streets decorated with flags, of bands and columns of Chinese armies marching down the streets. The Panthéon was hung with a red flag and stood wide open. A chain of flower-strewn trucks was parked by its front railing. On either side of the entrance two lanes of soldiers stiffly stood at arms. P'an Tsiang-kuei was surprised and asked a sentry why the ceremony was being held.

"We're transporting them to China," the soldier responded.

Only now did P'an Tsiang-kuei recall why he had come here, and cutting through the nave he ran quickly down to the crypts.

The crypts were open, and a festive crowd was crammed inside. Squeezing through, P'an Tsiang-kuei spotted a platoon of soldiers prying open Rousseau's sarcophagus with gigantic iron pickaxes. The sarcophagus refused to budge, as though nailed to the ground.

"One more time! All together! On-n-n-ne!"

Not an inch.

P'an Tsiang-kuei shoved aside the nearest soldier and leaned on the pickax with his whole stomach.

"Now! On my command! On-n-n-ne!"

Not an inch.

"On-n-n-ne!"

Again, nothing.

"On-n-n-ne!"

Beads of sweat appeared on his forehead.

The image vanished. For a long moment P'an Tsiang-kuei could not figure out what was happening, where he was, smothered in an impenetrable darkness. The first sensation, thrashing like a fish upon the glassy surface of his consciousness, was a sharp pain in the pit of his stomach. Wait a minute . . . What was that? Ah yes! He'd been leaning on the pickax with his stomach. When had that been, and where?

The pain was getting more unbearable with every passing moment. It helped to ground his thoughts in space. Darkness. Night. The bed. In the institute. Pains. Could it be?? . . .

The pain became inhuman. P'an Tsiang-kuei jumped barefoot onto the cool floor, groped for the light switch and flipped it. The light burst on, carving out a green tablecloth covered in papers, high-backed armchairs, a ceiling, the night.

The savage pain in his stomach would not give. P'an Tsiang-kuei staggered to the window where he'd left a bottle of cognac, and he drained its burning contents in one swig. The cognac swished in his gut in a fiery stream, killing the pain for a second.

P'an Tsiang-kuei went back to bed with slow, hesitant steps. His thoughts took shortcuts, interrupted themselves, like images in an old, damaged film. The sharp pain in his stomach declared itself once more.

P'an Tsiang-kuei stretched out stiffly and tried to rein in his thoughts. The cognac frothed under his skull, warmly splashing in rhythmical waves. His belly, a sack full of pain, dropped out somewhere, as if his whole body had been pulled past all limits, the space between his head and his hips stretching several yards. Cool waves of pain undulated rhythmically upward, one after another. His tired brain projected images dissolving and laboriously reconstructed onto the screen of his shut eyelids. For a moment he dozed off.

Half asleep, the real contours of objects seemed to blur and arch, creating fluctuating landscapes from new combinations of the same lines.

A chandelier of a thousand flames is now a gigantic, scorching ball-shaped sun, heavy as a drop of molten metal, ready to fall to Earth at any moment, burning it to cinders. A row of benches moments ago is now the furrows of a thousand fields languidly sprawled in the sunshine, peeking out from the murky enamel of the water. Up to their knees in the water, small, shriveled, Chinese in rags plant rice. As far as the eye can see, nothing but water, fields, and hunchbacked people stunted by centuries of labor, under the molten drop of sun, on the verge of collapse.

An enormous, painful wave of all-consuming love crawls slowly from the stomach to the larynx, a flush of warm, clustered tears. P'an Tsiang-kuei feels that at any moment he will throw himself face first into the drenched clay of the fields to kiss the white, sweat-stained grains of life-giving rice with burning, bitter lips, he will grasp the tiny, wrinkled face of a stooped female villager and press it to his heart with a sob.

Suddenly the image starts to glisten and fade, as if seen through tears. In the foreground a pair of monstrous feet flash by, hovering in the air, the whirl of spokes on a wagon nearby.

Sharp, searing pain, and darkness. The red-hot sundrop has fallen. Gray, biting smoke coats everything with a soft, predatory caress. White, grimacing human faces dangle in the lines of smoke, as though in nooses.

Whose is that swollen female face, her eyes wide with childlike fear? Such precious, familiar features. Chen! My dear! The words are inaudible, but a phrase he's heard somewhere perceptibly quivers in the sketch of her mouth: "I am so afraid to die!"

The smoke slowly dissipates, unveiling the red skeletons of buildings. Nanjing!

A flame devours the Chinese district and stops as though spellbound before the iron grille guarding the British Concession. From behind the grille the puffy white face of a pockmarked foreman gives a revolting grimace and lolls out its tongue over the smoking maw of a machine gun.

"Follow me!" cries P'an Tsiang-kuei to the crowd crushing behind him, crossing the square between him and the grille with giant leaps.

Suddenly he looks around. The square is empty, no one is standing behind him. The pockmarked face behind the grille bares its teeth to jeer over the whitish viper of smoke slithering from the barrel of the machine gun. The hideous pain in his belly is snapping his gut strings.

"Right in the stomach!" whispers P'an Tsiang-kuei, vainly struggling to break into a run.

The pain twisted in his stomach like a worm. The smoke had fallen. The chandelier burned bright on the ceiling. The green tablecloth. The telephone. A groan was heard squirming in the corners of the large, well-lit room.

"Who's that groaning in here?"

P'an Tsiang-kuei sat up on the cot. He noticed the groan was coming from him. The gnawing pain in his belly thrashed like a wounded bird.

"Ah, so this is the end?"

P'an Tsiang-kuei repeated the word twice out loud, unable to nail its significance. He began mechanically to dress, hissing from pain. He took a long time getting dressed, pausing to catch his breath after particularly sharp paroxysms. His clothes were still moist. P'an Tsiang-kuei suddenly froze in mid-movement. A vivid thought rewound itself, gathering up the scattered beads of the facts on a string. The stains from the corrosive sublimate. The broken beaker. The small Japanese assistant. Those taunting sparks. On his hand — the strange touch of dry, trembling lips . . .

P'an Tsiang-kuei buttoned his coat. He automatically pulled on his gray gloves and wrapped his scarf around his neck (to ensure that only the smallest surface area of skin came in direct contact with the pestilential air).

Now dressed, P'an Tsiang-kuei dragged himself to the table and searched for a pen and paper. The pain crawled through his gullet. It had already filled his whole mouth, and his chattering teeth helplessly sounded the alarm. He had to hold his jaw in place with his left hand to write straight. He composed two letters, slid them carefully into an envelope, and addressed it.

Only when he had finished did he pull a large revolver from the drawer, a comrade from his days as a Red in Nanjing, and sat himself in the armchair. The telephone rang on the table.

P'an Tsiang-kuei put down the revolver and picked up the receiver. For a moment he couldn't recognize the terrified voice on the other end of the line. It was the assistant who ran the professor's workshop.

"Tonight — unexpectedly — there were no symptoms — the professor — died. He hadn't slept — in the evening. — The nightshift assistants — found . . ."

P'an Tsiang-kuei hung up. A thin smile fought to the surface of his pale, chewed lips. P'an Tsiang-kuei put the black revolver back into the drawer and took a small, polished six-shooter from another drawer. He put the barrel in his mouth, his smile still fixed in place. His teeth vibrated like a tuning fork, rattling against the cool steel. The gun was locked firmly between his teeth, and the viewfinder found a place in his mouth that seemed specially carved for it.

The shot reverberated against the astonished, solemn walls of the empty, well-lit room, producing a hollow, uneasy echo.

•

P'an Tsiang-kuei was buried with military honors, with no music, to the rattle of snare drums. Thirty-three drummers played a lonely, ominous solo, like an alarm of drums raised suddenly amid the funereal silence of a circus orchestra hushed at the moment of the *salto mortale*, a roll of flashing sticks tacking a long grave path before him. By special decree of the national government his body was exempted from the cremation directive and temporarily lay in state in the Panthéon.

In the middle of the main nave, in a sculpted wooden crate covered with the red standard, he was placed alone behind a bolted iron gate. The solid white eyes of the marble figures gaped as if in surprise at the odd intruder.

In the simple wooden coffin, on a simple sackcloth pillow, P'an Tsiang-kuei lay prone and motionless in his gray gloves and scarf wrapped tight around his neck, as if to ensure that only the smallest surface area of his pestilential skin came in direct contact with the clear, life-giving air.

VII

BY A STRANGE TURN OF EVENTS, it was not only the Chinese Republic that was unusually animated that morning. Two districts west, across the Seine, the Russian monarchy of Passy was preparing to receive the Bolsheviks who were finally being handed over by the French government. They brought planks and hastily slapped together an improvised platform on Trocadero Square. In compliance with the resolution of the provisional government, the Bolsheviks' trial was to take place in public, in the open air. The whole Russian émigré community was to serve as the prosecution. Tables and benches had been haphazardly set out.

Excited and impatient crowds had been gathering on the road leading to Jena Bridge since eight o'clock that morning. Mainly women. Skipping their morning toilettes, chubby bejeweled women seldom seen in public before noontime took to the streets in a feverish haste, three hours before the designated time. Powdering their rosy faces, the women passed the time chatting.

They all brought up the same subject: How many were they bringing, and were they young or old? Dozens of names passed from mouth to mouth. As the words flew, they provided a wealth of commentaries on the fantastical bloodthirstiness or atrocities of this or that Bolshevik. The fortieth lady in the line said that the first secretary of the diplomatic mission had murdered three thousand families single-handedly. He had interrogated them in his own apartment, at a table set with gourmet dishes, and had plucked out the eyes of the more stubborn detainees with toothpicks.

A stalwart, bearded pope was giving his hungry listeners a hundredth litany on the sacrilegious desecration of the Church of St. Mitrofan: the sacred relics of the martyr had been tossed into a cesspit, and the church turned into a hospital — the Bolshevik Sisterhood was sullying the holy place with iniquity.

All the requisitioned furniture, the confiscated valuables, the shop-worn injustices and grudges were dragged out into the light of day from the bottoms of émigré trunks, from under countless layers of mothballs, and they bared their decayed teeth with an undiluted craving for revenge, for warm, frothy blood. Like a cat awaiting a mouse's release from a trap, the mob licked its paws in keen impatience.

Eleven o'clock and still no cars were visible on the French side. Exhausted from quelling its appetite, the mob started to grow restless.

At three minutes to twelve a large truck finally appeared on the other side of the bridge, with two motorcycles out front. The truck slowly drove onto the bridge, then halted midway. Two French officers hopped off their motorcycles and approached the waiting Russian officers. A lively conversation ensued. The crowd rippled restlessly. All eyes were turned toward the truck on the bridge. From their vantage point, they could not make out who was in it.

The conversation on the bridge dragged on. The officers made ani-mated gestures, spreading their arms. Finally, the Frenchmen saluted and got back onto their motorcycles. The truck slowly rolled across the bridge toward the Russian side. The crowd prickled with excitement.

When the truck drove off the bridge and onto the bank, a hollow roar of helpless fury tore out of everyone's mouths. The Red Cross flag fluttered at the front of the vehicle.

A tight circle surrounded it. Now everything was clearly visible. Over a dozen people lay side by side on the bed of the truck, their faces twisted and ashen, writhing like worms. They were infected.

Within a second, space was cleared. The crowd leapt back onto the sidewalks in fearful panic.

A few minutes later the crowd slowly and reluctantly dispersed and went home, gesticulating and swearing like an audience after the illness of a star actor causes the cancellation of a gala performance.

In the deserted square stood the lone, unwanted, black truck, filled with stifled moans and writhing.

•

Captain Solomin returned home as gloomy as a tenor booed off stage. The disappointment was too great to ignore; it threw a wrench into his daily routine.

It seemed to him he had been waiting years on end for this moment. He had wrestled with humiliation and adversity, he had dreamed about it at night, and here at the last moment fate had stuck out its tongue.

The handsome captain flew into a helpless rage, lost his composure, and snorted like a horse.

"Bastards!" he snarled through clenched teeth. "The frogs! They consciously postponed matters from one day to the next, extorting our money and waiting till they all croaked."

At that moment he hated the French as much as he did the others. They had made a real ass out of him. In one fell swoop they'd taken back all the tips he'd so painfully squeezed out of them, all their *sous*.

A hollow rage seethed on the Primus stove of his heart, like milk about to boil over and smother everything in a scalding white lava.

Everything suddenly lost its value and significance, necessity evaporated. His one hope of compensation for the long years of contempt, for his wasted life and derailed career, had failed. Nothing was left. He walked with leaden feet, not knowing where or why.

The dark, empty room swam in a hospital tedium, and the furniture with its cloth covers, like invalids dressed in gray, oversized operating gowns, were nagging reminders of sickness, of death, of a swampy hole in the damp ground. He wanted to vent his anger on somebody, even on the furniture in operating gowns, to gut the twisted springs from the bursting bellies of the armchairs with one thrust of his rusty saber, as never before — in this lazaretto far from the Reds.

An orderly happened to be tiptoeing by with a pillow. He kicked the boy in the stomach with a polished boot, sending him flying through the air and landing in the doorway. The boy's stunned gaze licked the shiny boot, and then he silently disappeared through the door.

He had to get out!

Slamming the door behind him, Solomin went out into the street. Desolate and hollow inside, he aimlessly wandered through the alleyways and squares as the night drew on. Hunger shook him from his numb stupor.

He went into a small corner bar. As soon as he entered he was greeted by a storm of voices:

"Solomin!"

Some of the boys were sitting at a corner table. Officers. Glowing red faces. They thronged around to exchange kisses. The rows of empty bottles explained the warmth of the shared affection. They pulled him over to the table and poured him a brimming glass:

"Drink!"

He drank heartily, without batting an eye.

Fifteen minutes later, to the accompaniment of a scratchy "Volga" from the gramophone, the clink of glasses and the gurgle of vodka, he went to pieces on the shoulder of a red mustached lieutenant — he wept on his prickly epaulette, soaked his uniform jacket with tears, his moist face sticking to its folds like a soggy blini.

The red-haired lieutenant leaned back his head with motherly tenderness and poured a glass of spirits down his throat.

•

How and when Solomin eventually found himself back on the street — he was not sure. Outside it was black as pitch. Struggling to stay upright, he groped with his hands along the walls. When he got under a streetlamp he noticed something sticking out of his pocket: an open bottle of cognac. The hiccups were killing him. He took a swig and, recorking the bottle, marched on. The alleyways twisted into bizarre figure eights beneath his feet.

When he finally stumbled into a square, it seemed he had emerged from a thick woods and into a clearing. Tripping and stumbling on his feet, he made his way across it.

But having walked only a dozen steps, he tripped over something. Under closer observation, it turned out to be a truck with double tires.

Solomin stopped, trying to recall something. Like a fisherman stooped over the pond of memory he clumsily tossed in his line, and a memory flapped in the clear water like a silver-scaled gudgeon: his dancing float partly vanished, then flashed into sight once more, shattering the water as it bobbed to the surface.

Suddenly, he heard a strangled moan from the truck bed above. The float ducked into the water like a falling stone, and at the end of his rod glimmered a massive, dazzling fish — it was too much: his whole life hung on that memory like a lead weight.

"Ah-ha, you little scamps! . . ." murmured Solomin. "Still breathing, are you? Well, well, I see you won't be leaving this vale without my help . . ."

The drunken captain started clambering up, his eyes bloodshot and cloudy. Progress was slow. His stumbly legs slipped off the spokes, his hands felt wooden as they struggled to heft up his inert body. Finally, with a mighty thrust, he hurled himself over the frame and smacked his face down into something soft. He pulled himself up and sat down heavily on a flattened heap.

A molting moon peeked out from behind the clouds. In the smoky light Solomin made out the bottom of the bed covered with a pile of black, stiffened bodies. From somewhere in the corner he heard the same groan.

Captain Solomin turned toward it, his swollen fingers pulling a revolver from its holster.

A man in his twenties lay supine with his head propped against the frame, sweat streaming down his bright, symmetrical face like tears shed beneath the surface of the skin. Clumps of blond hair clung to his brow in disarray. A groan escaped from his blackened lips like smoke through cracks in a clay roof.

Captain Solomin bent low over the man and, gripping him by the lapels, picked him up and set him upright.

"Ah-ha! That's a sad tune you're singing, brother. No playing dead, now. I've come to pay a visit. Let's chat."

Propped up helplessly like a rag doll, the man opened his dull eyes and hoarsely whispered:

"Drink!"

"Want to drink?" mimicked Solomin. "Well all right, suck on this!" he said, shoving the barrel of the gun into the sick man's mouth.

The sick man began greedily sucking on the cool barrel of the gun with his burning hot lips.

"Is it good?" croaked the captain. "How's it taste? Careful you don't swallow a bullet — you could choke on it."

His free finger groped in the dark for the trigger.

"You'll choke on it, I swear to God!" His finger found the trigger and stopped in thought. Solomin pulled the barrel out of the sick man's mouth and slid the revolver back into the holster.

"Oh no, brother! It's not so easy! You're too smart. That's how anyone would want it. Kill you off? What for? You wouldn't even feel it. You'd be grateful. No idiots here. Wait, first we should wake you up — we'll have a little chat. You want a drink? Why not? I've got something here for you. Look how kindhearted I am. That'll have you on your feet in a jiffy."

The captain pulled a bottle of cognac from his jacket, uncorked it, and put the neck into the sick man's mouth.

"Drink all that pours in, my dear boy. It's on the house! That's none of your Soviet ditchwater. It's Martel! Three stars! Divine, isn't it?"

The sick man greedily sucked the sparkling liquid from the bottle.

"You're no slouch! That's it, just a tad more. Don't be shy. You'll be shipshape in no time."

Solomin tilted the flask. The liquid flowed over the sick man's lips, and he choked with a violent convulsion. He coughed for a long time, unable to catch his breath. When he finally settled down, he turned to Solomin with keen eyes that shone with consciousness. His breathing was staggered and rapid.

Captain Solomin took his time recorking the bottle and slipping it back into his pocket, then took his revolver out again.

"There. Now at least you're looking at me like a human being. Now we can talk."

The captain sat himself comfortably on something that resembled a human back and, fiddling with his gun, began his interrogations:

"What's your name?"

The sick man kept staring at him ravenously, like a fish thrown ashore and gasping for air.

"Where am I?" he finally spluttered.

"In Paris, son, in Paris. Not in Moscow. In Paris, among the Whites. Before the Imperial Tribunal of the Russian Empire. Now you get the picture?"

The sick man squeezed his eyes shut, evidently collecting his thoughts. After a long pause he quietly asked, with an expression of mortal fatigue:

"What do you want from me? I've got the plague."

"That, brother, has got nothing to do with it. You think that just because you've got the plague there's no such thing as justice, you lowlife. Nonsense! You're going to dance just a few steps, brother, before we swing open the pearly gates. If you don't answer my questions — the barrel goes between your teeth. If you don't want your face all asplatter when you meet your Lenin, answer politely and succinctly. Understood?"

The sick man stared at Solomin in silence.

"What's your name?"

"Solomin."

"Trying to play jokes, brother? Want a laugh or two? I'll show you jokes, you son of a bitch! How do you know my name? Speak when I ask you a question! How do you know me?"

"I don't know you at all and I don't want to know you."

"How do you know my last name?"

"I don't know your last name."

"You said it a moment ago: Solomin."

"My name is Solomin."

The captain lowered his gun in astonishment.

"What do you mean, you weasel, that your name is Solomin? My name is Solomin."

The sick man furrowed his brow and took a careful look at the captain.

"Your name is Solomin?"

His eyebrows flew up like startled birds.

"What's your first name?"

The captain gave him a powerful slap with a stiff hand, with all his might.

"How dare you start asking *me* questions, you motherfucker? Who's the defendant here, you or I?"

The sick man covered his face with one hand.

"You're stinking drunk and you've clearly forgotten your own last name. My name is Sergei Alexandrovich Solomin. I'm the USSR's Deputy Secretary in Paris. You wanted to know whom you had the pleasure of meeting — there you are. Now go ahead and shoot. I'm not saying another word."

But Captain Solomin did not lift his revolver. He stared at the sick man, his eyes popping out of his skull. All the alcohol suddenly drained from him like a shed skin, and he sat there sober, his mouth hanging open, unable to utter a single word. The name clawed its way up out of the depths of his throat and fell with a clatter:

"Sergei!"

The sick man observed him in mute astonishment.

"Hang on, that's impossible," mumbled the captain. "That's impossible. I am Boris Alexandrovich Solomin, son of Colonel Alexander Vasilyevich Solomin."

The two strangers stared at each other for a long moment in bafflement.

"Brother . . . ," breathed the sick man, straining to lean on the frame. A long silence.

"I thought you died long ago," the sick man said finally. "Mama told me you ran off with the Whites. For so many years we heard nothing from you. It never occurred to me that you might be in Paris . . . An officer in the farcical White Army . . ."

He fell silent, slumping over from exhaustion.

Captain Solomin absently wiped the sweat from his face with a stiff and fumbling hand, as if wiping away the residue of the steaming alcohol.

"I didn't recognize you," he said after a long moment. "How could I? When I left Moscow you were maybe thirteen years old. Well, and now it's crazy to think . . . It didn't occur to me that you were alive, an adult, that you had sold yourself to the Bolsheviks. And is Mama alive? They haven't murdered her?"

"Mama died this year, not long ago."

"And Yula, our sister? I heard rumors. That she married a Bolshevik. No doubt she's a Bolshevik herself. Bad seeds, the both of you."

"Yula is a model worker and her husband is a good worker, too, one of the first. She's lived through a lot, learned a lot. But why bother telling you, a White Guardist? You wouldn't understand anyway."

"Sure, go work for the oppressors — smart move. Not everyone would understand. Like how they shot Papa — you don't remember?

You were too young. You've forgotten. I'm sure Yula's forgotten. Your memory's a short one, boy."

"It's not short. If they had shot more 'papas' back then, we wouldn't have had to go through those three years of hardship."

"You parrot their jargon like an agitator at a rally. You forgot to add: 'They've drunk enough of our blood!' You've denied your own father. Gone to serve the brutes. For a sack of barley, for an allowance payment — to lick the hand of the Jew. And this is a Solomin! I shudder to think this is my brother: a villain, a Bolshevik."

"You sadden me, Boris," said Sergei softly. "We don't understand each other. We speak different languages. I never suspected that by coming to Paris I'd meet you in this émigré crowd. No doubt you've spent your time taxiing people around the amusement parks or waiting tables and scrounging for tips. Like everybody else. Bowing and scraping your life away. Without even a shred of dignity left to pop a bullet in your head, like a real officer. Eh, Boris?!"

Sergei's face suddenly contorted into a grimace of inhuman pain and went completely ashen. The sick man groaned, and his body quivered with quick jerks like a bow cracking under strain. Foam appeared on his lips.

Captain Solomin felt as though his hair were standing on end, sharp as needles, and his heart were like a ripe orange crushed in a fist, stinging painfully as it squirted through the fingers. He could not understand the source of this pain. His bulging eyes were riveted on the man writhing in convulsions, and he wanted to scream, but the scream was like an oversized cork jammed in tight, refusing to come out the narrow neck of his mouth. He grabbed the dying man's arms with his clammy hands and gave him a shake, choking:

"Sergei!"

He wanted to say something warm and tender, but searching feverishly through a pile of words he found nothing. His hands just convulsively clutched at thc withered, powerless arms.

Then suddenly it came to him in a flash — he took the flask of cognac from his pocket, uncorked it with his teeth, and, carefully propping the dying man's head with one hand, tipped the liquid into his mouth with the other. Sergei drank greedily, to the last drop. A surge of life tore through his body. A moment later, the sick man opened his eyes.

The captain felt a strange humming chaos in his head, and it was only from afar that he heard the incoherent mumbling of his own mouth:

"Wait . . . You can't do this . . . I'll take you home . . . We'll call a doctor . . . You can't . . ."

The sick man's lips twisted into a wan smile:

"What's that, Boris? You want to save a Bolshevik? A fine White officer you make. Anyway, it's too late. It's day three already. The end's on its way."

The captain bent over and stared into that face, suddenly so close. His pulse beat in his temples. From somewhere above his thoughts, a flash: So much like his mother! The nose, the mouth, the curve of his chin . . . He wanted to howl. A warm surge of tenderness crept from somewhere in his entrails up to his throat.

"It's blood I feel, blood . . ." he thought, trying to somehow justify the unfamiliar stream gurgling within him.

With a mind of its own, his hand crawled toward the pale head leaning on the frame. It rested on the forehead, then slid down the silky, sweat-drenched hair . . . This gesture held everything: his mother's cheek covered in tears when he left her for the last time, the years of bitter, icy solitude, with never a warm word, never a loved one, and the soured tenderness of his sore, aging, unclaimed body, saved for no one.

The dying man shut his eyes, and a smile again lit upon his lips:

"You think, Boris, that I'm scared to die at twenty-five? You're all torn up: so young, etc. Give it a rest! Go cry for yourself. People like us don't die. We've grafted all our roots onto the masses, onto the species. Our every fiber has grown into them. Those who weren't there to experience the first years of building with us will only envy us when their time is up . . ."

The sick man's shaking hands clutched at the captain's lapels, pulled him near, and began whispering into his face in a voice rasping and excited. His eyes glistened with fever.

"Do you understand, Boris, what it means to mold clay with your own two hands, to fire bricks for your own house, to clear a construction site, to pull floor after floor from the very earth? To build a new, solid, perfected life . . . To feel you're the core of a marvelous human avalanche that has torn free and is flying into the future . . . it smothers you, like snow, in a churning, grainy mass. You are its heart . . . a cell in its bloodstream, slipping from vein to vein. You scoff at the laws of physics: at the same time you are permeable, and you yourself can permeate with no loss of material contours . . . Oh, Boris! You could have had it as well, you also were given the rare, the inconceivable fortune of being born and of living in these times, and you gave it up, you preferred, like some blind mole, in your thick, crude stubbornness, to try to knock down what was spreading before your eyes, hoisted up by the girder of a million hands, in spite of all the moles in the world, until you were driven from your hole . . .

"Oh, Boris," he added after a brief pause, in a tired, stifled whisper, "how lonely, unwanted, and homeless you must feel, like a stray, mangy dog . . . How are *you* going to die, Boris?"

Sergei leaned on the truck bed, exhausted, and a thin stream of foam trickled from his mouth. His narrow, blackened lips twisted into a horseshoe of pain. His face, white and wrenched in agony, became tiny, almost childlike.

The captain felt the iron hand of an irresistible paternal tenderness turn him toward that face. What to do? Just let him die alone? Get him out of here! Away! Stay by his side! Don't leave him! His pale lips spoke, repeating incoherently:

"Sergei! It's not true! This can't be happening! Grab my neck. I'll take you from here. I'll carry you home. We'll call a doctor. You'll recover. We'll get out of here. We'll go together, to your people. I won't leave you alone. I'll go with you. You hear me, Sergei? We'll go together. I'm going to work with you. Sergei!"

A strange yellowish shadow began to envelop Sergei's face. It was his lips, just his lips that wheezed out:

"No Boris, it's too late. It's the end . . . It's you, you I feel sorry for. If you don't die — go back there. Work. Try to make up for things, reform yourself, start over. Reform yourself, like I did. Like Yula did . . . Wait . . . I have no right . . . But you'll redeem my sin with your life, your years, your work . . . Here, take my Soviet passport . . . You look like me . . . They won't notice . . . Use it to get to Moscow . . . Find Yula . . . She's a brave comrade . . . Yula will help you, she'll understand . . . Only, swear to me on the memory of our mother that you won't misuse it . . ."

"I swear," mumbled Boris.

"Good . . . Now go . . . Don't touch me . . . You'll get infected . . . Tru–"

A sudden convulsion jerked his body and tossed him onto his side. A milky film stretched across his open eyes.

The captain reached for his flask. He wanted to pour his brother some more. It was empty.

A slender thread of dun foam and blood escaped Sergei's mouth.

Solomin felt as though something inside of him, some string whose existence he'd never suspected, had suddenly stretched and then snapped for good. At once he felt voided, as if all the sawdust inside him had been shaken out. His dull, absent gaze studied the dead face, and his mother's nose, chin, and the horseshoe of the pain stricken mouth pointed at him. He mechanically bent over and kissed the lips. He felt the salty aftertaste of blood. He sat there stiff and inert, like a puppet of straw.

The moon peeked out, illuminating the truck bed. The fallen, lifeless hands of Captain Solomin. In one, a crumpled wad: a booklet. What's this? Ah, of course! The Soviet passport. Sergei had given it to him . . .

The captain brought it to his eyes. A little red book. Where could he have seen it before? Not so long ago . . . Ah yes, the Jew. The red stamp . . . If I don't die, I'll return to Russia. Reform myself. Replace Sergei. No. Too late. At this age people don't get reformed. Hell of a communist I'd make! Why did I lie to Sergei?

The captain knelt down, gingerly unbuttoned his brother's shirt, and placed the red booklet on the cold chest.

A vacuum rattled inside the truck, hollow like the tin casing of a transformer.

His hand stroked the barrel of his revolver that protruded obediently from the holster.

When the following morning the sanitary workers drove the black truck of corpses to the crematorium, they found the body of a White officer in uniform and epaulettes among the Bolshevik cadavers to be thrown into the ovens. An officer from Central Command recognized it as Captain Solomin.

An investigation only ascertained that on the tragic night in question Captain Solomin had left the restaurant in a state of severe intoxication, heading in an unknown direction.

On orders from Central Command, his body was cremated separately, with full military honors.

VIII

THE BLINDS WERE STILL DRAWN in Mr. David Lingslay's antique salon, and in the trembling twilight, against the backdrop of bright red wallpaper, the motionless, upright silhouettes of Rabbi Eliezer ben Zvi and his corpulent companion in American eyeglasses seemed like a pair of wax figures some pranksters had brought in from the Grévin Museum.

"May I help you, sirs?" David Lingslay asked his peculiar guests, fiddling with his necktie. "Unfortunately, I'm just rushing out the door to a meeting and have only ten minutes to spare."

The hunched man with the gray beard and the unsightly, shabby frock coat said something in Yiddish to the corpulent man in the horn-rimmed glasses. David Lingslay studied the delicate Semitic, patriarchal features of the man in the frock coat with curiosity. The round man in glasses, clearly brought along as translator, repeated in faultless English:

"Our business won't take too much of your time. Please have a seat and give us your full attention."

"Go ahead," responded David Lingslay, planting himself in an armchair.

The strangers exchanged a few words, after which the man in eyeglasses translated:

"Our business shall be brief. You may choose to go along with it or not, it's up to you. Before we speak of it, however, you must swear to us that not a single word of our conversation will go beyond the four walls of this room."

"I generally dislike secrets, particularly with strangers," Lingslay responded dryly. "But if it is so terribly important to you, I will give you my gentleman's word of honor that I will not mention our conversation to anyone."

"Literally to no one," emphasized the man in the eyeglasses. "It is of the utmost importance to us. Not even to your friend, Miss Dufayel."

Lingslay furrowed his brow:

"I see that you are splendidly informed on my private life," he said in an icy tone. "I'm starting to catch a whiff of blackmail in all this. I am not the slightest bit interested in your business, and I think it best if you both left my apartment, keeping your secret to yourselves."

The man in eyeglasses seemed not the slightest bit disconcerted.

"Our business is simple and should interest both you and ourselves. We have come here to ask: Would you perhaps like to leave Paris and make it back to America?"

Lingslay stared at the speaker in astonishment.

"What do you mean by that? Speak more clearly, please."

"I mean that we are capable of facilitating your escape from Paris and return to America in the immediate future," repeated the man in eyeglasses.

Mr. David Lingslay blinked in disbelief:

"And how, if I may ask, do you plan to do that? I might tell you that all the members of our zone have already tried pulling every string they could imagine to achieve exactly that, without, as you can see, any results."

"That's beside the point," the man in eyeglasses responded calmly. "We ask for your reply: Yes or no?"

"But of course!" Lingslay said, somewhat forcing a smile. "I will give any sum of money to consummate this transaction. I simply don't understand why you've come to me alone with this enticing proposal. I assure you there are a good few hundred gentlemen who would pay any price to get out of here. Or maybe you have in mind some mass enterprise to take prosperous people across the cordon for an established sum? An extremely lucrative scheme! I'm in, no questions asked."

"We'll take no fee for the transport. On the contrary, we'd be willing to pay you any sum of money, should you require it. We know all too well, however, that you don't need it."

"So I see that the two of you are clearly philanthropists, or you are offering me this for my good looks — because surely I haven't had the pleasure of making your acquaintance before?"

"We are not offering you this for your good looks," the man in eyeglasses continued unflappably. "We are simply offering you a favor for a favor. We take you out of Paris and help you get to America. You promise us another favor in exchange."

"You have intrigued me, gentlemen. You have my undivided attention."

The man in eyeglasses turned to the gray-bearded old man in the frock coat and they spoke with each other for a short while in Yiddish. Mr. Lingslay listened impatiently.

A moment later the man in eyeglasses slid his armchair nearer to his host's and, leaning in toward him, said emphatically:

"We have come to you as delegates from the Jewish town."

"How did you manage, sirs, to get into the Anglo-American territory?" Lingslay cried in alarm.

"No matter. Please listen carefully. The Jews of the Jewish town are leaving Paris in a matter of days."

"How will you manage that?"

"Never mind the details. We paid off the army at one stretch of the cordon. The military will open the cordon for the Jews, who will go through metro tunnels to the outskirts to avoid drawing attention. Freight trains will be waiting on the other side of the cordon. The Jews will then travel to Le Havre in sealed boxcars, as if they were crates of ammunition."

"Marvelous, but rather improbable. How many inhabitants, if I may ask, are in the Jewish town?"

"Only the wealthy will be on board, naturally. The poor will stay in Paris. Only the healthy will go, after a three-day quarantine in the boxcars. All in all, we should count on around three thousand people. The rest have died, or will in the near future. We have to leave as soon as possible. Staying in Paris is increasingly risky. Over and above the hundred-odd Jews that die of the plague every day, another catastrophe is looming over the Jewish town, one even more infectious than the plague. The Jewish territory borders the Belleville Soviet Republic. Since its inception, we've noticed dangerous ferment among our rabble. Just yesterday, the whole République neighborhood broke away from the Jewish town and attached itself to the Bolsheviks. Over a thousand merchants fell victim to the mob, and their properties were looted. The dregs of the Jewish town are just waiting for the right moment to follow suit . . . Staying in Paris is out of the question."

"So you mean to say that an army of three thousand people will make it out of a cordoned Paris and no one will bat an eye?"

"That's right. Everything has been prepared and taken into account."

"It all sounds like a fantasy novel. But let's suppose it's true. If I understand you correctly, you want to take me with you, make room for me in your sealed boxcars. Am I right? And what favor will you demand of me in return?"

"A simple favor and something you'll scarcely find difficult. The thing is, resettling such a large number of Jews somewhere nearby, in Europe, would be impossible. In any case, the plague will sooner or later jump the cordon and flood the rest of the Continent. We Jews aren't fleeing Paris and paying all those millions just to have the plague strike us somewhere else. The Jews have to make it to somewhere totally safe: we must make it to America."

"Bah! Surely you've heard that America has closed all its ports in fear of the plague, and no ship could get through to its shores without being bombed."

"We know that just as well as you do. That is precisely why we are here. With your extensive contacts, you'll see to it that America lets one ship through."

"Nonsense."

"Hold on. You won't mention at all that the ship is carrying people from Paris, or even from Europe. You'll say that the ship is on its way from Cairo. Everything will indicate this. The ship is waiting in Le Havre. It will sail from Le Havre at night, with all its lights off, so that it attracts no attention. Along the way, it will change its name and flags. It won't be heading for New York or Philadelphia, but for some small port. It'll land, drop off its passengers, and drift off into the night. No one will find anything out. All you have to do is use your contacts to get the local authorities to avert their attention for one hour. That's it."

David Lingslay sank into deep reflection.

"You are asking, sirs, that I bring the plague to America, no more and no less; because there can be no doubt that, of the three thousand people leaving Paris, it will break out in at least a few on the way, or after we land. I refuse."

"You shouldn't refuse before you give it some thought. Consider it carefully first."

"I've already thought it over. I cannot accept such a responsibility. Why did you choose America? Go to Africa, or to Asia."

"There is nothing for Jews in Africa, or in Asia. Every Jewish family has relatives in America, and America is the most protected from Europe. Besides, it's in your interest that we Jews go to America. If we were to go to Africa or Asia, we wouldn't need your help."

"And you wouldn't have any reason to take me with you. I understand that perfectly. Nevertheless, I can't do what you ask of me. I am staying in Paris."

"You're suicidal. You want to kill yourself, even though you have the opportunity to be saved."

"A dubious sort of salvation. If I take the plague with me when I escape to America, it's not salvation, its only a deferral."

"You're a pessimist. Who says that one of the Jews on board will be carrying the plague? Doctors will examine everyone before we go. Everyone will undergo a three-day quarantine. If someone falls ill on the ship, they'll just be thrown overboard. And even if, let's suppose, one or two Jews fall ill after we land, you still can't call that an epidemic. All of America won't be infected by two Jews."

"Out of three thousand, it might be more like three hundred sick Jews than just two."

"Why be such a pessimist? You've always got to count on things turning out for the best. Give it some thought. We'll come tomorrow for your reply."

"I've already considered it, and I cannot agree to your proposal."

"Is that your final word?"

"Yes, it's final."

The man in eyeglasses consulted for a moment with the old man in the frock coat and then turned once more to Mr. David Lingslay:

"You, sir, are an idealist." (Lingslay smiled at the thought with involuntary pride). "We thought you were a practical man. You condemn yourself to die for fear of infecting a few Americans. You're not considering that you would be saving the lives of a few hundred worthy Americans with capital who are trapped here in Paris, whom we are prepared to take on board our ship bound for America. In any case, if you're such a humanitarian, why aren't you concerned for those three thousand Jews who will be infected and killed by the plague if they are forced to stay?"

"Why should I feel concerned for those three thousand Jews and not for the million other residents of Paris who are also fated to die?"

"You can't feel concern for everybody. You couldn't live that way. You've got to be concerned for those nearest to you."

David Lingslay's features clouded. "Why do you think Jews in particular are near to me?"

The man in eyeglasses responded with a diplomatic silence.

Lingslay took out a cigarette, lit it, and nervously inhaled the smoke.

"It seems that I'm starting to understand the real source of this visit. You have discovered, gentlemen, in collecting your information about me, that my father was Jewish, and you thought that if I didn't do it out of self-interest, I would do it out of sentiment. A *Yiddishe hartz*, as you say among yourselves. As for my Jewish heart, I'm afraid I'll have to disappoint you. I was brought up in America. America is where I made my fortunc. I am an American. I owe nothing to the Jewish people, we have nothing in common. Our lines, which may have crossed in previous generations, have gone entirely separate ways. The matter of origins is strictly one for the record books here. The Jewish community has no cause to expect anything from me."

The man in eyeglasses hastily objected.

"Who said anything about origins? I was just trying to suggest that you were behaving irrationally. A few Americans infected and dying is, in any event, no more than a possibility, whereas there is not the slightest doubt that you will die if you stay here another five or six days. Is that a logical equation? And what if not a single one of those three thousand Jews is sick? Such a possibility exists as well. Then not a single American would get infected. But instead of exploring this possibility, you prefer to resign yourself to the fact that in one week's time, rather than being at home, in America, surrounded by your family and friends, far from infested Europe, you'll be lying here, not even buried in the ground — the devil knows where, a mere heap of ash, because you are no believer in life after death. And don't tell me you doubt for a moment that such an end awaits you here."

David Lingslay pushed back his armchair with a scrape.

"I see this conversation is pointless. Please do forgive me, but I can devote no more time, I'm already late for my meeting."

Both men got up and hastened toward the exit. At the door the man in eyeglasses stopped and said with a kindly smile:

"There's no rush. You're in a hurry. We won't take your time. Think about it, weigh the options. We'll come tomorrow for your answer."

David Lingslay wanted to cut in, to tell these people categorically not to return, that they needn't waste their breaths any further, that his decision was final, but there was no longer anyone in the room.

Lingslay crushed his cigarette between his fingers, rifled through his pockets, noted that he'd forgotten his watch, returned to his bedroom, slipped the watch on the tabletop into his vest with anxious revulsion, mechanically stuffed a small steel object into his pants pocket and, pressing his hat down over his forehead, quickly ran down the stairs.

At the landing of the staircase he bumped into two hospital orderlies carrying down a stretcher veiled in black. Lingslay swiftly made way for them and, foregoing his morning coffee, hurried toward the American Express building.

•

A bellhop was already waiting for Mr. Lingslay at the entrance to the American Express building, ready to take him by elevator to the second floor (confidential meeting, office No. 7).

In the office Lingslay was slow to discern the shapes of his five American colleagues through the blue fog of cigar smoke and from the embrace of their comfortable club armchairs. He was struck by the absence of his British colleagues.

Lingslay sat himself in a waiting armchair, selected a fat cigar from the box obligingly presented to him, and fell into a quizzical silence.

The distinguished, rumbling voice of Ramsay Marlington came to him through the plumes of blue smoke as if through a muffler:

"I do believe, gentlemen, that as we have all arrived, and the purpose of today's meeting is known to one and all, we can proceed to discuss the details of the affair without any further ado. I should first like to hear the opinion of my worthy colleague Mr. David Lingslay on this matter, however, as it might serve as the basis for our discussion."

"I beg your pardon, gentlemen," responded Lingslay lackadaisically from the depths of his armchair. The silky-blue atmosphere of the room was having a narcotic effect. "I must, however, confess that I received nothing on the subject of today's meeting, and before I can say something, I'll have to be informed on the matter at hand."

All the heads leaned out from their cavernous armchairs and turned toward him, as if on command.

"Can it be?" spluttered Marlington, his voice astonished. "Weren't you visited by a delegation from the Jewish town this morning?"

Lingslay's armchair gave the stifled shriek of tortured springs.

Mr. Marlington, invisible in the clouds of smoke enfolding him, like a massive, two-hundred-pound Pythia, calmly continued:

"As we've just established, at the very same hour — more or less nine o'clock in the morning — each of us five received a visit from two delegates of the Jewish town with one and the same proposal. The delegates informed us that two of them had also approached you, as the deciding vote in this case. Did you not let them in?"

Playful wisps of smoke drifted over the armchairs to form five question marks.

Lingslay's armchair emitted a calm, bland voice:

"Indeed, I was visited by a delegation. But they didn't tell me they were going around to the other principal American members of our territory. I took it as something of an individual proposal and did not expect today's meeting to be devoted to this matter."

"Excellent," Marlington bleated out from his armchair, "so now that we have established the true state of affairs, could my colleagues and I please learn your reply to the Jewish delegation?"

"Of course," responded Lingslay phlegmatically. "I declined the offer."

Here each of the five armchairs produced a strangled scream. Silence reigned.

Then a kindly chortle rang out from one of the armchairs:

"Our colleague is pulling our legs! Ha ha! That was a good one!"

"I'm afraid you're mistaken, my friend," Lingslay dryly cut in. "I'm not joking in the slightest. I'm not sure if you all know the conditions the Jews have placed on the service they were offering us. The Jewish delegates told me that they were prepared to take us along only if, for our sakes, America admits the three thousand Jews who will be leaving plague-infested Paris with us — in other words, if America admits the plague. I didn't think I could take such a responsibility upon my shoulders."

"Well, of course," Mr. Marlington replied after a long moment had passed. "The import of three thousand Jews to America is undoubtedly the least enticing part of this proposal. But in this respect it would be hard to make any reservations. We mustn't forget that, when it comes down to it, it is not we who are taking three thousand Jews with us to America, but they who are taking us. We know full well that all of our efforts to get across the cordon have come to nothing. Rejecting this offer would be a kind of insanity. Be that as it may, the moment we find ourselves on the other side of the cordon our roles will change dramatically. After we hit the shores of America there should be nothing simpler than preventing the Jews from coming ashore, under the pretense of some medical commission. When we find ourselves safe on dry land we shall proceed as we deem correct and proper for the good of our dear homeland. Am I right, gentlemen?"

The heads in the armchairs nodded their approval.

Mr. Marlington continued in the pause between two puffs of fragrant smoke:

"In the interests of avoiding unnecessary rumors and assuming that this matter concerns only us Americans, we've decided to leave our British friends out of it, and have not, as you can see, invited them to today's confidential meeting. Let them try to get to their island on their own two feet. They're a lot closer than we are, and anyway, going with us would be out of their way. In all honesty, I confess that I see no reason to burden ourselves, so to speak, with a people who for the past few decades have been incessantly sticking a wrench into our global endeavors. Appeals to the kinship of our peoples are abstract and unpersuasive. I believe I am only expressing the opinions of all those gathered here today when I recall an old motto: America for Americans."

The armchairs nodded their heads in silence.

Mr. Marlington leaned confidentially over his armrest toward David Lingslay.

"I see that in this respect we're of the same mind. The matter is almost entirely up to you, Mr. Lingslay. You have the whole of the United States naval fleet in the palm of your hand. All it would take from you is a quick dispatch for the patrol boats on a given part of our shoreline to steam off on some maneuvers. You gave the Jewish delegation a hasty reply, without considering all the angles. All of us here are true American patriots. But it's not enough to be a patriot in one's heart. One must also be a rational patriot. Our return to America would no doubt be to our homeland's advantage, while our pointless death here would be an inestimable loss. In choosing our compatriots to take back to America from Paris, we shall not be thinking in terms of quantity, of course, but quality. Only those people whose means would place them among our great country's leading citizens and who provide sturdy support to its social order will be departing with us. My secretary will have a list prepared by this evening. I believe this matter should in no way be delayed, and that you should inform the Jewish town council of your consent as soon as possible."

Lingslay set down his cigar and rose.

"Allow me twenty-four hours for my decision. I will give you my answer tomorrow by telephone after thorough consideration. The matter is too important to be decided at a moment's notice."

The five gentlemen heaved themselves up from their armchairs. Lingslay said farewell and hurried to the door.

"As for those three thousand Jews coming into America," Mr. Marlington blew after him with a cloud of smoke, "don't pay them any mind. We'll have no trouble eliminating that tiny impediment once we get there. You just leave that to me . . ."

Lingslay heard only the first half of the last sentence. The end was cut off by the clatter of the elevator doors.

After he left, the gentlemen exchanged knowing glances.

"I wonder what sort of tricks old Lingslay is up to," one of the arm-chairs said as an aside.

"And how much we'll have to fork out for them," added a second.

"Or maybe Lingslay has made a deal with the Jews to go with them alone, leaving us in Paris? Did you notice his consternation, gentlemen, when he found out that we were all visited by the Jewish delegation today?"

"Yes, in my opinion we should keep an eye on Lingslay. No doubt he's hiding something. Lingslay's part Jewish himself. We would be unspeakably stupid if he made fools of us and we missed out on this plum chance."

"You can rest easy, gentlemen," said Ramsay Marlington's distinguished voice, resounding from a corner. "Lingslay and I have worked in related branches of industry for ages, and my detective has not left his side for a moment, out of longtime habit. We'll know about his every move and be able to intervene when the time is right. Meanwhile, let's start preparing our departure so that we aren't caught napping."

Unfortunately, Lingslay was not around to hear this noteworthy conversation. He was already on the street, and locating his Rolls-Royce in a row of cars, he threw himself down onto the soft pillows and grunted his usual:

"Champs-Élysées!"

An unfamiliar chauffeur's face turned to him from behind the steering wheel.

David Lingslay at first thought he had entered the wrong car by mistake. He glanced at his monogram stitched on all the pillows, he wanted to ask, but he didn't. As a headliner in this lunatic stage show, he was well accustomed to the daily changes in the cast of browbeaten extras made by that crazed director, Death.

He gave the exact address in a dry, metallic voice.

The chauffeur nodded in silence. The car moved.

The departing day, like a modeler able to wait no longer for a slowly dying patient, covered Lingslay's face with a plaster mask of scorching heat. Lingslay thought about soft silk pillows one settles into, like into a state of semiconsciousness, and of other cushions, even silkier and more intoxicating. He closed his eyes and slipped into reverie.

When he opened them he noticed his car was stopped in front of a palace he knew all too well. The blinds in the window were tightly drawn.

"She's asleep," thought Lingslay tenderly, and he smiled at his own thoughts. He rang the doorbell twice. A long moment went by. Nobody answered. Lingslay rang once more. The response was silence. Was it possible there were no servants? Lingslay impatiently held down the button. The bell clattered an alarm. Again: silence.

The head of an elderly, graying man peeked from the doorway of the neighboring palace. A rotten, peevish head. The head said loudly in broken English:

"No one home. The lady died today noon. They take her to crematorium. Servants all gone," and then it ducked away.

David Lingslay froze, his hand on the doorbell. He stood there, it seemed, for quite a while, because the next thing he noticed was the quizzical, surprised, slightly mocking face of the new chauffeur.

Lingslay went down the stairs and fell into his seat. The chauffeur turned toward him, the quizzical expression still on his face.

"Please drive just . . . you know . . . on . . ." Lingslay said slowly.

The chauffeur nodded respectfully. The car moved.

•

When late that evening David Lingslay's Rolls stopped in front of the gates to the Grand Hotel, the first floor of the Café de la Paix was already squealing with jazz, and goggle-eyed gentlemen with one foot in the grave were sitting around tables like gigantic mosquitoes sucking the red blood of cocktails through the proboscises of their straws.

Alone in his room, David Lingslay absently wound his watch, set it down on his nightstand, and slowly started to undress. The chilly touch of the sheets through the thin silk of his pajamas was the first stimulus to awaken from its torpor his consciousness of a strong, well-functioning body, and this consciousness, activated like a machine, started on its daily, infallible course.

It was only under the blankets that the forty-year-old man first clearly realized that the night before he had kissed, held, and taken a woman who was now dead of the plague.

This thought was so cold and sharp the man felt a slight chill go down his spine.

On the surface, the deceptive social "I" of this forty-year-old gentleman known as Mr. David Lingslay — a label on a bottle of chemicals, a jumble of notations stuck to its glass — staged a revolt: his lover had died, his one and only, etc. Sorrow, screams, and resignation would have been understandable, but not this vulgar egoism and fear: I've been infected! I'll die! But this, like every label, did and could not affect the chemicals inside the bottle (a careless chemist sometimes switches labels) — and the body of the forty-year-old man, totally unabashed, continued its thoughts according to its own unswerving logic.

One thought meshed with the next: so if I'm infected, the plague is in me. I'll die tomorrow at the latest. Maybe even tonight.

The forty-year-old gentleman abruptly sat up in bed. The thought was so simple, so irreproachable in its flawless logic, so transparent and filled with oxygen, that in comparison the air in the room seemed pure carbon dioxide, and for a moment the forty-year-old man struggled to catch his breath.

"Love," "lover," all those categories by which David Lingslay had once defined the levels of his emotions suddenly seemed incomprehensible, like words in a foreign language. There remained an unfamiliar, infected, dead woman — not even a woman, a few pounds of ash — who now lived only inside him, in the bacteria of the plague she'd passed on to him, which at this very moment were perhaps gnawing into his flesh and entering his bloodstream.

The forty-year-old man hit a switch to turn on the light. The grimace of a familiar pale face contorted in the mirrored wardrobe opposite.

"Is there no way out? Is there really no way out? Let's think calmly, now," reasoned the body of the forty-year-old gentleman. "There have even been cases of people who caught syphilis and burnt the infected area right after intercourse, thus preventing the spread of the disease."

"Too late," the brain tried to protest.

"No, it might not be too late at all. It hasn't been twenty-four hours yet. If I hurry . . ."

For the body, like all bodies, put the language of concrete action above abstract reasoning. The forty-year-old man leapt barefoot from his bed, tossing — or rather tearing — his pajamas from his body with superstitious revulsion, and ran naked to the dressing table. The hand of the forty-year-old gentleman snatched a jar of sublimate from the phials resting on top and, having prepared a powerful solution in the sink, started to splash himself with it, rubbing his hairy body covered in goosebumps until it went red from his genitals all the way to his face and ears.

Only when he had satisfied his need for immediate action and his energy had flagged, like a top losing momentum, could David Lingslay get a word in, and looking through the eyes of the forty-year-old man at the flushed, woolly body in the mirror, he concluded:

"I am ridiculous."

Yet this was but a timid observation that remained on the periphery, as if it in no way concerned the forty-year-old gentleman. Unaccustomed to this nakedness, the forty-year-old man felt a shudder of cold. Walking around the pajamas strewn across the carpet, he made for the wardrobe, took out a fresh robe, and wrapped it around his frame.

For a moment he wondered if he shouldn't go back to bed, but then it hit him: Change the sheets! He wanted to ring the bellboy, but here David Lingslay intervened once more, being ashamed to come face to face with a bellboy at that odd hour, and the forty-year-old man let him win, climbing into the armchair and resolving to stay there until morning.

Now settled, the forty-year-old man started carefully to probe his belly, pressing it with all his strength, and then feeling the glands under his arms. The survey yielded no definite results, and the forty-year-old man had no alternative but to wait.

David Lingslay tried to emerge again in this space of waiting, quickly formulating a thought:

"I'm a coward. I'm scared of death. What nonsense! Living these three weeks among plague victims I've known all too well that I could die any day."

Yet what David Lingslay knew in no way concerned the forty-year-old man, who refused to let this information sink in, and just squirmed all the more in the armchair.

"I'll die, I have to die," David Lingslay tried to convince the forty-year-old man. "What's so odd about that? It's simple: I was here, but soon I'll be gone."

But the forty-year-old man could in no way fathom this simple fact, and he squirmed all the more. And David Lingslay shuddered, sensing that the forty-year-old man wanted to scream.

"You must not! They'll hear! The servants will come! The shame!" he feverishly chided.

The forty-year-old man couldn't have cared less at that moment about the servants. He felt something black and slippery coating his limbs, and he gave a long bellow, like an animal, until David Lingslay plugged his mouth with a fist.

"They'll hear!"

David Lingslay listened carefully for a moment. Not a sound. Only now did he recall that he was the sole occupant of the entire floor.

"Hush! Hush!" he tenderly calmed the forty-year-old man, standing there naked in his brocade robe. He was cold, and his teeth chattered.

Taking advantage of his momentary apathy, David Lingslay tried to reason further.

As an experienced businessman, he was used to calculating the assets and liabilities before proceeding to liquidate a company. And now, from his armchair, as if on high, David Lingslay tried to look back over the life he'd lived and roughly balance its books. Peering over his shoulder, he saw an inconceivable mass of digits flowing toward him from all sides, an impenetrable, all-consuming lava, surrounding his armchair like a gray sea of billions of rats, and in instinctive horror he folded his trembling bare legs under him.

The only island of green flourishing amid this gray sea of digits was his love of the past few weeks, and like a castaway reaching for a plank, David Lingslay grabbed hold of this island and tried to stand on it, to secure himself on its narrow shores. But at that moment the forty-year-old man, who loathed this dead plague-ridden woman, seized him by the arm, fearing to set foot on her legacy.

His life had turned out to be a loss-making enterprise, and David Lingslay felt little regret at closing its ledgers. Had it been worth turning that heavy quern of millions, day and night, for twenty long years like a convict, amply lubricating it with sticky red grease, only to check the balance sheet to find that the laboriously built flour mills were infested with billions of rat-digits, a numberless, ravenous army, already whetting their teeth on the very man who had regarded them as his tool, as a means, and who now suddenly found himself little more than a means to their own mysterious end?

And Mr. David Lingslay, as if sitting an exam, duly replied:

"No, it wasn't worth it."

"So I'll die — I'll die and nothing will remain of me, not a trace . . ."

Formulated this way, the thought seemed indigestible even to David Lingslay, and like a stubborn case of hiccups it kept popping back into his throat.

"Hold on . . . Let's be sober about this: writers, thinkers, and artists all die. They remain forever in their creations. What have I created?"

Mr. David Lingslay answered:

"Money, possessions."

A thankless, nameless sort of creation. His heirs would carve up the possessions. There would be nothing left, not even his name. They would duly strike his name from his bank accounts the world over. What would remain? The dull hatred of millions of workers, for whom he had been a terrible legend? Even there they would efface his name, replace it with another. In five years he would scarcely be remembered.

David Lingslay for the first time comprehended what he had used to call the philanthropic psychosis of aging millionaires, all the Carnegies and Rockefellers who splurged enormous sums on worthy causes, establishing million-dollar foundations in their own names. He felt the hollering terror of their old age in the face of oblivion, their desire to be commemorated, to latch onto something at all costs, if only through the syllables of their surname. For the first time he understood, he empathized, he absolved them with a knowing smile. The poor devils! By financing someone else's idea, they deluded themselves that they were the ones being immortalized, as long as they could pin their calling card onto it, though it was only the balance in their checkbooks that brought the two together.

This made even the forty-year-old man a bit ill at ease, as if the earth were sliding from under his feet, while his fingers clutched at thin air. The forty-year-old gentleman was in no state to compete with the logical deductions of Mr. David Lingslay, and his blind animal instinct began convulsively searching for something to cling to, like a barnacle sensing the approach of a wave that would sweep it away, frantically searching for a protrusion, for chinks in the rock to latch onto and survive. Groping in the void of his consciousness, the forty-year-old gentleman suddenly stumbled upon a familiar face, and his back arched like a whipped dog . . .

David Lingslay was childless. This tiny anxiety gnawed at him like a worm, though he wouldn't have admitted it, not even to himself. Having confirmed in his thirty-sixth year that he would not be having children, Lingslay had thought about his family. He had once had a brother, but apparently he'd starved to death in some hole outside London. For a man as devoid of any family sentiment as Lingslay, this information made not the slightest dent. He was occasionally bothered by a twinge of guilt (he had once taken the opportunity to make a tiny correction to their father's will). Thus looking through his family, he recalled that his luckless brother had left behind some kin. Lingslay resolved to find them. After a long search, he discovered that of the whole brood, only a twenty-year-old boy named Archibald was left, earning a living in London.

Hurrying to send him first-class fare on an ocean liner and a few thousand dollars to wrap up his affairs in Europe, Lingslay wrote a laconic letter suggesting that his nephew move to New York to study.

What showed up was a tall, bony man with good hazel eyes, his face sunken and ravaged, cracked and cut with premature wrinkles, wisps of chestnut hair falling over his high, wise forehead. He moved into the left wing of Lingslay's mansion.

Mr. David Lingslay liked his nephew's open face, and decided that after a bit of fattening up he would make him his right-hand man. But things started to go awry at once. His nephew was an avowed communist, and he began agitating at his uncle's factories even before he had properly unpacked. Mr. Lingslay received the alarming reports from the sub-directors with a forbearing smile. Wanting to put a stop to the youthful whims of his nephew, he named him secretary general of one of his companies, explaining to him over a long, kindly, and confidential talk that he saw the young man as his partner and heir.

The nephew accepted the position but continued agitating in the factory. It all ended one fine day with the incensed workers occupying the factory and declaring it the property of the Workers' Committee.

The police were called in, and they only just managed to restore order and remove the instigators.

The nephew and uncle had a fiery confrontation, ending with a definitive parting of ways.

From that time forward, Mr. Lingslay wanted no more to do with his ungrateful nephew, who vanished without a trace.

Until one spring afternoon. On that day a few ringleaders were dismissed, which led to strikes breaking out in fourteen of Lingslay's factories. On Lingslay's orders the board of directors closed the factories, tossing all the workers onto the street. The dismissed workers tried to take the factories by force. The army was brought in. The mob expelled from the factory buildings poured out of the alleyways and from all sides, forming a procession that marched toward David Lingslay's mansion. The windows rattled.

Caught off guard, Lingslay called in the police. The police commissioner, who was in his pay, asked obligingly if weapons ought to be used. Lingslay grunted laconically into the receiver:

"I think it's high time we ended this farce. Your tear gas is useless. The mob expects blank cartridges, so they won't do any good. Two salvos of real ammunition will scatter the demonstrators and teach them a lesson for the future. In any case, it's your call."

The commissioner did not disappoint the trust vested in him. Hiding behind a curtain, Mr. David Lingslay watched the police cordon crawl out from a side street as the salvo boomed and the crowd panicked to escape. In the space of five minutes the square was evacuated, with a dozen people left lying motionless on the asphalt.

A moment later the commissioner appeared in Mr. Lingslay's office, crumpling his immaculately white gloves in visible consternation. It took Lingslay some time to understand the purpose of his visit.

"Your nephew," stammered the commissioner, "in the front line . . . We had no way of knowing . . ."

"Killed?" Mr. Lingslay dryly ventured.

"That's right . . ." choked out the commissioner, encouraged by his tone. "Should I order him brought here?"

"By no means!" said Mr. Lingslay, taken aback. "Or actually . . . quite right . . . Please have him brought to his room in the left wing."

Late in the evening, for the first time in a year, Mr. David Lingslay stood in the doorway to his nephew's room. His nephew lay on the couch. His head was thrown back, and two thin threads of blood ran from the corners of his mouth and trickled onto the expensive carpet.

David Lingslay had seen many faces since then, both living and dead, but this one stayed with him for good, artificially enlarged, nailed amid a hundred odds and ends to the wall of his memory.

He understood everything: the workers' revolt, the marching against police salvos with their chests exposed. He saw no heroism in it, nothing unusual in the wretched envying the wealthy their wealth. Just raise their salaries and they'd bow their heads and go back to work. It wasn't even hatred he felt for them, just contempt.

But here all logic ran aground. Lingslay's nephew, the future heir to his thirty factories, leading a bedraggled, rapacious mob to plunder the riches one day to be his . . . This Lingslay could not fathom, and his thoughts, accustomed to strolling the lengths of society as if it were his private office, rammed headfirst into an impenetrable wall.

The digits came flowing again in a wide stream, but they couldn't wipe clean or erase the pale face with wisps of chestnut hair and two threads of blood in the pained corners of his mouth. Nephew Archie, buried in a New York cemetery, in the Lingslay family tomb, clearly mocked the costly marble stones, carrying on his work where he had left off. From the crowd of assailed demonstrators, from the bulletins on the latest strike, from the pages of the morning gazette reporting the revolution in China, from every which way, Mr. David Lingslay felt the gaze of the pale face under the chestnut hair — alert, omnipresent, indestructible.

Sometimes, when Lingslay was reading reports on the workers' rising demands, when his impatient hand was just reaching for the receiver and his mouth was preparing to bark the order for a lockout, the face of his nephew Archie would emerge from the receiver like a snail from its shell, and he would drop the phone, take up the report once more, make some concessions.

Though not cognizant of this himself, somewhere deep down inside, beneath the unshakable foundations of his "principles" and "convictions," his nephew Archie remained forever in the small, fireproof safe of his soul as a symbol of disinterested idealism, and whenever Mr. David Lingslay, a crook and plunderer devoid of any scruples, happened to perform a truly selfless act in some critical situation, his fingers would, unbeknownst even to his own consciousness, touch the doors of this safe, as a Jew does a mezuzah, as if his involuntary pride were seeking sanction from within.

Much like the morning in question, when the gray-bearded Rabbi Eliezer and the corpulent gentleman in horn-rimmed glasses made their business proposal, the immorality of which was beyond question, Lingslay had been inclined to agree, but then his hand reached down to his strongbox and, much to his own surprise, he adamantly refused to comply.

Now, shucked from his clothing, the naked forty-year-old man found himself staring into the void, and with a convulsive scream his hands groped for something around him, something to cling to, something to leave his mark on, to make permanent, in defiance of the inescapability of death and the process of decay, and in this void his hand fell upon the pale face with the mop of chestnut hair, and the forty-year-old man shook as though he had touched a live wire.

Yes, Nephew Archie had known that secret. Smothered by the heavy, expensive slabs of the Lingslay tomb, he had lived an intense, grounded existence. In every square mile around the world, wherever a few hundred ragged and oppressed people assembled, joined by a yearning for a new order, he again shot vital, life-giving sparks.

For the first time his uncle felt the whole burden and poverty of his inhuman solitude, and he understood why his reckless, half-mad nephew had not wanted to inherit his thirty factories . . .

"Everything will remain the same, they'll just carry on without me," David Lingslay tried to imagine. "The mirror, the commode, the bed, all of it the same. The plague will pass. They'll disinfect and that will be that. Other people will sleep in this bed, men with women, who knows, maybe even acquaintances of mine. Everyone will see themselves in the mirror. And I won't leave a trace behind. It's comical! Or maybe something really does remain of a man after he dies? I'll have to remember the way I looked."

Mr. David Lingslay turned the chandelier on bright and looked into the mirror. What he saw terrified him. A forty-year-old man with disheveled, grayish hair stared out at him from the mirror, robe unbuttoned down to his naked chest, his knobby knees touching his chin, his jowls trembling.

"That's not me, it can't be me!" stammered a numb Lingslay, unable to locate his impeccable features in the pale, flaccid face of the forty-year-old man.

"Nothing will remain, nothing!" the forty-year-old man roared from the mirror. "They'll come, carry me off, throw me into a pit! Nothing, not even in the mirror! Tomorrow it will reflect someone else, not me! Not me? What does 'not me' mean? Wrong! I'll squeeze my way in! I'll hang on! I'll stay in the mirror! To watch! To see what others do here! Here, in this very room! Oh-ho-ho! Let's see them *try* to scrape me off the glass! Oh-ho-ho!"

The forty-year-old man with trembling jowls stiffened upright, taking up the whole mirror.

Mr. David Lingslay felt as though the earth were slipping from beneath his feet, that it was melting away like a phantom. In a last fit of self-defense he grabbed the phial of sublimate lying nearby and flung it at the mirror with all his might . . .

•

When the following morning the bellboy led Rabbi Eliezer ben Zvi and the corpulent gentleman in American eyeglasses to Mr. David Lingslay's salon, the two men waited a long time in silence.

Twenty minutes later, Lingslay appeared in the doorway to the salon. He was somewhat more pale than usual and even more stiff. Staring somewhere out the window he said in a flat voice:

"I have spent all night considering your proposal, and I have concluded that my reasoning yesterday was hasty. Indeed, why suppose that someone has to be infected? We have to hope that the doctors' scrupulous examinations and quarantine will keep the plague confined to Paris. I'll send a coded message to my secretary in New York today. The matter should not be delayed, and it would be for the best if we could set off this very evening."

Rabbi Eliezer and the gentleman in eyeglasses nodded their heads in silence.

•

A cold eastern wind tossed the unruly mop of the nighttime sea with the fingers of an adroit barber.

The RMS *Mauretania* was going full steam with its lights out. The last contours of the shoreline had long melted into the fog. The passengers had crowded the decks for the first hour, but now they were slowly shuffling off to their class compartments. In the ship's enormous hull, two windows glowed in the row of first-class cabins, like two glowworms fastened to its ribs.

The old shammes slept wrapped up in a ball on a couch in one of these cabins, and through his dreams his lips repeated the words of an unfinished prayer.

By the table, Rabbi Eliezer ben Zvi sat in an old striped tallith, like gray-bearded Neptune in a striped swimsuit, his torso swinging steadily in time to the sway of the ship as his lips whispered a prayer of thanksgiving:

"For I am Thine, Lord God, whom Thou hast taken from the lands of Egypt, from that house of servitude . . ."

Little by little Rabbi Eliezer's restless eyes began to droop, and the gigantic, bulging hull of the ship swung in time to the prayer, facing *mizrach*, toward Jerusalem.

David Lingslay was lying in the portside corner cabin, stretched out on his bed, a cigarette in his mouth, staring at the shadow of the lamp quivering on the ceiling. He tossed and turned, lighting his tenth cigarette from the burning stub of the ninth. The room swung like a hammock, summoning sleep, which then skittered away like ball bearings across the sloping floor of the hull. Every tilt of the floor was another mile away from Europe, from Paris, from the plague, from death — a mile into the depths, into the downy, flower-carpeted meadow of life.

An indifferent, ironic watch ticked on the nightstand: six hours since departure from Europe.

•

On the evening of the second day, the burning iron of the sun had utterly smoothed all the crumpled folds of waves. The ship was turning a wide arc to the west, an enchanted needle on the gigantic spinning gramophone disc of the ocean.

All decks were black with passengers.

From the upper deck a few hundred gentlemen in plaid caps, covered in blankets, were staining the immaculate blue of the backdrop with plumes of cigar smoke. The more spry gentlemen passed the time first with some golf, then a bit of tennis, then a simple game of bridge. Incorporeal stewards bearing trays balanced themselves piously between the couches, like tightrope walkers on invisible wires stretched over a precipice, fearing to lose a drop of the valuable liquid, or to breathe the slightest word or inadvertent sigh.

On the first-class deck, bloated, overstuffed gentlemen fingered their beaded pendants and took in the sea, leaning back on comfortable deckchairs. Fleet-footed, guttapercha stewards distributed cool drinks. A few enterprising youths slapped together an improvised jazz band from a pair of chance trumpets, a drum, and kitchen utensils, and the young people danced themselves ragged to the caterwauling sounds of the popular music.

On the third-class decks the poorer passengers sitting on bulging suitcases caught wind of the scraps of sounds falling from above and opened their mouths wide in astonishment, like fish catching bits of bread.

Suddenly the dancers went amok. The deck cleared as if blown by a violent wind. Everyone scattered into a wide circle. In the center writhed a young man sporting a pince-nez. The fall had broken a lens, and the staring, shortsighted eye, now exposed, gaped in horror at the fleeing crowd. The young man clumsily flapped the cumbersome fins of his arms like a fish on a sandy shore.

Seemingly from out of nowhere two men in white aprons suddenly came around a corner with a stretcher, upon which they threw the young man, twitching like a carp, and vanished back whence they came. The other lens fell out of the pince-nez and rolled along the deck.

A moment later the whole deck was a whirl of panic. The obese men, pushing each other and dropping their pendants, made a crush for the cabin stairs. For an instant all that could be heard was the clamor of voices and the clatter of doors slamming shut. Within five minutes, not a living soul was on deck.

Then a grayish man in a checkered sporting outfit rose from one of the armchairs tucked behind the smokestack. With a slow, absent-minded gait he walked across the deck and leaned on the rail.

The grayish man smoked a cigarette.

Down below, waves lapped against the side of the ship.

•

The following day the wind blew, and the sea swayed fearfully under its lashings.

The first-class decks were empty; drowsy, rubbery stewards ambled up and down them like butlers after a ball.

At around ten o'clock, the grayish man in the checkered sporting outfit appeared on deck.

He strode hesitantly, stumbling out of time with the wobbling of the ship. He went a few steps, made it to a comfortable deckchair near the ship's side, and collapsed heavily into it. Taking an expensive leather-framed mirror from his pocket, he carefully studied his tongue.

His face a blank, he tucked the mirror away, and cautiously glanced around the deck. It was deserted. Having confirmed that no one was looking, the gentleman in the sporting outfit performed a few strange movements with his arm that resembled Swedish calisthenics. Then, continuing to look around, he surreptitiously felt his underarms, like a man whose clothing was pinching him.

A steward appeared on deck. The grayish man swiftly took a book from his pocket and buried himself in it. From the corner of his eye he could see the third-class deck, where passengers were crowded together and kneeling on their suitcases to unwrap their provisions and wolf down their breakfasts.

On the deck where the grayish man was sitting, stewards were putting overturned chairs back in place.

The grayish man quickly leafed through his book.

It was already well after noon when a noise and commotion reached his ears from the lower deck. The commotion was so loud that the grayish man broke off his reading and leaned over the rail to have a look downward. The lower deck was seething like a trampled anthill. He could make out a pair of white smocks weaving through the black swarm. Shielding his eyes with one hand, the grayish man saw two other white smocks at the far end of the lower deck. A third pair of white smocks was carrying a load down the stairs leading to the cabins. A chorus of laments and confusion came from below.

The grayish man returned to his prior position and busied himself with his book. The commotion was clearly distracting him, because a moment later he set his book aside and, stretching out in a leisurely position, shut his eyes. He remained that way for a long time, and a chance observer might have assumed he had fallen asleep.

After some time he took a fountain pen from his pocket and jotted a few words on a piece of paper torn from a notebook. Then he got up and went downstairs with a decisive step.

Finding himself in the telegraph cabin, the grayish man asked the man on duty to send an urgent coded message to New York. The telegrapher nodded respectfully. The machine tapped away.

A moment later, the grayish man bumped into the corpulent gentleman with horn-rimmed glasses in the cabin doorway.

"Ah, Mr. Lingslay!" the gentleman in glasses said jovially. "I've been searching for you everywhere. We'll be there in three hours. Is everything in order?"

"Absolutely. After all, I showed you the reply. Everything's set. Just to be completely certain, I sent one more telegram to my secretary a moment ago."

"Splendid," said the gentleman in glasses, rubbing his hands.

David Lingslay glanced at his watch.

"In less than three hours we'll be crossing the perimeter where U.S. ships patrol the coast. Please make sure all my instructions have been followed to the letter. You haven't forgotten to raise the Egyptian flag?"

"Everything has been done according to your instructions."

"There might be an admiral on one of the ships who is not privy to the plan. If this is the case, they will be forced to fire on us. Using blanks, of course. Be so good as to inform the passengers of this, to avoid unnecessary panic. Let's not have anyone running for the lifeboats in the confusion! The sector commanders have been fully briefed, and they will fire a few rounds of blanks at most, to keep up appearances. We'll be sailing under blackout conditions and should be through the perimeter in about five minutes."

"So, we can rule out any complications?" asked the man in glasses anxiously.

"Absolutely. I showed you the bulletin. Everything has been prepared down to the smallest detail. My presence on board is, I believe, the best guarantee. You don't suppose, perhaps, that I would expose myself to uncertainties."

"Of course not. I'm just asking to make sure. You sent one more wire?"

"That's right. The reply should come at any minute."

A boy appeared on deck:

"Wire for Mr. David Lingslay."

Lingslay scanned the telegram.

"My secretary says that everything is prepared," he said, crumpling the paper. "Please be so kind as to inform the passengers what I have said and to give the final instructions. We'll meet on deck the moment we arrive."

David Lingslay climbed back upstairs.

Dusk fell quickly. In the gloom, Lingslay bumped headfirst into two figures dressed in white, carrying a bundle of some kind. He hastily made way and pressed himself against the furnace. A cigarette lighter flickered in the darkness. Lingslay held the telegram up to it, and then used the burning paper to light a cigarette. The slender flame illuminated his face for a moment — pale, harsh, almost stony. The fire went out. The face melted into the darkness.

•

It was midnight when the lights of the first cruisers appeared on the horizon. The deck sprang to life. Human figures darted here and there in the darkness and short bursts of commands punctuated the air. The *Mauretania* was sailing under blackout conditions and at full steam.

The twinkling lights on the horizon were getting closer every minute. The monumental black contours floating in the dusk were already visible to the naked eye. A spotlight sprayed from a tower. It anxiously groped the sea, resting on the hull of the *Mauretania*, blinding the crowd on deck with its shaft of light.

A second spotlight simultaneously illuminated the deck from the north side. In the hollow silence, a siren wailed mournfully, continuously, and the wail was picked up and joined by others further along, one by one. The tension on board reached a crescendo.

A whistling pillar of fire tore from one of the cruisers and soared in an arc over the *Mauretania*.

"They're firing blanks," the gentleman in glasses whispered in confidence to the group of portly men surrounding him.

"Isn't it possible for a real one to slip in among the blanks by mistake?" a gentleman with a pointy black beard asked nervously.

"Impossible," said the man in glasses with a forbearing smile. "When dealing with Mr. David Lingslay there can be no room for mistakes."

The *Mauretania* was sailing at full steam. Now pillars of fire streamed upward from three sides simultaneously, and roaring projectiles shook the overhanging sheet of the air like a sail. A scream rang out from the far end of the deck, followed by the rumble of crashing shrapnel. The ship erupted in pandemonium. Cannons blasted incessantly. A red shaft of smoke exploded from the middle deck of the *Mauretania*, propping up the collapsing sky. At that same moment the old shammes, his robes flapping, appeared on the spotlit deck and ran around screaming and flapping his arms.

"Killed! Rabbi Eliezer has been killed!" shrieked the delirious shammes.

"Mr. David Lingslay! Where is Mr. David Lingslay?!" screamed the man in the horn-rimmed glasses, seizing every gentleman he found by the lapels and staring him in the face.

An explosion of floorboards and smoke threw him onto the guardrail.

The man in glasses tried to get up, but a gigantic, invisible load was pushing him to the ground. The old, disheveled shammes bent down over him. The man in glasses was trying to say something. He managed to draw a scratchy whistle from his throat. The shammes bent down lower.

"A message . . . Today he sent a new message to New York . . . ," coughed up the man in glasses.

The shells crashed down relentlessly. The *Mauretania*'s rear hull, utterly pulverized, was submerging with lightning speed. Only the prow still protruded from the waves, pointing straight upward.

Mr. David Lingslay hung over the rail of the prow. An ample stream of blood was pouring onto the deck from his hand, which had been severed along with part of his torso.

Mr. David Lingslay felt no pain. He felt he was slowly spiraling downward, but not into the water — it was more of a soft, ambling elevator that was lowering him somewhere into the depths, past shifting floors of consciousness. Other glass elevators flew past him going up, filled with familiar, half-blurred faces. In the foreground, Lingslay made out the unnaturally enlarged face of his nephew, Archie, with those good hazel eyes and curls of chestnut-brown hair on his wise, broad forehead. Archie was smiling. David Lingslay tried to reflect that smile with the corners of his lips, now oddly stiff. He felt pride at having just performed some immensely important work, for which he had never found time in his life until then, and which should have made his nephew Archie very satisfied, but he could not even recall what this work was exactly. Fewer and fewer illuminated floors flashed by in the impenetrably black tunnel of the shaft.

The swaying elevator slowly and softly lowered him to his death.

IX

IN THE DARK, STARLESS NIGHT A SMALL BLACK BOAT sailed down the middle of the Seine, from Pont de Bercy heading east, like a gigantic floating catafalque with its candle-chimney snuffed.

Two men were leaning on the bow rail, the four points of their eyes piercing the gloom.

On the horizon a blinding smear of light gleamed like a thick white line of chalk on the black dress of the night.

"In three minutes we'll be at the first firing line. It's five minutes to twelve. We should wait two minutes before approaching the line," said one of the voices in a low whisper.

"It's a perfect night, as long as the wind doesn't scatter the clouds. I'd bet my head we manage to get through unseen. Have one more look around the deck, comrade, to make sure we haven't forgotten to shut off any lights. No one dare light a cigarette! I don't want to hear a single word! We're almost there."

Comrade Laval was forced to squint for a moment. The tugboat floated around the bend. The river a quarter mile away was flooded with light, seemingly on fire. Comrade Laval bent down to the speaking tube and said in a throaty whisper:

"Stop!"

The screws spun into place. The boat came to a halt.

Now, in contrast with the wall of light, the gloom seemed even blacker and thicker. The spotlighted strip of the demarcation zone stretched into the distance both left and right, like a white-hot iron poker.

Comrade Laval strained his ears. An infinite minute passed. From somewhere in the city, in the perfect silence, came the sound of the first clocks tolling midnight. At almost the very same moment, from behind the city, came the first bang, the clatter of a falling projectile a second later, and then again silence.

"Missed!" hissed Laval through his teeth.

Soon two new shots rang out. A moment later — a third, fourth, and fifth. The cannons roared one after another.

Suddenly, almost in time with the thunder of a bursting projectile, the wall of light dividing the river collapsed, and the darkness whistled as it funneled into the breach. The artillery boomed relentlessly.

"Go!" Comrade Laval roared into the speaking tube.

The tugboat shuddered, jerked forward, and flew full steam into the black tunnel of darkness. Somewhere in the distance a spotlight spluttered, groping at the indifferent sky with a blind man's trembling, open hand.

And then a black balloon swayed into the halo of light in the sky. Almost simultaneously, the tailed flare of a projectile shot toward it.

"Yes, everything's going according to plan," mumbled Comrade Laval, rubbing his hands. "Now they'll occupy themselves awhile with the balloon until we pass. Come on, once more!"

Rockets danced and dashed through the sky time and again, aimed at the swaying balloon. Smothered in darkness, Paris responded with cannon fire.

Like a panting sprinter, the tugboat swallowed the space in large gulps. It left the jagged wall of light behind. Now, from both right and left, the banks sparkled and flashed with a thousand lights, rumbling with the hollow blast of the alarm.

Suddenly kissed by one of the flares, the awkward black balloon burst in a ball of flames and started to plummet like a gigantic glowing butterfly.

"A bit too early, damn it!" murmured Laval with an angry glare. "Now they'll turn their attention to us . . ."

The cannons kept booming, though more weakly and at longer intervals.

Here the river visibly narrowed, and the lights falling upon it from the banks cut fantastical teeth in its uniform black braid. The cannons gradually grew softer. Just one, and then two last shots — like belated applause — and a thick curtain of silence fell into place for good.

His whole body tense, Comrade Laval held his breath and leaned on the rail, as if wanting to cover the noisy, panting tugboat with the stunted wings of his hands, like a hen with an unruly chick.

The lights on the banks gradually started to thin, the odd one popping up here and there, then scurrying behind the boat like will-o'-the-wisps. Just three or four more semaphores and the boat floated into the black crater of night.

They drifted for some time in total darkness, marking off the space with the tug's heavy screw propellers. At last, Comrade Laval lit a cigarette and sucked at it greedily. He could make out his watch by the flickering light of a match: five past one.

Laval bent over his speaking tube:

"All hands on deck!" he loudly commanded.

An instant later the deck was swarming with a dozen brawny figures.

"You may smoke, comrades. We'll be there shortly. Bring the lights on deck! We can turn on the smaller one. And now — careful! Somewhere nearby, on the left bank, there ought to be a dock with a few barges. Whoever sees it first, let us know. I fear we might've already passed it. Is Comrade Monsignac here? Didn't you serve in the light marines, comrade? Are you any good at climbing ropes? Good. I'll be needing you."

"A barge! There's a barge. There's two, three, four barges!" sounded a few voices at once. "And there's the dock!"

"Stop!"

The tug drew to a halt.

"Shine both lights. There should be a road by the bank."

"There is! There's a road!" came the voices.

"Good! Somewhere near the bank the road forks. One way goes inland. We must have missed it. Back up! Closer in on the bank! Right."

The boat slowly started moving in reverse.

"There's the fork!" shouted someone from the portside. "Stop!"

The tugboat halted.

"Turn on all the lights! Light up that place well for me! Good! Nice and bright. Now a bit closer! Stop! Enough! Comrade Monsignac, come closer. You see that junction telephone pole, with wires going out in three directions? How far do you think we are from it?"

"About thirty feet," said the stout sailor, judging the space with a trained eye.

"Can you throw a line around it?"

"Why not? If you could just move up a bit closer . . ."

The boat moved another seven feet toward the shore.

"Stop! Don't go right up to the shore!" Laval commanded. "Right. And now, comrade, try to toss the line over. Make a strong loop so that you'll be able to go straight from the deck to the pole. You're going to have to cut the wires on both the left and the right and attach ours to the remaining line perpendicular to the shore."

"Then why do we need the rope, comrade? I'll just jump ashore and be up the pole in a flash. The line will just waste time."

"Don't even think about jumping ashore! Whoever goes ashore gets a bullet to the head!" Laval warned. "If you're a sailor and not a wimp you should be able to walk the line from the deck to the pole."

"I can do what needs to be done, but it'll take time. It's a waste. The sun will rise on us."

Comrade Laval dryly interrupted:

"We'll discuss it when you get back, comrade. If it's time you're worried about, let's not stand around dallying. Throw the line."

Comrade Monsignac silently tied a lasso, aimed, threw, and missed.

"I said it wasn't going to be easy . . ." he muttered, getting ready for another toss.

After fifteen minutes the line was finally fastened. The stout sailor reeled the wire over his arm, slung a pair of pincers and scissors on his belt and, rolling up his sleeves, adroitly began climbing the line toward the pole.

Laval pulled a revolver from his underarm holster.

"Comrade Monsignac — just in case it should enter your head to jump to the ground instead of returning to the deck, remember that a bullet from this revolver will crack your skull before you touch the ground."

The sailor was busy climbing and gave no response. A moment later he was straddling the top of the pole. Two cut rows of wires flew to the ground like broken guitar strings. The sailor spent another long moment fiddling up top.

"Done?" asked Laval from on deck.

"Done!" shouted the sailor.

"So back you go!"

The sailor seemed to be measuring the distance to the ground for a moment, and then the distance to the ship and the black Mauser Comrade Laval had pointed at him, and then he obediently began sliding back down the line to the deck. When his feet touched the deck he spat through his teeth and growled:

"Put away your Mauser, Comrade Commander. You'd be better off shooting the line — I hear you're a pretty good shot."

Comrade Laval silently took aim and shot. The line fell into the water. It was pulled up on deck. The sailor mumbled some compliments and began unwinding the wires attached to the pole at the other end.

"Shunt off to the middle of the river!" commanded Laval.

The boat slowly floated to the middle, pulling after it two thin threads of wires.

"Halt! Comrade Monsignac, here's the telephone, attach it to the ends of the wires."

The sailor fiddled with the telephone, clearly having a rough time of it, as every other minute he cursed vehemently and spat through his teeth. After twenty minutes had passed, the phone apparatus was ready.

Comrade Laval picked up the receiver.

"Light all the lights! And silence!"

The crank of the field device gave a dry crunch.

An eternity flowed from the receiver before a patient, melancholy "Hell-l-l-o . . . ," came from somewhere far away.

"Hello! Tansorel!" Laval yelled into the mouthpiece.

"Tansorel . . . ," came back like an echo.

"Get the mayor on the line!"

"Who's there . . . ?" came the distant voice.

"It's the prefecture," Comrade Laval calmly continued. "Please wake the mayor and the parish priest immediately and call them both to the telephone. It's urgent."

"Please hold . . . ," came the echo.

Comrade Laval propped his elbows on his lap, held the receiver to his ear, and smoked a cigarette as he waited. Ten minutes passed.

Suddenly someone's hurried footsteps clattered in the receiver. From far away a voice raveled in a web of wires descended, fluttered, and rang out.

"This is the mayor of Tansorel."

"Is the parish priest awake?"

"He's on his way."

"Please hand him another receiver. This matter concerns him as well. I don't want to have to repeat myself," said Laval in a commanding tone.

"We're listening. Who's speaking? Is that you, Mr. Prefect?"

"Listen carefully. This is the expedition of the Paris Republic of Soviets speaking. At midnight we broke through the cordon and came here for food. The Parisian proletariat is dying of starvation. Our boat is on the river, across from the dock. I am speaking from its deck. Don't try to call the garrison for help. All the telephone lines have been cut. The only remaining line connects you to our boat. Now listen carefully.

We have come in peace. We are anchored in the middle of the river, and if you act promptly we won't touch shore at all. We have come to collect food for the starving poor of Paris. If over the next hour you do not supply and load barges with six hundred sacks of flour, we will come ashore, plunder, and bombard your village. We are giving you one hour. It is your job, Citizen Mayor, to wake up the village, arrange transport, and guide the shipment to the dock. You, Citizen Priest, will use your authority to convince the reluctant and ensure that everything gets done on time. Both of you set your watches. It is now ten to two. If by ten to three the first load of flour has not yet appeared on the road to the docks, we will disembark. Discipline and punctuality will keep you and all of France from becoming infected with the plague. Understood, Mayor? Six hundred sacks of flour in one hour to the docks."

The receiver was silent. After a long moment the first scratchy words came out:

"But our village doesn't have that much flour . . ."

"You'll find it. You won't have to look far. You can take it from the Plon brothers' mill. Then load it onto the sawmill barges. As you can see, we know your area as well as you do. Don't forget to bring some tarps from the mill to cover the barges. Is this clear?"

"It's clear . . ." groaned the echo.

"Perfect, I knew I was dealing with intelligent people. So let's not waste any more time. I'll give you an extra five minutes to check the truth of what I've said. You can spend that time making sure your telephone wires really are cut and your village is in our boat's line of fire. Just to be clear, I warn you that the first messenger who appears on the road, either on horseback or bicycle, will get a bullet to the head. And now — get to work. I repeat: if in an hour's time the flour has appeared on the shore and the barges are loaded in another half an hour, we won't come ashore and no one will get hurt. We have not come to pillage. We've come to feed the starving. The clock is ticking. Goodbye and see you in one hour!"

Comrade Laval hung up and anxiously paced the deck. He couldn't tell from the nervous voice on the other end of the line if they would follow his orders or stay put. He was riddled with doubt. What if it were all in vain? If no one turned up on the shore within an hour? What then? Then he would have to turn heel and sail off empty-handed. He knew all too well that he wasn't about to go ashore, no matter what. Then the whole expedition would be shot to hell.

Comrade Laval spat in helpless rage, his hand squeezing his sluggish watch . . .

Meanwhile, at the other end of the wire, the village was being turned upside-down — doors slammed open and shut, people cried and scampered, drowsy, bewildered figures with lanterns crowded the road to the mill.

Leading them was the pale, wild-haired mayor, his collar missing, his jacket askew, and sockless in his shoes, giving out feverish orders. The first horse-drawn cart loaded with flour was already heading toward the docks.

Suddenly the parish priest appeared, his robes in disarray, breathless in the illuminated circle of the road, pushing the crowd out of his way.

"Hold everything! Hold everything!" the priest cried from afar, waving his arms. "I have an idea!"

The mayor ran to meet him.

•

The hands of the watch were dragging forward to three when the hump of white sacks on the first cart became visible at the bend in the road.

Comrade Laval wiped the sweat from his brow with a handkerchief and, lighter at heart, slipped the watch into his pocket.

After the first cart, a second appeared on the road, then a third — a long bridal train, a white litany of carts squeaking a melody. In the glare of the lights, the flour-dusted and frightened peasants were hunched under their loads like so many worker ants, carrying the white, bursting bales to the floating anthills of the barges, the snowy hills rising higher with every passing moment.

Comrade Laval anxiously glanced at his watch. An hour had already passed, and they had only just finished loading the second barge. Somewhere in the distance the black seam of the horizon that binds heaven and earth unraveled before their eyes, like a shabby, threadbare fabric, and the gray lining of daybreak shone through the growing rift. Comrade Laval kept uneasily turning toward it.

When the third barge was finally ready, his watch showed four-thirty. The smear of daybreak to the east had already drawn a wide crack. The snowy hills of the boats, as if warmed by the sun's first rays, went green with the improvised lawn of the tarps. There was not another moment to lose.

Leaping between the rails of the barges, which had been shoved to the middle of the river with poles, the crew hastily tied them with lines and fastened them to the tugboat. The crowd squeezed onto the river-bank to observe their work in silence.

Comrade Laval picked up the receiver one last time:

"Hello! Who's speaking! A postal worker? Splendid. Please inform the mayor that before the lines are repaired tomorrow, the junction telephone pole should be burnt and a new one put in its place, just to be safe. Yes, that's all I wanted to say. Please send the residents of Tansorel a proletarian greeting from revolutionary Paris."

Comrade Laval put the phone to one side.

"All hands on deck! Line up! Are there fifteen of you? Good. Positions. Cut the wires! Take down the floodlights! Turn off all lights! We're on our way!"

The boat shuddered, wobbled on the spot, and heavily shunted forward, nosing its way like a massive camel with its three barge humps.

"Full steam ahead!"

Comrade Laval paced the deck. In the darkness he bumped into a figure leaning on the railing.

"Is that you, Comrade Monsignac? What do you think, will we make it to Paris before dawn?"

"Hard to imagine, with all this cargo . . . ," the sailor gloomily replied.

"But on the other hand, now we're sailing with the current, so it's easier."

The sailor turned away without another word and pointed at the bursting seam of the horizon. "Day is breaking," he said dryly. "It'll be totally bright before we get there."

Comrade Laval spent a long time uneasily staring at the flesh-colored gash growing before his very eyes.

"We're late . . . ," he whispered, sunk in thought.

On either side the gray riverbanks were already sketching themselves out clearly, now sown with the first glimmers of light.

What Comrade Laval did not know was that a small, hunchbacked man had left Tansorel on bicycle an hour before, taking the field paths toward town.

The small man arrived at the town when the gray thaw in the heavens had already spread wide.

Ten minutes later rubber words were bouncing like a ball, chasing the breathless tugboat. Hopping from wire to wire, the words overtook the tugboat and bounced onward, into forests of red blinking lights.

After another twenty minutes, the following dialogue occurred in a plush, smoky salon of an old palace — the headquarters of the cordon army:

Lieutenant: Should we fire on the tugboat?

Captain: Of course, I've already given the order.

Lieutenant: But . . . as long as they've already made it . . . and, as the telegram says, they didn't touch shore at all and observed all precautions . . . What harm would it do to let them bring food to the city? They present no danger for now, and by sinking them we would achieve nothing.

Captain: Have you gone mad, Monteloup? Let them arrive at the city unpunished? So that someone else breaks through tomorrow? What have we set up this cordon for, then? Their impertinence must not go unpunished. And perhaps you've forgotten that these are Bolsheviks, and that they are bringing food to their commune? Should we be allowing more supplies for their commune? Thank you very much indeed!

Lieutenant: Of course not . . . I simply . . . I thought . . . since they've already made it . . .

•

A crowd of curious onlookers started gathering around Paris's Pont de Bercy at three a.m., anxiously peering eastward, where the white gash of daybreak was shining through the parted lips of sky and earth.

At five o'clock the gash filled half the sky. The return of the expedition seemed more and more unlikely. The dejected crowd started slowly drifting homeward. Just then, the thunder of the first cannon shot was heard from the east. The crowd shuddered, swayed, and then jerked in that direction as one body.

"They're coming!" came a holler.

The cannons boomed one after another. The crowd poured along the riverbank in a churning wave. A woman, perched like a bird on the iron railing of the bridge, wailed at the top of her lungs. After ten minutes of cannon fire, the murmur had changed into a howl.

Suddenly, someone roared:

"They're coming!"

A silence fell.

A black tugboat with a shattered funnel and bits of deck boards dangling helplessly had appeared at the bend in the river. The tugboat was panting heavily and floating practically on its side, pulling two barges with the remains of its strength. In place of the third barge, a black sideboard listlessly flapped its fins of broken planks.

The tugboat slowly approached the bridge. The crowd's enthusiasm peaked:

"Laval! Long live Laval!"

The tugboat struggled to shore. A squat, blood-smeared sailor leapt off and onto the sand.

"Laval! Where is Laval!" the crowd roared.

The sailor pointed a bandaged hand to the deck.

A few Red Guard soldiers jumped on board. The crowd grew mute in expectation. A few minutes later two soldiers appeared on deck, carrying something on a trench coat used as a makeshift stretcher.

The crowd craned forward.

On the coat lay a man with eyes squeezed shut and head thrown back, a gory mess of ground meat where his legs should have been.

The crowd removed their hats and stepped back in silence.

The Red Guards carried Comrade Laval through this improvised passage to the corner pharmacy.

Then the turmoil began.

•

Four men in blue army trench coats paced between the hospital beds. The orderly in front stopped before one of them.

"Here he is, Comrade Commandant."

Comrade Lecoq bent down over the cot.

A shadow fell over the wounded man's eyelids. They quivered and fluttered like a flame about to die, while the great, glassy eyes opened and rested upon the face of Comrade Lecoq. Finding a familiar face, the filmy eyes lit up in a smile. The lips moved mechanically, flapped like wings, struggling to release some cumbersome words from the cocoon of the mouth:

"Is that you, Comrade Commandant? . . . You see? I brought . . . They only sunk one of my barges, the bastards . . . ," he spluttered, his lips already going blue.

Comrade Lecoq bent down over him and, without speaking, gave his lips a quiet brotherly kiss.

Comrade Lecoq did not tell the man, dying with a smile of contentment, that the four hundred sacks he had brought back were filled with sand, not flour . . .

•

Three days later, the starved population of the commune stormed the barricades of the Anglo-American territory. The terrified gentlemen mobilized the army of the French burghers still inhabiting their territory to come to their defense. The fight at the barricades lasted several days and was marked by uncommon resistance and cruelty. Among the casualties were Comrade Lecoq — who was not to finish his history of the Paris plague — and many other outstanding leaders of the commune.

The new commander-in-chief of the dwindling army of the Belleville Soviet Republic decided to force the barricade with heavy artillery, positioning their battery on Red Hill. When called upon to surrender, the Anglo-American territory refused.

Who can say what new and terrifying scenes, what fantastic battles our multilingual, war-torn Paris would have witnessed, had the merciful plague not outpaced its competitor — famine.

By the day of September 1, there was not one living soul in all the territories of over a dozen tiny states signified on the map by the single, solitary circle of Paris.

The plague, having consumed the last Parisian, left the city that very same day, just as suddenly as it had appeared.

3

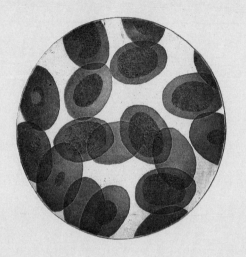

INTAGLIO · MICROGRAPH. *Stadii di ev. apu*
Magnified *260* *?* *diameters*
Prepared *CRISTIAN OPRIS, noiembrie 2007*

stad. incomplet. de
dev. a pers.

1/15

Ch. Opris

I

BEHIND THICK, TIGHTLY SEALED WALLS remained those who were beyond the reach of the plague.

In the death-flooded fields of Paris, in the silent hour of the tide's ebb, three islands of human life emerged, swaying on the ebbing waves like bald white shoals on the dead calm of the waters.

These were the islands of shaven-headed Robinsons, cut off from the rest of the world by the icy gulf stream of the law.

Lost among the deltas of streets, barricaded by the isolating liquid seeping from their walls, subject to their own internal laws like self-contained organisms in a different reality, they survived through the long weeks untouched, indifferent, like strange floating houses swept by flooding at night, bobbing to the surface in the morning, their inhabitants drowsy and unsuspecting.

The half-crazed prison guards, afraid of being held responsible and anticipating sudden orders, surrounded the inmates with a double ring of the tightest isolation. Their tongues were tied in fear of the crowded prisons learning about the epidemic and the chaos rampant outside, and of the cue to revolt.

The prisons had their own water reservoirs, so by sheer circumstance they avoided contracting the deadly bacteria from the outset. Their abundant supplies of food combined with the inviolable seclusion did the rest.

What had occurred was as improbable as it was undeniable: in its journey through the city the plague repeatedly bumped against the high medieval walls of these strange islands with their hermetically sealed gates, and then continued on into the night, into the gloom, into the tangle of streets and alleyways.

In the center and on the outskirts of the infected city, three untouched islands remained, surrounded by the dikes of their walls, inhabited by throngs of the shaven-headed pressed into their square allotments, long cut off from the outside world and fingering their monotonous rosaries of prison days, oblivious to what was taking place beyond the walls.

From the very first day of the epidemic, newspapers stopped seeping through the prison walls, causing the prisoners to protest and demonstrate. When this had no effect, a hunger strike was called. The hunger strike lasted four weeks and ultimately capitulated without bringing any results. Its only real outcome was to conserve provisions, which thus held out a few more days.

After the newspapers stopped arriving, the daily meals deteriorated, and then were reduced. Exhausted from the hunger strike, the prisoners saw this as another notch in the punitive regime. The deterioration of the food led to several more longer or shorter hunger strikes, which preserved some of the provisions but only delayed the inevitable.

The food portions grew more meager with every passing day. In fear of the prisoners' retaliation, the tiny group of guards who were also barricaded in this inadvertent Noah's Ark on the waves of the deluge suddenly cut the daily strolls, too afraid to release this riled human mass from their cells.

Denied their basic privileges and packed into the cramped barrels of their cells, the mob fermented until it seemed ready to blow, and the cells, filled ten times beyond capacity after the recent crackdowns, shuddered in their stone joints.

As the petrified prison guards scraped the bottoms of the food crates, terror filled their eyes. The certainty of execution at the hands of the despairing prisoners, ready to rip the bolted doors off their hinges, tempted them to flee for their lives, to the city. Yet their fear of the plague raging outside stopped them in their tracks.

A solution presented itself.

On the day of September 4, four days after the plague had claimed the last living Parisian soul and then marched out of Paris, the famished mob held at Fresnes Prison tore open the cell doors and poured through the prison building. Hiding in the attic, the guards were ripped to shreds. At ten o'clock in the morning the restless mob came crashing through the open gates and into the square.

To their considerable surprise, there was no police or military cordon to stop them. More disquieted than elated, the throng silently flowed toward the city without encountering a single living soul on their way.

Someone cried for the release of the fifteen thousand prisoners locked up in La Santé Prison. The stoked mob moved toward Boulevard Arago. The prison gates were taken by storm before reinforcements could be brought up. The astonished prison staff were put to death.

Upon hearing of the unexpected relief, the prisoners forced the cell doors and spilled into the yard. The brownish meat of the gathered masses boiled over from the narrow troughs of the courtyards and into Boulevard Arago.

On Boulevard Arago, the crowd formed a procession and drew upward in a sturdy wave. Someone piped up with *The Internationale*. That lonely, timid voice was like a match igniting the crowd. The alcohol of twenty-eight thousand voices burst into melodious flames. The mob had swollen as heavy as a lead-colored cloud, and now the rain of song poured from it. Like on a sweltering day charged with electricity, so dry that one seems to hear the crackle of sparks in one's hair, the refreshing downpour suddenly gave the air the fragrance of freshly soaked earth. With the protracted shudder of an electric current, the song ran through the gigantic serpentine body of the mass, from the head to the tail, joining the scattered human cells into one nimble organism, animated through the artery of its uniform rhythm. Twenty-eight thousand pairs of legs hit the hard shell of the pavement in unison with every turn of an invisible steering wheel, and the earth flashed sparks from the quick kiss of their feet.

The extraordinary procession moved through the deathly quiet of this ghost town, down the silent ravine of the boulevard, a demonstration of miserable men with shaved heads and gray prison garb. They had no banners, only the red flag of the sun raised high above their heads, and in the empty inlets of the streets this song of retribution struck an oddly menacing note, this song of the last fight, whose refrain hit the empty, shattered windows like the butt of a rifle.

At the end of Boulevard Montparnasse the front of the procession unexpectedly balled up in one spot, and the whole snake halted in its march and rippled with thousands of fists.

The crowd convulsed at the sight of what was unfolding before its eyes, as if the cold paw of terror had touched its naked heart.

On the streets and sidewalks, in the wicker chairs on the bistro verandas, human corpses lay in the twisted and incomprehensible poses chosen by death. They had begun to reek.

Consumed by fear, the procession continued on in silence.

The appeals and decrees in various languages plastered on the walls of the various district-states told the story of the past six weeks, it slowly unfolded before the crowd's wondering eyes in all its grotesque horror.

The procession turned onto Grands Boulevards, everywhere encountering the same tableau: a vast mortuary, staring through the glaze of one million eyes into the clear blue sky.

At the end of Boulevard Haussmann the crowd splintered into two groups, one of which flowed toward Saint-Lazare, to the women's prison. The closed prison gates met the demonstrators with a hollow silence. They forced them open using iron rails from the train station. Nobody inside tried to put up any resistance. The guards, it turned out, had fled to the city four days earlier in fear of the prisoners' revenge, condemning the three thousand women in their cells to death by starvation. The inmates hadn't eaten for ten days.

In ransacking the Gare Saint-Lazare, they unexpectedly found ample food reserves in its warehouses and stations, which had been stored there by the thriftiest of the district-states, the Anglo-American territory.

A provisions committee was assembled ad hoc, and they at once took to organizing food distribution.

Spontaneous patrols spread from the Gare Saint-Lazare to the rest of the city to inspect the remaining prisons. The patrols returned before evening empty-handed, one after another. The prisons were found open, full of rotting, plague-infested corpses. No other living beings remained in all of Paris.

Night fell, and the thirty-two-thousand strong crowd, preferring to stay clear of the apartments with their stinking corpses, bivouacked on the streets, the tireless tentacles of their sentries probing into the night.

II

THE FOLLOWING MORNING, a newly constituted Central Committee of the Party hastily convened in the grand hall of the former Ministry of War.

The day was sunny and the air as if dripping with spring. Thirteen people in gray prison shirts sat at the long table, green as the ruffled turf after a picnic, with scraps of notes tossed here and there like eggshells. The windows were thrown open wide, and the sunshine and the hubbub of the mass gathered in Place de la Concorde drifted in unceremoniously. The blissful atmosphere of this pseudo-springtime ushered in memories of April, interspersed by the distant rumble of turmoil and the thick, rushing downpour of applause, which would suddenly pick up, only to subside with equal swiftness.

Courreau, Secretary of the Central Committee, took the floor:

"We cannot be sure if the plague hasn't already managed to spread beyond the Paris city limits. Based on our current data, however, everything would suggest that Paris is still surrounded by tight military cordons, the intent of which is to isolate the city from the rest of Europe. This would indicate that they have managed to contain the plague. As soon as the government and the surrounding armies discover that the epidemic has vanished from the capital, they will surely advance on the city the very next day and throw the proletariat back into prison. After all the suffering they've endured to free themselves, we cannot allow this to happen. Given that Paris has ended up in our hands after such tragic circumstances, we have no right to hand it back to the capitalists and the exploiters."

"And how, may I may, do you intend to keep it?" cut in Comrade Majoie, anxiously scratching at his thin beard. "With thirty-thousand starving workers, we can't even dream of standing up to a proper army surrounding Paris from all sides. We have no right to lead these miserable remnants of the Parisian proletariat to the slaughter."

"Allow me to finish, comrade. We can hold onto Paris in a very simple way, without resorting to armed resistance, which is beyond our meager strength. At all costs we must make France and the whole world believe the plague is still raging through Paris just as before and is showing no signs of abating. All we need to do is have our people use the Eiffel radio station to send out worldwide bulletins every morning on the relentless devastation wrought by the infestation within the sealed confines of Paris. As long as the government and the army are convinced the epidemic is going full force, they won't dare set foot in the city."

"It seems you've forgotten, comrade, that the population of Paris is limited in number, and that it can only die once," smiled Comrade Majoie. "A simple calculation will tell them that every living soul in Paris should have been killed off long ago."

"I think not. By gradually increasing the reports, knowledgeably and with moderation, we should be able to keep Europe in the dark for a very long time. We have to inculcate our country, drop by drop, with the belief that for months and months to come, and who knows, for perhaps even years, Paris will be no more than a dangerous epicenter of plague, that all of its infrastructure has been destroyed, and that returning it to its former state would require billions in investments and years of labor. I assure you that nothing works so effectively as getting people accustomed to the status quo. Those who were initially unable to imagine the World War lasting for more than four weeks had already stopped believing by the end of the fourth year that it could ever come to an end. They had grown so accustomed to this state of affairs that it came to be entirely natural, and no other way even seemed possible."

"So, as I see it, you'd like to turn us into Robinson Crusoes on a desert island, condemned to fishing in the Seine and hunting monkeys in the Bois de Boulogne for years on end," quipped Comrade Majoie. "I see no point in this deception."

"Allow me, comrade," suddenly piped up Comrade Maraq, a withered, bony man with a drooping, angular face, a champion hunger-striker in prison, who could best anyone even with a week's head start.

Everyone turned to face him.

"I think I understand Comrade Courreau's idea. Just today I was doing a check-up on the Eiffel radio station, and the same thought occurred to me: keep Europe believing that the plague is still in Paris for as long as possible. Meanwhile, we occupy the city and establish the ideal commune. In the middle of France, in the heart of Europe, we could change a world metropolis into a massive communist city, a hotbed and a cell, radiating our system across the whole continent. As soon as we are organized, and before our deception is unveiled, we'll call out to the workers and peasants in France and the whole world behind the backs of the surrounding army. Let's not forget that behind the army cordon stand the French proletarian masses. The call from the East may not have reached them, it may have been drowned out by the whistle, roar, and swing of the capitalist jazz orchestra, but when it comes from Paris, it will shake all of Europe. Do I understand you correctly, Comrade Courreau?"

Comrade Courreau nodded his head.

After a moment's silence, Comrade Durail took the floor, having kept thus far to one side:

"Comrades Courreau and Maraq's plan is quite elegant, but I fear it is unfeasible. Comrades Courreau and Maraq are not considering one real, though unfortunate, fact: It won't be enough for Europe to leave us in peace if we want to survive for months behind the cordon. We also need something to fill our bellies. We have thirty-two thousand mouths to feed. They have already starved half to death in prison and cannot starve any longer. Comrade Duffy, who just today made a record of the provisions we found hidden around the city, is best able to inform us on the state of our rations and how long they might feed the whole commune."

All eyes turned to Comrade Duffy.

Comrade Duffy, fiddling with a pencil and tapping a beat on the table, began to speak in a monotonous, pedantic voice, as if reciting a report he'd chiseled into his memory:

"We haven't been able to record all the city's provisions in a single day. We found substantial rations of flour and sugar at the Gare Saint-Lazare. Around four hundred tons in total. The grain elevators contained one thousand two hundred tons. Larger or smaller stocks of provisions, mainly canned goods and pasta, were found in the cellars of factories and meat-processing plants. In the cellars of many private homes in the districts of Étoile, Grands Boulevards, Saint-Germain, and Passy, we found large quantities of flour, rice, and sugar. The residents there were clearly hoarding these items in fear of starvation. We'll need another thorough investigation to confirm the exact amount of these products. Roughly speaking, the total amount of foodstuffs unearthed over the course of the day can be set at two thousand tons. Considering the average human body requires a daily intake of 82g of protein, 100g of fats, 310g of carbohydrates and 26g of vitamins, this, when converted into numerals, tallies up to enough bread alone — in the absence of other substances — for at least 350g daily, meaning that the provisions discovered thus far should provide sustenance for thirty-two thousand people for four to five months at most. Of course, there is no way to tell how much food we still might find in the factory cellars and residential homes. Only a more thorough search will reveal . . ."

A new wave of applause came splashing in through the window, drowning out his remaining words.

Comrade Majoie lit a cigarette, paced the room in contemplation, and stood before the window. Down below, the square was obscured by the swarm of heads. A rally was underway. The ceremonial speakers climbed nimbly onto the sheer pediments of the eight symbolic virgin-cities and tossed handfuls of powerful and strident words like pills into the gaping mouths of the crowd, tickling their noses and spinning their heads.

A one-armed mustachioed man was speaking from the pedestal of the virgin symbolizing Strasbourg:

"Now, comrades, I would like to say a word about our comrades from the criminal profession. Among us there are around three thousand larcenous comrades who were released from prison with the rest of the proletariat. We do not intend, comrades, to drag them before a tribunal. Though they are criminals, as they say, we should view their crimes as having been committed against the old bourgeois order — and who then was *not* considered a criminal? Surely more than one of us has swiped a pound of sausage or a side of ham out of hunger, misery, or unemployment, haven't we? Such a man, their courts chewed him up — and then off to the slammer! He's a thief, end of story. But we do not intend, comrades, to bother ourselves with these details. A revolution's a revolution. What I'm trying to say is: freedom for everyone, no ifs, ands, or buts. In other words, the old sins, whatever they were, never happened — you might say it's amnesty, and that's that. From this day forward, everything starts from scratch, our way. Bygones are bygones, know what I mean?

"But comrades — now that our thieving comrades have their civil rights restored and so forth, they should show us their proletarian roots. We had various scores to settle with the bourgeoisie, and we swallowed a lot of grief — but now everything's been wiped clean. Now we're all equal workers, proletarians, period. If someone's stealing from the people — then beat it! We've got no time to be fooling around with the likes of them, comrades. The proletariat authority will unceremoniously punish every raid on communal property. Let all future comrade-thieves bear that in mind. What's past is past, and from this day on — no mention of it! We have no need, comrades, for courts or trials. If we catch a thief stealing from our communal stores — up against the wall! No one plays policeman here!"

"Hear, hear!"

"We don't have time to be keeping tabs on them!"

"It's not our job to police them!"

"Well said!"

"If they want to play along — there's plenty of work, enough for everybody. If not — it's their choice. Up against the wall, and that's the end of it."

"Exactly, comrades, that's just what I wanted to say. This is now a family affair, as they say. The Central Committee doesn't need to get involved, they've got enough on their plate. We're not going to put up notices or repeat ourselves. It's been said and that's it, right?"

The mustachioed speaker hopped down from the pedestal to a storm of applause.

Comrade Majoie smiled and walked away from the window with a lighter heart. A new eruption of applause and a thunderous "R-r-right!" drew him toward the last window. Comrade Majoie stole a glance back at the table. Duffy was still giving his report. Majoie tiptoed to the furthest window, leaned on the sill, and listened.

Down below, from a wooden crate that had appeared out of nowhere, a broad-shouldered farmhand with a pointy nose was bellowing away.

"Comrades! At this very moment our comrades in the Central Committee are deliberating on how to keep Paris for ourselves, to keep from handing it over to the bourgeoisie and the capitalists. The main hitch, comrades, is our provisions, mouths to feed. We've got a hell of a lot of them, and not a lot of food. I don't think we should bother our comrades from the Central Committee with this matter, comrades. We have starved, comrades, for the bourgeoisie of course, for their sake, and now we can starve for our own sake, for our workers' soviets. But we won't surrender Paris to the bourgeoisie!"

"Right you are!"

"We didn't fight to get it just to give it up!"

"And what about us? Right back to the slammer? We're no idiots! We'll hang in there!"

"The people know how to starve!"

"Comrades, Soviet Russia faced worse starvation in the ring of the imperialist blockade, but it survived and went on to build the first socialist republic. Is the French proletariat any worse off than the Russians?"

"Everyone's got the same stomachs."

"And didn't the Commune starve? They had to eat rats, but they didn't give up."

"Right!"

"No sense in idle talk, comrades. We'll just hold out and that's that. Just wait and see how the proletariat brings up the rear to help when they find out we've got Paris in the palm of our hands. We'll wait a month, or a year if we have to. If we're careful with our provisions, we can make it for a month or two. If necessary, we'll hold out longer. I saw for myself, comrades, that the bourgeoisie left us quite a bit in the grain elevators. If we play our cards right and keep our hands off the grain, we should be able to stretch it out till spring — and after that, piece of cake. We've got as much free space as we need in the city. The soil isn't all that bad. If we sow grain in the spring, by the end of summer we'll have a whole new field of crops. We could hold out for as many years as we like that way. The bourgeoisie won't lift a finger — they'll chicken out, all they think about is the plague. And meanwhile, we'll cause them so much trouble they won't know which way's up. The main thing to do here, comrades, is to hold strong."

"Of course we'll hold out, why shouldn't we?"

"We survived on prison grub, now we'll survive just as well on our own."

"We'll survive all right!"

"We haven't let one master die just to give power to another!"

Comrade Majoie turned away from the window. His ear caught the calm voice of Comrade Courreau:

". . . our armor of plague offers better protection from European intervention than any army we could have. The X-ray doesn't exist that's capable of telling from afar if the plague in Paris is eradicated, or if it's raging as fiercely as ever . . ."

Thousands of excited voices roared in the square below.

Comrade Majoie flicked away his cigarette and hurried back to his spot at the table. He saw from the looks of concentration on his comrades' faces that the final act was beginning. The face of the speaker wasn't turned to him, but he could tell that the gravelly voice belonged to Maraq.

"Comrades, in a moment we're going to put Comrade Courreau's motion to a vote. The fate of the French proletariat, perhaps even the European proletariat, hangs on the outcome. Let each of us weigh his own conscience. Do we have the right to hand over our own lives, and those of thirty thousand of our comrades, to the hands of the industrialists and imperialists in the hopes of mercy and amnesty? Do we have the right to squander this singular cataclysm in human history, this plague-broom that has swept Paris clean of the bourgeoisie and the magnates? Does fear of hunger, want, and isolation in the grip of the blockade give us the right to forego this opportunity to raise the foundations of a model commune in the heart of Europe, on the site of its former capital, the capital of bankers and prostitutes — a commune that will light the way for the proletariat of all countries like a pillar of fire, the first firebrand of the world revolution? Have we the right to forgo this historic mission, which our very circumstances have thrust upon us? Comrade Chairman, please put Courreau's motion to a vote."

Comrade Gaillard spoke up in a steady voice:

"Comrades, I am putting Comrade Courreau and Comrade Maraq's motion to a vote. Who's for? Please raise your hands."

Twelve hands rose.

Comrade Duffy abstained.

"Comrade Courreau's motion is passed," Gaillard laconically announced.

They proceeded to the remaining topics on the day's agenda.

III

AN ANIMATED CROWD WAS STILL BURBLING on the square outside when the first committee members appeared in the doorway to the ministry. Someone bellowed:

"They're coming!"

The crowd fell silent, swayed, and cracked open in a zigzag, only to close up again, swallowing the people exiting the building. For a moment the rafts of heads bobbed around the spot like ripples from a stone. Soon those who were sucked in started to flow out, one by one, onto the reefs of the monuments protruding above the surface. Their words were inaudible, you could only see the violent gestures of their hands slicing the air, as if twelve demented conductors wanted to capture the chaotic din of the polyphonic sea into the harmonious notations of a score.

A bony man was speaking from the plinth of the Strasbourg Virgin. The ongoing flood of applause dappled his face with great drops of sweat.

"Instead of the plague, which was to have spread across the entire world, but in fact only made room to start building anew, we hereby ignite the great plague of the idea that will spread across this old continent like a sea of cleansing fire, scorching the armies, cordons, and borders. Paris, the first to show Europe the great Commune, will be the first to blow the winds of change through all of Europe! . . ."

Leavened by the yeast of their enthusiasm, the crowd swelled and boiled over with a refrain of *The Internationale*. The thin, spindly man was carried forward, directionless, on swiftly flowing shoulders like a cork swept by a current.

The rushing human waves poured into the pools of squares and the straits of alleyways.

To tear this highly combustible crowd from its unbridled elation and channel it into concrete action, they had to yank out its seams and splice it with the scissors of organization.

By the afternoon, the mass had been segmented, yoked once more by the iron clamp of discipline, and was a viable source of power.

The first task was to clear the streets of the rotting corpses, which were threatening to cause a new wave of infection. Burying such a mass of bodies or burning them in small ad hoc crematoria was out of the question, so it was resolved to cremate them in the open air.

For the next three days, small divisions of shaven-headed, disciplined troops made gigantic pyres out of furniture and waste paper in the squares of Paris and piled the corpses on top. The work was completed on the fourth day. The mounds were doused with gasoline and oil and set alight.

There was no wind to put the neighboring buildings at risk. The fire punched the sky with a black spiral of smoke, and the burning heavens collapsed like a thatched roof in flames, covering the city with a fur cap of soot.

On September 8, newspapers all over the world carried news of the fire in Paris. Crowds gathered on the hills and highlands of France to see it for themselves. The black geyser of smoke gushed hundreds of feet up into the sky. It was an unforgettable sight.

A brave French pilot hit upon the idea of flying over burning Paris, but was forced by the plumes of caustic smoke to turn back, and was unable to say anything beyond the fact that Paris was ablaze from end to end.

Kindly old Grandma Europe was touched that day by the fate of the unfortunate city — and it was not crocodile tears she shed. Elderly gentlemen all around the world wistfully recalled the days of their youth: the Moulin Rouge and Maxim's, midinettes and mannequins. From high on their pulpits, priests made vague references to the Lord's wrath and exhorted penance. In the Chamber of Deputies, the gray-haired, immortal Briand railed against the communists.

The following day, the Continent's radios picked up the first signals from Paris after a long period of silence. The bulletins reported on the fire, the disorder, and the raging epidemic.

The events of the following months — during which the daily reports from Paris were as bleak as ever — turned French attention away from their capital for a long time.

Taking advantage of the turmoil in France, Germany categorically refused to make further reparation payments, as the Dawes Plan had outlined, on the pretext that their economy was struggling. War was in the air. The bourgeois newspapers, spearheaded by the socialists, called for the occupation of Berlin, to settle the score with their unruly neighbor. The sailors of the Mediterranean fleet responded with a revolt, hoisting red flags up their masts. The Lyon garrison clearly sympathized with them, and joined with the workers to demonstrate against war.

An emergency session of the League of Nations concluded with memos filling two cartloads of official stationery, an all-out attempt to mollify the swelling conflict. Under pressure from the working masses, the French government was forced into a compromise, thereby undermining the integrity of the Treaty of Versailles. The immediate threat of war seemed to have been averted.

Radio Paris continued to report the escalation of the plague and riots erupting in the infested city. According to the most recent news, the eastern quarters of Paris had been overtaken by an anarchonihilist cult bent on destroying the city. Three government aircraft that tried to fly over Paris were shot down by these alleged cultists. This deplorable incident took away the last of the government's desire to meddle with the plague-infested city, which from then on was abandoned to its cruel fate.

Months passed. France, a floozy with a short memory, slowly came to terms with the loss of its beloved capital city. More painful than the loss itself was the absence of tourists stuffed with dollars, who had proved quite difficult to lure back. It was imperative that they create a new capital as soon as possible, one that was in no way inferior to Paris in terms of its comfort and titillating attractions. A special consortium was established for the expansion and exploitation of Lyon.

Upscale, eight-story hotels soared up on either side of Lyon's boulevards with lightning speed. Theaters, dance halls, and cabarets opened up, and lavish brothels, for men and women both, sprang up from nowhere. Historical monuments were hastily transported from all corners of France.

Telegraphs trumpeted the sensational news of the new and glittering capital to all corners of the globe in the blink of an eye.

This extraordinary news met with a fevered response worldwide. Every country hustled to pitch in their two cents to the growing population of Lyon.

America, France's obliging ally, who had overcome its fear of the ongoing fires of the plague in the name of a profitable transaction, daily sent off huge ocean liners, loaded to the tops of their funnels with armies of jazz bands, dancing girls, hotel maître d's, stewards, and grooms. The more courageous Americans were already packing their bags to take the first Cook voyage and to be the first to set foot on a re-conquered patch of Europe.

From all the world over, cocottes, madams, and common prostitutes hurried to the Rhone on serpentine rails at breakneck speed, a live cargo of all nations and races, for whom the thoughtful French government was obliged to introduce additional train services.

In the shadows of the brand new homes, popping up like mushrooms after a rainstorm of dollars, appeared the immortal potbellied hoteliers.

The clatter of advertisements and signboards being hammered in place filled the entire city.

Day and night, from the streets and the alleyways, the familiar inscriptions of nighttime hotels blinked incessantly, enticing passersby. And on an evening filled with all the clamor of a Javanese orchestra, after a long hiatus, the fiery windmill of the Moulin Rouge spun its eternal circle where it had been reconstructed in Lyon, and Europe breathed a collective sigh of relief, as if to say: "So it's really spinning."

Champagne flowed in a pearl-white, all-cleansing stream through the gutters of the new Montmartre, and emaciated, ragged workers flowed in a black stream from the evacuating villages to the factories.

In the autumn of the second year, the government — the forty-sixth in a row — was stabilizing the franc. France's lousy economic situation had made people stop buying cars. Factories were being threatened with closure. The workforce was being cut by half everywhere you looked. To avoid any commotion, people were being dismissed a handful at a time and from different divisions, staggered throughout the day. Hiring more workers was out of the question.

In the Chamber of Deputies, a white-maned socialist by the name of Paul Boncour was forwarding a motion to double the police force.

One beautiful August evening, the streets teeming with that random and unsynchronized throng of extras cast every evening by Europe's rickety film projector onto the screen of Lyon's boulevards, on the corner of Rue Vivienne and Boulevard Montmartre, Jeanette informed Pierre that she would most definitely be requiring a pair of evening slippers.

IV

THE DUN LONDON FOG SLOWLY CREPT ACROSS EUROPE, spreading its vapors of damp toxic gasses.

During those years, scholars noted a marked change in the European climate. In the winter a slushy snow covered Nice, and the astonished palm trees, their leaves undulating under the frost like odd flat-chested skirt suits, swayed a phantom tango.

In London there was fog as always. The lampposts burned in the foggy daylight, and bristling figures flitted through the milky gelatinous haze — blind submarines with strangely short periscopes.

Londoners must have sponges for lungs, to soak up the fog and breathe it out, like factory smoke through pointy-faced chimneys.

In the noon fog, the pointy faces of the chimneys turned skyward and howled like dogs sniffing a corpse, then millions of human sponges poured out of the factories, the offices, and the government buildings to suck in the fog and carry it back to the six-story anthills of their offices.

Bloated ships roared into the coal-black ports daily, always at the same time, and on these ships soldiers, civil servants, and ordinary citizens of the British Empire floated off to their dominions, so that there, under the sweltering skies of India, they could exhale a bit of the fog that spreads across their land in a leaden vapor — for the sun-scorched Hindus, the London fog is more toxic than poison gas.

That summer a fine, prickly rain fell incessantly in Europe, and in August a fog swam in from the shores of Brittany. The fog pulled a heavy veil over the Channel, hugged the green coastline of Normandy, and pushed further inland, wrapping objects and cities in its soft, gray suede. The fuzzy gray puffs crawled through the valleys like smoke. Scientists predicted a damp autumn and ended their prophecies there, unlike the peasants, who recalled that smoke clings to the ground before a storm and began muttering of future calamities.

In the Channel, steamships blundering in the fog hailed one another with a constant scream of sirens.

In Dauville, the fog blew away the vacationers who had come to the beach to soak up the sun, and the greedy tongues of the sea lapped the white sand as if it were cold mashed potatoes left on a plate. Tourists wandered around the hotel terraces with tussled hair, flannel scarves wrapped tight around their necks.

In the restaurants, cafés, and hotel dance halls the jazz music started its barking in the morning, and hapless half-naked vacationers, dripping with the yellow, cadaverous light of the chandeliers, in dresses not unlike swimsuits, convulsed in syncopated bliss, latching like crabs onto the chests of the male divers, who shook themselves as they danced.

In the morning, the express train leapt out of the gray cloud in an electric zigzag, descending upon the station on the lightning-rods of the rails. Two men in black top hats were waiting on the platform, accompanied by some twenty photographers and a restless mob of journalists. A clean-shaven, grayish gentleman in a French kepi stepped out of the first-class car, accompanied by a few younger gentlemen. The men in top hats ceremonially rushed to greet him. Camera shutters clicked. The gentlemen tipped their hats politely and began speaking in English. Two cars were waiting at the entrance. They swayed gently under the weight of the gentlemen settling in their seats, and then drifted off into the fog. Reporters hopped into the first available taxis and gave pursuit, lured by the sweet hope of an interview. The gentleman who had arrived was the Prime Minister of Great Britain.

An hour later the prime minister's secretary went down to a hotel lobby swarming with journalists. He was dressed in a charmingly discreet pullover and a loose-fitting English suit, and with a politely bored expression on his face he informed the persistent reporters that the prime minister had arrived in Dauville with no particular political plans in mind, simply to relax for a few days from the rigors of affairs of state, and that he was rather distressed to see that the weather was not cooperating.

The reporters took all this down to the letter. They knew perfectly well that the President of the Council of Ministers of France had arrived from Lyon just the day before. They'd met him at the station, followed him to the very same hotel, and heard him make nearly identical remarks. They also knew that two days earlier a Polish emissary had come to Dauville by train from the Belgian border, though only one man in a top hat was at the station to greet him, with no photographers or journalists in sight.

So having urgently transcribed the secretary's statement, they all scrambled to send their editors news about the important political summit between the representatives of the three great powers. Then they ran back with all possible haste to lie in wait for the tight-lipped diplomats.

Both statesmen remained in their suites all morning. They ordered room service for breakfast, and each devoured it with gusto. At four o'clock in the afternoon, a reporter dressed as a butler noticed the British prime minister himself going to the bathroom, where he remained for a considerable time before returning to his quarters.

It was only around six in the evening that, to the delight of all the reporters patiently lurking behind their doors, the French president and his secretary left their suites in the left wing of the hotel and, without straying from their paths, headed straight toward the right wing, to the suites of the British prime minister. No matter how hard the reporters strained their eyes, they could not discern any kind of definite expression on his face. One of the reporters did notice, however, that the president was softly whistling a popular melody when he passed by the door behind which he hid.

The visit dragged on. Three times a reporter disguised as a bellboy brought cocktails to suite No. 6 and silently busied himself with the glassware for a long time. The whole time he was present the statesmen discussed the weather, complained about the poor harvests in their countries, and exchanged opinions on the most recent races at Wembley. In the end, the reporter accomplished nothing, though he did break a glass from his eavesdropping and his lack of professional training.

At around eight that evening a call was made, and ten minutes later the Polish emissary was knocking at the door to suite No. 6. Aristocratic in bearing and stylishly disheveled, a careful part ran right down to his collar between his sparse clumps of hair.

Cocktails were served once more. The conversation proceeded in English. The virtues of various types of cigars were discussed. The Polish emissary absentmindedly brushed flakes of ash from his sleeve.

The reporters behind the doors impatiently opened and closed their pocket cameras. They were eager to capture the facial expressions of the diplomats leaving the summit and they worried that, with the poor lighting in the corridor, this historic moment might slip through their fingers.

Finally, at around nine o'clock, the door of suite No. 6 opened and the Polish emissary came out, awkwardly adjusting his immaculate snow-white cuffs. His was absolutely expressionless, as befits the face of a diplomat. The Polish emissary took the elevator to his suite.

Only a good half hour after his departure did the French president appear in the doorway of suite No. 6, shown to the door by his English colleague. His face was slightly puffy and pink, like that of a man who has smoked too many cigars. Some of the less experienced reporters mistook this for a flush of excitement. Unfortunately, the lighting in the corridor turned out to be woefully inadequate, and these keen reporters were clearly not fated to capture for posterity the statesmen's facial expressions on this momentous evening.

Having trailed the French president back to his suite, the journalists dispersed: some to the post office, others to the restaurant to polish off Wienerschnitzel and scribble out their articles, and still others headed off for some dancing, to stretch their legs after a hard day's work. Both heads of state dismissed their servants and probably went to rest. The political day had come to an end. Nothing of interest could occur until the next day. The last reporter, who hoped to be the first at his post the following day, left the hotel.

And this was a pity. Had he only kept waiting until midnight, he would most certainly have noted an incident of some interest. A car pulled up to the hotel at ten to twelve. The Polish emissary came down the stairs, preceded by a bellboy carrying his suitcase. The emissary and the suitcase vanished through the car door. The car drove off to the train station.

A week later, buried deep on the back pages of the morning dailies, the word "Poland" appeared in print for the first time. By the end of the week the "Polish question" was cropping up with lightning speed, like quicksilver in the tubes of the newspaper columns, filling whole pages and creeping toward the headlines. The news became more and more detailed.

A newly contrived hetman had suddenly appeared in the territory of Poland — God knows how — and he was planning a march on Ukraine to liberate her from the yoke of Bolshevik rule. In his many interviews, this hetman proclaimed the resurrection of a "self-reliant" Ukraine, joined to Poland in its historical union. With the silent consent of the Polish government, this freshly baked hetman assembled a Ukrainian Liberation Army on the territory of the Polish state. The Polish newspapers sounded the reveille. They recalled the all-too-recent historical borders . . . The government maintained a dignified silence.

When it seemed as though the situation was reaching its climax, the government of the Soviet Union addressed the Polish government with a gentle note of caution, requesting that, in the interests of European peace and good relations between neighbors, the rabble-rousing organizations threatening the peace and integrity of the Soviet Union should immediately be dissolved.

The bourgeois press viewed this note as an outlandish provocation and began alluding to war. The Polish government was spurred to make an unparliamentary reply. An exchange of harsh ultimatums ensued.

A violent northwest wind blew in Lyon that day, and shredded scraps of fog flapped like wet underwear on invisible clotheslines. A gale furiously hurtled down streets, knocking unwary passersby off their feet. Wind-tossed hats flapped in the air like heavy birds, and headless pedestrians hopped strangely after them like rubber balls.

At around six p.m., special newspaper supplements appeared on the streets. Pedestrians twirled like tops at the intersections, clutching at papers that slipped between their fingers. They fluttered their awkward newspaper wings like butterflies trapped under the impenetrable net of fog.

Behind the thick glass of the café windows, hefty, shiftless clientele played Preference and, solemnly choosing their suit, poked at their hearts with sharp spades of spades.

"Whist."

"Naturally."

"But the trump is ours."

"Yes, monsieur, this is no laughing matter. Those bandits have provoked the Polish army into crossing their border. They're clearly threatening the integrity of our loyal ally, Poland. France won't stand for this kind of provocation."

"Pass."

"Tell me about it!"

"We'll aid our Polish friends with troops and ammunition. We'll drive out the Bolsheviks."

"We'll strike with our hearts! Yes, monsieur, that's the only way to finally return Europe to the old, prewar order. I always used to tell that to my deputy, Juliet. We'll never be rid of inflation until we finish off the Soviets."

"Queen of spades."

The wind was driving hard outside, it lashed the thick panes of glass, bounced upward, somersaulted over the rooftops, tripped, got tangled in the spider webs of antennae, and, freeing itself, pushed onward, while the vibrating antennae resounded long and dolefully.

In the industrialists' club that evening, the guests were playing Baccarat and indulging heartily in the buffet as usual, chewing slowly and drizzling Chablis on plump Portuguese oysters. In the smoking lounge, tuxedoed gentlemen sat in comfortable leather armchairs, smoked cigars and cigarettes, and held lively discussions.

Then a manager entered with two butlers, carrying a long scroll. When unraveled, it turned out to be a map of Europe. The butlers hung it on the wall.

The manager turned toward the graying gentlemen sprawled comfortably on the couch and jovially explained:

"When there's a war on, I know you like to have a map at the ready. During the last war we had to change maps six times. They were totally mutilated by all the thumbtack holes."

The men gathered in a circle around the map.

In the corner, on a sofa, a bald gentleman in a monocle was speaking to a gray man with muttonchops:

"Reportedly the English fleet set sail yesterday evening for St. Petersburg?..."

The man with muttonchops leaned confidentially toward his neighbor.

"A good friend of mine, the Minister of Internal Affairs, told me yesterday — just between you and me, of course — that the government plans to announce a mobilization tomorrow. A coalition of the whole civilized world is being formed, something like a crusade against those communist scoundrels. The Bolsheviks will be crushed in the next three weeks, and a rightful ruler will be restored to Russia. A provisional government made up of serious Russian émigré statesmen has been formed in London with the approval of the British and French governments. There's even talk of..." The man with muttonchops leaned in closer and concluded what he was saying in an inaudible whisper.

"Indeed!" exclaimed the bald gentleman. "Yes, that's quite conceivable. I, for one, have held that belief for ages. French industry will never get rid of this upheaval as long as the Soviets exist to the east. Dispatching the Soviets and bringing order to Russia will be a decisive blow to *our* local communists — it will mean a victory on our internal industrial front. All of level-headed France would not pale before sacrificing any number of victims for this cause..."

In the deserted streets outside, the blustery wind raced a lone motorcycle, and scraps of special supplements blew about like the gigantic snowflakes of a monster blizzard. Phantom-like policemen awkwardly danced on the street corners in their black oilcloth hoods.

The electricity burned bright in the print room of the workers' daily. Linotypes clattered and the tar-covered typesetters galloped the equine fingers of their calloused hands across the tiny cobblestones of the keys like some strange virtuosi. The levers and scatterbrained letters now leapt up, now dropped, soldiers instantly falling into line. And then, like divers from a springboard, the type thrust downward into the pool of liquid lead, a moment later emerging with the terse line of a sentence:

Today, at the hour of 12:00 noon, the first trans-

Again, letter chased letter, and, heated from their sprint, came out once more with another slender line:

port of arms and ammunition sent from Lyon to Poland

And further:

was held up 50 miles from the German border on account of a collective strike of railway workers, who refused to admit any transport sent to fight against the workers' Soviet Union.

Period.

"Way to go, boys!" smiled the typesetter.

The fingers flashed once more across the steps of the keyboard. Again, one after another, the letters climbed like acrobats along the lines, along the scaffolding of the levers, and moments later plunged headfirst into the bubbling pool, and emerged once more in another inseparable chain:

At 3:00 p.m. a decree was sent to town to mobilize the railways.

Immediately followed by:

The Central Committee of the United Labor Unions has called a general strike for tomorrow.

"Comrade, set a call from the Party C.C. to the working masses in pica."

Again the keyboard clattered:

Comrades! The bourgeois French government, under the beck and call of the English capitalists . . .

The roar of voices, the stamp of feet, and the rattle of machine guns came from the entrance to the print room. The staircase was swarming with navy-blue men.

The police.

That evening the red stains of posters appeared on the walls of buildings: The Communist Party's Central Committee was calling on all workers and soldiers.

Around seven o'clock special supplements with sensational news appeared on the boulevards of all the cities of Europe.

A British plane flying from London to Lyon lost its way in the thick fog over the Channel, flew off course, and unexpectedly found itself over Paris. It miraculously escaped being shot down and managed, in spite of a broken wing, to land beyond the cordon.

What the English pilot saw and reported was so unfathomable that even the tabloid press, which was not known for its adherence to scruples, conveyed it with a heavy dose of skepticism.

Wanting to establish where he was, the pilot had flown at only three hundred feet above the ground. By the time he had realized he was above Paris, it was too late — his curiosity had gotten the better of his caution.

He had flown from the direction of the Bois de Boulogne. A southerly wind was blowing the fog from the city, so everything was clear as a bell. The Paris that sprawled before his eyes was not burned in the slightest. The buildings, palaces, and monuments — everything seemed to be standing where they had always been, and yet he was also struck by all the changes that had taken place. The first thing the pilot noticed were the countless radio towers soaring above the city. The air was sliced on all sides by an infinity of antenna wires.

Passing the Arc de Triomphe, the pilot flew along the Champs-Elysées. What he saw there defied all probability.

Where once the Place de la Concorde had stretched with a measure-less sheet of polished asphalt, from La Madeleine to the Chambre des Députés, from Champs-Elysées to the Tuileries, a meadow of ripe grain now rippled in the gentle southerly wind. This grain was being gathered by mechanized harvesters driven by brawny, tanned men in white under-shirts. Men and women dressed in the same light harvesting clothes were nimbly piling the ready sheaves onto a waiting truck. At the edges of the field on all sides, women rested and breastfed their infants.

Seeing the airplane overhead, the harvesters stopped working, turned their heads upward, and gesticulated wildly.

When over the Tuileries Gardens, the pilot noticed a colony of a few thousand children playing in identical clothing, smocks, and small red caps — a field of poppies right beside the fields of grain.

Where the Luxembourg Gardens had once sprawled, now rows of cauliflower grew white in the sun in a chessboard of colorful plots, a gigantic vegetable garden.

The pilot was so astonished by what he saw that rather than continue his observations he flew a beeline over the city to share his discovery with his superiors a quickly as possible.

Over the Seine, right where the Métro Bridge spans it with a break-neck leap, he saw a train running across the viaduct, hauling freight cars loaded with goods of some kind. Virtually no one was in the streets, only in the fields and in the gardens — yet the slender streams of smoke coming from the factory chimneys indicated the area was pulsing with intense labor.

Flying over the southern suburbs, the pilot came under fire, and was forced to pull up. It was only through some skillful maneuvering that he was able to escape without much harm.

The pilot maintained that Paris was surrounded by formidable fortifications, and swore he had spotted long-range artillery on the bastions.

The pilot's incredible story was heard on radios across the globe that very same day.

Before evening, the sensational news of the day all across France was the mysterious people harvesting grain on Place de la Concorde and breeding whole ranks of children. Frivolous songs were sung about them in all of Lyon's cabarets.

V

THE EVENTS OF THE FOLLOWING DAY occurred at a truly dizzying speed.

At nine in the morning a decree appeared in Lyon ordering a general mobilization. In spite of the martial law and the prohibition on assembly, the streets were bursting with an agitated crowd, pouring out in processions, fulminating against war. A patriotic fascist militia was organized ad hoc to help the police maintain order in the city. Flocks of reserves cut through the streets, singing *The Internationale*. Three armored ships docked at Toulon put out to sea, waving red flags. In the cities: unrest and turmoil. A regiment ordered to deploy barricaded itself inside the barracks, hanging red kerchiefs from the windows.

At noon, the newspapers reported that a British squadron had set sail for Leningrad. The German government declared that they would maintain absolute neutrality in the ensuing conflict.

The general strike blocked evening editions of newspapers all across Europe. The febrile crowds, hungry for information, started mobbing the loudspeakers hung outside department stores, parks, and editorial offices to await the latest bulletins. At 7:15 sharp, the speakers coughed up the station's first broadcast signals.

And then, unexpectedly, over the minor accompaniment of the monotonous litany of numbers, smothering it like the brass roar of a trumpet, a muted string orchestra suddenly sounded, and then a booming voice:

"Hello! Hello! Paris speaking!"

These words were so startling that the crowds surged and fell silent, uncertain if they hadn't fallen victim to an aural hallucination.

For a moment all that could be heard from the speakers was a muddy echo, counting "eight, nine, ten . . ." The crowd leaned closer, feverish with anticipation. Then, through the sound of the countdown, the sonorous, metallic bass was heard once again:

"Hello! Paris speaking!"

By now there could be no doubt. Pushing and thrashing, people pressed closer to the speakers. The accompaniment fell silent. A moment later the same voice rang out a third time:

"Paris speaking!"

After the English pilot's unbelievable account, this sounded like the key to a baffling riddle. A second later the voice rang out again, emphatic and deafening:

"Paris speaking! At present, the city of Paris operates seven radio stations, built over the past two years, with an average capacity of 500 kilowatts apiece. We have set our machines to the frequencies of all the Continent's most popular stations. Tuning in to any of these, you will have no choice but to hear our voice, several times more powerful than their antennae . . ."

The words fell silent. For a second you could hear the broadcast of the smothered station, laconically announcing that the Japanese were declaring war against the Soviet Union. A moment later the same voice drowned everything out again:

"Workers! Soldiers! Peasants! This is the Revolutionary Government of Paris speaking. The Paris you thought dead is alive. The rumors of the raging epidemic are all lies. The Paris epidemic was eradicated two years ago. The only survivors were the thousands-strong Parisian proletariat who had been thrown in prison during the May crackdowns. The proletariat survived amid the ruins of the old Paris through their isolation in prison, and during these years they have erected a new Paris — a free workers' commune. Seeking to ga . . . the ti . . . start . . ."

Through the tangled web of words came the jaunty chords of a piano:

> . . . Madeleine, Madeleine!
> Shake up, wake up, and know my tears are true!

Fumbling my hands all under your dress,
I lost my head and I know just what to do.
Along the edges of your lacy frills
I'm a beetle that buzzes and trills,
To find the road I know so well,
Can't you see, I'm under your spell!
Oh, help me, oh, Madeleine . . .

crooned the tenor from the smothered station.

". . . the imperialist war, brought on by your bourgeois governments against the world's first worker-peasant state, the Union of Soviet Socialist Republics, thrusting a blade into the chest of the revolutionary proletariat of all nations, forces us to break this artificial isolation for the first time and turn . . . direc . . ."

. . . I aim for the target but all in vain,
I pray, I sway, my hands find the lock.
"Open sesame" I say, in the pouring rain,
Oh, Madeleine — knock, knock, knock! . . .

the stubborn tenor warbled on.

"This is the workers' Paris. Workers! Peasants! People bound by the yoke! A war against the USSR is a war against you, a war against our commune that you shall defend as an international revolutionary bastion in the sea of capitalist Europe. Pick up your arms! All for revolutionary Paris! For dis . . . pea . . . with the Uni . . ."

. . . Madeleine, Madeleine!

". . . live . . . your revolution of workers and pea . . . ! Down with the mili . . . pitalist . . . live . . . vil war! Long live Paris, capital of the French Socialist Republic of Soviets!"

The black maws of the speakers blared the brassy fanfare of *The Internationale*.

The crowds were consumed, it seemed, by a frenzy. People ran, shoving and trampling one another. Thousands of mouths agape with astonishment picked up the lingering refrain of *The Internationale*.

And under the billowing sails of the song the masses shuddered like titanic ships, creaking in their joints, swaying in the shallows of the roadways, and heaving forward.

At present, one of the few objects in Poland commemorating the life and work of Bruno Jasieński — a high school that bore his name in his hometown of Klimontów — has officially undergone a name change,* on the grounds that the writer in question is not "a role model for today's youth" and, indeed, has a "demoralizing effect" on their young minds. Leaving aside the question of the desirability of judging literature on such criteria, what seems most astonishing is that even now, over seventy years after his torture and execution in a Soviet prison, Jasieński is still such a socially awkward commodity, certain to make Anglophone readers as uncomfortable as Polish ones. Most of the greatest writers seem to have been born at the wrong time, but only a small handful of the truly odd ones feel as though they wouldn't be quite at home — or embraced — at any time.

OBJECTIVE SECTION

Bruno Jasieński arrived in Paris in the fall of 1925. In his last surviving statement for the Russian NKVD before his execution, he listed three reasons for leaving Poland: (1) he had graduated from university and was due to serve twenty months of compulsory military service, (2) he was being sued for alleged blasphemy during one of his poetry readings in Lwów (today's Lviv, Ukraine), which could have resulted in a year or two in prison, and (3) he was an unemployed literature graduate whose scandalous reputation scarcely promised him work as a high-school teacher. Difficult as it may be to imagine from today's perspective, his

---

*The school is now officially the Urszula Ledóchowska Liceum, named after the plucky Roman-Catholic nun-cum-saint.

293

poetry readings had been banned by the police in many Polish cities, and on one occasion an audience had even stoned him for his work.

Jasieński intended to learn French and to write novels in his new language. Instead, he immediately enrolled in Chinese and Japanese classes, and wrote freelance articles for the *Wiek Nowy** newspaper in Lwów. Among other events, he covered the exhumation of renowned Romantic poet Juliusz Słowacki's remains in Paris and their shipment back to Poland. He also worked as a director at the Polish Workers' Theater, where he staged an adaptation of one of his own poems.

The decision to write *I Burn Paris* is immortalized in Aleksander Wat's conversations with Czesław Miłosz in *My Century*. Wat claims that Jasieński misunderstood the title of Paul Morand's newly-published novel *Je brule Moscou* ("bruler" also has the idiomatic meaning, to "travel through quickly"), and was so enraged that he set about writing a retaliation piece: *Je brule Paris*. Poland's most untiring Jasieński advocate, Krzysztof Jaworski, suggests in *Bruno Jasieński in Paris* that this story might have been somewhat embellished: Jasieński had written positive reviews of Morand's work, a rarity in Jasieński's critical output, suggesting that the "rage" might have been colored in for effect. But such is the appeal of Wat's story that it retains its hold in the popular imagination.

Jasieński was indeed expelled from France for this novel, and import of the book (it was originally serialized in *L'Humanité*) was forbidden on the grounds that it "exuded blind and stupid hatred for Western European culture." Nor did it do much for his popularity in Poland, though in Russia it became a legitimate phenomenon: the first edition of 140,000 copies sold out in a matter of days, prompting a second edition of 220,000 copies.

---

*The New Age, remembered as Poland's first tabloid. Sample headlines from the period include: "Hypnotism Used by Human Traffickers," "Child Boiled in Pot, Cut to Pieces," and "Secret Den of Licentiousness Uncovered in Lwów."

I Burn Paris remains a reluctantly acknowledged masterpiece in part because of all its ambiguities. The effect comes from following moral impulses so obsessively that they sometimes become their own opposites. The novel marks what is generally thought to be Jasieński's transition from Futurism to Catastrophism. His Futurist poetry took the staccato rhythm and mechanics of typewriters, trams, factories etc. as their substance, a quality echoed in Part 1 of the novel:

the thousands-strong, hundred-street cities
pumping out thousands of papers a day,
the long black columns of words
shouting loud on the boulevards
written by little old men in spectacles.
wrong.
the City writes them
stenographing a thousand collisions.
in sync, in time, in blood.
a hundred thousand camera clicks
mark long forty-column epics.
[...]
power-plant strikes, suicide, adultery,
there's your big fat poetry.

[“Song of Hunger,” 1922]

The pulse in Jasieński's poetry is a mechanical one. It was (remains) shocking for its bold disregard of what this mechanization *means*, preferring merely to hand us a portrait of the state of things in the modern world and creating a poetry that reflects it. Yet in his works of prose the wonderment is gone, the machine has run amok, and the ramifications of this state of things has become the focus. Even so, the recurrence of these images retain some of the young Futurist's fascination for the factory-made man, and his prose holds onto the one-two punch of the poetry's mechanized rhythm. The repetition of such adjectives as "matte" and "flickering" tell us something else: Jasieński's novel is an early example of literature with a distinctly cinematic sensibility (Eisenstein is certainly a reference point), a narrative viewed through a camera lens.

A similar ambiguity emerges in Jasieński's treatment of the moral decadence and degradation of society, which takes many forms: brothels, child prostitution, racism, grinding poverty, jazz music, the lifestyles of the upper classes and the bourgeoisie, and so on. Pierre, the novel's initial protagonist (whose death occurs early, in a strangely offhand gesture), appears as a kind of interwar Candide, stumbling through the dark woods of modern French society, pummeled by its various mechanisms. Of course, in the midst of detailing the horrors that await Pierre in his descent into madness, Jasieński ends up writing passages that very much resemble a decadent novel. Everything is grotesquely bent out of shape, but the sections detailing the revulsion and vileness are, from a literary point of view, some of the most compelling to read. It is a dilemma familiar to the religious painter: Hell is more fun to paint.

Finally, there is a strange and unresolvable contradiction in the fact that a novel which culminates in celebrating the triumph of socialism and its potential to spread across Europe is also a novel whose central motif is the spread of a deadly and unstoppable plague.

None of this is to doubt the sincerity or conviction of Jasieński's aims. The violent imagery of anti-Semitism in the form of a Jewish refugee casually murdered by a Russian officer seems a precursor to the jarring images from World War II. The impression is made all the more powerful when one recalls how rare such graphic depictions were in European literature then. Jasieński's humane treatment of P'an, the Chinese communist, again runs counter to the period's common fear of a yellow horde ready to sweep across the Continent. What remains impressive in *I Burn Paris* is the fact that, whatever the moral or political status of the characters, Jasieński gives them full rights to our understanding and sympathy. In this disease-infested Paris everyone may well be cutting everyone else's throats, and the portrait of humanity as it stands might be dismal beyond repair, but as *individuals*, everyone gets a fair hearing, a fleshed-out literary existence.

But the ambiguities I have mentioned do seem to suggest that there is a subconscious, or subterranean, life to the narrative, one that goes unacknowledged by the writer as such, but which is perhaps the chief source of discomfort in reading the novel. Whether it is the Futurist undermining the Catastrophist, Jasieński casting doubt on his own best intentions, or a classic case of attraction/repulsion syndrome, it is a tension that runs through much of the book.

NON-OBJECTIVE SECTION

I should note in passing (though without the humility of a footnote) that the translator's introduction — surely the most conservative of all arts, save perhaps typography — has undergone a shift in demeanor over the past few decades, which is, not surprisingly, reflective of the shift in the so-called art of translating as such. This shift might broadly be defined as one from creative virtuosity to academic fidelity — both approaches with their own pitfalls — and accordingly, the sometimes disarming sincerity and eccentricity of translators' introductions of the 1960s and 1970s has largely given way to those that are at best blandly informative, and at worst larded with an academic rhetoric that puts the translator in a position of authority over his subject (i.e., the writer being translated). As I have no intention of playing such shabby tricks with the reader, because I am old-fashioned enough to believe that a translation should be motivated, above all, by a kind of bald enthusiasm for the author at hand, and ultimately, because this *particular* writer is one of painful and sometimes uncomfortable honesty, I should like to include the following.

Any introduction to *I Burn Paris* should explain what I see as the real tragedy of Bruno Jasieński, though I would like to refrain from wringing my hands and gnashing my teeth. The tragedy has less to do with the conventional pathos of a highly gifted writer sentenced to death in the vast slaughter of Stalinist Russia (though surely this is tragic enough), than with a more unconventional sort of tragedy: that of an artist pursuing his own delusions to the bitter end. From his earliest poetry, Jasieński was a writer with a powerful sense of his own showmanship and the manufacture of his own identity. This included the monocle he liked to wear, the pseudonym (real name: Wiktor Zysman), affiliation with various literary movements, manifestoes, public statements, rallies, and performances. Even as an aesthetic writer (as opposed to the politically engaged writer he later became), he had an acute sense of creating a persona — the writer himself was viewed as another fictional character. Jasieński's literary voice is seldom, if ever, an intimate one — it is that of a man holding forth from a tribunal or a podium. It is a Romantic impulse, a sign that a writer sees his role as a spokesman for the people (compare Bruno Schulz's "secretly clasping his reader's hand under the table").

There is a certain inevitability, perhaps, in such writers finding politics. Like many avant-garde artists of his time, Jasieński identified with Marxism. When he found himself expelled from France after the publication of *I Burn Paris*, the Soviet Union gave him a hero's welcome (a surviving photograph: crowds with banners at the train station, gathered there to greet him). His public addresses maintained the confidence and bluster of his early Futurist manifestoes. That is to say, one has the creeping suspicion that the character of Jasieński the writer (as opposed to Zysman — whoever he was) had not been fundamentally altered, it was only the rhetoric and the vocabulary that had changed. When the purges began in earnest in the 1930s and it became very dangerous to be a public persona, Jasieński had already made a few enemies, and he was soon fighting accusations of being a Polish spy and an enemy of the people. He was arrested on July 31, 1937, and executed on September 17, 1938.

There survive a few of his letters written from captivity directly to Stalin, begging for clemency. In his last letter of many pages, written in self-defense, he lists the shocking tortures to which he'd been subjected (fingernails pulled out, teeth kicked in), but just as shockingly, for the first time, we seem to hear Zysman speaking, begging to be allowed to die rather than continue the tortures. Zysman drops all the swagger of his character. And if I am not wholly mistaken, there is a dim recognition of the insanity of having arrived at this point simply for having played his role — and a confusion at the notion of all this fiction ultimately having such brutal consequences.

A warm clasp of the hand to Marcin Piekoszewski, Howard Sidenberg, Stan Bill, and Scotia Gilroy for their patient and intelligent help.

Soren A. Gauger
Kraków, 2012

Poet, novelist, and playwright, BRUNO JASIEŃSKI (1901–39) was born in Klimontów, Poland. Having authored in 1921 "To the Polish Nation: A Manifesto on the Immediate Futurization of Life" and "Manifesto on Futurist Poetry" he became the unquestionable leader of Polish Futurism, writing poetry that was marked by dynamism and absurdity. In 1925, he emigrated to France but was deported after his novel *I Burn Paris* was serialized in 1928. He spent the last decade of his life in the USSR working for the Union of Soviet Writers and producing work in Russian, chief among which were the play *The Mannequins' Ball* (1931) and the novel *Man Sheds His Skin* (1934). Arrested in 1937, Jasieński was expelled from the Party, put on trial, and sentenced to fifteen years in the gulag. Thought for many years to have died in transit some time in 1939, it is now known that he was executed on September 17, 1938, in Moscow's Butyrka prison.

SOREN A. GAUGER is from Vancouver, Canada and has resided in Kraków for nearly two decades. His translations include *Waiting for the Dog to Sleep* by Jerzy Ficowski, *Towers of Stone* by Wojciech Jagielski, and Bruno Jasieński's Futurist texts in *The Legs of Izolda Morgan*. His own writing has appeared in numerous journals and includes a collection of stories, *Hymns to Millionaires*, and a novel.

MARCIN PIEKOSZEWSKI studied at the English Departments of Opole University and Kraków's Jagiellonian University, graduating from the latter in American Literature. Having worked as a teacher, translator, journalist, and bookseller, he currently lives in Berlin where he runs Buchbund, a Polish-German bookshop.

CRISTIAN OPRIȘ is a graduate of the University of Art and Design in Cluj-Napoca, Romania. He has exhibited across Europe and his work has been included in group shows and presentations of contemporary avant-garde graphic artists. In 2002, he was awarded the Romanian Artists' Union's Prize, Youth Section, and in 2006 he took 2nd prize at the 5th International Lithography Symposium in Tidaholm, Sweden.

I BURN PARIS

by Bruno Jasieński

Translated by Soren A. Gauger and Marcin Piekoszewski
from the original Polish *Palę Paryż* published by
Towarzystwo Wydawnicze "Rój" (Warsaw) in 1929

First serialized in French in *L'Humanité,* 1928

Earlier versions of parts of the translation
appeared in *Antithesis, Asymptote,* and *Calque,*
to whose editors we are grateful

Artwork by Cristian Opriş
Cover by Dan Mayer
Design by Jed Slast
Set in Garamond & Futura

FIRST PAPERBACK EDITION, 2017

First published in hardcover in 2012

TWISTED SPOON PRESS
P.O. Box 21, 150 21 Prague 5
Czech Republic
www.twistedspoon.com
info@twistedspoon.com

Printed and bound in the Czech Republic by PB Tisk

Distributed to the trade by

CENTRAL BOOKS
www.centralbooks.com

SCB DISTRIBUTORS
www.scbdistributors.com

INTAGLIO · MICROGRAPH............................

Magnified...............diameters

Prepared.... *of. Osiris* *September 01*

1110